TROPHY

TROPHY

A NOVEL

STEFFEN
JACOBSEN

Translated from the Danish
by Charlotte Barslund

Arcade Publishing • New York

First North American Edition 2017

First published in Great Britain in 2014 by Quercus Editions Ltd

This is a work of fiction. Names, places, characters, and incidents are either the products of
the author's imagination or are used fictitiously.

Arcade Publishing books may be purchased in bulk at special discounts for sales promotion,
corporate gifts, fund-raising, or educational purposes. Special editions can also be created to
specifications. For details, contact the Special Sales Department, Arcade Publishing, 307 West
36th Street, 11th Floor, New York, NY 10018 or arcade@skyhorsepublishing.com.

Arcade Publishing® is a registered trademark of Skyhorse Publishing, Inc.®,
a Delaware corporation.

Visit our website at www.arcadepub.com.

10 9 8 7 6 5 4 3 2 1

Library of Congress Cataloging-in-Publication Data

Names: Jacobsen, Steffen, 1956- author. | Barslund, Charlotte, translator.
Title: Trophy : a novel / Steffen Jacobsen ; translated by Charlotte Barslund.
Other titles: Trofæ. English
Description: First North American edition. | New York, NY : Arcade
Publishing, 2017. | Translated from the Danish.
Identifiers: LCCN 2017000350| ISBN 9781628727876 (hardback) | ISBN
9781628727883 (e-book)
Subjects: LCSH: Serial murder investigation—Fiction. | Businessmen—Fiction.
| Clubs—Fiction. | Men—Societies and clubs—Fiction. | Denmark—Fiction.
| BISAC: FICTION / Thrillers. | GSAFD: Mystery fiction. | Thrillers.
Classification: LCC PT8177.2.A34 T7613 2017 | DDC 839.813/8—dc23 LC record available at
https://lccn.loc.gov/2017000350

Cover design by Erin Seaward-Hiatt
Cover illustration: iStockphoto

Printed in the United States of America

TROPHY

PROLOGUE

Finnmark, northern Norway
24 March 2011, 18.35
70° 29´ 46.97˝ N 25° 43´ 57.34˝ E

When they found him, he was watching the sun go down behind the mountains west of Porsanger Fjord, knowing that he would never see it rise again. The cold chased the twilight across the water. A few steps in front of him, the plateau dropped steeply down to the sea. It was his only escape, but in the fading light and the state he was in, he knew he couldn't make it down a hundred-metre-long wall with an overhang. This was the end and he chose to face it. He refused to be their quarry any longer.

He knew that the hunters had driven him towards this point all day: to the edge of nothing. He limped across loose granite scree, tossed aside the empty hunting rifle and sat down behind a boulder, polished by the wind into a comfortable curve that supported his back. Nearby a brook channelled meltwater away from the glaciers. It ran white, fast and smooth over the edge, hitting the shore of the fjord far below.

He could see headlights from the occasional vehicle on the other side of the fjord, less than fifteen kilometres away—and in another world. He tucked his hands under his armpits, rested his chin on his knees and inspected his hiking boot, which had been pierced by the client's bullet several hours ago. His foot was still bleeding; he could see blood being forced through the bullet hole, but it no longer hurt very much. He pulled off the boot and gritted his teeth when he did the same with his sock, stiff with congealed blood. He wedged the boot under the boulder and covered it with gravel and pebbles. Perhaps one day someone would find it.

They were good boots. Like all of his equipment—the camouflage jacket and the hunting trousers, the fleece jumper, the thermal underwear and the compass. He also had a laminated map of Finnmark with headlands stretching out into the Barents Sea between Porsanger Fjord, Lakse Fjord and Tana Fjord.

The first stars and planets started to glow in the sky. He recognized Venus, but none of the others. Ingrid would know their names. The plants, animals and constellations were in her genes.

He pulled out his hands from his armpits, and although he wasn't a man of faith, he folded them and said a prayer for his wife. Ingrid must have got away. She was faster on skis or on foot in the mountains than he had ever been, and he had managed to hold out so far. Until now.

They had embraced each other that afternoon when they heard the hunters' whistles and realized that they had been found. He had kissed her cold lips and pushed her away, into the meltwater at the edge of the glacier. She hadn't wanted to leave him but he pushed her again, hard, so she almost tripped. He would stay in full view on the ridge so that the hunters would come after him. She was to move along the glacier and then up into the terrain. If she ran for the rest of the day and through the night, she would reach Lakselv by dawn.

Ingrid had put on the skis and shot like an arrow down the snow-covered slope before disappearing between the dense pines where she would be hidden from view. She would outrun them.

He had seen his wife for the last time at the top of an elevation and at the same time spotted the hunters as they appeared over the next hilltop. The afternoon sun was behind them and the hunters cast long shadows. The ones at the front had caught sight of him, their whistles echoing once more through the lowlands.

His Norwegian wife had taught him to love the bleak landscape of northern Norway. They hadn't been to the mountains since the birth of their twins two years ago, and they couldn't wait any longer. When they saw a weather forecast for Finnmark that promised calm, cloudless days, he persuaded his mother to have the twins and booked two seats on the plane from Copenhagen to Oslo—and onwards from Oslo to Lakselv.

There they had dined at the almost empty Porsanger Vertshus. It was early in the season and the hostess had been delighted to see them. Afterwards they had shared a bottle of good red wine in their room, made love under cold duvets and slept a heavy and carefree slumber.

The next morning they had walked north along the east shore of Porsanger Fjord, hitched a lift with a truck going to Väkkärä, and then headed into the mountains. Their plan was to hike thirty kilometres north-north-east to Kjæsvatnet, pitch their tent, do a bit of fishing, take a few pictures ... just have a couple of days to themselves before returning to Lakselv.

They had walked under the spring sun, inhaling the scents which the thousands of lakes and moors, whose black ice cracked under their boots, released in the spring. He had caught a couple of winter-dopey trout in Kjæsvatnet and the fish lay heavy, cold and firm in his hands. He wrapped them in moss inside his creel and Ingrid lit a campfire. The frost made the trees creak, but they snuggled up in their sleeping bags close to the fire, leaning against the trunks of a small copse of birch while they ate.

Later that night he was woken up by the low, steady sound of a helicopter far away in the east, but thought nothing of it. They often heard helicopters fly patients to the hospitals in Kirkenes or Hammerfest, or taking supplies or crew to the oilfields in the North Sea. The county covered almost 18,000 square miles and was practically uninhabited, except for the two of them, a few windswept villages along the coast, the nomadic Sami and their reindeer.

He had fallen asleep again and had no clear recollection of waking up. From then on, everything was brief, disjointed fragments: a glimpse of a cold, starry night as their tent was cut from its frame above them; Ingrid's short cry; a blue crackling flash. Pain and darkness. He couldn't move a muscle, yet he could feel himself being lifted up in his sleeping bag and carried away under the stars.

Later he realized that they had been incapacitated with an electric stun gun. Just like in the movies.

The silhouette of the helicopter blacked out the sky above them. They were put on the floor inside it, and the aircraft wobbled as the men embarked.

Weightlessness. Transport.

Their kidnappers had not said one word, not to each other, not to Ingrid or to him. A few minutes later one of them leaned forwards with a syringe in his hand and stuck the needle through Ingrid's sleeping bag into her thigh, and her semi-conscious whimpering stopped.

He had seen droplets of a clear liquid being forced out of a second syringe. Then the man had kneeled down by his head and found his arm inside the sleeping bag.

He regained consciousness after swimming towards a glowing rectangle, and found himself sitting naked on a concrete floor, shivering from the cold and looking at an empty window frame, which was brighter than the surrounding wall. His body must have woken up before his mind because he had managed to stay balanced on his buttocks and heels. His hands were blue and swollen under the tight cable-tie around his wrists. A steel wire connected the cable-tie to a ring in the floor.

Stone slabs lay piled to the rafters at one end of the room and he guessed that they must be in one of the many abandoned slate quarries in the region.

He heard a sigh, a scraping of nails on concrete next to him, and rolled onto his side so that his face would be the first thing Ingrid saw.

They were pressed against each other, as much as the wires allowed, when the door was opened. Two dark figures appeared with the low morning sun behind them. Slate crunched beneath their boots as they crossed the hall; they ignored his furious questions in Danish, English and Norwegian. When he started swearing at them, a gun was put to Ingrid's head.

The bigger of the two men pulled him by the hair to a sitting position and took out their passports from his jacket pocket. In English, but with a Scandinavian accent, the man had checked their age and asked about their weight, if they were on any kind of medication, and if they knew what their oxygen uptake was.

He had briefly let himself be fooled by the man's calm, conversational tone. As his accomplice's gun was removed from Ingrid's head, he gathered a blob of saliva in his mouth and spat at his interrogator's boot.

The man didn't move. Not one word was exchanged between the two of them, but the heel of his partner's boot landed with a sharp crack on Ingrid's foot. She screamed, and as he threw himself away, against the wires, he received a kick to his stomach.

The man resumed his questions—and got his answers. The padlocks were unlocked, the cable-ties around their ankles cut, and they were pulled to their feet and led outside.

Ingrid had to be supported, but he insisted on walking unaided.

Four more men were standing in the yard between the quarry buildings: black ski masks, camouflage jackets and trousers, to blend in with the icy grey, black and dark green colours of the mountains.

He looked into the man's brown eyes.

"You think you're real heroes, don't you?" he said in Danish.

The man's eyes narrowed and the corners of his eyes disappeared into his crow's feet, but he made no reply.

The cable-ties around their wrists were cut and he held Ingrid close. She tried to cover herself with her hands.

Clothes, boots, equipment and food had been laid out on a table made up of doors resting on trestles. They were ordered to put on thermal underwear, T-shirts, fleece jumpers, socks, camouflage jackets and trousers. The leader encouraged them to eat as much as they could of the pasta, muesli and bread on the table. It would be their last meal.

They had been bought by a client who would hunt them across the mountains for the next twenty-four hours, the brown-eyed leader informed them. It wasn't personal. The client didn't know who they were and they didn't know who the client was. Other candidates had been considered, but the client had chosen them.

Ingrid buried her face in her hands, doubled up and sobbed. She kept saying the names of the twins over and over again.

He sensed movement behind a window. There was someone behind the filthy, broken pane. The blurred oval of a face, half shaded by a broad-brimmed hat.

Then the man slipped to one side and out of sight.

They would be given a two-hour head start, the leader continued. Then, if they were found within the timeframe, they would be executed by the client in whichever way he preferred. He pointed to a white, freestanding rock a couple of hundred metres away. At the foot of the rock they would find two pairs of skis and a hunting rifle with three cartridges in the magazine. He could use it if he wanted to. Did he know how to handle a rifle?

He nodded.

Ingrid collapsed and he pulled her brusquely to her feet. He led her between the buildings, past the heaps of slate and out into the terrain.

The sun released its grip on the mountains in the east as they started running.

He saw the reflections from their headlamps in the wet rocks in the brook and his heart started beating fast and hard. His bladder emptied and the warmth spread down his thighs. He swore from shame, his desperate fears for Ingrid, the unreality of it all.

Then he got up and stepped out from behind his boulder, clearly visible against the light evening sky behind him.

The hunters emerged from the darkness and he screamed at them. One of them was limping and he wished that he had hit the bastard in his heart and not in his thigh. One light shone harsher and more brightly than the headlamps and he shielded his eyes with his hands. A camera light. The arseholes were filming him.

The hunters stopped twenty metres away from him and started clapping in unison—at first quietly, then with more force. He bent down, picked up a rock and hurled it at them, falling short. There were seven men in the hunting party. The red and green beams of their laser sights danced playfully up and down his body, criss-crossing his heart.

Then they began singing—and his brain switched off. He was standing with his back to the abyss in one of the most deserted and remote landscapes in the world while his executioners bellowed, stomped and clapped their way through Queen's "We Will Rock You." The men raised their voices. Their boots slammed down on the rock. The semi-circle opened to make way for the client. He stumbled forwards with his hunting rifle in his hands; he seemed to be hesitating: he lowered the barrel—only to raise it again.

He tried finding the client's eyes below the broad-brimmed hat, searching for a glimpse of humanity, but was blinded by the floodlight. He shielded his eyes against it with his hands and couldn't see Ingrid anywhere among them. A wild hope opened his throat and he screamed out in wild, wordless triumph.

The client bent double and threw up. He rested the butt of his rifle against the rocks and leaned on the barrel. The leader barked something short and sharp to him and he nodded and wiped his mouth.

Then the leader turned to his prey and tossed an object through the air in a languid arc.

Instinct made him reach out to catch the heavy, black, closed sack and he looked briefly at the silent, motionless men before he opened the sack and lifted out its content.

His world imploded. A moment later, Kasper Hansen was dead.

CHAPTER 1

Michael Sander ran a comb through his hair and straightened his tie. He was walking along a three-metre-high white wall that surrounded one of Denmark's most exclusive addresses: the houses in Richelieus Allé in Hellerup were all in the sought-after category between "very large villas" and "mansions."

He stopped and studied a plate engraved with the name "Caspersen" sunk into the wall by the gate, checked his side parting in the polished brass, pressed the bell and flashed the surveillance cameras what he hoped was a trustworthy smile.

"Who is it?"

The question came from a loudspeaker built into the gatepost.

"Michael Sander."

"One moment, please."

The double gates swung open and the shingle crunched under the soles of his shoes as he walked up the drive.

Smiling dolphins spewed water on a naked, strangely lifelike nymph in a fountain in front of the house while an open garage displayed a rich man's toys: a sky-blue Maserati Quattroporte, a Mercedes Roadster and a dove-grey Rolls-Royce. The number plates were SONARTEK 1, 2 and 3.

An ordinary black Opel was parked in front of the main steps.

Michael began to realize the optical illusion. From the gates the white house had seemed merely indecently large, but he had been wrong: it was actually enormous.

He walked up the eight wide steps and had just raised his hand to lift the knocker when the door was opened.

A pair of grey eyes assessed him before the face granted him a reserved smile. The woman was tall and her build strong and angular. She had never been gracious or delightful. Her features were broad, but symmetrical, and Michael took her to be a few years younger than he was.

She offered him a well-practised handshake and introduced herself.

"Elizabeth Caspersen-Behncke."

Then she led the way across the white and green marble tiles in the hall and Michael sized her up: a string of pearls, black cashmere sweater, a simple, dark grey skirt and an unusual choice of wine-coloured tights which reminded him of the skinny legs of an oystercatcher. She was too tall to wear anything other than flat shoes, and she was a thinker.

He always divided potential clients into thinkers and doers. There were subdivisions, of course, but he rarely found it necessary to change his first impression. Michael knew that Elizabeth Caspersen-Behncke was the heir to a colossal family fortune, as well as being a partner in one of the biggest and oldest law firms in Copenhagen. For that reason alone there could be no doubt that she was academically gifted, but that wasn't the factor that determined whether she was a thinker or a doer: it was the way the hips connected to the upper body and the legs, the sway of the lower back, someone's posture, the length of their stride.

From time to time his wife would ask him in which category he would place himself, and every time Michael would feel a tad hurt. He regarded himself as a fortunate combination: sensuous, yet rational—a thinker *and* a doer.

Elizabeth Caspersen-Behncke continued to walk in front of him up the staircase. It was like walking through the Natural History Museum. The walls were covered with stuffed animal heads and every imaginable size and variety of antlers and horns from the deer and antelope family. Vacant eyes watched him from all sides.

At the first turn in the stairs, an African lion reached out his long claws towards him. Above the animal's front paws, its enormous head came crashing through a mahogany panel, its black lips peeled back over yellow teeth and its mane fluffed out; the furious expression in the animal's glass eyes momentarily stopped him in his tracks.

The woman glanced over her shoulder.

"My father called him Louis. Terrifying, isn't he?"

"Definitely, Mrs. Caspersen-Behncke."

"Elizabeth is fine, if I may call you Michael."

"Of course."

He was mesmerized by the animal.

"Imagine being a little girl with a vivid imagination trying to get down to the kitchen for a midnight snack."

"I'd still be having nightmares," he said.

They continued upstairs until Michael stopped again, just below a three-metre-high painting of the previous owner of the house, the recently deceased captain of industry, Flemming Caspersen. The portrait was executed with photographic accuracy. One side depicted bookcases with old, gilded volumes and Caspersen—in a contemplative pose—resting his hand on a round table. There were sealed parchments and yellowing manuscripts, maps and open folios, as if the billionaire had been interrupted in his study of the sources of the Nile or the meaning of everything.

A grey grizzly bear rose behind the billionaire and both the man's and the animal's shadows merged together on the wall. Caspersen's virile, energetic face was grave; his white hair stood up in short bristles, his brown gaze was directed at the spectator and the elevated position of the painting and his tall figure ensured him a regal dignity. His tie had discreet grey stripes and his suit fitted him as if it had been developed in a wind tunnel. "My father enjoyed playing the Renaissance man," Elizabeth Caspersen-Behncke said. "Though I doubt if he ever read a work of fiction. He used to say that his life was exciting enough as it was. He found fictional lives dull."

Michael pointed to a rhinoceros head hanging six metres above the floor. The animal squinted tragically at the grey, flat stumps that were all that was left of its horns.

"What happened to him?"

"Someone broke into the house a couple of months ago. They put the gardener's ladder up against the wall, cut off the horns with a hacksaw and scarpered. My mother was in hospital and the house was empty. According to the police, it was a professional job. We really ought to take him down. A rhino without its horns is really rather pointless."

She drew his attention to a cupboard down by the front door. "They forced the front door with a crowbar and cooled the alarm system with liquid nitrogen."

Michael leaned over the banister and studied the cream-coloured wall below the amputated trophy. He could actually see a couple of dark marks from the ladder.

"I've read that natural history museums and private collections are experiencing an epidemic of horn thefts," he said. "It's said to cure everything from impotence to cancer."

"Its horns were impressive," she said. "My father shot it in Namibia in '73. It's a white rhino. Or rather, it was."

"I thought they were an endangered species—protected by law?"

"This animal was shot for research, which everyone knows is just another word for bribery. My father always got what he wanted."

Michael stayed where he was. The prehistoric animal roused a strange kind of empathy in him.

"The horns weighed eight kilos and they were worth their weight in cocaine," she said. "The street value is exactly the same, incidentally. $52,000 per kilo."

Michael was impressed. Four hundred thousand dollars for half an hour's work was a good rate. Superb, in fact.

"And they took nothing else?" he asked.

"My mother's jewellery is in a safe deposit box and the only cash we ever keep in the house is for paying the gardener and the cleaner."

She led the way down a passage on the second floor. They passed a darkened bedroom and Michael caught a glimpse of an emaciated female face on a pillow, large birdlike eyes turning to the doorway. A nurse was in the process of attaching a bag of fluids to a drop stand.

"Flemming? Flemming?"

The nurse closed the door.

The voice kept calling out.

"My mother," Elizabeth Caspersen explained. "Alzheimer's."

Michael smiled sympathetically.

She opened the next door and Michael collided with the blinding sunlight bouncing off the surface of the Øresund.

"A beautiful room, isn't it?" she said.

The windows measured at least six metres from floor to ceiling.

"Amazing," he said, shading his eyes with his hand.

He recognized the interior of the library from Flemming Caspersen's portrait. An intricate wrought-iron walkway ran along the bookshelves three metres above the floor and formed the gallery. High above his head the huge, stuffed bear sparred with its front paws.

"A Kodiak bear, Alaska '95," she said laconically.

"I'm starting to understand why they're threatened with extinction," he said.

"You don't hunt?" she asked.

"Not animals."

"My father would have argued that if it weren't for the safari industry there would be no money for reserves and gamekeepers in places such as Africa, and poachers would have killed anything that moved long ago."

"He would probably have been right," Michael conceded.

She walked over to the windows, folded her arms across her chest and chewed a nail. This probably wasn't normal behaviour for a Supreme Court lawyer, he thought, and positioned himself by her side to offer a kind of silent support.

The tall white wall cordoned off the park from the neighbouring estates. He noticed thin alarm wires running along the top of the wall and several white surveillance cameras that would appear to cover every inch of the grounds. The problem didn't lie with the house's security, as far as he could ascertain. The weak spot was the open sea.

Out in the park, a black Labrador was sitting next to a flagpole with its nose pointing at the spring sky, whining pitifully.

"Nigger, my father's dog," Elizabeth Caspersen mumbled. "It has sat there, howling, ever since he died."

"Nigger?"

Elizabeth Caspersen smiled forlornly.

"He wasn't a racist. He only cared about whether someone could do their job. I think he found it amusing to walk around a neighbourhood like this and call the dog. Out loud."

Michael continued to examine the alarm wires and the cameras on the garden wall.

"Did the cameras record the break-in?"

"Yes. Two men arrived from the sea at two o'clock in the morning in a rubber dinghy. Hoodies, ski masks and gloves. They ran across the lawn and around the house, found the gardener's ladder, and broke down the door."

"And Nigger?"

She looked down at the grieving animal.

"He was probably just grateful for the company. He's a lonely dog, very friendly. Why don't we sit?"

He put his shoulder bag on the floor and took a seat in an armchair. Elizabeth Caspersen sat down in the chair next to his, crossed her red legs, looked out of the window, and began flexing and pointing her foot.

He leaned back.

She moved her foot faster.

He had seen this before, of course: the hesitation before exposing your life and secrets to a stranger. The client would either change their mind at the last minute and end the meeting before it had even started, or they would take the plunge.

This would appear to be something in between.

"You're not an easy man to find," she said. "What do you call yourself? A consultant?"

"Yes."

"You don't look like a private investigator," she said.

"I'll take that as a compliment."

"What? Oh, I see. Coffee? Water?"

"No thank you," he said.

"Are you married?"

Her fingers got very busy with the string of pearls.

"Very happily," he said.

"So am I."

Elizabeth Caspersen pressed her fingertips against her eyelids.

"So you don't follow cheating spouses, loiter behind people's garages with a camera at night, or rummage through their bins?"

"Only at the end of the month," he said.

"I'm sorry . . . I . . ." She blushed. "I'm sorry. It's just that this is all very difficult. You were recommended to me by one of my father's English lawyers who knew of a Dutchman who had used the services of a Danish security consultant. Everyone became awfully secretive and it took a long time before the Dutchman replied."

"He called me before he contacted you," Michael explained.

"I didn't think people like you even existed in Denmark?"

"I believe there are a few of us," he said. "But it's not like we have a trade union."

"Your name is Michael Vedby Sander?"

"Yes," he lied.

"And you know Pieter Henryk?"

"Of course . . ."

He had tracked down two incompetent kidnappers—father and son—to an abandoned farm south of Nijmegen in the Netherlands for Pieter Henryk. They had decided to kidnap the very wealthy Dutchman's youngest daughter, which was their first mistake.

Involving the police, risking media attention and a scandal, was unthinkable for Henryk, who was old-school and preferred a more discreet, permanent solution.

The kidnappers had raped the nineteen-year-old girl repeatedly while passing the time. They had shaved her head, beaten her up, stubbed out their cigarettes on her back, and she was more dead than alive when Michael and Henryk's team reached her. Michael's task had been to find the girl, while Pieter Henryk's men dealt with the kidnappers.

Michael had sat in his car at the edge of the wood a few hundred metres from the farm and seen her carried across the farmyard in the arms of a Serbian mercenary. The huge man delivered her to a Mercedes, where her father and a doctor were waiting. She was naked, limp as a rag doll, and looked like a flayed animal. The car left the farm with gravel spraying from the tires.

He waited. Half an hour later, a truck pulled up in the farmyard and the mercenaries started hauling bricks, mortar and buckets into the house where the kidnappers were still assembled.

Michael left the scene. He knew what was coming and he knew Pieter Henryk's crew. They were Balkan veterans and had seen everything. If they were feeling merciful, they would throw a gun with two bullets over the new wall—before laying the last brick. If they were in a bad mood, they would tie up the pair, brick up the wall and wait until the mortar had dried.

She clapped her hands with a bang that snapped him out of his memories.

"I'm sorry?"

"I want you to work for me," she repeated.

"And I may well want to," he said tentatively.

"Henryk said I could trust you unconditionally."

He nodded. "That's essential if we're to get anywhere."

"You'd be able to bring down me and my family if it turns out that you can't be trusted, Michael. We would have no future."

"That's often the case," he said evenly. "Perhaps I should tell you how I work. If I accept an assignment, I work on it 24/7 until I've achieved the desired outcome or you tell me to stop. My fee is twenty thousand kroner per day, plus reimbursement of my expenses for other expert assistance, bribes, travel, food, and accommodation. We won't sign a contract and I won't provide you with any receipts, you'll just have to trust me. I'll give you the number of my accountant's client account and he'll report the payments to the tax office. Is that acceptable?"

"What does the small print say?" she wanted to know.

"Not very much. I don't perform serious criminal acts if they go against my view of right and wrong. I decide how far I'm prepared to go on a case-by-case basis."

"Regardless of the size of your fee?"

"Yes."

"Agreed," she said. "So why are you so incredibly hard to find?"

"I'm picky," he said.

His wife sometimes asked him the same question. You wouldn't find Michael Sander's one-man consultancy anywhere on the Internet. Stubborn individuals might find the latest version of the firm's homepage somewhere in the Dark Web, the basement of the Internet, which wasn't accessible to search engines like Google or AltaVista, but only to specialized, vertical robots such as technorati.com. It was possible he lost out on clients by being so exclusive, but this was how he liked it. He knew of a beautiful, Danish escort girl in London whose intimate services cost as much as the Greek budget deficit, and she used the same method. It was a question of her and her daughter's safety, she said.

His homepage was brief and basic. It stated that Michael Sander was an ex-soldier and former police officer, and that he had worked as a security consultant for ten years for Shepherd & Wilkins Ltd, a well-known British security company. His remit had included personal security, hostage negotiations, financial investigations, and so on. His contact details gave only a mobile phone number, which was replaced at least once a month, usually more often.

"What do you know about me?" she asked.

"I know that you're the only child of Flemming and Klara Caspersen," he said. "I know that your father originally trained to be a radio mechanic and later studied civil engineering. I know that in the 1980s, he took out a series of ground-breaking patents for what later became known as the ultrasound Doppler, miniature sonar and laser rangefinders, used in virtually all military weapon systems from submarines to fighter planes, but also in civilian meteorological early warning systems. Quite simply, it's the core technology behind modern range calculation and target identification. The technology is crucial and has never been surpassed. Your father founded Sonartek in 1987 with a university friend, Victor Schmidt, and the rest, as they say, is Danish corporate history. A success story."

"One evening in Frederiksberg he heard an ambulance siren and spent the rest of the night sitting on a bench pondering how the siren's echo told him the exact location of the ambulance. That was the start. Then he started studying dolphins, bats, and the then fairly elementary Doppler technology. He improved and developed it."

"As far as I'm aware, only Sonartek's research and development department remains in Denmark, while production and distribution have been . . ."

"Outsourced to China, India, Poland, and Estonia," she said. "It was a business decision."

"And, finally, I know that your father suffered a heart attack and died a couple of months ago," he said.

"He had run a marathon only two days before. In just over three hours," she said. "He was seventy-two years old, but in really good shape. I don't think he ever took a pill in his life. He always said that genes were the only thing that really mattered."

She got up and walked over to the windows. The dog's inconsolable howling could be heard from the garden. Michael didn't stir, and he said nothing.

Elizabeth Caspersen dried her eyes and turned around.

"Bloody dog," she muttered.

"And your mother is ill?" he said.

"It started four years ago, and it has progressed incredibly quickly. She owns a large share of a company with subsidiaries in thirty countries, but she no longer remembers my name. She doesn't even know that my father is dead."

"What happened to the company?"

"The shares fell when my father died, of course, but they soon recovered. Sonartek produces great equipment. My father had been in charge of most things, and anything he didn't decide, Victor did."

"Victor Schmidt?"

"Yes. My father was the inventor and Victor the salesman. It was a brilliant combination."

"Did they get on?"

"I think so. When the business went public, Victor got his hunting lodge down at Jungshoved and my father this mansion."

"Are you on the board of Sonartek?"

"Yes, and as long as my mother can't represent her own interests on the board—which she'll never be able to—I represent her as well. My father was Chairman of the Board of Directors; Victor is currently acting Chairman and will be elected the new Chairman at an extraordinary board meeting next month."

"So the family is secured?"

"Not necessarily. Children or grandchildren of the company's founders aren't entitled to board representation or a job with the company. They must be 'suitable,' as it says in the articles and memorandum. The board decides if they are. I would appear to meet the criteria. No one wants a family feud, or to have some imbecile decide the company's future just because their surname is Schmidt or Caspersen. Then again, my mother did inherit my father's shares in Sonartek's holding company, so now I represent—through her—an actual majority share."

"Did your father want you to join the business?"

"Oh, yes! He was over the moon when I qualified as a lawyer. He had it all planned, and I expected him to shoot me when I said no."

Michael smiled. He was impressed. "And he didn't disinherit you?"

"He came round to my point of view. Like I said, I had prepared for the worst, but when push came to shove, he took it rather well. In that respect, he was really quite all right. Perhaps he always knew that I would end up working for Sonartek at some point. That I would come home. When I started attending board meetings, I did it mostly to please him."

Elizabeth Caspersen sat down. Her face was animated; several expressions were trying to upstage each other.

"Victor Schmidt has two sons?" Michael said.

"That's right, Henrik and Jakob."

"What do they do?"

"Henrik is Sonartek's sales director and has replaced Victor, who has taken over the day-to-day management of the company. He's hard-working and has built up an excellent network. He spends most of his time in New York or Washington courting the American defense industry. He's a workaholic and has no vices. Jakob . . ." She shrugged. "I don't know what he's doing at the moment. He's the black, but much loved, sheep. He was an officer in the Royal Life Guards. Now he's a logistician for large aid organizations. He's a free spirit and prefers being on his own, outdoors. The brothers don't see each other that often, but they have both been in Denmark ever since my father died. My father adored them and they're very upset."

"Adored?"

"Very much so. Their picture is over there."

She pointed to the wall behind the spiral staircase.

Michael rose and studied the black-and-white photograph mounted in a fine silver frame. He lifted it off its hook. The wallpaper around the picture hadn't faded. Either it hadn't hung there very long, or it was frequently taken down. There was a faded patch around the photograph next to it; it showed a long-dead leopard in the grass and a smiling Flemming Caspersen, in a safari suit, squatting on his haunches by the animal's head.

He examined the small picture in the silver frame: a grinning, gangly, dark blond boy of around thirteen was sitting at the rear of a canoe with a shiny fish as long as his arm. Behind the boy a sun-shimmering lake spread out. The boy was sitting on the border between the sunlight and the shade from a tree that hung low over the glittering surface. His brother sat on the trunk; a couple of years younger, very blond, skinny upper body, shorts, white teeth and bare feet dangling over the water. There was a tent in the foreground and the picture had a timeless, carefree summer feel to it.

"He took it in Sweden," she said.

"Your father did?"

"Yes. Victor never took a holiday, so he left the boys to my father who taught them all the usual boys' stuff: sailing, fishing, hunting."

"Is Victor married?"

"Monika. Swedish landed gentry."

"A trophy wife?"

"Far from it. She worked for Sonartek as a sales person. She's clever and well educated. She breeds horses now. Danish Warmbloods. Unless that's a contradiction in terms."

A bitter smile formed on her lips.

"My father was jealous of Victor's sons. He called me the third prize."

"The third prize?"

"First prize is a boy, second prize is a disabled boy, and third prize is a girl, he used to say."

Michael was starting to like Flemming Caspersen less and less. He would wait for the daughter to explain the job, as a matter of courtesy, but he had already decided to turn it down. Yes, Sara and he could do with the money, but they could also manage without it. They could tighten the belt another notch while he freelanced for Shepherd & Wilkins, even if it meant his travelling to some godforsaken hellhole in the Yemen, Nigeria, or, God forbid, Kazakhstan. And be away for at least one month. Michael had a standing offer to freelance any time he wanted, which sounded fine in theory, but meant in practice that he ended up doing the jobs that full-time staff avoided like the plague.

"This 'third prize' quip—is that another example of your father's catalogue of eccentric humour?" he asked.

"Yes. I don't think he really meant it. He was just . . ."

A callous, megalomaniac old bastard, Michael thought.

19

"Why am I here?" he asked.

The question appeared to take her by surprise.

"Pardon?"

"Why am I here?"

She looked at him and started saying something. Then she shut her mouth and steeled herself.

"You're here, Michael," she then said, "you're here because I think—no, because I know, that my father killed a man. For fun. For sport. On some kind of sick, twisted, depraved manhunt. That's why you're here."

She got up and took out a DVD without any label or title from the bookcase behind them—and burst into tears.

CHAPTER 2

She didn't move at all or say one word during the three minutes the footage lasted, but she never stopped crying. Without trying to hide it. Michael didn't stir, either.

He sat in the darkest corner of the library with his laptop on his knees as he watched the execution of a young man on a mountain. He heard men sing and saw an object fly through the air: a black sack tied with white cord. The hunted man caught the sack, stuck his hand inside it, and pulled out an object, which his body concealed from view.

The recording equipment was first-rate—picture and sound both crystal clear—and the camera was steady as it zoomed in on the man's ashen face. He limped as he ran out into the darkness, pressing something to his chest. The singing ceased—and half a second later the rifle rang out.

Only one shot was fired and it was impossible to see whether the man was hit. Then the camera found his body on the narrow, stony shore below the cliff. The victim's hand just about touched the water, but the object in the sack had disappeared. The light was turned off. Above the moonlit water he could see the starry night sky for a few seconds before the camera was also switched off.

Michael ejected the DVD from his computer, taking care to touch only the edge with his fingertips. Then he placed it on the keyboard and got up.

"Do you have a lavatory I could use?"

She didn't look at him. "Third door to the left . . . I'm sorry . . . I'm so sorry . . ."

The large house was cool, but sweat was breaking out between his shoulder blades. Michael walked down the passage with the high ceiling, locked the door to the bathroom behind him and splashed cold water on his face. His teeth chattered and his stomach churned, but he refused to throw up.

He had just seen a man hunted to his death, in sharp, natural colours, and he thought with a shudder about the indefinable, but chasm-deep difference between the most convincing Hollywood representations and the real thing.

However, it wasn't the DVD that made him feel sick, though he didn't doubt that the recording was genuine. It wasn't the film. It was the song. It took him back to Grozny, the dead capital of Chechnya. . . .

In September 2007, Michael and his regular partner on the job, Keith Mallory, had spent endless days in a rat-infested, partly collapsed church attic in a suburb of Grozny. Keith, who had a limp after a close encounter with a roadside bomb in Iraq, had been a major in a famous elite British regiment before becoming a senior consultant with S&W. He enjoyed literature, was Michael's immediate superior, and they had become good friends.

The Brit said it was the strangest conflict he had ever seen. To the north, a few hundred metres from the church, rested and well-fed Russian forces waited passively, while to the south, Muslim rebels strolled around without a care in the world among the city ruins. A row of singing women swept the street between derelict and long-abandoned tenement houses. Everything was surreal and everyone seemed temporarily indifferent to each other. The people would appear to simply be enjoying the clear, warm late-summer weather and the lull between bouts of fighting.

Michael and Keith had reached a stalemate in their negotiations with the Fedayeen about a suitable ransom for a British Red Cross medical team whom the Chechens had abducted from a field hospital a couple of months earlier. S&W were negotiating on behalf of an international insurance company who counted the Red Cross among its clients. They had one suitcase full of used dollar bills for the hostage takers, and a smaller suitcase for the corrupt officer in the Russian Air Force who would arrange for a helicopter to pick them up when they needed to get the hostages and themselves across the border to Azerbaijan. They had a floor covered with a thick layer of dried pigeon droppings, a short-wave radio, plaster angels and icons that had been evacuated from the church space below, machine guns, ammunition, their kit, a roll of plastic bags which served as their latrine, plenty of water and astronaut food.

There was currently a few thousand dollars between offer and acceptance, but the issue had become a matter of pride, and was impeded by faltering chains of command.

"He fishes 'cause he can't fuck Lady Ashley," Michael remembered Keith saying a moment before the song began.

"What?"

"Jake Barnes, for Christ's sake," Keith said, sounding tired as he pointed to Ernest Hemingway's *The Sun Also Rises*, the dog-eared paperback currently helping him pass the time.

"Right."

The former major sighed and put down the book. He was still hoping to persuade his young Danish colleague to read something other than weapons catalogues, ballistics tables, and car magazines.

Then he tilted his head to one side. "Who's singing, Mike?"

Michael had put his eye to the telescopic sight of the sniper rifle overlooking the Russian lines. Keith crawled under the low ceiling on his hands and knees and used his own binoculars.

Three hundred metres away a tank crew had grabbed a young Muslim mother and her daughter, who looked to be around seven. Spetnaz elite soldiers, easily recognizable in their blue-and-white striped T-shirts, jumped up and down on the tank and bounced and stomped their way through the old Queen classic "We Will Rock You." The woman was thrown between the soldiers in front of the tank. They tore off one colourful embroidered piece of clothing after another. The daughter was sitting between the legs of a soldier on the turret, turning her face away. The soldier had forced the girl's hands behind her back and put a gun to her neck while he tried to kiss her. By now the mother was naked, screaming, terrified.

Keith started pulling him away.

"It's not personal, Mike. It's terror. Now get the hell away from that window!"

The first soldier raped the mother against the side of tank. His camouflage trousers lay bunched around his boots, and the back of the woman's head bashed rhythmically against the armoured tank. Michael could see her limp arms and spread legs either side of the soldier's pumping body. The soldier's forearms and neck were tanned, while the rest of his body was white around his amateurish blue tattoos.

Four other men were queuing up.

The man on the turret had pushed his gun into the girl's mouth while he unbuttoned his fly.

For the second time Keith had grabbed his arm hard. Michael knew that he could send a bullet through the rapist's bobbing head from the church attic without hitting the mother.

But it meant losing the Red Cross team.

He had already slammed a cartridge into the chamber when Keith wrenched the weapon out of his hands. Then Keith Mallory had put on the headset, even though the radio was dead, and Michael crawled into the furthest, darkest corner of the attic and pressed his hands over his ears.

When he returned to the library, Elizabeth Caspersen was twisting a hand-kerchief hard between her fingers. He sat down on the armchair beside her, folded his hands in his lap and suppressed a shudder.

"What's your reaction to the film?" she asked him.

"I think the recording is real," he said, looking down at his hands. "What I'm saying is, I think someone filmed a crime. My guess is that the DVD must be some kind of hunting trophy."

"Oh, God."

She looked at the ceiling, and fresh tears rolled down her face.

"I presume that's what you thought as well," he said. "Otherwise I wouldn't be here."

She stared at the handkerchief, wound around a finger.

"Yes, only I was hoping . . . I don't know what I was hoping. Yes, I was hoping that you'd say that it was staged, that it was a movie . . . Just a really weird movie."

"Where did you find it?"

She got up and walked over to a Venetian mirror, swung it out from the wall and pointed to a white steel door with a keypad.

"My father's lawyers are winding up his estate. We've emptied the safe deposit boxes in town; all that remained was his private safe."

"Did you know the code?" he asked, wondering why the DVD had been kept in Caspersen's private safe. In his view, it belonged in a nuclear-proof underground bunker.

"The undertaker. My father had the code tattooed on the inside of his upper arm."

She blew her nose.

Michael frowned. "Really? If he went for a swim, anyone with a telephoto lens or good pair binoculars could—"

"Only if they also knew that the numbers must be multiplied by eleven and divided by three then followed by his date of birth," she said.

"Okay."

He still thought it was too obvious: like having the dog's name as the password for your computer.

"What happened to his body?"

"He had asked to be cremated."

"Was there an autopsy?"

"Yes."

"And?"

"Nothing. They said he had a coronary."

"I see . . ."

He rose and inspected the safe. It was a recent Chubb ProGuard model. An excellent safe, designed to be impossible to open in under three hours, even by Chubb's own engineers. The door was white, smooth and undamaged.

"Have you shown the film to anyone else?"

"Of course not! I can't even begin to understand that my father could do a thing like this. Although in some ways . . . unsurprising, isn't it?"

"What is?"

The tears dripped slowly from her eyelashes.

"How the super-rich . . . I know how easy it is to lose touch with reality when you lead a sheltered life, as my parents did at the end. Neither he nor my mother knew the price of a pint of milk."

"I don't know if it's typical. We can't even be sure that it was your father."

She stared at him. "But then why would he have it lying around? It must be him!"

"I can see half a sideburn, part of an ear, a hat and a bit of a sleeve, and a wrist," he objected gently. "It could be anyone."

"He had a hat like that! I know it was him."

"All hunters have hats like that," Michael said.

She swung open the door of the safe, took a flat jeweller's box from a shelf and flipped open the lid. The dark blue silk was embossed with the words "Cartier-Paris" in gold.

"It was in here."

"I wish you hadn't touched it," he said.

She looked at him, then it sank in and she nearly flung the box aside.

"Easy now," he said.

Michael took a clear plastic bag from his shoulder bag and she dropped the box into it.

"And I'm supposed to be a lawyer," she said. "Of course, fingerprints. God help us."

"And hairs, fibres, cells, dandruff, and so on," he said. "Don't be too hard on yourself. It's like a doctor ignoring a tumour about to grow through their own skin. It's a kind of blindness."

"You can say that again," she said.

"What do you want me to do with the DVD?"

She hesitated.

"I want you to find out if that really is my father. I want you to find out the identity of the man they killed. And I want you to find out who else was there. That's why you're here. I have to know if that young man had relatives who need my help."

"Financially?"

"In every way," she said. "How about you? Do you still want the job?"

He looked out of the window.

"I'd like to take the job, even though it's complicated and will require considerable outside assistance," he said. "But I wouldn't say yes if I didn't think I had a chance to work it out. The job doesn't contravene my personal rules. Your father is dead and can't be prosecuted."

"Not in this world," she muttered.

"Quite. I'll find out the victim's identity and as far as the hunters are concerned, I'll track them down, and when I do, they can be punished."

"If you can prove anything," the lawyer said. "Or make them confess."

"The latter might prove easier," he said. "My first impression is that they have military training. They use laser sights that are also available to civilians, but it seems unlikely that they would all come equipped with them if

26

they were just a bunch of stir-crazy hunters on a quest to kill a random victim. You can also see the sleeve of the person standing next to the cameraman. That sleeve is from a military camouflage uniform. Then there are other, less specific factors . . . such as the song. I'm fairly certain that they're soldiers, or ex-soldiers."

"Have you ever heard of hunting people as a sport? It's insane. Sick."

A safari with human prey? Michael had never heard of any such thing and previously he would have dismissed the suggestion as an urban myth, like the one about snuff movies on the Internet. Now he was faced with both, and he was sure that the film was real.

He also knew that some soldiers, despite remaining alive, never quite made it home. They had been different from the start, or the war had destroyed them. Some sought refuge in the wilderness as hermits; others found employment as consultants with security companies. In his career, he had met several professional operators who had forgotten most things about this world.

"I haven't heard about it before," he said at last.

"Do you have any idea where it might have taken place?" she asked.

"It's an Arctic landscape," he said. "But that covers a multitude of sins, as you well know. It could be anywhere from Patagonia to Alaska, but the recording could also be from any mountainous region outside the Arctic. He's screaming at them, but I can't make out the individual words or the language."

"Can you get to the bottom of it?" she asked, sounding despondent. "All of it?"

"Yes, I believe so," Michael said.

"How?"

"I'll examine the film on a series of digital photo programs. I have a hunch that I might be able to identify the crime scene from the constellations you can see just before they switch off the camera."

Again she dried her eyes with the handkerchief and looked up at the vaulted ceiling.

"Perhaps I should just go to the police."

"Perhaps." Michael smiled to encourage her. "But give me a couple of weeks first. I can't exclude the possibility that it might be necessary or relevant to involve the police. They have some resources that I don't. But they're also bound by certain civilized rules which I'm not."

"Are you uncivilized?"

"I can be fairly uncivilized."

"Fine. You have two weeks. What are you going to do with the jeweller's box?"

"Send it to a private forensic laboratory in Berne. If there are traces of anyone's DNA on the box they'll find it, and if there are fingerprints, apart from yours, they'll find them too."

"You can't send them the DVD," she said, sounding alarmed.

"Of course not. But I can check myself whether there are any fingerprints other than yours on the disc. I'm no forensic expert, but I do have some iodine powder and a roll of tape."

Elizabeth Caspersen nodded sceptically.

"I had no idea that they even existed," she then said slowly. "Private forensic laboratories, I mean . . . but then again, I didn't know that people like you existed either."

"Money buys you anything you like in Switzerland," Michael said. "Which reminds me. You ought to get someone to go through your father's private accounts. It would be interesting to know if he had transactions with Liechtenstein, the Channel Islands, the Cayman Islands, or some other tax haven."

She inflated her cheeks and let the air escape in a thin stream. "Of course. How far back do you want them to go?"

"I'll let you know as quickly as possible. May I see his guns, please?"

"Of course."

She made to get up, but sat down again.

"I just don't understand!" she burst out. She pointed at the DVD. "How can anyone do that?"

"You're normal, Elizabeth. So, naturally, you don't understand. I don't understand it either, but I have hunted people—scum who deserved it. Anyone who lives a secluded life, like you say your father did, who only surrounds themselves with like-minded people, easily develops a sense of superiority and invulnerability. They no longer move in the ordinary, agreed reality, and they don't feel that its laws apply to them."

"You mean billionaires?"

28

He flung out his hands. "Or politicians who have never had a real job, Saudi princes or twenty-two-year-old football players who make in a week what an ordinary person earns in a year by kicking a ball around for a few hours, and only see the world from a team coach or an Aston Martin. We tell them they're special and they end up believing it. They're surrounded by an entourage that keeps reality at bay, and suppliers ready to fulfil their every wish."

"Such as a human safari?"

"Or virgins, vintage Bugattis, or powdered rhino horn," he said.

There wasn't just an ordinary gun cabinet, but an entire weapons arsenal, in the basement of the house. Michael saw more hunting trophies, comfortable leather armchairs, bookcases with hunting literature, and magnificent, locked glass-and-mahogany cabinets, custom-made for the room. An almost defiantly masculine haven.

Michael liked weapons. He admired their functionality, performance and precision, and he even found their development fascinating. Behind the cut-glass doors in Flemming Caspersen's weapons room there were rifles and shotguns that would set you back an average Danish annual salary or two, and which made his mouth water. He asked for the keys and unlocked the first cabinet, having put on a pair of latex gloves before he touched anything. Michael lifted out the weapons, unlocked bolts, studied the inside of the barrels by holding them up to a light in the ceiling, and sniffed boxlock actions, magazines and bolts. In the last cabinet he took out a hunting rifle with a telescopic sight, went through the unloading sequence and, to his amazement, caught the unused cartridge as it was ejected from the magazine. He pulled the bolt all the way back and looked closely at the breech before carefully leaning the weapon against the wall.

He examined every cabinet, opened drawers, and studied cartridge belts, various types of sights, and boxes of ammunition.

Michael pointed to the rifle propped up against the wall: "That one. I want you to keep an eye on it. Leave it where it is and make sure no one touches it, okay?"

"Of course, but why?"

"It's a fine weapon," he said. "It's a Mauser M03. It's an excellent, modern, yet ordinary hunting rifle, compared to the magnificent samples your father also owned. Note there's no engraving on it, as there is on every other weapon here, and it doesn't do anything the others can't do just as well, or even better. It has a fine Zeiss telescope with night-vision sight. It's probably the gun I would choose if I . . ."

"Wanted to hunt down and kill a human being," she said.

He nodded gravely. "It wouldn't draw attention to itself and it's the only weapon here that hasn't been cleaned and oiled, which is odd, or at least worth noting. There's gunpowder residue in the breech and there are still cartridges in the magazine—a mortal sin. I've removed one of the cartridges, which I'll send to Berne, along with the jeweller's box. We might just get lucky, who knows. Incidentally, I'll need something with your father's fingerprints. And something with yours."

"A fountain pen, for example?"

"That will do nicely."

He pointed to a small table with a three-quarter-full bottle of whisky and a crystal glass with a brown, dried membrane on the bottom.

"I presume it was your father who enjoyed a dram of whisky?"

"I don't think he ever invited anyone down here," she said. "This was where he came to think. Oddly enough, I haven't been in here since his death. It was his room and I was brought up knowing that it was out of bounds."

"If I could have the glass," he said, "I think it might provide us with the fingerprint we need."

Michael looked around for some tools and found a fine selection of the screwdrivers and pliers used to make rifle ammunition. He pinched the end of the rifle cartridge with a pair of pliers and eased out the projectile with another pair, tipped the gunpowder into a drawer and dropped the cartridge case into a small plastic bag.

She looked at the weapon with revulsion. "Is that what he used, do you think?"

"Could be. I would also like to see the recordings from the break-in, if that's possible?"

"I'll get them to you."

He gave her the address of the hotel where he always stayed when he was in Copenhagen.

"Preferably tomorrow," he said.

"Of course," she said mechanically.

She walked him out onto the main steps, attempted a smile, but ended up folding her arms tightly across her chest and staring down at the tiles.

She was only one thoughtless word away from a complete breakdown, Michael thought. She had been on her own with that bloody DVD for far too long and was obviously juggling all sorts of conflicting demands. She had no idea if she could trust him. If the public ever saw the DVD, she, her husband and their children would have to live in its shadow. The media would crucify them and she would never be allowed to forget that her father, the renowned financier, had turned out to be a psychopathic killer.

He admired her for contacting him, rather than simply destroying the DVD and then crossing her fingers that no copies existed. He knew he wouldn't have been able to do the same.

CHAPTER 3

After the meeting, Michael sat in his car for a long time under one of the avenue's trees, which were already in bud. He had taken off his jacket and loosened his tie. He felt strangely feverish. He stuck a CD in the player, listening to Joan Armatrading while he mulled things over, smoking three of the eight cigarettes that constituted his daily ration: an agreement his wife had entered on with herself, on his behalf. He looked at the shoulder bag containing the computer, aware of what Keith Mallory would have said if he knew that he had taken the job: *"Don't forget your Kevlar, Mike."*

But he didn't own a bullet-proof vest and he wasn't armed. Weapons had a habit of turning unpredictable situations into unpredictable tragedies.

He was convinced that the hunters were soldiers, or ex-soldiers. Professional soldiers created their own subculture with specific songs, phrases, haircuts, tattoos, and slang, and he had heard that song in places other than Grozny. It was a hymn to victory used by elite soldiers from many countries.

Young soldiers who had been on high-risk missions never again experienced a sense of comradeship like that they had experienced at war. Going off to fight was easy, but coming home could be impossible, especially to a country divided in its views on the necessity of the war.

Michael had met young men and women who had become almost addicted to deployment, who pleaded to be sent out again. In the field they had been in charge of sophisticated expensive equipment, while on Civvy Street they might be reduced to sweeping floors in a warehouse. And they were a generation without authority figures. Their parents and teachers no longer had the ability or the guts to discipline them, so they grew up in a world without demands, boundaries or rules. The Armed Forces gave them skilled, stable role models, responsibility, a purpose and a sense of belonging. Some of them found their first family in the military.

Life was harder for this generation in so many ways: their perception had already been warped. Until they witnessed their first real-life fatality, they believed that everyone would get up again, without a scratch, the moment someone restarted the computer.

Michael found a parking space near Hellerup Station and took the S-train to Nørreport. He always stayed at the Admiral Hotel on the Copenhagen waterfront when his clients were paying. Its location was central, it was expensive and comfortable, and it offered a soothing view of the harbour.

He strolled down Frederiksborggade and looked at all the people who had come out to enjoy the spring sunshine on Kultorvet. It was warm, there was no wind, and Denmark was in the transitional phase from puffa jackets, boots, and knitted caps, to shirts, T-shirts, jeans, and summer shoes. He noticed three women about to sit down at a café table in the middle of the square. The second woman had chestnut hair, long legs in jeans, broad hips, a fine bust, even shoulders, and a classic, hourglass waist. She had the pale, clear complexion of a redhead, and large freckles generously scattered across her face. The upper curves of her cleavage, down to a white lace bra, showed in the gap of her shirt when she bent down to pick up a mobile that was ringing in her handbag. She brushed back her hair, put the mobile to her ear and let her green gaze glide indifferently across Michael. Her face and eyes hardened.

Michael's own mobile started ringing. When he answered it, he heard small, bubbling sounds which stopped him in his tracks.

"Hello?"

The moist bubbles were interrupted by an abrupt sneeze.

"This is Michael Sander . . ."

"Did you hear that?" his wife asked him.

"Heard what?"

"Julie said, *Daddy, how are you?*"

"She's eighteen months old, Sara. It sounded like someone stepped on the hamster."

"No, she really did say it, Michael."

"I'll take your word for it."

"Are you smoking?"

33

"Not at the moment," he said.

"What did she want?"

Her voice darkened.

"A job," he said, wiping the sweat from his brow. "I said yes."

"Any travelling involved?" she asked.

"I think so."

He put down his shoulder bag and looked at a shop window.

"Will you be gone long?" she continued.

Michael pulled off his tie and stuffed it in his jacket pocket.

"I think so. It's complicated."

"Dangerous?"

"Yes."

He heard her put down the toddler, whose big brother, aged four, shouted something to the dog.

"You take care of yourself," she said.

"Of course."

"I love you," she said.

"I love you, Sara."

The lobby at the Admiral Hotel had Wi-Fi, and Michael found a quiet corner and sent a long e-mail to the forensic lab in Berne. Then he wrapped the plastic bag with the cartridge case from Flemming Caspersen's hunting rifle in tinfoil, asked the porter for a large, padded envelope, and put the bags with the whisky glass, the cartridge case, the fountain pen and the jeweller's box inside it. He asked the porter to FedEx everything to Switzerland as quickly as possible and put five hundred kroner on the counter to stress the urgency. The porter smiled, promising to take care of everything immediately.

In his room, Michael opened the door to the small Juliet balcony and looked across Copenhagen harbour, the harbour entrances, Christianshavn, and further out at the calm surface of the Øresund. He took a long shower, put on one of the hotel bathrobes and set out his laptop, pen, and a notebook on the desk.

Michael dusted the DVD with iodine powder, carefully blew excess powder off the disc, and dotted circles and swirls from the fingerprints emerged. He

34

lifted the prints from the disc with special tape and held it up against the light from the balcony door. The prints were small, uniform and oval; a woman's prints, he presumed, and from a single individual, he felt certain of it.

He would send the tape sections to the lab in Berne and ask them to compare them to the prints from Elizabeth Caspersen's fountain pen.

Afterwards, he watched the film repeatedly, noting down various details he had missed the first time round. He isolated the only brief, distorted image of the client himself: seen from the right and diagonally from behind; half a broad-brimmed hunting hat with a feather in the hatband. Under the brim he could see part of an ear, a white, well-trimmed sideburn—exactly like on the magnate's portrait in Hellerup—a greenish sleeve, a gloved hand, and part of the butt of a rifle. Michael cut and pasted extracts from the film, added various degrees of brightness, resolution, and contrast to them, but the result was at best ambiguous. The human ear is highly individual, but most of this man's ear was hidden by his hat and jacket collar.

He tried to work out if there was a wristwatch between the jacket sleeve and the glove, but concluded that there wasn't. The weapon itself was impossible to identify. He examined the flash from the muzzle almost a dozen times, from the front and from behind. There was no doubt that it was a hunting rifle. The flash was longer and more yellow than that from a finely calibrated army carbine.

Of the other hunters, he could see only twisted random shadows in the terrain when the beam from a headlamp or the camera light happened to find them. They appeared to have lined up in a semi-circle and there were six of them, besides the client, judging by the number of laser sights. The cameraman tripped, and the camera swept across the nearest bystander, but was quickly steadied again when he regained his footing. Michael replayed the short sequence. He had caught a glimpse of something red and white. He froze the recording: it was a leg, a camouflage-clad right leg with a bloody field bandage wound tightly around the thigh between the knee and the groin.

The cameraman must have been injured.

He played the ending over and over: the young, dark-haired victim. His mouth a screaming hole. How he turned and ran out into the void beyond the cliff edge clutching the contents of the black sack. The victim was a well-built, tall, and athletic man in his late twenties, dressed in appropriate outdoor clothing. When the camera found him again, he looked like a rag doll someone had casually dropped on the shore of what could be a fjord, the mouth of a large river, or a section of an archipelago.

Michael again replayed the film, and zoomed in on the victim's right foot. It was naked, white, and stained dark brown with what looked like dried blood. He didn't think that the young man had appeared restricted in his movements, but then again he was likely to have been pumped so full of adrenaline that he could have run with a broken leg. On his left foot he wore a sturdy hiking boot with blue laces.

It wasn't much, and yet Michael felt strangely optimistic: the constellations in the background on the recording were sharply defined in the last few frames, and he could see the whole figure of the young man.

He paused and started pacing up and down the room. Then he unpacked his travelling bag on the bed, and smiled when he saw Sara's suggestion for bedtime reading. She and an old school friend owned and ran a small but densely stocked second-hand bookshop with strange opening hours, in the high street of the small market town on Fyn, where they lived, and where he himself had grown up. Like Keith Mallory, she was hoping to drag Michael out of his bottomless literary ignorance, but her recommendations inevitably centred on suffering, wasted opportunities, delicate, female sensitivities, and longings. This time it was Flaubert's *Madame Bovary*. On his last trip it had been a Jane Austen novel, and on the trip before that, a poetry anthology by Emily Dickinson. He tossed *Madame Bovary* back in his bag and took out a smuggled crime novel by Jo Nesbø, which he put on the bedside table.

He sat down in front of his computer again. It was a question of geometry, or, rather, trigonometry—as he had said to Elizabeth Caspersen when she asked if he could locate the crime scene. And that was his starting point: based on the pixels on the screen, he calculated the victim's height to be 1.85 metres by comparing his height to the size of his wristwatch, the buttons on his camouflage jacket, and a pair of sunglasses that hung around his neck on a string. He studied the landscape in the background in the few seconds between the camera light going off and the camera itself being turned off, and spotted a set of yellow beams across the water: surely head-lights from a car or truck. There would appear to be a road across the water, while the shore below was bare and stony. A few reflecting ice floes floated on the water. By comparing the height of the dead body on the shore—and again by counting the pixels—he worked out that the cliff must be approx-imately one hundred metres high.

He zoomed in on the stars and planets above the low mountains in the background and manipulated the images until he managed to include even more constellations. If he could find someone who knew how to make calculations based on astronomical almanacs of the stars' individual posi-tions and elevation over sea level, he would be able to determine the geographical position of the crime scene to within a radius of a few kilo-metres and the time the crime was committed to within minutes or even seconds.

He felt he was making headway. He copied the night sky images to a USB stick and looked around for a safe place to hide the DVD. He could always leave it in the hotel safe deposit box, of course, but that would be to run the risk of a prying employee unable to resist the temptation to sneak a peek. He looked up. The ridge of the ceiling in his room was four or five metres away, and the original beam construction was exposed. He dragged the desk to the middle of the floor, placed a chair on top, popped the DVD into a hotel envelope, stuck it between his teeth and started climbing. He found a beam with a thick layer of undisturbed dust on the top and wedged the envelope into a crack. He inspected the hiding place from every angle, but it was impossible to see the envelope from below.

Satisfied with his progress, Michael checked Sonartek's latest annual accounts and share-price trend on a couple of financial websites, and then called his favourite financial oracle, Simon Hallberg, a journalist with *Ber-lingske*. The young man was a born researcher and he had an impressive international network of contacts. Michael had made use of his expertise for several years—as when examining the credit ratings of firms, on behalf of S&W—and knew that the journalist would cooperate on one condition: the sum of two thousand euros paid into an account in Liechtenstein. Simon Hallberg was a gourmet, a wine connoisseur, and a fan of luxury hotels. His Liechtenstein account enabled him to travel in style.

They agreed to meet the following day, and Michael transferred his fee.

He spent the last few hours of the afternoon roaming around the Dark Web, hoping to get lucky. He tried every possible combination of words—"safari," "snuff," "man hunting," "live," "soldier," "mercenary," "real," "target," "human," "killing," "bounty," "experience," "unique," "lifetime." Michael came across a wide range of imaginative and inexhaustible human idiocy and perversion, but found nothing that warranted closer scrutiny.

He had room service send up a sandwich and a beer, and kept on searching until he nodded off in front of his laptop, by which time his brain had long since given up. His bed was starting to look remarkably attractive so he decided to take a break, lie down for a couple of minutes before getting back to work, and that was the last conscious thought Michael had before Sunday, April 15, turned into Monday, April 16.

CHAPTER 4

The song woke him. Or perhaps it was his hangover. Or his bladder, demanding to be emptied. Kim Andersen pulled himself up on his elbow and looked at the face of his new bride, fast asleep.

He sat up and fixed his gaze on the chest of drawers to stop the bedroom from spinning. His uniform jacket lay on the floor, but he was still wearing the pale blue, full dress uniform trousers of the Royal Life Guards, whose braces had got caught up between his legs. They had been driven back to their cottage at four o'clock in the morning after the wedding party. Drunk—extremely drunk—but happy.

He looked down at the lovely face once more. Louise had always been there for him. When he had returned from Kosovo, Iraq, and Afghanistan; heaven after hell on earth. She was there when he felt lost and alienated, when he drank too much, when he had nightmares that drove him out of their bed and into the woods, walking until everything became bright and normal again. And now they were married. He was happy; it was a fresh start.

Kim Andersen looked at his face in the mirror while he relieved himself. His hair was damp from sweat, but newly cut, his chin unshaven and his eyes raw and bloodshot. It had been a great wedding and everyone had been there: their families, Louise's colleagues from school, old army buddies, friends from the hunting syndicate, his colleagues from the carpentry firm, his boss, and his wife.

The song.

He buttoned up his uniform trousers thinking that he must have been dreaming. It was strictly forbidden here. He went into the living room and looked out of the window. There wasn't a sound to be heard. He breathed a sigh of relief—it was only a bad dream.

He hobbled into the kitchen, made himself a cup of Nescafé and looked out into the woods that bordered their property, an old forester's cottage. The box van belonging to the carpentry firm was stationed at the far end of the drive and Louise's new cream-coloured Alfa Romeo was parked close to the cottage with a blue silk ribbon around the body and a massive bow on the roof. He had woken her yesterday because he couldn't wait any longer. He had made her close her eyes and had led her out into the garden while he walked behind her, guiding her with his hands on her shoulders. They were only two metres from the car when he told her to open her eyes. She was thrilled, she said—but could they afford it? They still had to pay for the wedding. He had been upset and they had argued a little.

Kim Andersen narrowed his eyes when he saw through the living-room window that the door of the Alfa Romeo was open. The dashboard glowed red inside the car. He took his mug of coffee outside and was walking up to the car when the song started playing again. He dropped the mug and started running, the braces slapping against his legs. The song filled his ears and his brain with nauseating fear. The key was in the ignition, the stereo was on and the volume turned right up. He fumbled with the controls and finally managed to eject the CD with Queen's old rock number; a blank disc with no information or label.

Kim Andersen flung the disc into the grass, sat down in the driver's seat with his feet on the gravel and his face in his hands. His stubble scratched his palms as he threw up.

Much later, he got up and walked back to the cottage, through the porch and into the hallway. He opened the door to the children's bedroom; he had decorated it with lions, giraffes and zebras and a little girl and boy who were running through the tall grass of the savannah. The children were staying the night with Louise's parents; their beds were neatly made, and on the smooth pillows lay a shiny, 9-mm bullet: one for the head of five-year-old Lucas and one for three-year-old Hanna.

Two hours later Kim Andersen's new wife found him hanging from a rope tied to one of the lower branches of an oak tree. A white garden chair was lying under his dangling feet.

CHAPTER 5

Three hours later Superintendent Lene Jensen's mobile rang just as she had sat down outdoors at a café on Kultorvet in Copenhagen with her two best friends. Lene had been looking forward to this for ages. A good six months had passed since their last meeting. She looked at the display and groaned.

"Now what?" she exclaimed, pushing her spoon through the thick white foam on the caffé latte that had just been placed in front of her. Lene pulled an apologetic face to Marianne and Pia as the voice down the other end ruined everything.

A couple of hours ago, a thirty-one-year-old carpenter, Kim Andersen, had been cut down from a tree in his own garden in a forest south of Holbæk, the voice informed her. He had hanged himself.

The voice belonged to Chief Superintendent Charlotte Falster, Lene's immediate superior in Denmark's national police force, the Rigspolitiet. As usual, she spoke clearly, succinctly and a little too loud, as if deep down in her managerial soul she regarded her subordinates as a little slow. Charlotte Falster disliked misunderstandings and favoured clear and concise communication. She had attended courses on it.

"The poor sod probably just killed himself," Lene grunted. "Surely that's his right."

She spoke quietly and muffled her words deliberately, because Charlotte Falster hated muttering, but she knew perfectly well that the chief superintendent wouldn't have interrupted her own body-flow class or museum weekend in Berlin to trouble herself with a simple suicide on west Sjælland.

"His hands were handcuffed behind his back," the chief superintendent informed her. "Incidentally, he was married only yesterday, so his timing is rather odd. He's a highly decorated war veteran, so we should expect considerable media interest. The public feels that the Armed Forces don't do enough for veterans. That they've washed their hands of them, even though they're traumatized and sick. Holbæk Police has requested assistance. Please, would you take a look at it?"

Lene was tempted to ask if Charlotte Falster could call back tomorrow, but restrained herself.

"What about Torsten?" she asked.

"Paternity leave."

"Jan?"

"Knee injury. Football."

"Christian?"

"On a course. You can bring Morten if you like," her boss said. "Technically, two of you should attend."

Lene wouldn't get out of a burning car if Morten Christensen asked her to, and Charlotte Falster knew it.

"I'll set off in half an hour," she said. "Is that okay?"

"I'm delighted you can spare the time, Lene," her boss responded. "I'll call Holbæk to let them know you're on your way."

Lene plopped the spoon into the cup. She no longer felt like drinking coffee. She felt like screaming. She leaned back with her hands in her lap and stared into space.

"Your boss?" Pia ventured.

"The power bitch." Marianne nodded. There was only one person who could make Lene pull that face.

"It's your birthday," Pia fumed. "Why the hell didn't you tell her?"

"She's not a bitch," Lene said. "She's all right, really . . . a bit uptight, possibly, but she's all right . . ."

"No, she bloody isn't," Pia said.

Pia Holm was a psychiatric nurse, of Mediterranean ancestry, dark-haired and temperamental, and her love for Lene knew no bounds. They had met in a stairwell in Istedgade many years ago when Lene was still in uniform, driving patrol cars out of the old Station 1 in inner-city Copenhagen. Pia's front door was being kicked in by an ex-boyfriend who had been released on licence earlier that day. Her daughter, who was five years old at the time, had huddled up in a corner of the hallway in her nightdress with her hands pressed over her ears as Pia called the police. The other residents had turned up the volumes of their televisions, hoping that the man would get it over with and go away.

Pia had been in the process of pushing a chest of drawers in front of the door when she heard quick, light footsteps on the stairwell, an exclamation of surprise and a calmly admonishing female voice. When she opened the door an inch, a young woman with red hair in a police uniform was smiling at her. She had her foot placed firmly between the shoulder blades of the ex-boyfriend, who was lying on his stomach on the landing with his arms crossed in front of the officer's black uniform shoes.

Her daughter had poked her small, serious face into the gap under Pia. The redheaded police officer broadened her smile, asked her what she was called and how old she was. Then she looked at Pia.

"Do you know him?"

"Yes, I mean no . . . I did. We had a thing once. He's out on licence. He stalks me. I've tried moving."

She started to cry.

The officer looked into Pia Holm's eyes and said that he would never bother her again. She told them to go to bed and get the door fixed in the morning.

"Promise?" Pia asked.

"Cross my heart," the officer said.

"Fucking slags," the ex-boyfriend snarled from the floor.

Pia Holm closed the door and heard a noise like a dry twig snapping. The ex-boyfriend howled. Shortly afterwards she heard something heavy fall down the stairs.

She ran to the living room and looked into the street. The police officer's red hair shone like copper under the street lamp as she dragged along a limp human shape by his feet. Her partner was leaning against the bonnet of the patrol car, smoking a cigarette. The car doors were open, the blue flashing light swept rhythmically across the front of the buildings, and Pia could hear the crackling of a police radio from inside the car. The police officer flicked aside his cigarette and proceeded to calmly help his colleague tip the remains of the ex-boyfriend into the back of the car. The doors slammed shut, the flashing light was turned off and the patrol car disappeared around the corner.

A couple of days later she happened to bump into the police officer, now dressed in civilian clothes, in a supermarket and asked if she fancied a cup of coffee. The rest was history.

Marianne, whom Lene had known ever since she sat down next to her on their first day at school, and was now living in the apartment block next to hers on Frederiksberg, put her hand on her arm.

"Where are you going, darling?"

"Holbæk."

"It's not a kid, is it?"

"I don't think so."

Lene took a deep breath and forced a smile. "Next weekend? Promise me! Both of you!"

"Of course," they said.

She looked at the mobile on the table, pulling at her long red hair in anger.

"Why the hell . . . Why the hell can't people take a break, for once?"

"Because then you would be out of a job, darling," said Marianne, always the voice of reason.

"I could go back to Crete and rent out surfboards," Lene grumbled. "Or make jewellery to sell to tourists."

"You tried that twenty years ago," Pia pointed out. "Time for your presents!"

Her friends rummaged around their handbags. A gift card for Cinemateket—Lene loved movies—and a pair of beautiful silver earrings with pearls and dolphins. Lene was on the verge of tears.

"You're such nice people," she stammered.

"Yes, we are, aren't we," Marianne said. "Happy birthday!"

Lene found her little old Citroën in Nørre Voldgade and spent a moment studying her reflection in the visor. She stretched out the laughter lines around her eyes, refreshed her lipstick and heaved a sigh. The new earrings suited her. She found a hairband and gathered up her hair in a thick ponytail. She was forty-three years old, but didn't feel it. Her daughter Josefine was twenty-one and worked all the hours she could get at a café in order to to save up enough money to backpack with a friend for six months around South America, where she would hopefully find out what she wanted to do with her life. Exactly as Lene herself had done after leaving school with—as her father had pointed out—a set of mediocre exam results. She had spent six months in Crete before returning home to Vordingborg and an uncertain future. She was the first person in her family for several generations not to enter higher education. Police College didn't count, according to her father, who was a pharmacist, and her mother, who was a classical philologist.

She and Niels had divorced when she was thirty-nine and Josefine was seventeen. There had been no drama and they later agreed it was at least five years overdue. Niels had remarried while she drifted on, relatively content with her demanding job and single life. She hadn't been seriously in love for years and she was hopeless at flirting.

She drove home to Kong Georgs Vej, parked, and walked up to her third-floor flat. It was a lovely, bright, four-room, shared-ownership flat, which Lene had bought with the money she inherited from her father. She opened the door and shouted out that she was back.

She could smell popcorn. Her daughter and a friend, the potential South America travelling companion, were sitting at the dining table in the living room, eating popcorn while studying maps and travel brochures.

"How come you're back?" her daughter asked. Then she saw Lene's face and no further questions were needed. She held up the bowl.

"Popcorn?"

Lene grabbed a handful.

"They're lovely," Josefine said, pointing to her new earrings.

"Thanks, sweetheart. I'm going out again straight away."

"Where are you off to?" Josefine's friend asked.

"Holbæk." Lene scowled.

"Well, it could be worse," Josefine said.

"Really? Greenland?"

"Exactly."

"Christ."

Lene went into her bedroom and started hurling underwear, clothes, and toiletries into a sports bag while she debated whether to pack her running shoes. She was in excellent physical shape. She did combat boxing two or three times a week in the Police Officers' Athletics Club—mouthpiece, helmet; full contact—and she weighed the same as she did when she was twenty-five. She had never felt stronger, more supple, or been faster than she was right now. She opened the small steel cabinet built into the wall behind the wardrobe and went through the motions of unloading the service pistol that lived inside it; a grim looking 9-mm Heckler & Koch pistol with eighteen bullets in the magazine. She put it in her bag, added a belt holster and two magazines, and zipped up the bag.

She was ready.

CHAPTER 6

Lene turned off the sat nav when she spotted the patrol car at the end of the small forest track. Gærdesmuttevej was the name of the road; it sounded idyllic, and the white, half-timbered cottage with the thatched roof did indeed look cosy and inviting. A box van belonging to a local firm of carpenters, an ambulance, one of the police's crime scene vans and a brand-new Alfa Romeo with a huge blue ribbon on the roof were parked in front of it. Next to the ambulance was a stretcher with a covered body and, next to that, two paramedics were waiting, watching her car.

As she approached, she noticed the uniformed officer standing under a tree in the back garden and a CSO in white plastic coveralls squatting on his haunches next to the Alfa Romeo, taking samples from a substance that looked like vomit. He dropped something into a test tube.

Lene parked her car on the verge of the dirt track. The garden bordered the woods and there was a long, waterlogged meadow behind the property. A roebuck raised its head and watched her for a moment before it carried on grazing.

She held up her warrant card to the older ambulance man, who nodded to his younger colleague. The younger man pulled down the sheet to the dead man's hips.

Slim, well-built, muscular. His chest was hairless and the hairs across his stomach pointed down to his belly button in a black triangle. His head had rolled unnaturally far to the left. His cervical vertebrae must have snapped just below the skull, she thought. The rope was tied in a knot under his right ear and had left a deep, blue groove around his neck. Kim Andersen's eyes were half closed and his mouth open. The body was lying partly on its side, partly on its back; the position was due to the cuffed hands at the small of his back. Lene bent over to study the handcuffs, which looked very similar to the ones she had in a drawer at her office. The CSOs had wrapped the victim's hands in plastic bags and tied them with string to preserve nail scrapings and other forensic evidence.

The dead man's body was covered with a dozen tattoos. *Rege et Grege*, it said above a red heart near Kim Andersen's left nipple. On the body's left upper arm she found the motto *Dominus Providebit*. Under the crosshairs of a telescopic sight aimed at the head of a Taliban fighter, it said *RLG keeping hell busy*, and under another, empty crosshairs over Kim Andersen's right nipple, *You can run, but you will only die tired*.

Kim Andersen was wearing a pair of thick, pale blue uniform trousers with a broad white cavalry stripe.

"The Royal Life Guards," said the younger of the ambulance crew.

"Yes, I can see," she said. "Thanks for waiting. You can take him away now."

The body would be taken to the Institute of Forensic Medicine in Copenhagen. Lene would go there tomorrow and with luck, be presented with some findings by the forensic examiners. Apart from the obvious, of course.

Red-and-white police tape had been stretched out between the trees in the garden and the CSOs had marked two sets of footprints in the grass with green and red wooden pegs. Lene ducked under the tape, walked past a geometrically perfect log pile under a lean-to and onwards to the young police officer by the oak. Here she studied the upturned white garden chair and the end of a thin braided rope that had been cut off one metre below the branch.

The young, bearded officer pointed to the open garage, where a dinghy was sitting on a trailer.

"I think the rope came from the dinghy," he said.

They entered the garage.

"The jib sheet is missing," the officer explained. "Or, more accurately . . . it's hanging from that branch."

"You sail?" Lene asked.

"Yes, I have a small boat."

He walked in front of her back to the oak.

"What's your opinion of that knot?" she asked.

"It's a fine bowline knot," he said. "The universal knot for everything between heaven and earth, if you sail."

"Did you know him?"

The police officer shook his head.

"Who found him?" she asked.

"His wife. She had made coffee for him. She cut him down and gave him mouth-to-mouth resuscitation and CPR before she called. The call came in at ten fifteen."

Lene frowned. This was highly unusual. Most people would have been paralysed with shock, or panic.

The officer pointed to the cream-coloured Alfa Romeo in the drive: "Some gift, eh?"

"You can say that again," she said. "I should have been a carpenter. Where's your partner?"

"With the wife. Or widow, I guess we should call her, though they didn't even get to be married for twenty-four hours."

Lene looked at the sandpit and the tricycle by the garage.

"Yes, I suppose she is. And the children?"

"With her mother."

She slipped the blue plastic covers over her shoes before she entered the cottage. The first door to the left in the hallway had been hand-painted with African animals and was ajar. Lene pushed it open with a fingernail. It was the tidiest children's bedroom she had ever seen. Two white beds, one with bed linen from *Toy Story*, the other from *My Little Pony*. Perfect. A boy and a girl. Their toys were lined up on lean-to shelves or stored in plastic crates neatly under their beds. The duvets were tucked under the mattresses, but the pillows lay on the floor without pillowcases as if someone had taken a dislike to them, torn off the pillowcases and hurled them at the wall. Lene found the pillowcases under a play table, but didn't touch them. She went outside and asked one of the CSOs to bag them and the pillows.

The man looked at her. "What are we checking them for?"

"If I knew that, you wouldn't have to check them, Arne."

Arne groaned and climbed inside the crime-scene van for more evidence bags.

"What else have you got for me?" she said to his crouched back.

49

"Someone threw up next to the Alfa Romeo," he said. "And we've found this." He held up a plastic bag with a CD. "It was lying in the grass, but it hasn't been there for very long."

Lene looked at the grey plastic disc. "I look forward to hearing what's on it. Tomorrow?"

"Of course. Nothing would give me greater pleasure than staying up all night subjecting it to every acoustic test I can think of. All I had planned was a dinner party followed by a game of bridge. But don't you worry about that."

"I won't, Arne. And you're not the only one who had plans. It just so happens to be my birthday."

"Congratulations. The victim's wife used lopping shears for the rope. We'll take them with us."

"Anything else? How about computers?"

"I haven't found any."

Lene looked at him.

"Surely everyone has a computer these days?" she asked.

"I wouldn't know. Not these two, apparently."

Lene threw up her hands. "Of course they do. It's got to be somewhere, Arne."

"You're welcome to look for it," he said.

"Do I have to do everything myself?"

He grinned. "You're the detective."

"Jesus! . . . How about the footprints in the garden?"

"Two sets. Size eleven, bare feet, and size six, stockings."

"Thank you, Arne."

Lene opened the door to the living room. A woman police officer with short blonde hair was perched on the edge of an armchair with her hands folded in her lap and her legs pulled under the chair: one of those positions people instinctively assume when they know their presence is unwanted. Lene had sat like this more times than she could count.

At the far end of the living room, a young woman was pacing up and down with a mobile pressed to her ear. She didn't look at Lene, but continued her fraught journey between the couch and the bookcase. She held her dressing gown tightly around her throat with her free hand and tears dripped from her round chin. She was shorter than Lene and had a pretty, but pale, drawn face framed by long dark hair. She was wearing delicate flesh-coloured stockings. Lene assumed they had formed part of her bridal attire. Her feet were stained with dew and soil and she still had grains of rice in her hair. The heavy bridal make-up was ruined: stripes of mascara streaked all the way down to her neck and her lipstick was smeared.

"I don't know why," she screamed into the mobile. "He's just dead, Mum! Dead, dead, dead! Someone killed him!"

Lene waited inside the door.

The woman stopped for a moment to draw breath through an asthma inhaler.

"Who are you?" she asked suddenly, and glared at Lene. Her nose was red and her eyes swollen, but the superintendent still saw a hint of something in her eyes, a glimpse of something rational and cool.

"I'm Superintendent Lene Jensen from the Rigspolitiet," she said. "I'm sorry for your loss."

"It's so bloody unfair," the young woman whispered. "Just so bloody unfair. All those wars and not a single scratch and then . . . Yesterday was such a great day. I know that we would have been really happy."

She finished her conversation with her mother, sat down on the sofa, and stared numbly into space.

Lene studied a black-and-white photograph of the deceased on the top shelf of the bookcase. Forage cap, full dress uniform jacket, a cheeky, devil-may-care smile, pleasant facial features. The usual. It looked like every other soldier portrait she had seen over the years. *To my darling Louise*, Kim Andersen had written across the picture. Lene shifted her gaze to a larger colour photograph in a silver frame on the second shelf: a group of soldiers in a distant desert, sweltering in the sun. There were brown, bare ridges in the background and the sun hung vertically above the five men's heads. It was almost impossible to tell them apart: they were all tall and muscular, and they wore broad-brimmed desert hats that shaded the top half of their faces, and close-fitting, very dark or reflective sunglasses. The soldiers were deeply tanned, long-haired and bearded, and didn't look like they were dressed according to regulations: two wore sand coloured T-shirts and loose-fitting camouflage trousers, two were bare-chested, and the last wore an open uniform shirt hanging outside his trousers. Four out of the five had red- or black-chequered partisan scarves around their necks, and all wore black pistol holsters on their thighs.

Kim Andersen was standing in the middle. Lene recognized his tattoos.

The tallest and strongest of the five was standing slightly apart from the others with his arms folded across his chest. A small, but significant distance. Bare-chested, no partisan scarf, no one's arm around his shoulder. He was handsome, she thought. And heavily tattooed. Images, text, and runes meandered up his arms, over his shoulders, and popped up under one ear. Like the others, he was smiling, but his smile was different. Guarded.

She sat down on the sofa next to Louise Andersen. The widow's forehead was pressed against her knees and Lene waited until the strangled sobbing finally ebbed out.

"Louise?"

The head nodded.

"Where are your children?"

"With my mother."

"Would you like to go and see them?"

"Yes, please."

"Then that's what you should do. Can I ask you a question before you go?"

"Yes?"

"You were married yesterday?"

The air was quickly sucked in. Louise Andersen used her asthma inhaler again and wiped her cheeks with the palms of her hands.

She sent Lene a terrible smile. "And put asunder today."

"They tell me you cut down Kim yourself and tried reviving him. You did really well, Louise."

"Thank you . . ."

"Have you seen the handcuffs before?"

Louise Andersen curled up again.

"They were a joke," she sobbed. "One of his friends gave them to him because he was getting shackled to me for life."

"Who?"

"Someone or other. I don't know."

"Okay. Where is your computer?"

52

Louise Andersen gestured in the direction of an antique bureau between the windows facing the garden. Lene nodded to the officer, who got up and raised the lid. She held up a couple of unplugged cables.

"The computer, Louise, what kind was it?"

"What?"

"What make was it?"

"Toshiba. It's a laptop. It's old. Is it not there?"

"No, but I'm sure we'll find it."

"Can I go now? I want to see my kids."

"Of course. We'll take you."

Louise Andersen quickly got up, ran through the living room, and disappeared into the bathroom.

Lene looked at the police officer. Young. Very young. And completely out of her depth, though she tried to exude a quiet competence.

"You can take her to her mother's, can't you?"

"Of course."

"I think you need to get her seen by a doctor," Lene said. "One who can give her a sedative."

CHAPTER 7

A secretary had booked her a room in a small hotel outside Holbæk. It looked like every other hotel room where Lene spent roughly two hundred and fifty nights a year: tidy and sterile.

She ordered the dish of the day—which five minutes later she couldn't remember—and ate in the almost empty restaurant with a fine view of the fjord. A small white ferry glided across the dark blue water towards the island of Orø. The slow-moving lights of the ferry and the cultivated voices of the other diners had a calming, almost soporific effect on her. Lene started nodding off over her plate, until the waiter gently asked her if she would like some coffee.

She had received a preliminary report from Arne, the senior CSO. The CSOs had drilled open the gun cabinet and found a shotgun and a hunting rifle with a telescopic sight. Though the weapons were well-maintained, there was a fine layer of dust on the butts, bolts, and barrels, and they showed no signs of having been fired for a long time. A couple of unopened boxes of shotgun and rifle cartridges were also covered in dust.

They had searched the bathroom and found a bottle of Sertraline, an antidepressant, and a blister pack of sleeping tablets, a brand Lene sometimes took herself. Both prescriptions were in Kim Andersen's name. The seals on the packaging had been broken and Lene looked forward to the results of the forensic blood tests.

Arne had given her the prescribing doctor's name and address.

Apart from that, he said, the place had been unremarkable, furnished like thousands of other Danish homes.

Lene drank her coffee in the deserted hotel bar while she studied her notes and sketches and pondered the inconsistencies. There was more to Kim Andersen, the super-fit carpenter and highly decorated ex-Royal Life

Guard, than met the eye. And though the young widow was distraught at her husband's death—her emotional outburst had seemed completely genuine to an experienced and cynical observer like Lene—her actions after finding his body were downright improbable.

Having drunk yet another cup of coffee at the taxpayer's expense, she left the hotel via a side exit. She walked around a hedge behind the parking lot and continued down the tarmac footpath to the fjord. Lene spent a couple of minutes watching the lights in Hørby on Tuse Næs. The ferry was now on its way back to Holbæk. The water was still wintry cold, but the low hinterland was warmer and turned the sea breeze into dense fog.

She shivered and walked back to the hotel. A couple of sleepy yellow streetlights lit up the almost empty parking lot. A light grey Volvo Estate with a solitary figure in the driver's seat was parked under a lamp post. The windows were rolled down to let out cigarette smoke, and the man's leather-clad arm hung out of the open window, a cigarette tip glowing between his gloved fingers. He had a mobile telephone pressed to his ear. Classical music from the car radio drifted through the darkness. Lene cast a tired, automatic glance at the figure and saw short, dark hair, a shirt collar, then caught his eyes in the car's rear-view mirror. They followed her for a moment before his gaze was averted. The man laughed softly at something on the phone, but didn't speak himself. Lene yawned and went back to the hotel to go to bed.

She removed her make-up, cleaned her teeth, took a quick shower, put on clean underwear, and slipped under the soft duvet.

She woke up long before dawn and sat up, wide awake, as if something had bitten her. The room was cool. It was raining lightly and drops trickled down the windowpane, leaving bright tracks where the reflection from the streetlights hit them. Her heart was pounding and her body was soaked in sweat. She had to make an effort to breathe, and found her pulse on her wrist. She counted while the second hand on her wristwatch circumnavigated the dial. Far too high.

Every police officer knew this fear. At first you assumed that the attacks were random, but Lene had learned that they always had a cause: a small leak from the cupboard crammed full of the deaths, tragedies, violence, and mutilation she had witnessed during eighteen years of service.

Her pulse started to come down, her breathing relaxed and she leaned against the headboard with her hands folded across her stomach, her knees pulled up to her chest. No, that wasn't it this time. There were no faces in there, no voices or swearing or sirens or running footsteps. No dead children.

But there was a man's muscular neck in the sleepy light from a lamp post. A neck with the black, articulated tail of a scorpion crawling under the shirt collar. The neck belonged to the man in the Volvo that had been parked in the parking lot behind hotel. The man whose eyes had followed her in the rear-view mirror. She had seen that scorpion tail before.

In the forester's cottage. She was almost certain.

The mist drifted white and ghostlike across the meadow; above Lene's head Ursa Major was halfway through its gigantic rotation. She walked around the dark, quiet cottage, nearly tripped over the ever-present plastic tape put up by the CSOs and swore nervously. She had roused a sleepy duty officer at Holbæk Police Station to get the key.

She was standing in the porch, rummaging around in her jacket pocket for it, when she heard a faint snuffle right behind her. The warm air molecules from a body very close to hers made the tiny hairs on her neck stand up and she spun around with her pistol drawn and her flashlight at shoulder height. The beam caught the two round bloodshot retinas in the roebuck's wide-open eyes. The animal snorted with contempt, gathered up its legs, and leaped away with long strides through the mist.

Lene squatted down, pressed the cold steel of the pistol against her forehead and stared at her black brogues. Her heart was beating too fast again and she swore for a long time, fluently, despite her terror, and wished that she had shot the damn thing.

Then she let herself in, walked quickly through the hall, across the living room, and stopped at the bookcase.

The desert photograph was still there.

She turned it over, pulled the small metal clips back, and extracted the photograph. Lene sat down on the sofa and studied the soldiers once more in the light from her flashlight. She focused on the tall, broad-shouldered man standing apart from the others. Legs slightly akimbo, arms folded, muscles bulging under his tanned skin. His eyes were invisible behind the reflective, close-fitting sunglasses. The tattoos continued from the shoulder up under his right ear: the scorpion and its poisonous sting.

A guarded smile at the camera. He was definitely not like the others. The man at the edge of the forest removed his night-vision goggles and the world ceased to be made up of grey-green surfaces and shapes. He smiled at the thought of the roebuck that had startled the superintendent. He had actually been impressed by her reflexes, though he had seen better, obviously.

He walked back through the forest, wondering if he should have taken her there and then. It was a very attractive, almost irresistible thought. She was alone. The nearest neighbour was more than a kilometre away. He stopped on the narrow forest path and solemnly reviewed every single thing he would have done to her.

Then he walked on. Some other time. Superintendent Lene Jensen was resilient and strong. It would take a long time to reduce her to an animal.

CHAPTER 8

No one had to tell Michael that a good disguise didn't mean a fake beard, a wig, sunglasses, or shoes with built-in elevation, but rather a well-rehearsed combination of voice, posture, and expressions. It was a question of presenting a character who would block out the person behind the disguise in people's memories. Keith Mallory used to say that people would always see Mickey Mouse, but forget the man inside the costume.

Today's first appointment required him to play the part of a harmless, anxious father. Michael combed his hair forwards to a fringe that ended a finger-width above his eyebrows. He dabbed a little glycerine on his temples to make it look as if he were sweating nervously, and put on a pale, slightly too big, flat-woven linen jacket (which his wife referred to as his "pottery-maker-from-Møn-at-an- exhibition look"), a brown, stripy shirt, and brown sandals (his "biology-teacher, closet-paedophile, 1973 look"), along with a pair of grey checkered socks and baggy, non-descript trousers that even Sara couldn't find words to describe. A pair of sturdy spectacles with plain lenses completed his look.

He might be overdoing it, but this assignment was unusual and he didn't want anyone to be able to reconstruct his movements or uncover his identity. Not to mention the risk of exposing his client's identity.

After a hearty breakfast he had gone to FOTO/C behind the Royal Theatre: a specialist shop for cameras, darkroom equipment, film and photo editing. A staff member had made a copy of the best and clearest images from the starry sky in the last few seconds of Elizabeth Caspersen's DVD. Using advanced software, he had emphasized the constellations even more clearly and produced a set of high- resolution black-and-white photographs.

Michael walked up to Kongens Nytorv, took the metro to Nørreport Station, and decided to walk the rest of the way to the Niels Bohr Institute on Nørrebro.

He had called ahead with his request and after being put through to various extensions had ended up with a young and helpful PhD student with the romantic name of Christo Buizart, currently on loan from the Observatoire de Paris. Michael had introduced himself as Knud Winther, a desperate father in need of Buizart's help to find his daughter through the constellations on a DVD.

He looked at the renowned institute's grey walls before he checked the note with the young Frenchman's directions. On the first floor he soon got lost in a labyrinth of small passages, strange changes in levels and adjacent wings, and he had to ask for directions several times before he was finally able to knock on the door with the name of the astronomer written on a yellow Post-it note.

It appeared to be an informal place.

The Frenchman ruled over an office that was slightly smaller than two telephone booths put together. Stacks of papers, humming electronic cabinets, and several large computer screens made the office practically impassable, and there was only one chair, occupied by the young scientist himself. He rose, nearly knocking over a coffee cup, swore in his mother tongue and held out his hand.

"*Bonjour.*"

"*Bonjour,*" Michael said. "Could we possibly speak English?"

"*Naturellement, monsieur.*"

Michael began his cover story about a twenty-year-old daughter with an unhealthy fixation with goth rock, who had convinced herself that she was in love with the lead singer of a German band called Styx. The daughter referred to the singer as "the Master." Judging by his publicity photos "the Master" was at least sixty years old.

Christo Buizart smiled sympathetically.

"After a concert in Berlin in 2012, my daughter became obsessed with this wretched band and its strange world, and took off. We only heard from her through text messages and e-mails. Styx is worse than a religious cult. It's every father's nightmare."

The Frenchman, who was twenty-five years old at most, nodded as if he understood.

"But how can I help you?" he then said.

Michael wedged his shoulder bag under his arm and fumbled with the envelope containing the constellations. At the sight of the shiny photographs, Christo Buizart quickly gathered up his papers and reports and made room on the desk.

"One of my colleagues suggested I had these photos made," Michael said. "He's an amateur astronomer and thought you might be able to locate my daughter using the constellations. The recording is from a short film she sent my wife a couple of months ago."

Michael's face assumed a desperate expression while the astronomer closed the blinds and studied the photographs through a magnifying glass.

"Can I draw on them?" he asked.

"Of course."

With a white pencil the Frenchman quickly joined the stars to form their constellations.

He pointed to the largest glowing spot at the centre of the picture.

"This is Venus, of course," he said.

Michael smiled, impressed, and leaned forwards.

"Above Venus we have Sheratan in Pegasus and here we have Sheratan in Aries," Buizart continued. "So we're somewhere north. Very far north. We're looking at the western sky? Somewhere in the high latitudes. There is Pisces. Fine . . . very fine, in fact."

He glanced at Michael.

"There's water, a sea in the foreground. It looks as if it lies below the point of observation."

"She wrote something about standing a hundred metres above the water and *greeting the stars*," Michael informed him gravely.

The Frenchman nodded and clicked through different databases, tables and endless rows of green, constantly changing digits on a computer. Then he entered some numbers into a sophisticated pocket calculator.

"This is an astronomical calculator," he explained.

"I see."

The young man was lost in his private universe for a few more minutes before he looked up.

"Latitude seventy degrees, twenty-nine, forty-six North, longitude twenty-five degrees, forty-three, fifty-seven East," he said, scribbling down the coordinates on a notepad. "If we assume that the elevation above sea level was 102 metres."

"Where is it?"

"There." Christo Buizart opened Google Earth and moved the cursor to the coordinates. "Just east of Porsanger Fjord. The northernmost part of Norway, *monsieur. Voilà.*"

"What th—?" Michael cleared his throat. "Sorry, when?"

The astronomer swiftly entered more numbers into the calculator.

"At precisely eighteen forty-five local time on March 24."

Michael looked at him.

"What year?"

A Gallic shrug.

"*Je ne sais pas, monsieur.* Within the last few years. The constellations and their exact position in relation to the Earth repeat every year, obviously. More or less. If I could be absolutely sure of the elevation and if there were comets, satellites or other distinctive objects on the photographs, I would be able to tell you which year. But you said yourself that your daughter disappeared in the autumn of 2012, so surely this could only be 2013 if you received the film a couple of months ago?"

"Of course. You're right. Thank you so, so much!"

The astronomer smiled. He had some of the nicest teeth that Michael had ever seen.

"My pleasure. I hope that you'll be reunited with your daughter very soon," the Frenchman said solemnly.

Michael found a café with a small outside area overlooking the paths by the lakes. He drank black coffee, wiped the glycerine off his temples, combed his hair and put the glasses in his shoulder bag. He watched joggers and young women with prams while his mind processed the latest developments. The spring sunshine appeared to be enticing everyone outside.

Finnmark. Porsanger Fjord. Michael didn't know very much about northernmost Norway, other than it was sparsely populated, had few roads and exerted a magnetic attraction over hikers and climbers—though in his view March seemed rather early in the year for hiking in the mountain. But the date would explain the ice floes on the water below the cliffs. Perhaps the man had been skiing. Perhaps he had come from a nearby ski lodge. Or maybe he had been brought there from another location.

Michael wondered if there might still be human remains on the rocky shore of the fjord, but thought it most unlikely. The local wildlife had had time to consume it, and the tide, the ice, and the winter storms had presumably taken the rest. Finnmark could probably swallow up whole armies without anyone knowing.

Still, at least he now possessed a set of exact coordinates, provided that the elevation—which was crucial for the accuracy of the calculations—was correct.

He got up, paid for his coffee, and walked along the lakes to his next appointment.

Michael spotted Simon Hallberg easily. As agreed, the young journalist from the *Berlingske* was waiting under the famous white lamps outside the Boghal bookshop on Rådhuspladsen. He was wearing a short brown corduroy jacket, jeans, yellow sneakers, and a pale blue shirt, and had a tattered grey bag over his shoulder. Half street, half graduate. In other words, a journalist. His shoulders looked as if he rarely lifted anything heavier than a pen, and along with many of his contemporaries, he had shaved his head. Michael had the impression that more and more young Danish men were losing their hair prematurely. He had heard it attributed to phthalates in teething toys. Or maybe they chewed their iPhones?

Michael placed his hand on a corduroy shoulder and made the journalist jump.

"Are you thinking of defecting, Simon?" he asked.

"Hi, Michael! What? No, no, Christ, no, I'm very happy where I am. Absolutely. How are you?"

"Great."

"And your son?"

"Fine. We had a little girl eighteen months ago," Michael said.

"Ace."

Simon Hallberg, who was still single, ran his gaze up and down Michael's outfit with a pained expression.

"Undercover?"

"Very much so. Let's walk."

"Coffee? I know a . . ."

"I think we should walk," Michael said.

They crossed Rådhuspladsen diagonally, passed the statue of Hans Christian Andersen and continued down the boulevard. They found a vacant bench in the beautiful, but usually deserted town hall garden. Michael looked around. There was no one within earshot. Further away, on another bench, a couple of town hall employees were eating their packed lunches.

"Sonartek," he said. "What's the story, Simon?"

The journalist leaned back and pressed his fingertips together. His eyes were half closed in concentration. Michael knew the boy had a photographic memory.

"A sheltered island in the middle of the global, financial tsunami, Michael. Seriously. Solid, like Fort Knox. They appear to be almost unaffected by the crisis. They produce a range of products that will always be in demand and they're innovative and quick to adapt. They constantly bring out new software and improved hardware, and the stuff practically sells itself. Sonartek has a virtual monopoly in their particular niche market. They're the textbook answer to Gillette."

"But can they retain their position following the death of Flemming Caspersen? I thought he was the brains behind it?"

"It would seem so. Their engineers are the best in the business. A sensible mix of people who have been with them right from the start. Young Danish, Chinese, and American talent. So they're future-proof not only in terms of experience, but also in terms of creativity. They moved all the cost- and labour-intensive parts of the business out of Denmark before anybody else."

"To China, India, Lithuania, and Poland?"

"Precisely. They have a gold-plated brand; Sonartek's future looks bright and beautiful. In as much as . . ."

"In as much as?"

"A company such as Sonartek will always face external and internal threats," Simon Hallberg declared. "The founder dies, and then what? Danish industry is filled with stories of renowned family companies that split into atoms once the founder is gone. Factions, spoiled heirs who have never done a day's work in their life and can't stand each other. They wreak havoc in the boardroom. It's practically the rule rather than the exception. But standing between Sonartek and dissolution are Victor Schmidt, a solid holding company, a bullet-proof foundation which favours rationality rather than emotion, and a board of professional directors who look after the interests of the company, rather than those of the heirs."

"And external threats?"

Simon Hallberg smiled, lit a cigarette, and offered one to Michael, which he decided to exclude from that day's tally.

"Very interesting and unusual. What you need to bear in mind, if you're interested in Sonartek, is who wants to preserve the status quo and who doesn't. Their biggest customer is the US Department of Defense—the DOD—but the technology is also essential to the arms industry in many other countries: Bofors in Sweden—or the Celsius Group as it's now called—Thales in France, BAE Systems in the UK, and so on. Imagine a situation with no Sonartek. It would be catastrophic. There would be no maintenance of weapon systems, no spare parts, no engineers, no automatic software upgrades. Three-quarters of all the world's fighter planes, tanks, submarines, and warships would be grounded. They simply couldn't be guaranteed to work properly."

Michael whistled. "Not to mention meteorological early warning systems."

"Exactly. Airports across the world, civilian as well as military, would have to close. They wouldn't know how to get the aircraft up in the air or down again. Every system is fitted with Sonartek's Doppler technology. The Americans worry about it constantly. They don't like the company's monopoly. The vulnerability."

"So why don't they just buy Sonartek?"

"Oh, they've tried, along with everyone else. Now, the DOD isn't in the business of overt acquisitions, but they could ask a big investment company to do it on their behalf against guarantees of future market shares and contracts, discounts, favourable prices, the smooth processing of patent rights and so on."

"And have they?"

"Several times. In 2010, an offer of sixty billion kroner for the whole business came in from Bridgewater Associates, followed by a sixty-five-billion bid from Blackwell—two huge American investment companies. No one ever said it out loud, but everyone knew that the Pentagon was behind it. Victor Schmidt and Flemming Caspersen turned them down."

"And if they hadn't?"

Michael tried visualizing sixty-five billion kroner.

"Sonartek would have been broken up in less than five minutes," Simon Hallberg said. "The military part would be sold to, let's say, Raytheon, US-owned and a major supplier to the defense industry. They would create a subsidiary with the DOD as the main shareholder. The meteorological part would be sold to Philips or Siemens, and the optical division to Sony or Samsung. The investment company would earn billions in a few seconds, and the DOD could sleep soundly at night knowing that their aircraft and submarines would also work tomorrow. Happiness all around."

"Who on earth says no to sixty-five billion?" Michael wanted to know.

"Flemming Caspersen and Victor Schmidt. It's their life's work and they already have all the money they will ever need. I believe one of Victor's sons, Henrik Schmidt, will carry the baton. He's Sonartek's sales director and most people think he does a very good job."

"But he has two sons, doesn't he?" Michael asked.

"Yes, but I don't think Jakob Schmidt has ever shown much interest in the business. I believe he's a big game hunter somewhere? Or maybe he works for aid organizations in Africa? He's most definitely out of the equation when it comes to Sonartek's future, is what I'm saying."

Michael looked at his watch. There were so many things he wanted to get done today. Such as finding out the name of the man murdered in Porsanger Fjord.

"What about Flemming Caspersen's heirs?" he asked.

The journalist held up one finger.

"There's just the one. Elizabeth Caspersen-Behncke—note the sequence of the double-barrel. She's on the board of Sonartek, but has her own career as an attorney and she doesn't appear to be very interested in the company. Then there's Caspersen's widow, who has Alzheimer's, but legally she now controls Flemming Caspersen's share of the business until someone can get a power of attorney approved. She's no longer capable of making any decisions."

"And if her daughter is appointed her guardian?"

"With her own shares and those of her parents, Elizabeth Caspersen would have a majority shareholding in Sonartek's parent company and therefore all the power."

Michael looked pensively at his hideous sandals. That was interesting.

"How did the Americans react to the death of Flemming Caspersen?"

"No idea. There has been no official reaction, as far as I know, but you can be absolutely certain that they'll be against any change in Sonartek. They prefer knowing where they stand."

Michael nodded. Did the US Defense Department or one of their countless intelligence services have anything to do with Elizabeth Caspersen's DVD? New, complex possibilities and angles sprouted all over his brain.

He got up and held out his hand.

"Thank you, Simon. You are, as always, well-informed."

The journalist also rose to his feet. "Why are you so interested in Sonartek? Do you know something I don't?"

Michael smiled. "I couldn't possibly say, Simon."

CHAPTER 9

"A manhunt?" Keith Mallory sounded unconvinced. "Are you taking the piss, Mike? You are, aren't you?"

"No, I'm serious," Michael said. "Is that really so hard to believe? People ski down Mount Everest, have themselves smuggled across the Afghan border to play soldiers. Game hunters order a hybrid of a lion and a Bengal tiger to get a trophy for their mantelpiece that no one else has. And don't forget there were people who paid the Serbs to be allowed to shoot women and children in Sniper Alley in Sarajevo in '94. Just for the sport."

A pause followed on the other end of the line; Michael hoped it indicated serious consideration.

"And we're not talking New Guinea or Matto Grosso? Blow pipes and clubs?" asked the Brit.

"No, we're talking about a possibly psychopathic billionaire; we're talking the Arctic and laser scopes . . . and Queen's 'We Will Rock You.' Professionals, Keith. Ex-soldiers."

Michael knew that they both had the usual suspects in mind: consultants from the multinational security companies that got the contracts in Iraq, Kosovo, and Afghanistan when the regular army units were pulled out, and who then poured in to guard oil installations, foreign diplomats, aid organizations, parliament, the fledgling democracy, to train said new democracy's security forces, police, and army, and make sure that the ballot boxes were filled with ballot papers rather than plastic explosives.

"The guys from Pax," Keith Mallory suggested.

"Could be," Michael said.

Pax was the most notorious of all the security companies. It was banned in many countries, but sought after in others. Pax got the job done, but their methods were highly dubious and there were never any witnesses around once the dust had settled.

"I need a little more to go on," Mallory said.

Michael followed a water bus with his eyes. "Norway," he said.

"Norway?"

"Finnmark, Keith."

"When?"

"Sometime in March in the last two years."

"Can you be a little more specific?"

"Not at the moment, but once I find out the precise time, you'll be the first to know."

"How many?"

"Six hunters and one client," Michael said. "Please, would you take a look at it? The money is good. I mean, really good."

"Did they catch anything?"

"A man around thirty. He jumped from the edge of a cliff or was shot when the bastards had finished singing."

"Danish?"

"No idea."

"How sick. That's tragic, Mike."

"Yes."

"I'll look into it."

Michael got up, opened the balcony door and leaned against the balustrade. He looked at his newly purchased mobile phone with the prepaid SIM card, swung his arm back, and threw it far into the harbour's waters. He had three others waiting, still in their unopened boxes. From now on, he would use a new one every day.

Talking to Keith was the smartest move he could make right now. The Brit's contacts were fresh and far-reaching. If he dug deep enough, something would turn up eventually. This was the way things worked in Mallory's shadowland. No text messages, phone calls, or e-mails. Someone would contact the ex-major by tapping his shoulder in the pub or while out walking his dog, and Michael would subsequently pay a substantial finder's fee. Someone was bound to know something, or know someone who did. It was who you knew. Everything in this business was about who you knew.

He lay down on the bed and stared up at the ceiling.

Sixty-five billion.

That blasted film would hang over Elizabeth Caspersen's head and deter-mine everything: her own, her family's, and Sonartek's fate. It wasn't just a plastic disc with zeros and ones. It was a remote control with somebody else's finger on the button.

Thoughts buzzed around his head like angry bees and collided with the inside of his skull. He reached out for a newspaper and reread the headline on the front page, which had caught his eye earlier when he passed the 7-Eleven: MYSTERY DEATH OF YOUNG DAD. There was a photograph of a smiling man wearing the Royal Life Guards' full dress uniform. Forage cap with a tassel, uniform jacket, shirt and tie. Nice teeth.

"Suicide or murder?" the journalist speculated on page five. Kim Andersen, a thirty-one-year-old carpenter, who had previously been deployed as a combat soldier with the Royal Life Guards to Iraq, Bosnia-Herzegovina, and Afghanistan, had been found hanged by his new wife the morning after their wedding. The Rigspolitiet were involved, which meant his death was being treated as unexplained. The timing was extraordinary, Michael thought. The dead man had lived with his girlfriend for six or seven years before they were married and they had two young children. The journalist hinted at yet another maladjusted, burned-out veteran who couldn't find his way home.

There was a photograph taken from a helicopter of a thatched cottage in a forest, of ambulances and crime-scene vans, and the journalist had sniffed out that one of the Rigspolitiet's most experienced investigators, Superin-tendent Lene Jensen, was currently staying at Hotel Strand- marken, a few kilometres from the potential crime scene.

Michael's eyes widened when he saw the archive photo of the police superintendent on the steps leading up to Copenhagen's District Court: black suit, high heels, sunlight bouncing off sparkling red hair gathered at the nape with a hair slide. Serious expression.

He smiled when he realized where he had seen her before: at a café on Kultorvet yesterday.

He pushed the newspaper aside on the bedspread, stuffed an extra pillow under his head, and resumed his study of the ceiling.

CHAPTER 10

Lene yawned behind her surgical mask as she looked at Kim Andersen's dead body on the steel slab. She was so tired she was about to keel over. The smell of formaldehyde made her feel nauseous and the constant hum from the ventilation fans above was giving her a headache. She hadn't been able to sleep when she got back to the hotel. She had put the desert photo on the bedside table and spent the rest of the night either tossing and turning in bed or switching on the bedside light and studying the picture again.

The forensic examiner on duty today was a young woman whom Lene knew from previous cases. She folded the heavy sheet down to Kim Andersen's feet. Blue and reddish livors had formed where the skin touched the table. He had been freed of the handcuffs, the plastic bags around his hands, and the rope around his neck. The indentation from the rope below the ears had now turned black.

The forensic examiner looked at her.

"I expect you're here to find out what killed him?"

"He broke his neck, I presume," she said.

The doctor's eyes smiled above her mask. "Yep. Lunch?"

"Why not."

She followed the pathologist to a series of light boxes on the wall where X-rays of the dead man's cervical vertebras were displayed. Lene had once asked the young woman why she had chosen this macabre specialism, populated by abused children, rape victims, and drowned and charred bodies, rather than a more lucrative and sheltered career as a plastic surgeon or an Ear, Nose, and Throat specialist, but couldn't remember her reply.

The pathologist pointed. "Here's the top cervical vertebra, Atlas: he carries the globe, that's the skull, on his shoulders. It's displaced in relation to the underside of the skull, and the vertebra below, Axis, has broken. Do you follow?"

Lene nodded.

"So what killed him is the fracture on this section of the second cervical vertebra," the forensic examiner explained.

"By falling from a garden chair?"

"It's enough. He weighs eighty-five kilos and fell from a height of roughly forty centimetres. There was enough force, acceleration, and gravity to break his neck."

Lene leaned against the sink for support.

"What about his wrists?"

"That's *your* problem, Lene, and good luck with that one," the pathologist said, shaking her head.

"Someone handcuffed him after he was dead," Lene declared.

The forensic examiner nodded, went over to the section table, and lifted up one of Kim Andersen's arms. Rigor mortis had come and gone.

"There are no skin lesions or bleeding underneath the handcuffs, which there would have been if, say, someone handcuffed him while he was alive and then hoisted him up from the ground with the rope. If we imagine that he handcuffed himself because he was worried he might change his mind halfway, there would still have been some marks. His nervous system would have carried on working even after he was brain dead and he would instinctively have fought the handcuffs. Besides, we found polyester fibres that match the rope on the palms of his hands. He tied the knot himself, but didn't try pulling himself up by using the rope. There are no burn blisters in his palms, as you can see."

The forensic examiner pulled off her gloves, took off her sterile gown, scrunched everything up, and threw the bundle in a bin.

"I've heard of cases where a killer has tried to make a murder look like a suicide," she said pensively. "But I've never heard of anyone trying to make a suicide look like a murder."

"So this is unusual?"

"It is. Why would someone want to do that?"

Lene smiled. She really liked the forensic examiner. When she smiled, she revealed a charming gap between her front teeth which she could easily have had fixed. Lene liked that she had simply let it be.

71

"Elementary, my dear Watson," she said. "Someone wants Kim Andersen's suicide investigated as if it were a murder. So that's what I'm going to do. What do the blood tests say?"

The pathologist opened the file.

"A quite respectable level of alcohol following the excesses of the wedding, but not alarming or in any way life-threatening."

"Sleeping pills?"

The forensic examiner shook her head.

"No benzodiazepines or barbiturates, but Sertraline, a bog-standard anti-depressant in a therapeutic concentration. Happy pills. You don't kill yourself when you're taking happy pills."

"You just get even happier?" Lene mumbled.

"Sorry?"

"Nothing. What about his tattoos?"

"The Royal Life Guards. *Pro Rege et Grege* is the Guards' overall motto: 'For king and people.' Then we have the words *Dominus Providebit*, which means 'The Lord will provide.' Very pious. I looked it up. It's a secondary motto for the Royal Life Guards' First Armoured Infantry Company. It says *ISAF* on the inside of his right forearm, which stands for the 'International Security Assistance Force'—the NATO-led mission to Afghanistan."

"The Coalition?"

"Yes. He was a veteran."

"He was, and not just from Afghanistan. He had also been to the Balkans and Iraq. What about lipstick?"

"Excuse me?"

"His wife claims that she gave him mouth-to-mouth resuscitation once she had cut him down. She wore heavy make-up left over from the wedding, including smeared lipstick and mascara, which was far from waterproof. I couldn't see lipstick anywhere on his nose or his mouth. And there should be, shouldn't there?"

The doctor's eyes widened slightly and she nodded slowly.

"You're right," she said. "I mean . . . there isn't any."

The two of them looked at the dead man's stern, introverted face. The eyes had sunk deep into their sockets.

"You're saying the wife is lying?" the forensic examiner asked.

"I think that the only thing she has told me that's true is her name," Lene said.

She removed her surgical mask, even though it took the edge off the stench, and hid a fresh yawn behind her hand. Her mobile vibrated silently in her jacket pocket, but she ignored it. She knew who it would be. Chief Superintendent Charlotte Falster wanted her daily briefing so she could step in with her superior intelligence if she felt it necessary.

"Any fingerprints on the handcuffs?" she asked.

"Your CSOs have got them."

Lene pointed to an irregular, deep scar on the dead man's right thigh.

"What's that?"

"Yes, that's also very interesting. I'd say it's a bullet from a hunting rifle or an army carbine."

With some effort the forensic examiner raised the leg from the steel table. "The bullet brushed the top of the thigh, which broke its trajectory, so it went into the leg. The bullet passed straight through the flesh without hitting the bone or any of the vital structures in the back, such as a nerve or major artery."

The exit wound at the back of the thigh was considerably larger than the smallish, star-shaped scar at the front.

Lene frowned.

"And that's not shrapnel from an IED?" she asked.

"No. And it hasn't been treated by a surgeon. I'm sure it was thoroughly cleaned, but it wasn't stitched. It's been allowed to heal right from the bottom, which would have taken a couple of months. I would estimate it to be a few years old."

Lene nodded. She could see that the forensic examiner had taken tissue samples from the edge of the scar.

"So he wasn't treated at a hospital or an emergency room?"

The doctor shook her head vehemently.

"I'm absolutely sure that he wasn't. If a surgeon had treated this injury, the first thing he would have done would have been to cut through the soft tissue and open the bullet trajectory in order to ensure there was no soil or textile fragments inside it."

Lene nodded again. Now, what was it Louise Andersen had said? Something about all the wars her husband had fought in without ever getting so much as a scratch?

Lene stopped for a moment outside the low building and looked towards Fælledparken. Small figures from a nursery were making their way across the grass as a jogger in tracksuit bottoms and a hoodie did stretches against a tree about a hundred metres away. She took deep breaths to get the stench out of her nose.

Her mobile vibrated again.

"Where are you?" her boss demanded to know.

"Outside the Institute of Forensic Medicine."

Lene started walking towards her car.

"What have you found out?"

Lene could visualize Charlotte Falster sitting in her office at the Rigspolitiet's new headquarters in a dreary industrial estate in Glostrup, behind a big desk with a silver triptych frame displaying pictures of the senior civil servant to whom she was married and their good-looking and successful son and daughter. There were Impressionist posters on the walls, a Vibeke Klint rug lay on the floor, and an unflappable grey-bob hairstyle graced the chief superintendent's head.

She wasn't, as Lene's friends Pia and Marianne claimed, exclusively an irritating bureaucrat or a lousy boss. It was simultaneously more straightforward and more complicated than that: quite simply, the two of them didn't get on, and had both known it right from the start. Still, they tried to make the best of things, if only out of mutual professional respect.

"Kim Andersen killed himself," Lene said. "There's no doubt about it."

She unlocked her car. The energetic jogger in the hoodie had left the tree and was slowly running along the path, away from her.

"And the handcuffs? How do you explain them?" her superior said.

"Someone handcuffed him after his death."

"To make us investigate the case?"

"That would be my view."

"Any idea who it might be?"

"The wife. There are no footprints in the grass other than his and hers. The dew had fallen and the soil was wet and soft."

There was silence at the other end of the line while her boss sifted through her thoughts. "Do you need help?" she asked. "Jan is back at work after his football injury. You know that . . ."

She didn't complete the sentence, for which Lene was grateful. Yes, of course, each team ought to be made up of at least three staff: one to collate the information from the crime scene, one to read all the reports, and one to question witnesses. At this point, Charlotte Falster would usually start lecturing her about teamwork, synergies, facilitators, ownership, mutual evaluation, and other meaningless business school terms, but mercifully she refrained from doing so.

"It's just a suicide," Lene said. "I'll talk to the widow."

She heard a rustling of papers down the other end. Today's newspapers, no doubt. Charlotte Falster's relationship with the media was ambiguous. On the one hand, she performed well in print media or on television with her cool, reserved, articulate, and well-schooled manner. On the other hand, she hated the fact that journalists, whom she universally regarded as a tribe of grotesque, puffed-up, self-important, lazy fools, wasted her resources with their Freedom of Information Act requests, interviews, enquiries, and corrections.

"I'll handle the press," Lene hastened to add. "I'll call a press briefing tomorrow. You were right. They're really interested in this story. They're buzzing around Holbæk like flies."

"Thank you," Charlotte Falster said, sounding as if she actually meant it. "Why don't I issue a bland press release, and find a room at Holbæk Police Station. Is two o'clock tomorrow afternoon good for you?"

"Of course it is," Lene said. "And thank you."

She got into the car and pressed the speed dial on her mobile for Arne, the CSO, and asked him to compare the fingerprints from the handcuffs to those of Louise Andersen.

Then she wondered why it hadn't even crossed her mind to tell Charlotte Falster about her night-time visit to Kim Andersen's cottage, about the photograph of the invincible, young warriors in the desert, or about her feeling of being watched all the time. There was no easy answer. It was just the way it was. She didn't want the chief superintendent looking over her shoulder.

*

The jogger in the hoodie walked over to a motorbike parked behind the Institute of Forensic Medicine, removed the chain from the helmet he had locked to the handlebars, retrieved a leather jacket and a pair of gloves from one of the panniers, and put the key in the ignition. He was in no hurry. He knew he could find Lene Jensen any time he wanted to: the previous night he had attached several hidden GPS senders to her old Citroën. The police superintendent was utterly predictable. As was her pretty, twenty-one-year-old daughter, Josefine.

The flat in Kong Georgs Vej was empty, and clean. Josefine had aired it after the popcorn, no underwear was drying on the shower rail in the bathroom, the floor had been vacuumed, and the kitchen gleamed and smelled fresh. Even the daughter's room looked as if it had been visited by a Feng Shui consultant. Lene wandered around, slightly stunned, in her own home. It was as if her daughter had taken a quantum leap from being a messy and totally self-absorbed teenager to the headmistress of a domestic science college.

She would miss Josefine when she started travelling and when, in due course, she left home. She would even miss their strange, black arguments, which flared up out of nothing and into which they both threw themselves with passion. Neither of them ever asked for mercy and they took no prisoners. They would rather die than admit that they might have been wrong until they reached the far corners of their irrational fog, happened to look at each other, hit the *fast rewind* button on the conversation as they heard themselves spout the most ridiculous rubbish—and collapsed in laughter.

She would miss all of it.

Lene slept for a couple of hours on the world's best sofa in her living room and woke up deeply resenting her next task: a long, hard talk with the grieving young widow with the false tongue.

First, however, she had to go to Holbæk and talk to Kim Andersen's doctor.

CHAPTER 11

The doctor's practice was located, very conveniently, above a pharmacist and below an eye specialist, in a white building in Holbæk's high street. It was like travelling forty years back in time. The corners of the grey linoleum tiles in the waiting room curled up, and Lene inspected the worn furniture critically before sitting down on a sofa that looked as if it were made entirely of green sponge. She had introduced herself to an elderly, shapeless secretary in the front office, but wasn't convinced that the woman had heard her.

While she waited, Lene watched a small boy in the play corner of the waiting room, with thick glasses and cotton-wool balls in his ears, try to press a square peg through a round hole in a wooden board while his mother read a women's magazine. As the boy struggled, it struck Lene that this was how returning soldiers might feel: like a square peg trying to fit into a round hole.

Without warning the woman got up, grabbed the boy, and disappeared through a door. Lene hadn't heard anyone call out or seen a light go on, and she wondered if only the initiated could secure an audience with Dr. Knudsen. She heard a piercing cry from the doctor's office, followed by the sound of a mother's telling-off. A moment later, the sobbing child appeared in the doorway, freed from his cotton-wool balls. The mother had a firm grip on his arm and was dragging him through the waiting room.

The door to the office was left ajar, and Lene's name was whispered from inside.

She closed the door behind her and squinted into the gloom. A pale hand protruding from the sleeve of a medical gown appeared under the cone of light cast by the desk lamp, and the doctor asked her to take a seat.

Her eyes slowly adjusted to the darkness and she was able to see Dr. Knudsen's gaunt face. An old, grey computer monitor was sitting in a corner of his desk, and a cheroot was smouldering in an ashtray.

Lene sat down and the doctor retreated once more into the shadow.

"Hello," she said. "I'm Police Superintendent Lene Jensen from the Rigspolitiet."

"Hello, Lene Jensen."

Then nothing.

"Kim Andersen is, or was, one of your patients," she said. She reeled off the dead man's civil registration number and the doctor flexed his fingers, which emitted a series of small cracks. Lene hated that sound. Her ex-husband had had the same habit. And her father. The doctor's hands moved across the keyboard; his drawn face glowed green in the light from the monitor.

"I heard that he committed suicide," he said in a low, almost disappointed voice.

"He hanged himself yesterday morning," she nodded.

"I'm very sorry to hear that. Such a shame. I've known him since he was a boy. He came here very rarely. He was in excellent physical health."

"And mentally?"

Dr. Knudsen leaned back.

"As you know, I'm bound by patient confidentiality, Superintendent. I don't know if—"

"He's dead and there are some medical questions in connection with his death that I'd like you to answer."

"Are there?"

"Yes. We found antidepressants in his house. Sertraline. And sleeping pills. The blister pack of sleeping pills was half empty. You had prescribed the medication yourself."

"Stilnoct," the doctor said. "That's relatively harmless."

"For how long had he been taking sleeping pills, Doctor?"

"A couple of years."

"When did he start?" she asked.

"June 2011."

"And the Sertraline?"

"The same."

"June 2011?"

"Yes."

"Did you refer him to a psychiatrist?" Lene asked.

Dr. Knudsen remained silent and she was about to repeat her question when he leaned forwards.

"He didn't want a referral, Superintendent. I believe he trusted me. It's standard practice these days that we, the patient's general practitioner, undertake the treatment of patients with mild to moderate depression. There aren't enough psychiatrists and the waiting lists are too long. So many people are prescribed happy pills nowadays that we should consider adding the active ingredient to our drinking water."

He coughed quickly, and continued.

"I don't mean that, of course . . . but depression has become a national epidemic. Either because we're better at diagnosing it—and that in turn means that we previously didn't treat enough patients—or that people today are more depressed than they used to be. Or . . ."

"Yes?"

"That people are better informed of treatment options and consequently demand to be seen. The *Internet*, Superintendent."

The doctor spoke the word as if it were the name of a disfiguring venereal disease.

"Or it's possible that we over-diagnose the condition. It would appear to be an unstoppable trend. According to the current norms into which we must all fit, no one is ever well. If you're shy, you suffer from social phobia; if you're naturally introspective, you're morbidly repressed; if you're melancholic or going through a divorce, you're depressed; the irritating boy with no boundaries has ADHD; and people with a stiff neck or a bad back have got whiplash syndrome or fibromyalgia, or what have you. There's no longer room for good old-fashioned grief in people's lives these days, Superintendent. In my opinion. Today we call it post-traumatic stress disorder—PTSD. I prefer the word 'grief.'"

Lene nodded briefly. "And what was he mourning?"

While the doctor prepared his reply, she looked around. She wouldn't have been surprised to see a surgical instrument being sterilized in a glass of whisky, and she tried to imagine a gynaecological examination on the black, antique, and cracked examination couch in the corner, but her imagination simply didn't stretch that far.

"Who knows? He lost some friends in Afghanistan," Dr. Knudsen said at last.

"But he left the army in 2008 and he didn't start taking Sertraline until 2011," she objected.

"That's correct. I'm afraid I can't offer you a satisfactory explanation. But I do know that Kim was assessed by psychologists at the Institute for Military Psychology. I think they all were."

"Do you have a name?"

"I'm afraid not, but they're based at Svanemøllen Barracks in Copenhagen."

Lene closed her eyes. She was clearly doomed to spend the rest of her life commuting between Holbæk and Copenhagen. She could, of course, take up Charlotte Falster on her offer and get a colleague to speak to the military psychologists, Kim Andersen's superiors, and his old army buddies, but she knew that she wasn't going to. A crucial detail might be missed if several investigators got involved, and deep down, she trusted no one but herself. That was her nature and, besides, she hated depending on other people's speed and accuracy. They were never quick enough and always did things a little bit wrong.

"The autopsy revealed a healed wound on Kim Andersen's right thigh," she said. "The forensic examiner thought it was a bullet wound from a rifle or military carbine. They took some tissue samples and the wound is about two years old. Did he ever mention it to you?"

Dr. Knudsen's head moved closer to the computer monitor. His lips moved as he read through his own patient notes.

"It's not something I ever treated him for and he never said anything to me. Nor have I received a discharge letter from a casualty department or a hospital regarding a leg injury. I should have. How strange."

Lene agreed. Strange indeed.

"Thank you, Dr. Knudsen."

"You're welcome, Superintendent."

The doctor sank back into the shadows.

CHAPTER 12

As always, the CCTV picture quality was grainy, and besides, it looked as if the two thieves knew exactly where the cameras were located on Flemming Caspersen's property. They stayed in the border between light and dark and moved with speed and confidence. The rubber dinghy emerged from the darkness just before 2:00 a.m. that January morning. The men jumped into the water before the dinghy reached the beach, pulled it up on the pebbles and sprinted through the park. There were no white spots from faces or hands on the footage, and Michael presumed that they must have been wearing gloves and some kind of ski mask. They ran through the field of one camera and into the next until they reached the main steps. One of the men was limping very slightly on his right leg.

The taller of them stood still while his partner with the bad leg produced a crowbar from his rucksack. He wedged the crowbar under the hinges of the front door and eased it off. The door fell into the house and it was the man with the crowbar's turn to stand still while his buddy pulled a pressurized container out of his rucksack, containing liquid nitrogen no doubt, which they used to cool down the alarm system. The men ran down the steps and vanished behind the garage. A few seconds later they reappeared, holding the gardener's aluminium ladder between them, and disappeared inside the house.

And that was pretty much it. There were no cameras inside the house.

They had executed the job exactly as Michael himself would have done.

The poor quality of the CCTV footage really was frustrating. The two men—and surely it had to be two men, dammit, judging by their size—had been inside the house for exactly six minutes and twenty-three seconds, according to the digital clock on the recording.

Had they had enough time to plant the DVD?

Unlikely. Besides, there had been no signs of unauthorized access to the safe behind the Venetian mirror, according to Elizabeth Caspersen.

Nigger the dog had been conspicuously absent.

Michael ejected the CD out of his laptop, put it to one side, and stared glumly at his mobile. He had spoken to Sara and was tormented by homesickness and feelings of guilt. Their son, Axel, had needed a trip to Casualty after cutting his forehead. Michael should have been there. Sara had had to go there with a screaming toddler under one arm and a four-year-old needing eight stitches under the other.

This was the unintended consequence of his job, but he hated it, cursing himself for not becoming a baker, a chef, a schoolteacher . . . or something equally useful that was compatible with a normal family life.

When he moved back to Denmark, he had applied for regular jobs, but had either been under- or overqualified, or else his experience had been impossible to define—so that eventually Sara had insisted that he did what he did best: finding people and things. He had attended job interviews with various companies, but the interview always nosedived in exactly the same place: ten years working for a security company in England—what had his job entailed, exactly?

He couldn't tell them that, unfortunately.

Couldn't tell them what?

Every time, Michael was reduced to an apologetic smile and a shrug. Shepherd & Wilkins would set the dogs on him if he ever revealed operational information. It was like waking up from a ten-year coma. How did you sell a coma on your CV?

Michael poured coffee into his cup and started looking for missing persons in the Internet editions of Norwegian newspapers. Especially people who had last been seen in the northern parts of Finnmark.

He knew it would be difficult. People going missing attracted readers, while people who were found rarely made the headlines. Nor did there prove to be a shortage of tales about hikers, climbers, skiers, people on snow scooters, berry pickers, or ornithologists who had got themselves lost in the north Norwegian wasteland.

A thirty-nine-year-old Dane had disappeared for almost a week in late July 2011, somewhere near the Finnish border, before being found safe and sound by a rescue helicopter from the Norwegian Air Force. In late March the same year, a young Danish-Norwegian couple had gone missing during a hike in Finnmark. There were several articles about the couple in both Danish and Norwegian newspapers, and there were hyperlinks to various clips on You-Tube where the couple's friends and family asked for information, but Michael paid little attention to this particular case. The victim on Elizabeth Caspersen's DVD had been alone.

Then he checked the Rigspolitiet's missing persons homepage, but it clearly hadn't been updated in the last twelve months. There were very few names on the list. Michael clicked until he found the three heavyweights: the Red Cross, the Red Crescent, and the UN's Missing Persons Tracing Service; finally he tried a dozen smaller organizations, but to no avail.

One hour, two cups of coffee, and three cigarettes later he discovered that he had read the same eight lines at least four times; they were from the Danish newspaper *Ekstra Bladet*, dated April 4, 2011:

A 31-year-old Dane and his 29-year-old Norwegian wife are still missing in Norway. Relatives reported the couple missing on March 27. The couple, who are experienced hikers, disappeared in Finnmark near Lakselv. Norwegian police say that they were carrying both GPS and a satellite telephone. They arrived at Lakselv on the flight from Oslo on March 22. The couple's route is not known.

Norwegian police and army search and rescue teams have initiated a search in the area north and east of Lakselv. (Reuters).

His instincts started flickering. Sometimes they were right, other times not, but he had learned to heed them. Experienced hikers, GPS, satellite telephone . . . a Norwegian wife. Norwegians learned to survive in the mountains as soon as they could walk. It didn't add up.

Michael knew he had made a breakthrough. He knew it because something inside him calmed down and his brain developed tunnel vision. Any doubts he might have had vanished when he found a long article in the Norwegian newspaper *Verdens Gang*, dated May 3, 2011, with a sharp colour photograph of the missing couple.

DANES LOST IN FINNMARK was the headline.

The journalist, a man called Knut Egeland, summarized historical incidents where Danes, used only to their flat country, had got themselves lost in the vertical, northern wilderness. They were usually found safe and sound, but not Kasper Hansen and Ingrid Sundsbö, who disappeared east of Porsanger Fjord in the final days of March 2011. Ingrid Sundsbö was of Sami stock and a very experienced hiker. She was twenty-nine years old when she disappeared. Kasper Hansen was a Danish civil engineer, who had spent many holidays in the mountains with his wife. The couple had left Porsanger Vertshus on the morning of Wednesday, March 23. Hotel staff had stated that the couple appeared to be well equipped with a tent, sleeping bags, a hand-held GPS, and a satellite telephone. They had left their telephone number with the hotel reception they had last stayed at.

A truck driver who had picked them up remembered them clearly. In his opinion, the young couple had been cheerful and excited. The woman had spoken Norwegian, obviously, but her husband's Norwegian had been almost as good as his wife's. The truck driver, who was on his way to Murmansk, had dropped them off at a lay-by a few kilometres south of Lake Kajavajärvi. The woman had been wearing a red parka and the man's was black. Their kit had been top-notch, the driver recalled, and they had seemed happy, healthy, and well rested. The driver appeared to have been the last person to see them alive.

Michael studied the photograph accompanying the article: a mountain landscape, unsurprisingly. Kasper Hansen and Ingrid Sundsbö were standing on a hilltop with distant, snow-covered peaks in the background. Kasper Hansen had his arm around his wife's shoulders, and she looked up at him with a smile. White knitted cap, long, straight black hair, a red parka with a fur collar, slim. Kasper Hansen looked straight at the camera. A pair of snow goggles dangled from his neck. Black parka, dark, short hair, white teeth. Both of them looked healthy and contented, and he had no doubts about the identification: it was the young man from the DVD. Kasper Hansen was the man who had been chased to his death on the shore of Porsanger Fjord.

He leaned back in his chair and lit a cigarette. His fingers were trembling and it took him several attempts to work the lighter. But Ingrid Sundsbö . . . what the hell had happened to her?

No calls had been registered from the couple's satellite telephone in the period from March 24 onwards, but there were plenty of incoming calls from Kasper Hansen's mother, who was looking after the couple's two-year-old twins, and from Ingrid Sundsbö's parents.

Norwegian police and army units had carried out a thorough search. At a long, narrow lake called Kjæsvatnet police had discovered the remains of a campfire; an empty leather and wicker creel had been found by a nearby brook. It had the initials KH. There were no other leads that could be traced to the couple.

The weather had deteriorated at the start of April with strong winds and snowfall. The search had finally been called off on April 10.

Michael logged on to Facebook and studied the pages dedicated to Kasper Hansen and Ingrid Sundsbö. There were numerous pictures of the missing couple and pleas to get in touch if you had information that could lead to any kind of resolution, no matter where in the world you might be. There were pictures of the couple's now four-year-old twins, a boy and a girl. They were handsome and dark-haired. There were photographs of the couple's parents, grandparents, brothers and sisters, and dozens of pictures from a kind of memorial service arranged by relatives in the Norwegian Seamen's Church in Copenhagen. It was heart-breaking in all its simplicity and dignity.

The most recent information stated that Kasper Hansen's mother lived in Vangede, a suburb of Copenhagen, and had been granted custody of the twins, even though Kasper Hansen and Ingrid Sundsbö were still theoretically alive. It could take up to seven years for the probate court to declare the couple legally dead.

Michael visited the homepage of the Norwegian Meteorological Institute and checked historical weather charts on a couple of international weather services. Everyone described an unseasonably favourable high pressure area moving from the Karelian peninsula across northern Norway in the last week of March and the first days of April 2011, after which it would disperse somewhere over the Norwegian Sea, between Iceland and Jan Mayen. The weather had been clear and, considering the time of year, warm, and there had been no significant precipitation in the area around Porsanger Fjord. The nights had been starry, exactly as on Elizabeth

Caspersen's DVD: stars; clear weather; no wind; no whooshing in the microphone.

He searched various Norwegian and Danish homepages to see if there were any hostels near the location, but the nearest official hostel was thirty kilometres from the crime scene. As the crow flies.

Michael switched off his laptop, lay down on the bed, got up again and started pacing up and down the room. Then he called Elizabeth Caspersen, told her to buy a new mobile and a prepaid SIM card, and to call him with her new number. He left a short message on Keith Mallory's answering service, giving him the time of the couple's disappearance.

He felt the need to burn off some excess energy, so he put on a T-shirt, shorts, and a pair of running shoes, went down to the hotel gym and spent the next hour and a half on the treadmill.

CHAPTER 13

While he showered after his workout, he received a text message with Elizabeth Caspersen's new telephone number.

She didn't waste time on pleasantries. Michael could hear traffic in the background and presumed that she was in a car.

"I was redirected to your new number by a female English voice," she said. "How often do you change your phone?"

"Every day."

"But it's still you?"

"I think so," he said.

"What have you found out, Michael, and why did I need a new phone? Who would want to bug my calls? How can that even be done?"

She sounded stressed.

"Yes—to answer your last question first," he said. "In fact, it's frighteningly simple. As for who would benefit, there's no shortage of candidates. I can easily imagine that someone would want to bug your phone if, say, the DVD had been planted in your father's safe to blackmail you."

"Blackmail me? Why?"

"The holding company. I presume your mother needs a legally appointed guardian and you're the obvious choice?"

"Of course. The lawyers are working on it as we speak. It could go through at any time."

"And what will Victor Schmidt say to that?"

"He'll suddenly become very, very friendly. Or not."

He waited for her to continue, but she didn't say anything else.

"Sonartek produces extremely valuable technology, Elizabeth. Valuable to several powerful players," he said. "If anything were to happen to the company, if it becomes the subject of a family power struggle, for example, or it's broken up and sold, the American Department of Defense will have to get involved. Once you control your parents' shares as well as your own, you will, at least in theory, become a key player in these considerations because you'll be Sonartek's main shareholder."

"Why on earth would I do something to harm my father's company?" she asked. "It makes no sense. I'm not even particularly interested in Sonartek, Michael. I already have a life, just so you know."

Michael sighed.

"We can't be sure that every decision-maker in the arms industry or the American Defense Department share that view. In fact, I think you can assume the opposite."

He smiled, hoping that his smile would spread to his voice. He had read somewhere that telephone salespeople were instructed to smile when they tried to talk people into buying whatever they were selling. It was claimed that you could hear them smiling.

"Like I said, it's just one explanation, but the DVD would be an excellent blackmail tool."

"Brilliant," she said in a flat voice. "I can't imagine anything more effective."

"Good, so we agree about that," Michael said in his business voice. "As regards your first question, I've found a possible crime scene."

"Where?"

"Northernmost Norway. Finnmark. On the eastern shore of a long, narrow stretch of water called Porsanger Fjord. And I have the date and time."

He held a rhetorical pause.

"The man was killed on March 24 at six thirty in the evening," he said.

"Are you sure? Last year, the year before? When?"

She had given him the very answer he had been hoping for. If she had known more than she had told him, she would have been unlikely to ask about the year so quickly and sound so sincere.

"I'm quite sure about the location, the date, and the time," he said. "And it probably happened within the last three years. We identified the location from the position of the stars at the end of the film."

"The stars? Are you quite, quite sure about this?"

"Yes, actually, I am," he said.

"But that's shocking. Do you know who he was?"

"Not yet."

He didn't think it was the right time to tell her about the Danish-Norwegian couple. He told himself he needed to turn over the identification in his own mind a few more times. The truth was that he was afraid to tell Elizabeth Caspersen that her father might not have had one, but two young people's lives on his conscience. The parents of two small children.

"What do you want me to do?" she asked, blowing her nose.

"I want you to find out if your father was away from Denmark in late March during the last three years."

"I've been more involved in his life in the last three months than I ever was while he was still alive," she said. "I practically didn't see him for the last ten years."

"Why not?"

"I think we quite simply didn't like each other any more. Does that sound strange?"

"No."

Michael thought about his own father, the alcoholic vicar, an intolerable, unreliable dreamer who had shagged everything with a pulse and broken his mother's heart. Michael had worshipped him.

"He didn't really get on with my husband," she said. "Perhaps they were just too alike. Or perhaps it was a delayed teenage rebellion on my part. I've thought about it a great deal recently."

"Can you find out if he went abroad in March around that date?" he asked.

"Maybe. The company has a private jet, which was his second home. Along with a house on Mallorca and a flat in New York."

"I'm sure you can think of something," he said. "I've got another job for you."

"What?"

"Your father must have had a gunsmith. Look for receipts for adjusting and repairing his weapons or a business card from a gunsmith."

"Why?"

"I'm interested in that Mauser rifle. I want to know when it was bought and if it was customized for your father. The gunsmith might have changed the length of the butt, for example, or maybe they have never heard of it. That in itself could prove useful information."

"You're saying he bought it for this very purpose?"

"Yes."

"And you really have no idea who the young man is?" she asked.

"No."

"But you'll find out, Michael?"

"I will. Elizabeth, are you absolutely sure that you want me to continue? We could very quickly reach the point of no return," he said, thinking of Ingrid Sundsbö and her twins.

"What are you saying?"

"If I stop now, you can hope that all this will go away of its own accord, but if I carry on I might find a name. He would have a history, a family, relatives, maybe children. Right now, he's a character on a plastic disc. It's a terrible film, no doubt about it, but he's just a character. A stranger. If I were you, I'd take a moment to consider very carefully if this is what I really want."

"Somewhere, someone wants to know what happened to him, Michael," she responded immediately. "If one of my girls disappeared, I'd want to know at any cost."

"I understand, and of course you're in charge," he murmured.

"There's more," she said.

"What?"

"The others. The men with my father. Perhaps they have done it before *and* after Norway. Someone has to stop them and I'd like it to be me. I can see no other way of atoning even a little for my father's insane actions. I'm rich and I'm prepared to spend every krone I have to find those men."

And you may very well have to, Michael thought.

"I'll find the gunsmith and I'll speak to my father's pilots," she said. "So I want you to continue, is that understood?"

"Yes," he said. "By the way, thank you for the recordings from the break-in."

"Were they any use?"

"I'll go over them again, but like you said, they knew what they were doing. I'll take another look at the footage."

Michael rubbed his forehead hard before his next question.

"Victor Schmidt and his sons. Would it be possible for me to meet them?"

"I don't know. It would be difficult. Why do you want to meet Victor?"

"It's possible the DVD is what it is. A bizarre hunting trophy, which your father put in that safe himself. But maybe it's something else, something more. I want to form an impression of anyone who was close to your father. Are they all in Denmark at the moment?"

"Yes, but it'll be rather awkward. Victor is no fool. Don't underestimate him. Who do I tell him you are? A journalist writing my father's biography?"

She tittered nervously.

Michael had actually considered that option, but rejected it.

"No. The trick of any good lie is to make it as close to the truth as possible. You said your mother has been ill for quite some time?"

"Yes, four years."

"Did she travel with your father?"

"Not often. She doesn't like flying and came to enjoy the social side less and less. She used to say that she had drunk her last martini. She had plenty of friends. She played bridge and tennis, painted and read, and she was a fantastic grandmother. She had her own life."

"Great," he said. "Was your father fond of women?"

"Women?"

"Women."

"Yes, I think so, but I've never heard any rumours of infidelity, if that's what you're implying. If there was someone, he was very discreet. As far as I was aware, my parents got on fine. I've never thought of him in that way."

Michael had a flashback to the naked marble nymphs surrounding the palatial Caspersen home.

"Let's pretend that your father had an affair on one of his business trips," he said. "Or a permanent mistress. On Mallorca, or possibly in New York. Let's say New York. And I'm not talking about a call girl, but a well-educated woman from a good family . . . A woman of a certain class."

"Go on," she said drily.

"Good. And let's pretend that their relationship had . . . consequences."

"You're saying I have a baby brother or sister in the US? That would be wonderful!"

"It's just a cover story," he said. "An introduction to Victor. If you can come up with a better one, that's fine by me."

"I don't think my imagination stretches that far. All right, my father had an affair with a woman from a good family in New York, and then . . . what?"

"The woman in question wants to claim her rights for herself and her son. She's one hundred percent sure that he's the fruit of Flemming Caspersen's loins."

He heard a door slam shut and the traffic noise grew louder.

"I've started smoking again," she said. "I quit ten years ago, but now I'm standing in some godforsaken lay-by off a motorway smoking cigarettes by the packet; I blame you entirely."

Suddenly she giggled—a little nervously, but she sounded liberated.

"The fruit of his loins? Christ . . . Is your father a vicar, Michael?"

He laughed in surprise.

"Actually, he was. Please don't tell anyone. He drank himself to death."

"And you? Do you drink?"

"I've retired Jack Daniels. More or less. He stops by every now and then."

"I'm glad to hear that. The retirement, I mean," she said. "It's such a waste."

"It usually is," he said, without quite believing it.

"Do you know what I'm thinking right now? No, of course you don't. I'm imagining Victor's face when I present him with an unknown heir to Sonartek."

Michael laughed with her. Briefly.

"How old is the little tyke?" she asked, and tittered like a schoolgirl again.

Michael interpreted her reaction as the beginning of a big, beautiful, and classic nervous breakdown.

"Let's make him six months," he said. "You've received a letter from a . . . a Miss Janice Simpson . . ."

"Simpson?"

Elizabeth Caspersen laughed out loud this time, but her laughter was drowned out by the roar from a truck. It sounded as if she were standing in the middle of the motorway.

"Or whatever. You choose. A nice, handwritten letter. Write it your way. She expresses her condolences on your loss, which is also hers and junior's loss, she's empathetic, but still manages to include several, highly personal details about your father, Sonartek, and you. Information known to only a few people. She has even included a photograph of the baby, who looks like any other baby, of course. She's heartbroken at your father's . . . and her

92

lover's death, but obviously has to consider her son's future in every sense of the word."

"Of course," she said.

"She believes your father would have wanted him to have an appropriate upbringing. Miss Simpson isn't going to be unreasonable, not at all. On the other hand, she would like to give you the opportunity to respond before she involves her lawyers. She's prepared to provide you with every DNA test imaginable."

"Michael, that's brilliant," she said.

"It's just a cover story."

"But it could be true."

Neither of them spoke for a moment.

"Where do you fit into the picture?" she then said.

"I play myself. A private investigator recommended to you by a Dutchman. You're distraught. First your father dies, your mother is ill, and now this. What will Miss Simpson want? Money? Your father's name? A seat on the board? Official recognition of her son? Obviously you want to discuss various scenarios with Victor and his family, who were so close to your father, and with me, as a kind of expert investigator. As a lawyer, you understand the legal implications for the estate, but you've asked me to establish if Miss Simpson is just some con artist or if she's the real deal. You want to know more about Miss Simpson's background, family . . . Who she is and where she comes from."

"You're right," Elizabeth Caspersen said. "I really would. If the story were true, I would have found someone like you."

"There you are," Michael said. "And I bet Victor Schmidt will want to know if he needs to heat feeding bottles for the next board meeting."

She giggled again for a long time until Michael interrupted her.

"One last thing, Elizabeth."

The laughter died away.

"What?"

"Your father's hospital records. Where did he actually die?"

"At Victor's estate where he had been hunting. He spent a lot of time doing that. He practically lived there when he wasn't travelling. They found him dead in his bed one Sunday morning. Why?"

93

"No reason in particular. I presume he was taken to the nearest hospital."

"Where he was declared dead on arrival," she said.

"Of course, but there must be a hospital record or a casualty note, a death certificate, and you've already told me that an autopsy was carried out, so there must be an autopsy report. You're his next of kin and you're entitled to see his medical record. I'd like a look."

Elizabeth Caspersen's voice acquired an edge: "And again I'm asking you why? I've no reason to think he died from anything other than a heart attack."

He phrased his next sentence carefully.

"I think there are too many unrelated incidents. An otherwise healthy man suffers a heart attack, then there's the break-in, the theft of the rhino horns, the hunting rifle with ammunition still in its magazine. The film. You have to agree, it's all a bit odd."

The pause was extra long.

"You're right, and you're wrong," she said at last. "But I'll get hold of the papers and have them sent to you."

"Thank you."

Elizabeth Caspersen had finally stopped giggling, something for which he was grateful.

After their conversation Michael fetched his travel bag and took out a scratched, white plastic press pass the size of a credit card. It had a microchip and a blurred passport-sized photo of him. Using adhesive letters he could alter the name on the pass as and when he needed it. It wouldn't stand up to professional scrutiny, but few people had ever seen a press pass and no one had ever looked at it twice.

He would be Peter Nicolaisen from Danmarks Radio, he decided, and prepared the lettering.

Michael wasn't a believer in the traditional sense. His father, the fallen vicar, had cured him comprehensively of Christianity, but he still hoped that someone somewhere would understand and forgive the step he was about to take: bringing false hope to grieving relatives.

CHAPTER 14

Lene parked some distance from the fine, classical redbrick building that was the home of Holbæk Police Station. The sun had passed its zenith, but it was still warm. She pulled up the hood on her sweater and donned a pair of sunglasses. The death of the veteran along with the Rigspolitiet's presence had made crime reporters flock to the west Sjælland market town, and they could spot Superintendent Lene Jensen's red hair from miles away. She had no wish to be besieged by clamouring journalists right now; they would have to wait until tomorrow's press briefing.

She entered through a side door and popped her head round the duty office, exchanged a few words with the duty officer, and was allocated a room on the first floor.

The room was furnished with a faded blackboard, an old poster of Storstrømsbroen, fire evacuation instructions from 1983, a scratched desk, and two chairs. She hung her anorak over one chair, put her shoulder bag on the floor, and sat down at the desk. She took off her wristwatch and put it on the desk next to her notebook and a ballpoint pen.

She had had another brief chat with Arne, the CSO, on her way to Holbæk. In many ways, a disturbing conversation which had confirmed her own suspicions.

At four o'clock there was a knock and the young female officer whom Lene had met in the forester's cottage opened the door to allow Louise Andersen to enter. Then she closed the door behind her. Lene didn't get up, said nothing and carefully kept her facial expression neutral. She gestured to the chair opposite the desk and the widow sat down.

Louise Andersen's face was freshly scrubbed, the bridal make-up had gone and she had aged ten years. She had dark circles under her eyes and the corners of her mouth were turned down in a way Lene suspected might be permanent. She didn't look the superintendent in the eye.

"How are you, Louise? Where are the children?"

"With my mother."

"Have you managed to get some sleep?"

"No."

Lene tried, and failed, to catch the other woman's eye.

"Can you remember what happened yesterday?"

"How could I forget?"

She glanced at Lene before staring down at her red Converse sneakers. She was an attractive woman, Lene thought. She had great hair, dark brown and naturally curly, high cheekbones and her big eyes were slightly slanted, though they were currently stripped of life.

"You made coffee for Kim when you woke up yesterday. You called out for him. You looked for him in the bathroom, you went back to the kitchen . . . Please, would you take it from there?" Lene prompted her.

"I went out into the kitchen," the widow mumbled. "I felt sick, and I had a headache. We'd had far too much to drink. I drank half a carton of orange juice and made some coffee. I can't remember if I called out to him. I thought he might have gone for a walk."

"A walk?"

"Yes. He often did. I drank my coffee and poured a mug for him. Two sugars and a dash of milk. Kim can't drink coffee without sugar."

Her mouth began to twitch.

"Then what did you do?"

Louise Andersen shielded her eyes with her hand.

"I went out into the garden. I found him. Someone had hung Kim from a tree . . ."

Her hands dropped into her lap, her face dissolved, and the tears flowed. She got up without warning, crossed the floor, and pressed herself into a corner by the door. Her shoulders started heaving.

Lene leaned back and looked out of the window. In the parking lot below, an officer was opening the back of an station wagon to let an Alsatian out into the sunshine. The animal rose on its hind legs and planted its paws on the man's chest. The officer pushed the dog down and it licked his hands. A young dog. Still a playful puppy.

"No . . . no . . . no . . . no . . ."

The widow was whispering softly to the wall.

"Louise . . . ?"

The head nodded.

"Do you know what I see when I look at you?"

"No."

"I see someone very special. I see a strong, brave woman. You're very like me. And you *have* a future on the other side of this. After Kim. Even though it's going to take time. It's up to you to decide if the start of that future will be very hard or just hard."

"There is no future."

The widow was still facing the peaceful, green corner.

"But there is. Look at me, Louise."

The widow still didn't turn around.

"Bloody well sit down on that chair!"

Lene put on her street voice. Police frequency. It was a long time since she had used it on protesters armed with cobblestones or agitated football hooligans, but its effect was still remarkable. The young woman jolted upright as if she had been given an electric shock, marched across the room, and sat down on the chair. She looked at Lene with wide open eyes.

"Do you think it's the first time I've sat here with someone in your situation?" Lene demanded brusquely.

"I guess not."

"No. And you *have* a future. I know that right now everything is shit and it's going to stay that way for some time. Serious, fucking shit, okay? The question is: are you going to let it win? You're in shock. Of course you are, anyone would be, but that's a healthy and normal reaction, and you had damn well better believe me when I tell you that it *will* pass. One day you'll start a new life and it won't be because you don't honour or love your husband."

"Have you ever lost someone?"

Lene blinked. She had been asked that question before. She had lost her father, but he had been old, chronically ill, and at peace with the world. He was ready to go. And she had had an abortion when she was seventeen, but that didn't really count. Her greatest loss had been her beloved cat that disappeared when she was eleven. She had cried for three weeks. She had always believed that the cat, Valium, named by her father, who was a pharmacist, had been the victim of a crime, that their evil neighbour who loathed animals had killed Valium and buried it. While he was at work, she had vainly searched his garden. In a way, that had been her first case.

"No," she replied.

"You're lucky," Louise Andersen said.

"I know. What did you do when you found Kim?"

"I cut the rope."

"What with?"

"I ran back to the house, found a knife in the kitchen and then I returned. I stood on the chair, but I couldn't reach the rope . . . Oh, God . . ."

"Then what did you do?"

"Then I ran to the garage, found the lopping shears, and then I could reach."

"I'm impressed," Lene said, kindly. "No, really. I presume you couldn't carry Kim? He was a big, heavy man."

"No, he fell onto the grass. I tried holding on to him, but the chair fell over."

"What time was it?"

"No idea."

"Okay. Kim is lying on the grass and you do . . . what?"

Her face lost all expression; she avoided looking at the superintendent.

And here it comes, Lene thought.

"I tried giving him mouth-to-mouth resuscitation and CPR. But it was no use. He was cold and he didn't move. He just stared up at the sky. I don't think his heart was beating."

"Where did you learn how to resuscitate someone, Louise?"

A vertical frown appeared between the widow's fine brows, freshly plucked for the wedding.

"I'm a teacher. I did a first-aid course at work."

"Did you see the handcuffs straight away?"

"I saw them straight away."

"Do you remember if you touched them?"

"I didn't."

"Coffee?" Lene asked.

"What?"

"Would you like a cup of coffee? A glass of water? Can I get you anything?"

"A glass of water, please."

"Just a moment."

Lene left the office, walked down the corridor, found the lavatory, held her wrists under the cold tap and splashed water on her face. She stared at her reflection in the mirror for a long time before she turned off the tap.

The kitchen lay behind the duty office. The dog handler was sitting at the kitchen table and the dog was lapping up water from a plastic bowl that jerked across the slippery linoleum; a long-legged puppy that had yet to learn to coordinate four legs, a tail, and its big head. It sniffed Lene eagerly until the handler summoned it. Lene poured coffee into a mug and added three sugars. Then she found a Snickers bar in her pocket and tore off its wrapper. Her hands were shaking. Low blood sugar.

She munched the chocolate, drank the coffee, and looked at the dog.

"Is he going to turn out well?"

The handler gazed at it with fatherly pride.

"I think so. I trained his big brother from an earlier litter, and he was very good."

"King?"

He smiled.

"No. And not Rollo, either. His name is Tommy."

Lene smiled at the dog. "Good name."

"Yes."

She poured water into a glass for Louise Andersen and walked back to the small, dusty office.

Lene placed the coffee mug next to her wristwatch, put the water glass in front of the widow, and glanced at her shoulder bag on the floor. It was untouched.

"You can smoke if you want to," she said.

"I have asthma."

"Oh, that's right. I think your house is the cleanest I've ever been in. Including my own."

"It has to be clean."

"Of course."

Lene looked into her mug as she sipped the black liquid.

"Louise, when I said that it's up to you to decide if day one of your future will be very hard or just hard, I was being serious."

The widow twirled a dark curl around a finger, pulled it hard, and Lene grimaced. It seemed as if the other was enjoying the pain. The distraction.

"Okay."

"There is something called interfering with a dead body, Louise. It means you mustn't touch or move a dead person unless there's a really good reason. You're not allowed to pose a body in any way, undress it, apply make-up, put it on a motorbike or anywhere else. Do you understand? It's a criminal offence."

"Of course."

"Good. There's also something called obstruction or perverting the course of justice. That's also a criminal offence. And then finally there's something called perjury, or giving false evidence. It's when you say something during a police investigation or in court which you know to be untrue."

The widow looked attentively at Lene. Her lips were moist and slightly parted.

"I know what it means."

"I'm glad to hear that, Louise. I really am. Unfortunately it's my view that you're guilty of all three, and I want to know why."

"What are you saying? Just what the hell are you saying?"

Lene looked her right in the eye. "When I called you strong and brave, I actually meant it. There were no marks on Kim's wrists from the handcuffs. We would have expected him to struggle if someone had put the handcuffs on him before pulling him up into the tree, for example. We would also expect to find bleeding under the skin if he had put them on himself because he was afraid he wouldn't be able to go through with it. It would be an instinctive reaction. Inevitable, in fact."

Louise Andersen pushed back her chair abruptly and was halfway to the door when Lene ordered her to sit down. The widow stopped as if she had walked into a wall, and Lene was about to get up to forcibly push her back into the chair when Louise Andersen spun around with blazing eyes and sat down without saying a word. She crossed her arms and legs and her knuckles turned white against her upper arms.

"Thank you," Lene said gravely. "This isn't going to go away just because you walk out of that door, Louise. There was only one person's fingerprints on those handcuffs. Yours. And as far as the alleged resuscitation attempt goes, we would have expected to find traces of your lipstick on his face. We didn't. We did find your fingerprints on the lopping shears, so that part of your story holds up. Now I want to hear the other part. The truth."

"I want a lawyer," the widow said.

Lene nodded.

"Of course. But if you want a lawyer, I'll have to charge you first, and if I charge you, you'll go to court, and if you go to court, you'll be convicted. I can guarantee you that."

The widow's lips started to tremble. Again she buried her face in her hands.

Lene looked at her watch. Would this never end? She suddenly got very angry with Louise Andersen's inexplicable excuses and refusal to cooperate.

"So what's it going to be?" she asked harshly. "Very hard or just hard?"

The other muttered something.

"Speak up. I can't hear you, sweetheart."

"I think just hard is more than enough."

"That's what I think, too," the superintendent said. "Let's start with the handcuffs."

"I don't know . . . I don't know what I thought . . . Yes, I thought that if I handcuffed him, you, the police, might find out what was wrong with him. I'm sorry. I shouldn't have done it."

"What was wrong with him?"

"Oh, fuck . . . Everything!"

"His depression? We found the pills, and I've spoken to his doctor."

"No, no . . . I think they helped him to begin with, but then he became more and more withdrawn and miserable, he isolated himself; he couldn't even be bothered with the kids any more. And he had always been crazy about them. It wasn't just his depression. I got that, and I could handle it, but some days, some days he didn't say one word to me or the kids, he didn't eat, he didn't shower or change his clothes, he would wander around the forest or go sailing in his dinghy and wouldn't come home until he was sure that I had gone to bed. We stopped having sex, we never talked, we did nothing."

"How long had he been like that?"

"The last year was terrible. Getting married was my idea. I actually proposed to him . . . I thought it would make things better. That it might convince him that I would never leave him. He had started dreading that. I thought that the party and planning the wedding, him seeing his old friends, would help. And it did, it really did. I thought he cheered up even though there were still lots of days when he just didn't get out of bed. His boss put up with it. Kim was a veteran and his boss was prepared to make allowances for him. But of course he has a business to run and other carpenters to think of. The others had to work extra hard because of Kim. He knew it, and he felt really bad."

Lene knitted her brow.

"I still don't understand, Louise. And I don't follow the timing. As far as I know, Kim came back from Afghanistan in November 2008, am I right?"

"Yes."

"And Dr. Knudsen started him on antidepressants in June 2011, and Kim also started taking sleeping pills around June 2011? Why?"

"He could only sleep if he took a pill. He said he took them so he wouldn't dream. He didn't want to dream, he said."

Lene nodded. "It's just that I had expected his problems to stem from his discharge from the army. I presume he was a combat soldier? He wasn't in logistics or catering, for example?"

Louise Andersen smiled miserably.

"Kim? He would rather break both arms than do paperwork. It didn't interest him. And he couldn't boil an egg. He wasn't very good at reading or writing. He never read a book for pleasure. He read manuals. All he cared about was being in the field with his mates. Kim is one of the most highly decorated privates in Denmark. He was a skilled soldier and very experienced. He had been to Iraq, Bosnia, and Kosovo; the Division was his family."

"Did he have any brothers or sisters?"

"He has an older half-brother, whom he rarely saw. He lives in Jylland. They liked each other all right, but there was ten years between them and they didn't have very much in common. Kim's parents divorced when he was nine and he barely saw his father after that. They never really got on.

His father moved to Thailand and married a local girl, and his mother also remarried. She lives on Bornholm."

"So how was he after Afghanistan?"

Louise Andersen sipped some water and stared into space.

"Well, it takes time, doesn't it? They're still pumping with adrenaline . . . bouncing off the walls when they get home. It's like they've got ADHD. They're either up or they're down, but it usually wears off. And so it did for him. After Afghanistan, I mean. He got a job and it looked as if he was getting his act together. He always got his act together."

"Was he seen by the Institute for Military Psychology?"

"They all were. They screen them for stress, both before and after missions, to see if they can handle it and if they need treatment when they get back. He didn't have therapy or anything like that, if that's what you're asking."

The widow paused.

"People like him are worth their weight in gold," she said.

"Why?"

Her face and eyes had become more animated. Kim Andersen had been a lucky man, Lene thought. Relatively lucky.

"There is no substitute for experience," Louise Andersen said. "People like Kim help young and inexperienced soldiers by showing them the ropes. He was in the First Armoured Infantry Company. They're the most experienced, I think, and the ones they deploy when the going gets tough."

"Okay," Lene said. "So it was all right to begin with. What happened in the spring of 2011?"

"I honestly don't know. He liked going hunting. He was a member of the local hunting syndicate and he and a couple of ex-army mates had game rights at a country house on south Sjælland. Pederslund it's called. He went there often. Otherwise it was mostly deer hunting with rifles. Sometimes he would travel to Poland or Sweden to hunt wild boar or elk. He was in Sweden in March or April 2011, where he injured his leg. He got a limp as a result, but said that nothing could be done about it. He had been to Casualty in Sweden. But I don't think that was it. In May, he was told that two of his best friends, who were still in Afghanistan, had been killed by a roadside bomb. Kenneth and Robert. The Taliban had filled a pressure cooker with plastic explosives, ball bearings, nuts, nails, broken glass and pebbles, and they sat on some hilltop nearby and triggered it with a mobile phone. There were five of them on patrol. Kim's best friend was at the front and was killed instantly, and his mate, who was three metres behind him, died later from massive shrapnel injuries to his neck. He took it badly."

"Christ."

Louise Andersen looked up.

"Yes. Christ indeed," she whispered. "I think he felt he could have prevented it if he had been there. That somehow it was his fault. It was madness. He said it was a punishment for something they had done. Something they had all done. Kenneth and Robert were due to come back the following week."

"A punishment? What for?"

Louise Andersen gave her a pale smile.

"I've no idea. He refused to say any more about it. A punishment. That was what he called it. I made him go to the doctor. And that was when he got the pills."

Lene nodded and wrote a couple of words on her notepad.

"Okay. Incidentally, we found a rifle and a shotgun in the gun cabinet," Lene said. "They didn't look as if they had been fired for a while."

"He hasn't been hunting since that time in Sweden," the widow said. "And it was after that trip he started feeling bad."

"Who was with him?"

"Some of his friends from the country house, I believe. He hardly ever spoke about it, and he hated being interrogated. He would just close down. He was very stubborn."

"How did he injure himself?"

"He told me he had tripped over a tree that had been knocked down by the wind and a branch had gone through his thigh."

"And he was never injured in Kosovo, Iraq, or in Helmand?"

"Never. He used to say he was invulnerable because he loved me so much. He was incredibly lucky."

Lene leaned back. This was less than she had expected—and much, much more. All sorts of doors began to open. Perhaps she ought to write it all down, but she knew that the thin thread between her and the widow might snap if their intimacy was replaced by official procedures. Louise Andersen might dissolve in grief again or sink back into mute defiance. Right now they were on a safe, little island.

She mustered up her friendliest smile.

"A note, Louise?"

The widow looked at her.

"Did he leave a note?"

The young woman took a deep breath and, for a moment, Lene thought that she had lost her, but then she lifted her handbag up on her lap, found an envelope and handed it to her across the desk.

A single sheet, blue squares. Torn off a cheap spiral pad.

You have my heart, Louise. Always.
I'm sorry.
Dominus Providebit.
Kim

Lene turned over the note. There was nothing on the back, nor was there anything on the envelope.

Louise Andersen stared at Lene's hands. Her eyes welled up.

"It's my letter. You can't keep it."

Lene gave it back to her.

"Of course not."

The widow folded the note and returned it to the envelope. She kept her handbag on her lap and rested her hands on top of it.

Lene scrutinized her.

"Your story, Louise. I might be able to understand why you acted the way you did. Cuffing him, I mean. But your husband *did* kill himself. He took a rope from his boat, climbed a garden chair, tied the rope to a branch, put the noose around his neck, and kicked away the chair. I don't mean to be brutal, but that was what happened. Suicide or attempted suicide falls outside the penal code. And though it's difficult, impossible perhaps, for the rest of us to understand what can drive someone to that point, it is and will remain a private matter. I just don't see how the police can help you. With your new and improved explanation, the case is pretty much closed."

Louise Andersen nodded. She sat for a while without saying anything. Then she stuck her hand into her bag and placed her clenched fist in the middle of the desk.

"So how about these?"

She uncurled her fingers. Two 9-mm cartridges were lying on her small palm.

CHAPTER 15

The cartridges rolled across the desk until they came to a standstill. Lene didn't touch them.

"Where did you find them?" she asked.

"One was on Lucas's pillow, the other on Hanna's."

"Do you think Kim saw them?"

"The door was open."

"And you threw the pillows on the floor?"

"Yes."

"Who put bullets in their beds, Louise?"

"I don't know. Some psycho."

"Do you know any psychos?"

"None that I'm aware of."

The widow was calm. Her voice was assured, low, but clear.

"The same person who took your computer?"

"Who else?"

"But why?" Lene asked.

"That's why I put the sodding handcuffs on him, do you get it now?"

Lene nodded, fetched the photograph of the five soldiers in the desert from her shoulder bag and placed it on the desk. She turned it so the young widow could see it.

"I helped myself to this photograph from your house. I recognize Kim from his tattoos. Who are the others?"

"Robert Olsen and Kenneth Enderlein are standing on Kim's left. They were the ones who were killed. Kim's best friends."

"When was the picture taken?"

"The summer of 2006, somewhere outside Camp Bastion, or Camp Viking, as the Danish part of the camp is known. Sometimes there would be Brits,

Americans, and Canadians there as well. And the Danish special forces unit, the Jægerkorps. There are almost eleven thousand men in that camp. It's hard to know everyone."

Lene pointed to the soldier with the open uniform shirt. Unlike the others, he didn't look like someone who could feature in a tattoo magazine.

"Who is standing next to Kim?"

"Allan. He's a sergeant in the Royal Life Guards. I think he's still in the army. Allan Lundkvist. Kim said he was a good soldier. He keeps bees."

"Bees?"

"Sometimes he would give Kim honey when he had done some carpentry work for him. It tastes great. He lives on an old farm near the barracks."

Lene smiled.

"What does it mean to be a good soldier, Louise?"

"That people can trust you and that you don't do things that endanger the lives of others. They had to be both, right?"

"Please explain?"

"I mean they have to be level-headed—other people need to know that they'll think before they act—but they also have to be ready to fight and make split-second decisions under pressure. It's not easy. They must be able to do crazy stuff, while at the same time looking out for each other. That's the only thing that really matters: looking out for your mates."

"What about civilian losses?" the superintendent asked.

"It happens. They might request aerial or artillery support if they were in danger, and this would sometimes hit the target, other times not, or civilians might be killed by a grenade. The problem is you can't tell the enemy and the civilians apart. They wear the same clothes, speak the same language and go to the same places. Kim said that was the hardest thing about being out there. It was easier in Kosovo, in Bosnia-Herzegovina, and Iraq. You knew who the enemy was."

"Right. And the fifth man? The one standing apart with the scorpion tattoo on his neck."

Louise Andersen picked up the photograph.

"Tom," she said, putting it back on the desk.

"Tom?"

"I think he was just someone who happened to be there that day."

"Did you ask Kim about him?"

"He never talked about him. I don't think he knew him very well. I don't even know if he's Danish. He could be Canadian, British, or American."

"So he never mentioned him . . . Tom?"

"Never."

Lene watched her closely. The widow sounded completely sincere. She wasn't lying.

"Who took the picture, Louise?"

"I don't know. Kim never said. I presume they put the camera on a rock and used the self-timer."

"Okay. So how about this?"

Lene held up the plastic bag with the CD. The disc was covered with red spots from the CSOs' fingerprint powder.

"We found it next to the Alfa Romeo," she said. "Kim's fingerprints were the only ones we could find a match for."

"What's on it?"

"Queen's 'We Will Rock You.' On a loop."

"What?"

"You heard me, Louise."

The widow's face drained of all colours except ash grey.

"It was their song . . . in the company, I mean. They sang it when they got drunk. They sang it on their return to camp when things had gone well."

"Gone well?"

"They were there to kill the Taliban, Lene."

It was the first time she had addressed her by name.

"Of course. So it was a kind of battle hymn?"

"You could say that."

"Did he listen to it at home?"

"Never. He wouldn't dream of it. Some things are off-limits. They're deeply superstitious. I think it's common for soldiers, sailors, and others in dangerous professions. Are police officers superstitious?"

"Not especially. By the way, congratulations on the Alfa," Lene said. "Nice car."

"I hate it," the widow said and burst into tears again.

Lene leaned across the desk and handed her a paper tissue.

"Why? It's a fantastic car."

"But that's just it! We can't afford a bloody car. It's madness. We haven't even paid for the wedding. I don't know what the hell he was thinking. And I've no idea where the money came from. He just said that he had been lucky."

"What money?"

"I pay the bills. I manage our finances online and a couple of months ago, 1.3 million kroner suddenly appear in our account. Out of nowhere. It turned out to be the krone equivalent of two hundred thousand Swiss francs from a bank in Zürich."

Lene leaned forwards.

"What was the name of the bank and was there any message with the transfer?"

"Credit Suisse. And no, there was nothing. There was an account number, but no link that I could click on. Kim called it compensation. He wanted a big wedding, to give me a day to remember."

"Compensation for what?"

The woman squirmed.

"Please, can I go now? I want to be with my kids."

"Compensation for what, Louise?"

"I don't know! God dammit, can I go now?! Compensation for his leg, his depression, the nights in the forest. I don't know! And there was more, there was much more where it came from, he said. We could travel. We could move to Argentina or New Zealand. Start a new life. A wonderful, new life!"

"Did that ever happen before this time, Louise?"

"Never."

"Never?"

"No. We never had very much money. Or, at least, not more than our friends."

Lene looked at her.

"Was this before or after you proposed to him?"

"I don't know. Hang on . . . I think it was right after. Oh, God, do you think that . . . ? Did I . . . ?"

Louise suffered with her.

"I don't think so, Louise. It would have happened sooner or later, I'm sure of it," she said, placing her hand on the other woman's forearm.

Louise Andersen took a deep breath and put two items on the desk: a gilded box with the word ROLEX in silver on the lid and a blue velvet box from Hertz Jewellers.

"He went to Copenhagen three weeks ago," she said. "And he came back with these. A Rolex and a diamond ring. Do you want them?"

Lene looked at the boxes and considered the offer. It was probably the closest she would ever come to owning a Rolex. She massaged her temples.

"Go home, Louise. And keep your presents or sell them on eBay and give the money to the Red Cross."

The widow was halfway across the room before Lene's last sentence had ended. She turned and looked at Lene.

"Will there be anything else? Will you need to talk to me again . . . ?"

Lene mustered up a kind of smile.

"Go home to your kids."

"Thank you."

"You're welcome, Louise."

"I shouldn't have asked him, should I?" The widow spoke out into the air. "I shouldn't have proposed. I know I shouldn't."

"Drive safely," Lene said.

She sat there for a little while, then got up, stretched out and walked over to the window. She watched Louise Andersen cross the parking lot. The widow walked quickly with her shoulders hunched and didn't look right or left. Lene turned back and examined the bullets on the desk: one for the boy and one for the girl. The bullets . . . the song . . . trained reflexes. Kim Andersen had hanged himself because someone had activated his trained response. Someone had remote-controlled him.

Tom . . . Danish, Canadian, American, British? Shit!

She put the bullets in her pocket. If there had been any fingerprints on them, they would have been wiped off long ago. But Lene knew that the bullets had been clean.

Now she needed court orders. She would turn Kim and Louise Andersen's personal finances inside out and she would find that account in Zurich, even if it meant going there in person and putting a gun to the head of some oily, obstructive Swiss banker. Or perhaps she should follow procedure and ask a case officer in the Rigspolitiet's COM Centre in Glostrup to handle the matter. The case officer would ask the Danish public prosecutor to submit an official request to a Swiss judge for an order, which the COM Centre and Europol could bring before a court in Switzerland.

But Lene would be dead and buried long before the Danish public prosecutor got a response. Perhaps she should pretend Kim Andersen converted to Islam. That tended to speed things up.

CHAPTER 16

Lene had lost count of the number of times she had commuted the sixty-five kilometres between Holbæk and Copenhagen, and she was thoroughly fed up with it.

Everywhere she went, she scanned her surroundings, but failed to identify the source of her feeling of being watched and she told herself over and over that she was getting paranoid. No one followed police officers in Denmark; the very thought was insane. She parked her car close to her flat and took her shoulder bag from the back seat as she glanced up and down the street. A motorbike drove slowly across the junction of Kong Georgs Vej and Kronprinsesse Sofies Vej, but the driver didn't look in her direction. A man was walking on the opposite pavement, but away from her. She stayed where she was until the man let himself into an apartment block.

Josefine was on the sofa watching a reality TV show in which a group of plain, anorexic-looking girls competed to be the country's next top model. They were cheered on by the equally plain-looking hostess, who spoke a curious mixture of Danish and hyperbolic English.

"There's food in the fridge," her daughter said.

"You've opened a tin of tuna?"

Josefine shot her wounded look. "I cooked spaghetti carbonara. There's enough for you *and* for tomorrow night's dinner."

Lene stood very still and closed her eyes.

"I want my daughter back, please," she whispered.

"You're so funny," Josefine said.

She glanced at her watch and got up.

"I'm off."

Josefine worked in a café near Frederiksberg Town Hall and wouldn't be back until two o'clock in the morning. Though the café was only a fifteen-minute walk away and Josefine was twenty-one years old, very sensible, and perfectly capable of looking after herself, Lene knew she would lie awake until she heard the key in the door.

When the front door had slammed shut downstairs, Lene went to the kitchen, lifted the lid of the saucepan containing Josefine's spaghetti carbonara and cautiously sampled the food. It actually appeared to be edible so she helped herself to a plateful, opened a bottle of red wine and sat down on the sofa in front of the television with a blanket around her legs. She channel-hopped until she found Hitchcock's *Notorious* starring Ingrid Bergman as the Nazi honey trap and Cary Grant as the world's most attractive and foolish agent. She had seen the film many times before, but she loved it. She always feared that the fleeing couple would be exposed at the last minute and caught on the endless stairs in the Brazilian Nazi palace.

After the film and two glasses of red wine, she dozed off, as her subconscious continued to process an inconsistency just beyond her reach. She had seen something that didn't add up, didn't make sense, but though she knew it was important, she couldn't pin it down. The harder she tried, the more the missing piece seemed to elude her.

He was squatting on his haunches next to his motorbike, whose engine cowlings were spread across the pavement. He had a flashlight between his teeth and heard her stop one metre away. She had to clear her throat before he looked up. Josefine Jensen smiled as she gestured towards the engine cowlings and the bicycles leaning against wall, blocking the rest of the pavement. He returned her smile, got up, muttered an apology and let her pass. It was a cool evening and the girl tightened her thin jacket about her. She smelled nice.

Twenty metres on, she stopped again and glanced over her shoulder at him, but he pretended once more to be completely absorbed by the engine, which was in fact in perfect working order. When she disappeared around the corner at Falkoner Allé, he quickly reattached the cowlings, started the motorbike and pulled down the visor of his helmet. He saw the girl run across the road a few hundred metres in front of him; he counted to fifty and pulled out into the street. The girl weaved fluidly in and out between the evening's pedestrians.

In another context she would have made a fine trophy, he thought.

He followed her to the café where she worked. She sprinted across a pedestrian crossing, ignoring the red light, and a taxi sounded its horn indignantly. She didn't look back and the man on the motorbike smiled when she gave the taxi driver the finger behind her back as she ran on without breaking her stride.

He took a deep breath before he opened the door to the café, mentally preparing himself for the unfamiliar noises: the ecstatic, self-important chatter of young city dwellers, clattering glasses, cups, cutlery against plates, excessively loud music. He hated cities and knew that people's eyes would be on him.

He found a vacant table at the back near four young women. He hung his biker jacket over the chair, took a newspaper from the stand and ignored the women, who were discreetly checking him out. He was used to it. Women had told him that he was handsome, though he couldn't see it himself. He never paid much attention to his appearance. He rarely shaved, didn't shower every day, and cut his own hair whenever he thought it had grown too long. Home was currently an old camper van.

Josefine Jensen emerged from the kitchen behind the bar, tying her apron around her waist and pulling her hair into a ponytail. There were no customers at her end of the bar, so she started putting glasses into holders above the counter. Her face showed no emotion and her movements were fast and practised. The other waiter whispered something to her and they both laughed out loud.

He got up, crossed the room and waited until she noticed—and remembered—him before he smiled. He sat down on the bar stool and picked up a cocktail menu. He knew that she had recognized him because she began moving with a slight hesitation. She reached up on her toes and her breasts pressed against her thin, white shirt.

He closed the menu, put it aside, and looked at the shelves behind the counter and her figure in the mirror. Fine waist, nice arse, long legs.

She had finished putting the glasses away and was looking at him.

"Did you get your bike fixed?"

"Sorry?"

"Your motorbike. I just saw you on Kong Georgs Vej with most of the engine in bits all over the pavement?"

115

She gestured towards his hands.

He saw the oil stains and smiled. "Was that you? Sorry. Yes, it's fine. It's just old and temperamental."

He opened the menu.

"You'll stain it," she said.

"What would you order?" he asked.

"I don't know. Are you driving?"

"Yes."

She took the menu from his hands, even though she could have taken one of the other half-dozen, brushed a blonde strand of hair away from her eyes and frowned. He leaned forwards and spotted a book on a beer crate behind her. *Lonely Planet Guide to South America.*

Brilliant.

"A mojito?" she suggested.

"Too many plants," he said.

"Black Russian?"

"Do I look like someone who drinks Kahlúa?"

She looked at him closely.

"No, not really."

She turned over the menu, furrowed her brow again, and he wondered if she might be slightly short-sighted. She had her mother's green eyes.

"Singapore Sling?"

"Pineapple juice? I don't think so."

She grinned.

"No . . ."

He looked at the whisky bottles behind her.

"Give me a double Glenlivet with ice," he said.

"All right, but didn't you just say you were driving?"

"I'll walk."

She took a glass from above the bar, poured the whisky and started looking for a spoon for the icebox.

"Use your fingers," he said.

She looked at him and dropped three ice cubes, one by one, into his glass with her fingers. She placed it in front of him and he paid with a new two hundred-krone note.

"How about one for yourself?" he asked.

Josefine could feel her colleague's eyes on her back.

"I've got to last a few more hours."

"Some other time?" he asked.

"I don't think so," she said as she gave him his change. The coins dropped slowly into his large hand. She slammed the till shut and smiled at a woman in a fur coat behind him.

He didn't move. He kept watching her until she was forced to look at him.

"Some other time?" he repeated.

She gave him a deadpan look.

"Will you be here tomorrow night?" he asked.

"I guess so," she mumbled.

"I'll wait for you outside. Tomorrow," he said.

He grinned, slid off the bar stool, and went back to the table with his whisky. Josefine took the oil-stained menu and put it behind the bar.

"Sorry, what did you say again?" she asked the next customer.

The woman in the fur coat looked at her: "Two lattes," she repeated very clearly.

He had gone back to reading the newspaper and sipping his drink when his mobile vibrated in his pocket. He glanced at the girl behind the bar when he had read the message. She blushed under his gaze; her clear, green eyes avoided looking at him while she served the line of queuing customers.

Pity.

He put his mobile back in his pocket and emptied his glass. The superintendent had spoken to Kim Andersen's widow at Holbæk Police Station for a long time. Far too long, it would appear. Her investigations had to be stopped.

It was a matter of indifference to him. He was paid so well that he could live the way he wanted to most of the time, and freedom always came at a price. It was a no-brainer.

Lene woke up when she heard the key in the door. The television was a flickering, grey surface in the darkness. She felt even more tired than before she fell asleep. She sat up and looked at the luminous hands on her watch. Two thirty. The light came on in the passage and she heard Josefine hanging up her jacket, the door to the bathroom, a rustling of toilet tissue, the tap and the electric toothbrush; soon afterwards the door to the living room was opened.

Lene turned on the lamp next to the sofa.

"Hello, sweetheart," she mumbled.

"Hi, Mum, did I wake you? You really don't have to wait up for me. I can find my own way home."

"I don't mind. Christ, I'm knackered. How was work?"

She patted the cushion seat next to her.

Josefine flopped down on the far end of the sofa and stretched out her legs until she was almost horizontal.

"Fine."

Lene yawned behind her hand and watched her daughter's quiet face.

She recognized the symptoms so easily.

"Who's the lucky guy, sweetheart?"

Her daughter shot her a belligerent look.

"I don't know what you're talking about."

"Oh, come on, Josefine . . ."

"What?!"

"Nothing. Your dinner was lovely. The spaghetti tasted great."

Her daughter got up.

"You're welcome. Good night."

"Sleep tight."

The door to her daughter's bedroom was shut with slightly more force than strictly necessary.

Lene emptied her glass. The red wine tasted bitter. She was angry at herself, of course she was . . . but, for crying out loud! Hadn't she been just like Josefine? Or was she a little bit jealous? She dismissed the thought. Josefine was no angel, and Lene didn't expect her to be. Lene hadn't been exactly sexually restrained herself until she met her husband, Niels, and there had been a few occasions during their marriage when . . . oh, well, she sometimes longed for another body, other hands, another's mouth. She was aware that she was turning into a workaholic, and she would definitely welcome romance back into her life if she actually tripped over it. Only it was never the right time, or she couldn't be bothered to play the dating game or lacked the energy to bounce back from a new, complicated and protracted disappointment. Perhaps she ought to find herself a married lover, but she knew that she wasn't the type. Sex without a minimum of feelings and healthy expectation was death.

Lene switched off the light, left the living room and opened the door to her daughter's room a crack. Josefine was lying on her stomach, the duvet twisted around her legs and she was hugging a big pillow. Lene sighed and closed the door.

CHAPTER 17

"Norse paganism?" Lene said in disbelief. "Are you kidding me?"

The chief psychologist at the Institute for Military Psychology, Dr. Hanne Meier, smiled. Lene had discovered that smiling came easy to her.

"Absolutely," she said. "Thor and Odin, Loki and the whole shebang. If you took away their uniforms, you would think you were seated at a table in Valhalla or on a longship with a bunch of Vikings. They're covered with runes and old Norse designs and the tattoos are historically accurate. There's no street cred in sporting the wrong ones. They're a tribe."

"What do the army chaplains say?"

"They deal with it surprisingly well. I think some of them have even studied Norse rituals and ceremonies so they can perform them, if needs be."

Lene, who was baptized and confirmed and went to church as often as she could, was horrified.

"But they're pagans!" she exclaimed.

Hanne Meier was a woman of her own age. She looked at the superintendent and they burst out laughing.

"If the army chaplains can live with it, surely so can we," the psychologist suggested very sensibly. "Not all of them share that belief, of course, but many of them do."

"Why?"

"Why what?"

"Why Norse paganism."

"It's a very militant faith, don't you think? A warrior religion. They're warriors. It all fits. They'll meet again in Valhalla. I can't really see them as Buddhists or Taoists, can you?"

Lene still couldn't see the attraction and wondered how deep the soldiers' transformation really went. Did they return to more traditional values when they left the army, or continue to see themselves as a chosen tribe with its own, sovereign rules?

"What happens if they're killed? I don't imagine they're launched in a boat with a funeral pyre lit by a burning arrow shot from the shore?" she asked.

"No, but the Ministry of Defense will go far to meet their wishes, both while they're alive and if they die. Military personnel make their wills before they're sent out and they write letters for their next of kin in case the worst should happen. If they have specific wishes for their funeral, the army will try to accommodate them. Within reason, of course."

The psychologist smiled to herself.

"There was a major who wrote that he wanted to be cremated and his ashes dissolved in Dom Pérignon."

Her infectious laughter erupted again and Lene joined in.

"Wait!" Hanne Meier held up a hand. "That's only the half of it. He also requested that the champagne be drunk by Naomi Campbell. He wanted permanent residence in her body!"

"I hope he came back in one piece," Lene said.

"He did. And thank God for that. That would have presented us with something of a challenge."

"How do you feel about it?" Lene asked. "Norse paganism?"

"As long as it helps them, I don't care if they believe in Father Christmas or the Easter Bunny. Of course, there *is* a point where they stray too far from the world which has deployed them and expects them to come back. But, as far as I know, no one has crossed that line yet. Danish soldiers are very good. They know perfectly well why they have been sent out. They know it's a foreign policy decision. They're some of the best soldiers in the world. Everyone says so. They're democratic and creative. The segregation in the mess into privates, non-commissioned officers, and officers is only for show. I've been to Afghanistan myself and it wasn't unusual to see a junior officer deep in discussion with the chief of a battalion in the officers' mess over a beer. That just wouldn't happen in other armies, possibly with the exception of the Israelis. They're professionals and they know and respect the chain of command. Serious disciplinary problems are very rare."

"So they see themselves as modern-day Vikings?" Lene asked.

"Apart from the bit about raping and pillaging and stealing the church silver, well, yes . . . I think so. A cross between Vikings and aid workers."

Lene nodded and looked around the austere office. There were removal boxes labelled "2007" in a corner. The building in Svanemøllen Barracks had an atmosphere of permanent transition; as if the Institute couldn't make up its mind whether to stay or go.

"A brotherhood," she said slowly.

"Very much so. And highly skilled."

"You screen them prior to deployment?"

"Yes, we've started doing that. And we debrief them when they come home. We've no experience of the horror stories you may have heard about Vietnam veterans in the US who have become marginalized and live as outcasts in the woods. Many of them suffer with mental health issues or are downright psychotic, insane. And have never been treated."

Lene frowned.

"But surely some of them fall apart. Mentally? I mean, how well can you really prepare yourself for war?"

Hanne Meier leaned back.

"It's not often, but you're right. A few go mad. They experience psychotic episodes. It has happened."

"What do you do with them?"

"If it happens at the base or in the field, they're cuffed, sedated, and sent back to Denmark on the first plane."

"Come again?"

"Army doctors carry plastic ties. Plastic handcuffs. You use them as well, don't you?"

"Yes."

"Right, they're cuffed, given a shot of Ketalar—that's a sedative—and, well . . . they're flown home as quickly as possible."

"Who are the ones who can't handle it?"

"As we gain more experience, we become better at spotting them. Active field duty is like a microscope, for better and for worse, and there's nowhere to hide. Your strengths will be magnified, as will your weaknesses. So if you're a victim of neglect or abuse and have a fragile sense of self, even if you now inhabit the body of a bodybuilder, it will out. Not surprisingly, some of them can't cope when their mask is torn off. They're confronted with their own inadequacy. They collide with reality," the chief psychologist continued. "Sometimes people lose it when the gap between who they thought they were and who they really are proves to be too wide. I think we all know that feeling. If your whole sense of self comes crashing down while you're on active service, you can go insane. At least temporarily."

"How do you treat them?"

"The most important thing is to tell them . . . convince them that even if they weren't born to clear dark houses of Taliban guerrillas in labyrinthine villages, even though they're scared of leading a patrol in an area notorious for roadside bombs, even if they break down when they see their best friend maimed or killed, yes, even if they're not the perfect combat soldier, they can still be a worthwhile human being." Hanne Meier nodded pensively. "That's what we do."

"Does it work?"

"Sometimes. Usually. It's not macho to have a nervous breakdown; surely you know that from your own line of work?"

Oh, God, yes, Lene thought as she thought about colleagues whose masks had been torn off over the years. She wondered what had happened to them and how close she herself had come.

"I do," she said. "But I imagine we also need people who are unemotional and possess certain qualities which would get them into trouble in civilian life, but are useful in war . . . who will thrive in combat, but nowhere else?"

"Psychopaths, you mean?"

"Perhaps. What's the current definition of a psychopath?"

The psychologist threw up her hands: "Pretty much the same as it always was, I think. They're callous, manipulative, exist outside ordinary, social norms, and lack empathy. They act only in their own interests and use every available means. Without consideration for others."

"Have you met some of them here?" Lene asked.

"Both in the Armed Forces and outside. Of course I have. It's a deviation from the norm, and there is a spectrum. On the other hand, sometimes it's much easier to define deviancy than normality. I mean, what's normal?"

"Would they thrive in the military?"

"They could be used for certain tasks. Black ops, for example—missions where it's best not to have too many feelings or where ethical concerns would only get in the way. I'm speaking generally now, not specifically about the Danish Armed Forces."

"What about Kim Andersen?" Lene said.

Hanne Meier reached for a slim, green case file and put on her reading glasses.

"He definitely wasn't a psychopath or a sociopath. I don't remember him all that well, but I spoke to him in January 2009, a couple of months after he was sent back for the last time. To be honest, I'm surprised to hear that he killed himself. Very surprised."

Everyone seems to be, Lene thought.

"He wasn't very academic, but he was highly disciplined and got on well with the NCOs and his friends," the psychologist continued. "A cheerful disposition, would be my initial assessment, and nothing can replace an innate, cheerful disposition. He was in excellent physical health, incidentally. He had practically no disciplinary notes, except the usual pranks such as hoisting the battalion chief's bicycle up a flagpole and throwing flash-bang grenades into the dormitories at night. That kind of stuff."

"Did he go on black ops?" Lene asked.

"He completed specialized sniper training here at home and in England. He would appear to have been a natural."

"He was certainly an experienced hunter," Lene said. "And he was pre-scribed antidepressants for the last two years of his life. Something seems to have upset his cheerful disposition. By the way, he married his girlfriend of seven years, Louise, the day before he hanged himself. They have two children, aged three and five."

"I'm shocked," Hanne Meier said. "I really am. We use various tools, a range of psychological questionnaires, including a depression index, and Kim Andersen's replies never gave us cause for concern."

"He began treatment for depression in June 2011," Lene informed her. "Around the same time he started having trouble sleeping. He took sleeping tablets every night, his wife told me. His doctor has confirmed it."

Hanne Meier nodded and pensively looked out of the only window in the office. Young men and women from all three services strolled towards an auditorium. Chatty, laughing, athletic-looking. Lene watched them as well.

It was comforting to see so many passionate and enthusiastic young people. Good to know that they still existed.

"What do they do in the camps in Afghanistan when they're off duty?" she asked.

"They watch porn or action films, play computer games, work out. Pretty much what they would do at home."

"How do I join?" Lene mumbled.

"I think you'd get bored pretty quickly."

Lene smiled. "Surely you expect them to experience some psychological problems when their tour of duty ends?" she asked.

"Soldiers have a range of problems," Hanne Meier said. "And not all of them are caused by active service, though Kim Andersen was deployed the maximum number of times."

"Of course not. But some find it tough to come home, don't they? They miss their friends, life on the edge, the daily adrenaline kick, the structure?"

"I think most of them feel that way, to be honest," the psychologist said. "To a greater or lesser extent. There's a world of difference between clearing a village of heavily armed and fanatical Taliban fighters and spending your Saturday going to the DIY store with your wife to buy insulation or spending the day cleaning the gutters. The majority want to go back. But Kim Andersen had tried it before, several times, in fact. He knew exactly what coming home would be like."

"Okay, then, thank you. . . ."

Lene stuck her hand into her shoulder bag and found the desert photograph. She had studied it endlessly and every time she felt its significance. She had folded back the left quarter of the picture to ensure the psychologist would focus on the bigger section.

She pointed.

"That's Kim Andersen. The guy with the most tattoos. Do you recognize him?"

"Not really," Hanne Meier said. "They all look the same. Heavily tattooed, long beards, and long hair. They must have been away from camp for a long time to look like that. Perhaps they've been on an investigative mission. Someone is missing."

"Who?"

125

"A platoon commander, I would say."

"Like this one?"

Lene unfolded the picture and pointed to the man with the scorpion tattoo.

The psychologist pushed her reading glasses up the bridge of her nose and narrowed her eyes.

"Yes, perhaps. He looks like a leader."

"Do you recognize him?"

"No. But like I said, I'm not sure even their own mothers would recognize them."

Lene sighed.

"He's a ghost," she said, putting the photograph back in her bag. "Kim Andersen's wife doesn't know him either, even though the photograph has been on their bookcase for years. Can you tell me if he's an officer?"

"He's not wearing any badges, so no, I can't."

"Are officers tattooed as well?" Lene wanted to know.

"Of course. It's not limited to the lower ranks. Who are the others?"

"Two of them died in May 2011. Robert Olsen and Kenneth Enderlein. A roadside bomb. And the fifth is Allan Lundkvist."

"Is he the beekeeper?" Hanne Meier asked.

Lene smiled.

"I believe so. Do you know him?"

"One of my colleagues has spoken to him."

"And?"

"I can't comment on the psychological profile of living soldiers, Lene."

"No, of course not."

She got up, shook hands with the psychologist and had reached the door when Hanne Meier said softly, "I think he's okay, the beekeeper. He gave my colleague some honey. And I imagine he must know who the fifth man is."

"Well, I certainly intend to ask him," Lene said. "I've phoned him dozens of times, but he hasn't returned my calls."

She opened the door, but the chief psychologist continued. "Your ghost . . ."

"Yes?"

"Is he Danish?"

"No idea."

"I thought . . . Oh, I don't know . . ."

"What?"

Hanne Meier hesitated.

"I tell myself that I have some experience by now, Lene. With oddballs, dangerous men. I think he stands out, in a weird and totally unscientific way. Perhaps you should stay away from him."

"I don't think I can," the superintendent said, as something dark and cold stirred inside her.

"Well, in that case, watch your back," the chief psychologist said gravely.

"I will. Thank you."

CHAPTER 18

"Why are we here, Lene?"

Oh, so we're on first name terms, are we? Lene bristled. Charlotte Falster had called a press briefing at Holbæk Police Station and Lene definitely couldn't complain about the turnout. The station's canteen was packed to the rafters with journalists. Holbæk's own chief of police had offered to take part, but Lene had declined. She could handle it, she assured him, and she had detected a certain relief.

She looked coolly at the man who had asked the question, a journalist from a Copenhagen morning paper. They grew younger and younger—or perhaps she was getting older. Shaved head. Small architect's spectacles. Black T-shirt with a Metallica logo on the front.

"What do you mean?"

"Let me rephrase: Why are you here? If this is 'just' a suicide?"

Good point.

The other journalists looked at her. The boy was only saying what everyone was thinking.

"Initially, we believed that there were some . . . that the technical evidence from Kim Andersen's suicide could be interpreted in several ways," Lene said. "It's not uncommon for us to be involved in an apparent suicide until the forensic examiner's report is ready. In this case, it was clear and unequivocal."

She smiled at an older, female journalist from *Ekstra Bladet*. They had followed each other's careers for quite a while now, and Lene found the reporter's work to be balanced and sober. The woman smiled too, and made a note of something on her pad.

"Interpreted how, Lene? Was there anything to suggest that a crime had been committed? . . . In terms of the technical evidence?" the skinhead continued.

He stressed the word "technical" and looked around the room, like the classroom star he had undoubtedly always been.

Hungry. On his way up.

"I'm unable to give you any details . . . Janus? All I can say is that we no longer doubt that Kim Andersen committed suicide. So, as far as we're concerned, the case is closed."

The boy nodded his dissatisfaction and Lene pointed to a plump, middle-aged man in a pale blue shirt and tweed jacket. The buttons looked close to bursting. He was holding up a broad, red, farmer's hand.

"Isn't it strange that Kim Andersen, a tough veteran from the Royal Life Guards, decides to kill himself the day after his wedding?" he said. "He left the army four years ago. Was he being treated for some kind of depression?"

Lene's hands stayed calmly folded on the grey Formica table. These days anyone who knew a doctor, a pharmacist, or a personal carer could access other people's medical records if they knew the civil registration number of the individual concerned. It wouldn't be difficult for an experienced journalist to find out everything there was to know about Kim Andersen's treatment for depression.

"I can't give you any information about that," she said, knowing full well that the journalist already had the answer.

"But you would agree that the timing is unusual?"

"That would be my initial reaction. But for obvious reasons, we won't ever know why Kim Andersen took his own life."

"Did he have financial problems?"

"I have no information about that, so I can't comment."

"And you're not linking his suicide to his military service?" The journalist flicked through his notebook. "He had been deployed to Iraq, Bosnia-Herzegovina, and three times to Helmand. Have you spoken to his company commander, for example? Fellow soldiers?"

"I haven't." Lene looked directly at the journalist: "I want to emphasize that we have no reason to think that a crime was committed in connection with the death of Kim Andersen. Suicide remains a private matter. And the case is closed as far as the Rigspolitiet is concerned. I'm not here to speculate about his motives."

The reporter from *Ekstra Bladet* asked the next question. "Kim Andersen had two young children, Lene. And he had been with his wife, Louise, for seven years before they were married. You've spoken to his widow. How is she coping? I understand it was she who cut down her husband and tried to resuscitate him. I believe that you had a long conversation with her here at the station yesterday afternoon."

Lene nodded gravely and moved the salt shaker towards a bottle of ketchup.

"I think she's coping remarkably well," she said warmly. "It's a huge shock, obviously. It would be for anybody. Suddenly finding herself alone with two young children . . . but her parents live nearby and she has a good support network. Louise Andersen will get through this, I know she will. For years she has lived with the knowledge that Kim Andersen could be killed in action and those mental preparation will benefit her now. And I'm sure that the Armed Forces will assist in every way they can."

The journalist smiled. She might just have got her headline.

"Do you think that the Armed Forces do enough for veterans?" asked the journalist with the farmworker hands. "It's not the first time that a veteran has committed suicide."

"I'm not a sociologist and I don't feel that I'm qualified to express an opinion about that," Lene said.

She got up.

"Any more questions?"

She looked around the room and knew that every single journalist was frustrated at having driven all this way for so little. They had been hoping for a crime or a human interest story about a traumatized war veteran whose past caught up with him, propelling him to a final, irrevocable action. Yet another broken soldier.

They got up and she had picked up her duffel coat from the table when Metallica said, "I've spoken to Kim Andersen's friends and colleagues, Lene." The boy was brimming with confidence and was the only one still sitting down. "He was injured."

Lene dropped her coat. Don't blink, she told herself.

"What do you mean?"

"He was never wounded in action, but he was injured—" Metallica consulted his notepad—"in the spring of 2011. He was on sick leave for three months before getting some kind of protected work." The journalist ignored

130

Lene's death stare. "According to my sources, he started taking antidepressants in June 2011. He was very open about his treatment."

"So it would appear," Lene said. "And?"

None of the other journalists stirred.

"No one can quite understand how he could afford to invite eighty guests to his wedding and buy his wife a new Alfa Romeo."

Metallica paused for effect.

What did the little pipsqueak expect, she wondered. A standing ovation? Cheerleaders?

"What was your question?" she asked.

"Well . . . Do you have any comments on that information?"

She smiled at the boy, despite a strong urge to put him over her knees and give him the thrashing his parents had clearly never managed.

"You shouldn't believe everything you hear. People might have been jealous of him, what do I know? I have no further comment."

There was a flash of anger behind the architect spectacles. Lene recognized the type. She came across it more and more often. A spoiled generation of children with helicopter parents and an overdeveloped sense of entitlement, brought up in a loving home—far too bloody loving and indulgent. No one had ever said no to him. Wooden toys. Rudolf Steiner nursery. Wobbly masculine identity. In short, an arsehole.

"But you haven't given me anything!" Metallica protested. "His friends from the shooting syndicate and his colleagues told me he boasted of having lots of money. Surely that must mean something!"

"I fail to see how," Lene replied. "He killed himself. And perhaps he died rich, who knows? Have a nice day."

She left the canteen with a grim face and didn't start breathing properly until she stepped out into the rain. Then she trod in a pothole, her shoe filled with water and she swore all the way to her car. She got in, grabbed the steering wheel with both hands and shook it as hard as she could while she screamed.

"Good job, Lene," she muttered to herself when she eventually calmed down and was staring blankly out of the windscreen. "You're a real pro."

CHAPTER 19

Peter Nicolaisen, a journalist with Danmarks Radio, also known as Michael Sander, had called Tove Hansen in advance. She was the legal guardian and grandmother of two orphaned, four-year-old twins and the mother and mother-in-law of Kasper Hansen and Ingrid Sundsbö respectively. He hadn't bothered with a disguise, and was wearing his usual anorak, hoodie, jeans, and running shoes when he rang the doorbell of the small yellow house. He knew he could easily play the part of an investigative journalist looking for two of the many Danes who had vanished without a trace in 2011.

It didn't sound as if the twins were at home and he was grateful for that. He looked down the garden path. A couple of well-maintained children's bicycles were leaning up against a tree in the front garden; there was a swingball stand in the lawn and a big garden trampoline with half its springs missing. The herbaceous border was invaded by weeds and a broken basement window had been patched up with a yellow supermarket bag and gaffer tape.

He smiled at the woman who appeared in the doorway and introduced himself. She nodded and Michael made a move to take off his shoes, but she shook her head.

"There's no need."

"Thank you. I hope I'm not disturbing you?"

The woman shrugged. She untied her apron and hung it on an already heavily burdened row of pegs in the narrow hallway: children's winter clothes, snow suits, a beige ladies' coat, woolly hats, and an orange bobsleigh that had made it as far as the pegs on its spring journey from the garden to the basement. Tove Hansen opened the door to a living room with a low ceiling.

She took a seat in an armchair and a small white poodle wandered over to Michael and sniffed his leg. He would appear to have been accepted because the dog padded out of the door without barking.

"That's Perle," she said gravely.

"Cute dog," he said.

He sat down opposite her.

"I can make coffee if you like," she said with a nod to the kitchen.

"I've just had some, Mrs. Hansen. But thank you very much."

"Tove," she said.

"Tove."

She looked at him with tired grey eyes, and Michael checked out the room. The bookcases were filled with book-club purchases. The furniture was nice, but shabby. Toys lay neatly sorted in blue and red IKEA boxes. He looked at a photo showing a younger, slim, and tanned version of Tove Hansen next to a dark-haired man on a hotel balcony with a blue shimmering sea in the background. He could see Kasper Hansen in both of them, and there was a photograph of their son on the day he left sixth form on the wall above the sofa. His sixth-form cap was pushed cheerfully back and the young man looked ready to take a big, gluttonous chunk out of life with his white teeth. Next to Kasper Hansen hung another student photo of a blonde, long-haired girl with very similar features to her brother, but in a softer and feminine version.

"It's Kasper to the left and Sanne to the right," Tove Hansen said.

"Yes, I recognize him. A couple of weeks ago I came across a photo of Kasper and Ingrid in an article in *Verdens Gang*. My editor thought it might be worth following it up."

"It has been two years now," she said. "It's strange . . . I still can't get used to it. Every morning when I wake up, I think he's still alive . . . the moment I hear the kids, I know that Kasper is gone, of course, but at other times I think he's still here."

"They're four years old now?" he asked. "A boy and a girl?"

She looked at him as if she registered the words, but hadn't quite taken them in. Then she nodded. "They're at nursery. I can pick them up, if . . ."

"There's no need," Michael said with a weak smile, while fighting a feeling of profound self-loathing. He produced a notebook from his inside pocket, though he had no intention of writing anything down, and opened it.

"They disappeared in Norway in March 2011?"

"March the 24th or 25th," she said.

"What were they doing in Finnmark?"

133

"Hiking. They loved the mountains."

"Did anyone invite them or were they travelling with other people?"

"No, it was a last-minute decision. They hadn't been up there for two years and they were missing it. Ingrid missed it the most, seeing as she was born and bred up there. Kasper had saved up some holiday and Ingrid worked part-time, so she could look after the children. She was a graphic designer. They told me that the weather up there was unusually mild. A kind of early spring. They were only going to be away for a couple of days and asked me if I could have the kids. They dropped off the twins on the morning of the 22nd and I drove them to the airport."

Without warning Tove Hansen started to cry, but there was no reaction in her face. Michael watched her, wondering when she would realize. She jumped when a tear landed on her wrist. She muttered something and half ran out of the living room. He heard her on the stairs to the first floor.

Michael quickly got up, took out a small digital camera from the pocket of his anorak and photographed all the pictures on the walls: the twins right from when they were born to when they could stand on the trampoline in the front garden, Tove Hansen's wedding photo, Kasper Hansen's student pictures, yet another portrait of her son, this time in his army uniform, a picture of Kasper and Ingrid at a party; she looked lovely with her raven-black hair done up, a green silk dress and bare, tanned arms.

Michael put away the camera and slipped back into his chair a moment before Tove Hansen returned.

"I get upset," she said.

"Of course you do, Tove. Did Kasper grow up in this house?"

"My husband and I have lived here since we were married. Sanne lives in California. She's an engineer, just like Kasper. My husband . . . their father died five years ago."

Michael pointed to the picture of Kasper Hansen in uniform.

"Where did Kasper do his military service?"

"He was with the Horse Guards in Slagelse. It didn't interest him. I think he was bored."

Michael almost did a double take. He himself had been a first lieutenant, and later a military police captain, at Antvorskov Barracks in Slagelse, but that was long before Kasper Hansen had completed his training there.

"What do you think happened to them?" he asked, closing his notebook.

Tove Hansen moved a candlestick on the coffee table.

"Everything. I've imagined everything. Sometimes it's a happy ending and I see him again . . . Other times, not so good."

"I understand."

"Did you say you work for Danmarks Radio or TV2?" she asked.

"Danmarks Radio."

"Danmarks Radio, fancy that. Kasper's father was a butcher and I worked in a shop. But our children went to university, Sanne and Kasper both . . ."

Her voice ebbed out.

"Were Kasper and Ingrid in good health?" Michael asked.

"Pardon . . . ? Yes, they were. There was nothing wrong with them. They loved to exercise. They ran and cycled, Kasper played squash with some colleagues twice a week. There was nothing wrong with them. Nor was Kasper ever ill when he was little."

"And they never called you from Norway?"

"They just vanished. No one has ever heard from them."

"Did they know the area?"

"They had been there several times. I've never visited it myself, but I've seen their recordings and photographs. There are rocks, glaciers, and bogs. I imagine it's easy to have an accident if you're not careful."

Michael nodded.

"Does anyone help you with the twins?"

"I prefer to look after them myself. Ingrid's parents travel down here every now and again, and the twins spend some of their holidays with them. Ingrid was an only child. Then there's my daughter, whose children are the same age. She visits from the US as often as she can. I think the twins are doing well, they don't remember their parents any more."

"And financially?"

The woman straightened up.

"I manage. What is it you're going to do?"

Michael leaned forwards: "We've done a series of programmes about missing Danes. The concept is very popular and we've managed to reunite friends and family on many occasions. This is different because Kasper and Ingrid went missing in a remote and dangerous area. The most obvious explanation is that they had an accident of some kind. Most of our other stories have been about people who had mental health issues or chose to disappear for financial reasons."

"I understand," Tove Hansen said.

Michael sent her as much of an encouraging smile as he could muster.

"On the other hand, it's a good story, Tove. Don't get me wrong, but we have some options. We can send a team up there to talk to the police, the army, the locals. We might find some leads and perhaps we can help raise awareness of the dangers of hiking in northern Sweden or Norway. Kasper wasn't the first Dane to go missing up there, and he probably won't be the last."

She nodded.

"I think that would be good. But I still want to know what happened."

"Of course you do."

"I would like to have a place where I can take the twins and tell them that this is where their parents are buried. I think it's important for them when they grow up. The way we live now is so strange. As if they were lost at sea."

"Of course it is. I do understand," he said. "I'll carry on with my investigation if that's all right with you, and I'll be in touch. We'll need some interviews with both families, friends and colleagues."

She got up and looked at her watch.

"It's time for me to go get the children."

Michael got up as well.

"Of course."

"Would you like to see Kasper's room?" she asked. "It hasn't been touched since he left home. It's in the basement."

Every cell in Michael's body was screaming to get out of the small, quiet house.

"Yes," he said. "I would like that very much."

CHAPTER 20

"How did it go?" Charlotte Falster wanted to know.

"Hang on."

For once Lene was delighted that her boss had called. She had found it hard to move on from the press briefing and welcomed the interruption. She put the earphone in her ear, the jack in her mobile and rested the mobile in the car's ashtray.

"Are journalists even human?" she wondered out loud.

"Not if you ask me," the chief superintendent said. "What have you found out?"

"Kim Andersen killed himself. His wife handcuffed him when she found him hanging from a tree. She was and still is worried about some trouble he appears to have got himself into."

"What kind of trouble?"

"Depression, insomnia, excess drinking . . . and an unknown sponsor who used Credit Suisse in Zurich to transfer a small fortune to Kim Andersen's account. The wife says she has no idea who it came from and I believe her. All that money spooked her. *She* proposed to him, and now she's afraid she inadvertently pushed him into doing something criminal in return for money, so that he could give her a big wedding."

"How much money are we talking about?"

As always, Charlotte Falster sounded composed, but Lene thought she could detect a certain fatigue in her voice.

"Two hundred thousand Swiss francs just over a month ago."

"Nice. Any ideas?" the chief superintendent asked.

"None, other than to get the public prosecutor and the COM Centre to request information from Zurich."

There was a pregnant pause down the other end. Lene could sense that Charlotte Falster was intrigued.

"You and I will be long gone before we ever get a reply," she said. "Why don't I try?"

Lene smiled.

She had been hoping that her boss would make such an offer. Charlotte Falster's husband was a permanent secretary in the Ministry for Justice and a member of the Danish Management Society, along with the governor of Danmarks Nationalbank and God himself. He could definitely pull a few strings completely beyond the reach of a humble superintendent.

"Yes, please," she said. "I'd really appreciate that."

"What could he have done that was worth two hundred thousand Swiss francs?" Falster mused. "It's not likely he built someone a garage, is it?"

"No, I don't think so, but I would like to find out. I've spoken to an army psychologist who described him as completely normal. She was actually very surprised to hear that he had killed himself. As was his doctor. He was sent home in the autumn of 2008, but didn't develop depression that needed treatment until the summer of 2011, after a hunting trip to Sweden and learning that two of his closest friends had been killed in Afghanistan. He was never wounded in action himself, but sustained a serious leg injury in Sweden. The forensic examiner says it looks like an untreated gunshot wound. My problem is that I want to file the case as a simple suicide so the media will leave me alone, but carry on investigating it as if it were a murder. By the way, someone put a 9-mm bullet on each of the children's pillows. Kim Andersen found them just before he hanged himself. I'd say that's sending someone a clear message."

"You're saying someone told Kim Andersen to kill himself and save them the trouble? And why didn't you tell me about the bullets earlier?"

The professional sparring with Charlotte Falster was one of the aspects Lene liked most about her job, even though she didn't particularly like the chief superintendent. Falster's thinking was just as sharp as her words were direct, and few topics were off limits when the two of them discussed a case.

"It must have slipped my mind," she said.

"You don't say," Charlotte Falster remarked drily. "This is highly unusual, Lene."

"It is. You're right."

Falster fell silent and Lene knew that her boss considered, assessed, and dismissed possibilities and scenarios with the speed of a computer.

It was Charlotte Falster's right and duty to allocate her scarce resources in an optimal manner in relation to the targets imposed on her from on high, and Lene was only too aware that the department was chronically understaffed and that there were other cases that could easily keep an experienced investigator busy. She accepted it and she rarely developed proprietorial feelings for her cases, but the Pavlovian response that was Kim Andersen's suicide was too important to be left to others.

"Okay," the chief superintendent said at last. "Stick with it and stay away from the press. If anyone asks, you're taking the next few days off as leave. What are you going to do?"

"If you deal with the money and the Swiss, I'll look into the family's finances and speak to Kim Andersen's army mates and officers."

"And Sweden?"

"And Sweden."

"And the person who left the bullet . . . Who is he or she? It doesn't sound like someone you would want to meet in a dark alley."

Lene thought about the man with the scorpion tattoo. The guarded smile. The small, but significant distance between him and the rest of the world.

"I'll find out."

"Take care of yourself," her boss said casually, and Lene nearly drove off the road. Concern? Charlotte Falster? All that was left now was for Brøndby to win the cup again.

"I will," she said, and ended the call.

Then she tried the beekeeper's landline once more. By now she had made at least a dozen calls without getting a reply and had left a similar number of messages on his answerphone, ranging from informal to borderline pleading. As far as she knew, Allan Lundkvist was no longer abroad with the Royal Life Guards and there could be a million other reasons why he didn't answer his phone, but surely someone had to look after the damned bees? He lived on a farm in Ravnsholt, not far from the Royal Life Guards' barracks in Høvelte.

Lene looked at the clock on her dashboard. She wondered whether to swing by Ravnsholt on her way home, but decided she would rather have an hour with Josefine before her daughter went to work. Allan Lundkvist would just have to wait.

On the way home, she shopped for dinner in Copenhagen's best foodie shopping street, Værnedamsvej. She bought a couple of delicious cheeses, French mineral water, grapes, artisan bread, big, fresh olives, and Spanish ham. They would have time to eat together before Josefine had to go.

"Jose?"

Lene put the shopping bags on the kitchen table. Her daughter mutilated a Shakira hit in the bathroom while Lene arranged the delicatessen food on a carving board, tipped the olives into a bowl and poured red wine for herself and a glass of mineral water for Josefine. She carried the plates and glasses into the living room and put on a Nina Simone CD.

"Jose . . . Ham! . . . Olives! . . . Bread!"

A hairdryer started up and Lene knew that her daughter hadn't heard a single word. Lene ate a couple of olives, dipped a chunk of bread in olive oil and sprinkled it with coarse sea salt. She realized that she was starving. And that she needed the lavatory. She went out into the passage and slammed the palm of her hand against the door to the bathroom.

"What?"

"I need the loo, Josefine. Now! Dinner is ready."

"I'm not hungry, Mum."

"Of course you are."

Her daughter had the metabolism of an incinerator, and when she was little, she would consume her own body-weight every day. She could still eat whatever she liked without gaining weight.

Josefine emerged from the steaming bathroom, buttoning an indigo blue silk shirt over a white lace bra that Lene didn't remember seeing before. She got a quick hug and was enveloped in a cloud of Chanel Mademoiselle. Her daughter's face was glowing after her bath and she had applied discreet make-up, while her lips were blood red.

"Can I borrow your new pearl earrings, Mum?"

"Is David Beckham in town?"

"Too old for me. Can I?"

Lene sighed and pulled her birthday present out of her ear lobes. David Beckham . . . too old? Christ, he was still a boy.

"Can I use the bathroom now?"

"Of course."

While Lene washed her hands, she noticed the exclamation marks, the zigzag lightning, and the hearts drawn in the condensation on the mirror and felt a lump in her stomach. She took a deep breath and scolded herself. Get it into your skull, Lene! The girl is twenty-one . . . she's an adult, for God's sake! Though as far as Lene was concerned, Josefine would always be five years old.

She blew the hairs from her daughter's eyebrow plucking off the bathroom shelf and put the mascara wand back in its tube. Contraceptive pills? She opened the medicine cupboard and checked Josefine's blister pack. Well, at least it was up-to-date.

When she returned to the living room, Josefine was bent over the coffee table. She carefully popped olives and tiny pieces of ham into her mouth so as not to ruin her lipstick. She had pulled back her hair in a tight ponytail and the earrings suited her. Her black jeans fitted as if they were painted onto her long legs, and she was wearing her new, hip-length suede jacket, an olive green scarf and her new, black boots.

Lene was proud of her daughter. And worried sick.

"Will you be sleeping in your own bed tonight?"

"I sincerely hope not! No, Mum, joke! . . . I think . . . yes, I will. See you later."

"Be safe," Lene said automatically, but her daughter was already gone.

Lene stood for a moment staring at the door.

Then she tried calling the elusive beekeeper, Allan Lundkvist, again, and for the umpteenth time heard his slow drawl on the answerphone. She left a new message and flung down her mobile in frustration.

CHAPTER 21

Michael returned to the hotel in a terrible mood after interviewing Kasper Hansen's mother. He cursed himself: he was a smooth-tongued fraudster. A snake. Poor woman. Now she was waiting for a call that would never come, a journalist who would never contact her again, a program that would never be made.

In reception, the porter handed him a thick, yellow envelope with no return address, sealed with several staples. He started opening it as soon as he reached his room and spread the photocopies of Flemming Caspersen's medical records across his bed.

He started with a brief note from Næstved Central Hospital. Flemming Caspersen had been found in his bed at eight thirty in the morning on January 14, 2013, in the east wing of Pederslund. He appeared to be dead. An ambulance had arrived fifteen minutes later. Victor Schmidt and his wife had given Caspersen CPR and mouth-to-mouth resuscitation while they waited for it to come. On arrival, the paramedics took over the resuscitation and continued during the journey to the hospital. They administered adrenaline directly to his heart and made several attempts to shock it back to life. Flemming Caspersen had exhibited no vital signs. His pupils had been non-reactive during transport and it was presumed that his brain had been deprived of oxygen for a long time.

The duty doctor at Næstved Central Hospital had declared him dead on arrival. Time of death was called at 9:33 a.m., and the cause of death was attributed to *institutio cordis*, cardiac arrest—probably due to a massive, acute, myocardial infarction. The duty doctor and the medical officer who examined the body six hours later both agreed.

Michael assumed his favourite position at the balcony. Heart failure. Ultimately wasn't that what we all died from? The autopsy report was brief and cursory: the pathologist had discovered an unusual hardening of the arteries given the patient's age and a coronary thrombosis which had caused a major part of the heart's left side to die. Flemming Caspersen had passed away in his sleep. There were no outward signs of violence. His blood alcohol level was what one would expect to find in a man who had consumed a few drinks the night before. No toxin screens had been carried out and no one had examined the body for hidden needle marks between toes or fingers, under the tongue, in his scalp, in his ears or the mucous membrane of the anus.

Michael was far from impressed by the pathologist's work. Hardening of the arteries, coronary thrombosis, dead, the end. There were literally hundreds of ways to make a murder look like a natural death, but not one of them had been considered in the report.

And now Flemming Caspersen's body had been cremated.

Michael had dissolved two Treo painkillers in a glass of water when his telephone rang.

He swallowed the bitter, white liquid.

"Hello?"

"You're invited to dinner at Pederslund tonight," Elizabeth Caspersen said without introduction. "We both are. Victor almost had a fit when I told him about Miss Simpson in New York. Can you make it?"

"Of course I can, Elizabeth. Great. Did you write the letter your-self?"

"Yes. It was devastating."

"And the picture of the little one? Do you have one?"

"One of my secretary's grandchildren. Ugly little brat. He looks like Winston Churchill."

"With the cigar?"

"Yes, Michael. I pretended one of my daughters needed it for some homework about overpopulation. I don't think she believed me."

"When should I get there?"

"Drinks are served at six o'clock, on the dot, and dinner is at six thirty. They eat early in the country. They're all there. I can pick you up from your hotel at four thirty. That's in one and a half hours. We can talk in the car. Any news?"

"Yes," he said. "But let's save it for later. Dress code?"

"I don't think there is one, but if you're out of clean shirts, perhaps you should invest in a new one."

Michael closed the door to the balcony.

"I will, and while we're on the subject of money, I need to ask for you for an advance. I've already had some expenses, and I'm about to incur a lot more. For starters, I need to charter a helicopter."

"A helicopter . . . ?"

Elizabeth Caspersen sounded taken aback.

"It's just for a couple of days," he added.

"A couple of days?"

Her voice faltered, and Michael pulled a face.

"Do I have to remind you that yesterday you were willing to spend all the money you have to get to the bottom of this? A case which might prove that your father was responsible for the murder of a random hiker in Norway. I can make do without the helicopter when I visit Finnmark, of course, but I think that the cost will be more or less the same. When you factor in my fee."

Her silence was eminently expressive.

"Of course . . ." came the self-possessed response. "Of course, I am. And I apologize. I just have to . . . I just have to get used to this level of expenditure. I came to you and you're doing an excellent job. How much?"

"Two hundred thousand kroner should cover it for now."

"I'll transfer the money immediately," she said in her newly humbled voice.

"Thank you."

He gave her the number of the client account with his accountant in Odense. He knew that Sara would be thrilled. Or she would be, until he started renting helicopters in Norway.

"I'll see you at four thirty," she said.

"I look forward to it," he replied.

"I wouldn't if I were you," she said and hung up.

Michael flicked through that day's newspapers. The Rigspolitiet were still investigating the veteran's apparent suicide in Holbæk. There was a new photograph of the deceased, surrounded by his army mates on the bonnet of an armoured personnel carrier outside Baghdad. Kim Andersen's naked chest glistened beneath the Middle Eastern sky, a black-and-white-chequered partisan scarf tied around his neck. Michael smiled at the sight of all the tattoos that covered the soldier's arms, shoulders, and torso.

Michael himself had a single tattoo on his shoulder, which was more than enough. He had been blind drunk one night in Manila when Keith Mallory had dragged him into a small, unhygienic tattoo parlour.

Michael only discovered what had happened twenty-four hours later when, still somewhat under the influence, he was drying himself in front of the mirror after a shower. He had screamed when he noticed his right shoulder, where a big, orange Homer Simpson looked over his shoulder with a smirk. The character had his trousers around his ankles and was baring his naked backside to anyone who cared to look. Sara hated it.

In another newspaper, there was a new picture of Superintendent Lene Jensen in a parking lot outside Holbæk Police Station. She was photographed midstride and she was looking at the photographer. As always, her face was grave.

Lene Jensen was a doer, Michael concluded.

The journalist had spoken to Kim Andersen's colleagues from the carpentry firm, a couple of old school friends, and fellow hunters, and everyone expressed surprise. Coming home must have proved tougher for Kim than they had all realized. In the past year he had become introverted and morose. He had been limping, his leg was hurting, and he could no longer climb scaffolding or roofs. Perhaps his suicide wasn't so hard to understand after all.

Michael flicked through the other newspapers without finding anything except speculation and predictable coverage.

A dead, highly decorated veteran. With a limp. Just like one of the rhino horn thieves.

Elizabeth Caspersen's black Opel Insignia pulled up in front of Admiral Hotel at exactly four thirty. Michael opened the passenger door and got in. He had managed to buy a clean shirt and the hotel had pressed the only suit he had packed.

She looked tired and stressed. The driver's seat was pushed right back to make room for her long legs. She wore black, perforated driving gloves and drove with skilful concentration. They crossed Langebro, passed the SAS Hotel and headed east down Ørestads Boulevard.

Neither of them spoke until they joined the motorway.

"You look very nice, Michael."

"Thank you, so do you."

She smiled feebly.

"What have you discovered? You look terribly serious."

Michael sighed and stared at his hands.

"A young Danish-Norwegian couple disappeared on a hiking trip north of Lakselv around the March 23, 2011. Kasper Hansen and Ingrid Sundsbö," he said, without looking at her. "Thirty-one and twenty-nine years old. He was an engineer and she was a graphic designer. They arrived at Lakselv from Copenhagen via Oslo on the eve of March 22 and spent the night at Porsanger Vertshus. The following day they headed north and caught a lift with a Norwegian long-distance truck driver. Since then no one has seen them, except their killers. They were experienced hikers with good equipment and the weather was fine and warm."

The car swerved into the middle lane and she straightened it up with a jerk.

"Two people . . . ? Please, not two?"

"I'm afraid so. Like I said, a young couple. She was probably killed the same day. Her body has never been found. Neither has his, obviously."

"Michael . . . Jesus Christ . . . oh, God."

She leaned back and closed her eyes. Michael kept a nervous eye on a truck in the wing mirror.

"Do you want me to drive?" he offered, but Elizabeth Caspersen didn't appear to have heard him. "Two . . ." she whispered again in despair, and he felt genuinely sorry for her. "They didn't have any children, did they? Michael . . . please tell me they didn't have children . . ."

"Two. Twins. A boy and a girl. Four years old now," he said mercilessly. "I'm sorry. Kasper Hansen's sixty-five-year-old mother was granted custody of them. They live in a small house in Vangede. I visited her this morning, pretending to be a journalist interested in the case."

"Michael, that's awful! What do I do? And it is them? You're one hundred percent sure?"

"There is no doubt. Family and friends held a memorial service last autumn for two empty coffins in the Norwegian Seamen's Church in Copenhagen. They were well-liked. Facebook is full of requests for information. Like you said, people want to know."

"Stop it . . . I get it, okay . . ."

Her eyes were blinded with tears; Michael put his hand on the handbrake.

"No more details?" he asked.

"Not right now."

"I tried telling you, Elizabeth, I really did. Now they have a face and a name."

"I know, and I want to know everything, I just want you to ration it. I didn't know . . . It never even crossed my mind that there could be others. At the same time, I mean."

"Of course not, but you didn't do anything wrong, Elizabeth. You're doing the right thing now. Remember that."

"Yes, but it's *my* insane, murderous father. I can't help feeling responsible. I know perfectly well that it isn't rational, but I do."

She started crying again. "Those poor kids, I feel so sorry for them." She blinked away the tears on her eyelashes. "Do you have children of your own?"

"A four-year-old and an eighteen-month-old," he said.

She nodded and stared straight ahead while her mind tried to process a storm of fresh horrors. Michael watched a tear make the journey from the corner of her eye; it fell from her jawbone and left a small, dark stain on her silk collar.

Eventually she regained control of her emotions—and the car—and he leaned back and noticed that his nails had left small, red crescents in the palms of his hands.

"And the others?" she asked. "The hunters. The murderers?"

"Nothing yet."

"But you'll find them?"

"I think so."

"You have to find them, Michael!"

"Of course."

"My father was a customer of Guns and Gents," she said a little later. "Their gunsmith looked after his weapons. They ordered the Mauser rifle for him in January 2011, and they sighted it in for him with the telescopic sight it's fitted with now. All the stamps, receipts, and numbers match. You still don't think it was him?"

Michael said nothing.

"Sonartek's Gulfstream flew my father to Stockholm on March 20, 2011 in the morning," she went on. "It returned without passengers in the afternoon, flew back to Stockholm on March 27, and returned with my father."

"I see," he said.

"Is that all you have to say?"

"It is for now."

"I can't work out whether you're listening to me and understand what I'm saying, or if you simply don't want to believe that he did it," she exploded. "Seriously. It was just him and a bunch of crazed killers, not a conspiracy dreamt up by the CIA, or Victor, or anyone else, to blacken his name or cause me problems. They killed two innocent people, Michael!"

"I hear you and I understand you, Elizabeth," he said. "But—"

"But what?! Isn't that enough, for God's sake?"

He sighed and desperately wished that he could smoke.

"Nothing."

"I'm not an idiot, Michael. What is it?"

"I don't know. I really don't, it's just something I've learned along the way."

"What?"

"Patterns, Elizabeth." Michael made a helpless gesture. "When something is too easy, when everything fits, it's because it's too good to be true. Always."

"If you say so," she mumbled. "I know it was him."

He changed the subject: "What should I be expecting down at Pederslund?"

"Victor will try to intimidate you. He'll never trust you—or me, for that matter. No one, least of all him, likes outsiders prying into their private lives. He'll resent it deeply. As far as his wife, Monika, goes, she'll be a great hostess. Unless Victor has knocked her about recently."

"Recently?"

"It happens," she said. "If you hear strange noises during the night, don't open your door."

"Tonight?"

Michael stared at her.

"It'll be too late to drive home tonight. Victor won't be satisfied until every stone has been turned. An illegitimate son of his business partner, a baby in the US, with *their* insane legal system? Forget it."

"I didn't pack my toothbrush," he said.

"The guest bedrooms are well equipped. I think you'll find everything you need."

"And the sons?"

"Henrik will barely notice you. He'll be hunched over his mobile phone or his laptop. He works all the time. If he does notice you, he'll be hospitable, but distracted. Charming, but wise beyond his years."

"Is he married?"

"He's asexual, I believe. I've certainly never heard of a girlfriend, or boyfriend for that matter. He works."

"And Jakob, the army officer?"

"Reserved. Doesn't take after his mother or his father. He travels all the time. Lives very frugally."

"Single?"

"He finds it hard to fall in love. To my knowledge he has only had one serious relationship in his whole life."

"Who with?"

She furrowed her brow. "When he was on leave from the army, he travelled around Nepal and met a girl. A girl just like him. An explorer. And worth exploring, clearly."

"What happened?"

"It was five, six years ago. Jakob came back from the army and had lost ten kilos. He locked himself in his room for a month. He refused to talk to anyone and never about her. I don't remember her name."

"She dumped him?"

"Jakob isn't the kind of guy you dump. But I don't know the details. No one ever talks about it."

"Did you read the autopsy report?" she asked when they had driven for a while in silence.

"Yes."

"And?"

"Nothing. Your father just died."

CHAPTER 22

The hunting lodge was beautiful and enchanting, and there was nothing along the narrow, private sunken road to reveal its existence. Hedges and trees grew together above the road and blocked out the light evening sky.

Elizabeth Caspersen threw the car through a gap between two hedges, an opening that Michael would have missed. He caught sight of a set of red gateposts and black cast-iron gates overgrown with ivy. They drove a few hundred metres on a rust-coloured gravel track before the park opened up with its winding waterways, ponds covered with water lilies, thatched and darkened tenant-farmer buildings, ruler-straight flowerbeds and lawns so smooth you could play billiards on them.

The park and the buildings were just as well kept as the entrance to the hunting lodge had been wild and discreet. The main house was white, harmonious, light and crisp. It had an Italianate feel to it, delicate like pastry. Behind the buildings, the park sloped towards the sea. White enclosures and neat red stable buildings stretched to the right of the main house. A couple of thoroughbreds with clean, blue blankets were grazing in the enclosures.

"How marvellous," he said.

"It's a lovely place," she agreed. "The horses are Monika's hobby. She breeds Danish Warmbloods and leaves Victor to his own devices. That's the deal. Pederslund is a hunting lodge built by King Frederick VI for one of his four illegitimate children by his mistress, Frederikke Dannemand."

"More illegitimate children." Michael smiled.

"Yes, and while we're on the subject," she said, "the boy—my American half-brother—is called Charles, named after Ms. Simpson's grandfather."

"Nice detail," Michael said.

She parked between a Volvo Estate and a dark BMW. Michael got out and stretched his back.

"Does Victor work from home?"

"He has a flat in Copenhagen. It's mainly Monika who now lives here."

Elizabeth Caspersen walked around the car to Michael. "It's an open secret that he also has a mistress in Copenhagen, and Monika, well . . . she takes the occasional lover. An arrangement that suits them both, I believe."

A pair of large lamps either side of the front door came on automatically as they walked up the main steps and the door was opened by a tall, lean man. Iron-grey hair, well-trimmed moustache and a hawk nose. Light brown Italian loafers, a soft, cinnamon coloured pullover, and a pale blue shirt, rolled up his sinewy forearms. The man's movements were fast and energetic and he greeted Elizabeth Caspersen profusely, but his dark eyes were busy scanning Michael.

"Come in! So nice, Elizabeth. So nice to see you. You're well?"

He didn't wait for an answer, but pulled her through the doorway so he could concentrate on her companion.

Michael smiled politely. Victor Schmidt's hand was long, cool, and dry. He looked to be in excellent physical shape even though he was in his late sixties.

"Welcome to Pederslund, I'm Victor Schmidt."

"Michael Sander."

"Elizabeth's mysterious . . . what, exactly?"

"Adviser?"

"Michael is helping me," she said.

Victor Schmidt released Michael's hand. He smiled, but his eyes didn't join in.

"Welcome anyway."

"Thank you."

Michael looked around the hall. He saw a white double staircase opposite the front door with two sections that floated, as if weightless, up through the different floors. There were antlers and centrepieces arranged in fans and rosettes around particularly impressive trophies, but this collection of skeletal remains seemed to belong exclusively to the Danish fauna.

As Victor Schmidt helped Elizabeth Caspersen out of her trench coat, he glanced at Michael, who looked back at him without expression. There was something wrong with Victor Schmidt's eyes, he thought. The enormous crystal chandelier suspended from the ceiling at the centre of the hall reflected differently in them. It took him another moment to work out that Victor Schmidt's left eye was prosthetic.

The businessman flung out his arms as a sign of comic surrender.

"A completely outrageous story, Elizabeth. The old goat. I don't know whether to laugh or cry . . . or envy him. You would think that Flemming had heard of condoms, for God's sake. Your poor mother. Perhaps it's just as well that she is . . ."

"Gaga?" Elizabeth Caspersen suggested.

"Yes. A blessing. Drinks?"

He led the way through a set of dark double doors and Michael edged closer to Elizabeth Caspersen.

"He has a glass eye?" he whispered.

"What a brilliant detective you are, Michael."

She gave his arm a quick squeeze.

The estate's library bore comparison to Flemming Caspersen's, but Michael got a feeling of stepping onto a stage set, something he hadn't had in Hellerup. The sense of belonging and ownership which he knew from large English houses, and which only several generations of unchallenged, inherited privilege could create, was missing. The library at Pederslund was simultaneously too much and not quite enough.

It wanted for nothing: there were comfortable Chesterfield sofas, a fine-looking fireplace where a fire crackled merrily, bookcases from floor to ceiling filled with impressively titled, weighty tomes—he suspected they had been bought at an auction by the yard. There were oil paintings from the Danish romantic golden age, silk lampshades, huge Chinese vases, oriental ivory and wood carvings, and even a varnished college rowing oar above the mantelpiece. But there was no soul.

A slim, dark-haired woman got up from the sofa and crossed the room. She exchanged continental kisses and a stiff hug with Elizabeth Caspersen before looking at Michael with large, soulful eyes. She was wearing a tight-fitting beige silk skirt with pearl embroidery, a black silk blouse whose neckline was gathered with a pearl over her décolletage, and a short jacket of the same material as the skirt. She moved beautifully, even though she was wearing very high, thin stilettos. Slim silver bracelets jingled down her forearm when she extended her hand towards him, and he didn't know whether to shake or kiss it, but chose the former.

"Monika," she said in a husky voice.

"Michael."

She was a sun worshipper and the skin at her throat had thickened and turned slightly leathery, but her neck was smooth, long, and elegant, and her face still beautiful. Her black hair was gathered at the nape of her neck in a tight ponytail that made her look like a dressage rider.

"I'm Swedish," she said. "Victor abducted me from Stockholm."

"I can see why," Michael said gallantly.

She smiled.

"Thank you. What would you like to drink, Michael? I understand that you're some kind of private eye, so I guess it has to be whisky?"

"Yes, please."

"Ice?"

"If you have it."

"Come and meet my son, Henrik," she said, and walked over to the drinks cabinet. She had a beautiful backside and strong, slim legs. When she turned, he noticed large, round breasts that seem to defy both gravity and age. He put her in her mid-fifties, but carefully preserved. Then again, he imagined all that riding must keep her fit.

A young man with blond, sandy hair and very light blue eyes had got up from the desk. A laptop displayed long, green columns of numbers. Michael recognized the blond boy from the summer picture in Flemming Caspersen's library. He was still slim like a boy, lanky, and he had his father's narrow shoulders, but his face was open with an easy smile on his lips. He brushed the fringe from his eyes and extended his hand.

"Hello. Henrik. Welcome."

"Michael. What a great place."

"It's a bit off the beaten track, but my father grew up in a tenement block in Vesterbro, he claims, and always wanted to have a castle. Now he has finally got it, he spends most of his time in Copenhagen. It doesn't make any sense, does it?"

"But your mother lives here?"

"She dotes on her horses."

"Do you ride?" Michael asked.

"Never. In my opinion, horses are neurotic reptiles. They're overrated and unpredictable."

Michael's nostrils caught a hint of Monika Schmidt's perfume as she touched his shoulder lightly. Over by the fireplace, Victor Schmidt and Elizabeth Caspersen were deep in conversation.

"Your drink, Michael," Monika Schmidt whispered. She was very close and the scent was overpowering. She looked at her son.

"Have you had the reptile speech?" she asked.

"Just the headline."

"The truth is, he's scared of them," she said.

Henrik Schmidt smiled. "Yes, Mother. No, Mother. The horse is a noble animal, I know."

"It really is," she said.

Michael looked out at the enclosures that glowed strangely white in the last rays of the low evening sun. The horses were dark, calmly grazing silhouettes. He sniffed his whisky and detected notes of saltwater and seaweed. Islay Malt, would be his guess. It was like biting into tarred hemp rope. In a good way. What a shame he couldn't drink tonight.

"You . . . have a stud farm?" he asked.

"I have a wonderful stallion," she said, and eyed him up and down. "Cavalier of Pederslund. We freeze his semen and sell it across the world. Or we let the mares come to him. A mare from Germany is here at the moment. I think we'll let him mount her tonight."

She raised her glass to her mouth and Michael observed the lipstick on the rim.

She smiled: "I love *deckara*, Michael . . . 'procedurals' you say in Danish? Are you really a private eye?"

"Not in the literary sense," he assured her.

She sized him up again as though she considered bidding for him at an auction.

"Are you sure?" she sounded disappointed.

"Quite sure."

Michael looked around frantically for Elizabeth Caspersen.

Henrik Schmidt watched his mother with pale, flat, inexpressive eyes. Then he flashed Michael a boyish smile, made his excuses, and returned to his laptop. There was something monastically ascetic and isolated about his slim, hunched figure. Henrik Schmidt looked like someone who was in his element.

Michael was finally rescued by Victor Schmidt and Elizabeth Caspersen. The financier put his arm around his wife's shoulders, pulled her close and smiled to Michael.

"I have to warn you, Michael," Victor Schmidt said. "When my wife spots a fine stud, she'll stop at nothing to get him."

Monika Schmidt blushed and didn't smile.

"He's an investigator, Victor," she mumbled. "He's his own man."

Victor Schmidt squeezed his wife harder and looked at Michael. "So what are your qualifications? I've tried looking you up. You must be the only person on earth who can't be googled."

"Stop it, Victor," Elizabeth Caspersen said. "I can vouch for Michael."

The financier shot him an inquisitorial look with his working eye, while his glass eye happened to be aimed at his son at the desk.

"Surely I need to know something about the man before I let him into every nook and cranny of my company."

"*Your* company?"

"Our company, Elizabeth, for God's sake."

"I think Victor is right, Elizabeth," Michael said smoothly. "I would feel exactly the same." He smiled. "I worked for Shepherd & Wilkins in London and New York for a decade before I started working for myself. Perhaps you've heard of them? Before that, I was a military police captain with the Horse Guards, and after that, I worked for Hvidovre Police's Serious Crime Unit."

Schmidt nodded. "How hard was that, Elizabeth?" He drained his glass and let go of his wife. "I'm satisfied. In the circumstances. And you have the letter from this Miss Simpson?"

He set down his glass on a coffee table as Elizabeth opened her handbag and handed him a pale blue envelope made from good quality paper. He found a pair of reading glasses, put them on his long nose and pulled out a single, densely written sheet. A small photograph fluttered to the floor.

Michael picked it up and looked at it before passing it on. Elizabeth

Caspersen was right. The surly-looking chubby baby in the picture did have a remarkable similarity to the late, eminent British statesman.

Schmidt took the photograph from Michael. His lips moved while he read. He turned over the letter and carried on reading. Then he looked at Elizabeth Caspersen over his reading glasses.

"This is not good, Elizabeth."

She nodded calmly.

"I agree. It's very unfortunate."

"Unfortunate? It's a shit storm. If your father wasn't already dead, I'd happily shoot him myself."

He held up the letter to Michael.

"Have you read it?"

"Yes."

"And?"

"And what?"

"All of it, damn you! Is it genuine? Does she exist?"

Monika Schmidt smiled apologetically to Michael from her position behind her husband.

Michael nodded.

"Miss Janice Simpson lives at the address stated," he said calmly. "She's thirty-three years old, works as an editor at a publisher's near Bryant Park, she almost owns her apartment on 58th Street West outright, and publishes books on modern art. Her mother is a librarian at the New York Public Library and her father is a judge at New York's Criminal Court. It's an old family with a fine lineage. They have been New Yorkers for seven generations. That makes them aristocracy in that town."

He looked at Victor Schmidt in the hope of fanning a social inferiority complex, but the other man just nodded vaguely.

"I'm waiting for some bank information," Michael continued. "Simpson Junior's birth certificate and various photographic evidence."

Schmidt looked a little bit impressed, despite himself.

"Excellent," he said slowly. He looked at the photograph. "Hideous kid."

"May I see?"

Monika Schmidt held out her hand. She looked silently at the photograph before handing it back. Her gaze was downcast and her eyes half closed.

Michael looked at the large oil painting above the mantelpiece: a happy, younger version of Monika Schmidt in a long, pale silk dress, near an open window with light curtains. Her two sons stood next to her: blond Henrik with the sky-blue eyes who looked like his father, and the stronger, darker, and introverted Jakob, who took after his mother. The painting had photographic accuracy and detail. It was the same artist who had painted Flemming Caspersen with the Alaskan bear in the house in Hellerup.

He sent Elizabeth Caspersen a loaded glance, but she ignored him.

"I think he's cute," she said. "Charles . . ."

"Charles Caspersen?" Victor Schmidt burst out. "What sort of name is that?"

"I don't think she'll insist on the surname, Victor," Elizabeth Caspersen said. "There really would be very little point."

"The whole thing is pointless," he said. "What an old fool."

"I would appreciate your not discussing my father in those terms, Victor. If it weren't for him, you'd be selling second-hand cars in the suburbs of northwest Copenhagen instead of owning half of Sonartek. Remember that."

"Less than half, Elizabeth, dear. You and your demented mother now own the rest," he said maliciously.

Monika Schmidt intervened.

"*Snälla, ni båda!* Victor, you'll apologize to Elizabeth immediately, and you, Elizabeth, will forgive Victor. As usual."

She glowered at her husband until he obeyed orders and mumbled an apology.

Michael felt a pair of eyes staring at him and turned around. From the chair by the window, Henrik Schmidt was watching him with almost myopic intensity. When he discovered that Michael was looking at him, he smiled broadly, but then he spotted something behind the security consultant. His face brightened and he made to get up.

"Hi, Jakob!"

Michael turned around, astonished that someone could be that silent. Keith Mallory was fond of saying it: "Sooner or later you'll meet the new talent, Mike, and though you think you're one hell of a tough guy, you can only hope to God that you're on the same side or he'll fuck you up the arse until you can no longer remember your own name."

Michael thought that day had just arrived.

CHAPTER 23

"Michael Sander," he said, and stuck out his hand.

"Jakob."

The other man looked at Michael's hand for a moment before he shook it, almost warily. No pissing contest was required. He didn't blink and his face was imperturbable and serious. Dark suit, black roll-neck jumper. He was tall, almost a head taller than Michael, broad-shouldered and well-built, with dark blond hair, and an impassive, weathered face, a long hawk nose and dark eyes that didn't smile.

Michael watched the faces around him. In Victor Schmidt's, irritation seemed to do battle with genuine affection.

"You went down to the sea?" his father asked.

"My usual walk."

"The boy's name is Charles," Victor Schmidt said. "Try to get used to it."

"Charles?"

"Yes, God help us. Charles Simpson-Caspersen."

"Stop it, Victor."

Monika Schmidt's voice was sharp and long-suffering.

Elizabeth Caspersen was almost as tall as Jakob Schmidt. They embraced warmly.

Michael jumped when a woman's voice right behind him announced that dinner was ready in the kitchen. The woman shook hands with him and introduced herself as Mrs. Nielsen. She looked after the family. Or at least made sure that they got enough to eat. She had a pasty face, wore a dark, simple dress and was strangely devoid of personality.

"Lovely, Mrs. Nielsen," Monika Schmidt said. "Henrik, Jakob, are you coming? Victor?"

Michael passed Jakob Schmidt at a distance of only a few centimetres. The man smelled of cold air and grass.

"You work for Elizabeth?" he asked as they headed for the door.

"Yes," Michael said.

"As a . . . ?"

"Consultant."

"That's not a protected title, is it?"

"Not at all."

"Do you think you'll be able to do it?"

"Do what?"

Jakob Schmidt smiled, and something fast and lethal swam across his eyes. "Get to the bottom of things?"

"We're talking about Flemming Caspersen and his son Charles?"

"Of course. That's what we're talking about."

"I sincerely hope so," Michael said steadily.

The tall young man held open the door for Michael, who again passed him at very close quarters. Jakob Schmidt moved with the economy of an athlete and Michael wondered if he could take him, one on one.

He doubted it.

Michael was seated opposite Monika Schmidt at the long table in the kitchen. There was no tablecloth, but the stoneware and the glasses were exquisite and you needed strong muscles to lift the heavy silver cutlery. There were rustic Italian bread baskets, brown Spanish wine jugs and blue, hand-painted Portuguese plates.

He spread his starched linen napkin across his lap, realized how hungry he was, and smiled at his hostess.

Behind him, pots were bubbling on the vast Aga.

"It smells fantastic," he said.

A bowl of bouillabaisse was placed in front of him, large chunks of lobster and fish floating in the soup, and Michael inhaled the aromas expectantly. Monika Schmidt poured him some white wine, and Victor Schmidt raised his glass and looked around the table. He put his hand on his younger son's shoulder.

"A toast to heirs. Old and new."

"I understand that Pederslund is a hunting lodge," Michael said, making conversation. "Do you still hunt or . . . ?"

"Frequently," Victor Schmidt said. "We have pheasants, snipe, some wild boar—vicious bastards—ducks and geese on the coast, roe deer, obviously, and a few red deer. Do you hunt?"

"No."

Michael was tempted to add that he was still sexually active, but stopped himself.

"It's a good business," his host said after giving the matter some consideration. "We have some syndicates down here and a gamekeeper who deals with most of the feeding, releasing the pheasants, minding the dogs, and so on. He's an old friend of Jakob's. Quite a few ex-soldiers come here."

Michael broke off a chunk of bread. "And he lives on the estate?"

"Of course. When he's not travelling. He's away a lot, isn't he, Jakob?"

Michael couldn't interpret Victor Schmidt's face.

"I suppose he is," Jakob Schmidt said. "Thomas co-owns a safari company. He arranges hunting trips to Africa, Canada, and the Himalayas. When he's not here, he gets one of his friends to look after the dogs and the game. Peter is covering for him at the moment."

"It's an excellent arrangement," Victor Schmidt declared, and Michael realized that the matter was closed.

He smiled to Jakob Schmidt instead. "Elizabeth told me you were an officer?"

The young man merely nodded, but Victor Schmidt glowed with pride. "Captain in the Royal Life Guards, First Armoured Infantry Company. Jakob was in Bosnia-Herzegovina, Iraq, and Afghanistan, and these days he's usually anywhere but home, isn't that right, Jakob?"

The son stared into his bowl.

"He's a ghost," Monika Schmidt declared.

Henrik Schmidt looked from one to the other and smiled to Michael: "We played at Scarlet Pimpernel all the time when we were boys. Jakob was the Scarlet Pimpernel, of course. He was older and he could beat me, so he was in charge. I was either an aristocratic oppressor who must be guillotined, or a revolutionary trying to catch him. Do you remember, Mum?"

Henrik Schmidt was the family peacemaker, Michael thought. Wedged in like an airbag between his father and big brother's unyielding, potentially explosive egos.

Monika Schmidt moistened her lips.

"You bet I do, darling. *They seek him here, they seek him there, those Frenchies seek him everywhere. Is he in heaven? Is he in hell? That damned, elusive Pimpernel!*" she quoted, while gazing lovingly at her older son.

"And he still is," Victor Schmidt said. "A quite useless ghost."

"Jakob has never been interested in business, Victor," his wife said, to mollify him. "You have Henrik and you should count yourself lucky. Jakob would hate every minute in the boardroom. He can't stand being indoors. You know that."

"And of course I am—grateful for Henrik, I mean," Victor Schmidt said. "I think we all are."

"And, anyway, you have a new heir now," Elizabeth Caspersen quipped sweetly.

"And so close to Wall Street," Jakob Schmidt said with a smile.

"Have you seen her, Henrik?" his father asked. "She said that she used to visit Flemming in the apartment on 3rd Avenue. You practically lived there. Did you ever meet her?"

"It's a big apartment," Henrik Schmidt pointed out.

"Surely it's not so big that you wouldn't notice a frantically copulating couple? Not to mention the pallet-loads of Viagra?" He looked at Elizabeth Caspersen. "I'm sorry, Elizabeth, but really . . ."

"It's all right, Victor," she said with a sigh, as she, too, turned her attention to the younger son.

"Have you met her, Henrik?"

"Of course not. Flemming was always out, usually with me. We had meetings all the time. We *did* work when we were there, just so you know. I find it hard to believe that he could have had an affair without my knowledge. And, no, I've never seen her in the apartment or anywhere else."

And you're right, Michael thought. He almost felt sorry for Henrik Schmidt.

"She writes that they met at an exhibition at the Guggenheim Museum," Victor Schmidt said. "The Guggenheim? Since when was Flemming interested in modern art? Unless someone had painted a dead animal, he would never—"

161

"I think there was a Congress Defense Committee event the summer before last," Henrik Schmidt said. "We weren't the only ones to seize the opportunity to do some lobbying. Flemming was there."

Michael looked at Elizabeth Caspersen. It was an excellent detail she had included in her letter. Highly plausible. He was impressed.

"So what does she want?" Victor Schmidt said to no one in particular while the soup bowls were cleared away and a dish of roast pigeons was placed on the table.

"She wants a secure future for herself and her son," Elizabeth said. "And if my father really got her pregnant with . . . with Charles, if he really is the child's father, then I can see her point. She writes that she's not going to be unreasonable."

"Unreasonable? A New Yorker? What the hell does that mean? A couple of billion dollars?"

"At least," Henrik said. "Her father is a judge. Oh, what fun."

Victor Schmidt exploded.

"This is no joke! It has taken thirty years of bloody hard graft to build Sonartek, and now Flemming is dead, and then some . . . some . . ."

"Calm down, Dad," Jakob said. "Perhaps it won't be so bad."

His father pulled himself together with considerable effort and turned his attention to his older son.

"Tell me, for how long do we have the pleasure of your company this time?"

Jakob Schmidt pushed the sleeve of his jacket away from his wristwatch with a twisting motion, as if he wanted to strangle his own wrist or didn't quite trust it. A scratched Rolex on a steel strap slipped up his wrist and Michael noticed white skin underneath.

"I'm leaving around eight thirty."

"Eight thirty?" His father scowled at him. "Listen, boy. Flemming, my business partner, whom you may vaguely remember, has screwed around and fathered a child—not in the hereafter, but in New York. Now. 'Charles.' We're facing a massive crisis here. His mother could sue us for millions. She's an American, Jakob! Her father is a judge. Do you have any idea what that means?"

Jakob Schmidt calmly returned his father's gaze and shrugged his shoulders.

There didn't seem to be much love lost between them, thought Michael, who was following the exchange. In fact, there was a strange alienation in Jakob's eyes when he looked at his father. Perhaps he just didn't like him; after all, his father beat his mother. Or maybe it was something else. Michael had seen it before: one child plays by the rules, while the other, usually the more loved, can't or won't, and recklessly breaks away so as not to go under. Elizabeth Caspersen had done it as well. The two of them seemed to understand each other.

"Define 'us,'" the son responded flatly.

Victor Schmidt drained his glass and filled it up again. The wine spilled across the table. Mrs. Nielsen got busy with a cloth, but the financier didn't even sense her presence.

"*Us*, God damn you! Your family. Your mother, brother and me. And Elizabeth. What could you possibly be doing tonight that's more important than this?"

"Meeting someone," the son said.

"Could you give me a lift to Copenhagen?" his brother asked.

"Sure."

Victor Schmidt looked exasperatedly from one to the other. Betrayed.

"As for Flemming's American offspring, surely it's only fair that the mother receives some form of maintenance?" Jakob said.

He looked at Michael. "Are you going to talk to her?"

"I believe that's the plan."

"But Jakob, you'll be back later, won't you?" his mother asked.

"Of course, I'll be back before you know it."

"Promise?"

He reached out a big hand and squeezed one of his mother's small ones. But his father hadn't finished.

"Fair? You think so? And what does that entail? A seat on the board? Just what exactly do you mean by 'fair?'"

The son smiled.

"Isn't there some sort of lower-age limit, Elizabeth? When it comes to board members of a quoted company, I mean. You're the corporate lawyer."

"It's seventy, I believe," she said. "But you also have to be a member of Club 300, the Danish branch, and be the CEO of a company where every board member is one of the boys. Or that's how it seems. Inbred. After all, Victor is also on the board of TDC, Carlsberg and Brødrene Hartmann. They make a living out of telling each other how brilliant and clever they are, and how they would have been headhunted as CEOs of Pfizer or Morgan Stanley long ago if they hadn't been so damned patriotic."

Her cheekbones were glowing.

Monika Schmidt placed a calming hand on her husband's forearm, but he snatched it back angrily. He seemed to jump at the chance to vent his fury on his son and Elizabeth Caspersen—as if anyone had any doubts—but then his glance swept across Michael, the outsider, and he shut his mouth hard as if an insect had flown into it.

"Come on, Dad," Jakob Schmidt said, trying to appease him. "Let's wait and see how bad it is. Send Michael to New York. Find out what the woman really wants. May I see the letter?"

Elizabeth Caspersen passed it across the table.

Jakob Schmidt began by looking at the little photograph. He smiled and put it to one side. His dark eyes jumped from line to line. Then he carefully put the letter back in the envelope, slipped in the photograph and handed it to her.

"Do you mind if I smoke?" he asked.

The housekeeper didn't wait for him to be granted permission, but pushed a silver ashtray across to his elbow. Jakob Schmidt lit a long, brown cheroot, blew the smoke up to the ceiling and watched it drift towards the doorway.

"Henrik said that Miss Simpson is an editor," he said.

"Michael has already found that out," Elizabeth Caspersen said. "Why?"

The older son gave her an inscrutable look.

"Nothing. She's probably okay. Seventh-generation New Yorker? Give her our best wishes."

"I will," Michael said.

"Don't include me," Victor Schmidt said in a thick voice.

"I can have a DNA test analysed by a forensic laboratory in Berne," Michael said. "I understand from Elizabeth that Miss Simpson is willing to supply a sample of the child's DNA. Perhaps we should await the result of the DNA test before we get ahead of ourselves."

Monika Schmidt smiled warmly around the whole table.

"Listen to what Michael is saying, Victor, before you blow a gasket," she said. "That seems reasonable, doesn't it, Elizabeth? The whole thing might turn out to be a storm in a teacup."

"Good advice," she replied. "I suggest we send Michael to New York for an initial interview with Miss Simpson. He can form an opinion of her, see the child, and gain a sense of where we stand. And get a DNA sample."

Victor Schmidt stared at Michael with his working eye while the false one randomly looked at a plate of grapes. He ran both palms across his face.

"All right," he said. "Even though Flemming was cremated and I haven't got a clue how you intend to get his DNA."

"We'll find a way." Michael turned to the housekeeper: "What delicious grapes."

"Mrs. Nielsen always prepares enough to feed a whole army," Henrik Schmidt said. "If it was up to her, we would be waddling rather than walking."

Michael forced a smile, eased his chair over a groove in the floor and got up. "Where's the lavatory, please?"

Henrik Schmidt rose as well. "Upstairs, third door on the left. Do you want me to show you?"

"Thank you, I'll manage," Michael said.

He walked quickly up the stairs and opened the door to the corridor on the left. It was like walking through a luxury hotel. There were tall, white-painted panels, green silk wallpaper and matching doors to either side. Michael opened the first door and found a guest bedroom with an untouched but made-up bed. The next door revealed an enormous bathroom with a sunken tub with steps, golden taps, and murals. Roman scenes of bathing women in flimsy, damp clothes, and naked young men holding out amphorae suggestively spurting water. Colourful birds courted each other in the mosaic border. Michael opened every cupboard, but found only a pile of exclusive, fragrant towels, dressing gowns, various oils, lotions, and soaps.

He closed the door to the bathroom and tried the other doors down the corridor without finding anything other than linen cupboards, a sewing room, and several identical guest bedrooms.

The last door to the left was the only one that was locked. On the doorframe someone had put up an enamelled Royal Life Guards crest with the motto *Dominus Providebit*.

The others were drinking coffee by the time he returned. Michael smiled at the women and sat down.

"Coffee?" Mrs. Nielsen asked.

"Yes, please."

"Coffee for the detective," Victor Schmidt intoned, but apparently without resentment. He winked humorously to Michael.

Maybe someone had defended him in his absence. Even Jakob Schmidt received him with a small, if still skeptical smile. It was almost like an ordinary dinner in an ordinary house with an ordinary family.

CHAPTER 24

There was a light tap on his bedroom door. Michael looked at his watch and frowned. It was two fifteen in the morning and the house was as quiet as a mausoleum. Jakob Schmidt had left Pederslund at eight thirty with his brother.

They had discussed the legal implications of Flemming Caspersen's fruitful, albeit imaginary infidelity until Victor Schmidt became too drunk and incoherent and his wife had helped him upstairs to bed. Michael had said good night to Elizabeth Caspersen outside her bedroom, which was opposite to his. Even she was slightly tipsy and, frankly, he couldn't blame her.

Michael had drunk nothing. He was very proud of himself.

He flicked that evening's first cigarette out of the open window. The glowing tip trailed an arc in the darkness over Jungshoved. Then he opened the door to Monika Schmidt, but blocked her path. She was now wearing some kind of negligee, one transparent layer upon another, which reached down to her bare feet. It was like butterfly wings. Michael could see the contours of her slim, petite body against the light from the lamps in the corridor.

She had changed her perfume to something lighter, more floral—and anaesthetizing. She looked gravely up at him, but he didn't remove his hand. A small, fearful smile played on her lips while the rest of her face was calm and expectant.

"Are you just going to leave me standing here?" she asked.

Michael scratched the back of his head. He had freed himself from the stiff new shirt, jacket, shoes and socks, and was standing in the cool evening air wearing only his trousers.

He tried to smile.

"Monika, listen . . . I think you are . . . you're a very beautiful . . . attractive . . . but . . ."

She performed an ironic curtsy, fluttered her long eyelashes at him, and held up a bottle of Talisker and two crystal tumblers. Her thin bracelets jingled.

"A whisky, Michael? *Snälla, snälla*, Michael. You can't send me away now. It just wouldn't do."

She ducked under his outstretched arm and continued into the darkness, where her contours dissolved. Michael popped his head out and glanced up and down the dim corridor. The gap under Elizabeth Caspersen's door was dark. There was no key in his door.

"Doesn't anybody ever lock their doors around here?" he grumbled.

"Jakob usually does," Monika Schmidt said behind him.

She turned on the bedside lamp, climbed up on his bed and stretched out her legs on the bedspread. She smiled and poured a whisky with a steady hand.

Michael closed the window and sat down in an armchair a safe distance from his hostess. Then he crossed his legs as if to signal that perhaps she ought to do the same. She didn't. Instead, Monika Schmidt watched him with a little smile. She held out a glass to him, and he got up and took it.

Then she leaned back against the headboard, sighed and pulled up one leg. Michael kept his eyes on his glass. He suspected that her studied movement had caused the negligee to slide up her thigh.

"Please don't get me wrong, Michael," she said.

"What on earth is there to get wrong, Monika?" he asked.

He sipped his whisky without looking up. He noticed that she had pulled down the negligee so it covered her crotch.

"Are you married?" she asked.

Michael muttered something affirmative.

"Happily?"

"I think so."

"So there's still such a thing as true love?"

"I hope so."

"Like in the fairy tales. Children?"

Michael held up two fingers. "Two."

Monika Schmidt nodded and folded her arms across her breasts.

"Lucky woman, your wife," she said.

"I'm not so sure. I know I'm the lucky one, but I don't suppose that she is."

She smiled, but said nothing.

"Cheers," he said.

She raised her glass and took a sip. This was a different version of Monika Schmidt, he thought. Serious, balanced. Her hectic quality had gone.

"The whole thing is insane, isn't it, Michael?" she said, and let her gaze glide across his naked torso with an expression of some alarm.

"The baby in New York?"

"Yes. Do you believe it?" she asked.

"I think I do. It wouldn't be the first time a married man fathered a love child."

"Not Flemming."

"I guess he had balls and urges just like everybody else," Michael mumbled. "What more does it take?"

She looked at him gravely. "He wasn't like that. He really wasn't."

"If you say so."

She nodded, emptied her glass, and refilled it immediately.

"Michael, please don't think ill of us."

"Of course not, Monika. Why would I?"

"*Asch!* Because . . . we always clash. Victor . . . me . . . Victor and me, Victor and Elizabeth, Victor and Jakob. It's not as bad as it looks. Victor is a good man, really. He's a product of his upbringing, we all are. His father beat him and his mother didn't care. Do you know how he lost his eye?"

"No."

"One day his father picked him up, put him on the kitchen table, told him to jump and promised to catch him. He was five years old. Victor jumped, but his father didn't catch him and he lost his eye. His father said that would teach him never to trust anyone. And he learned that lesson all right. They were very poor. No matter how rich, powerful, and comfortable Victor is now, in his head he'll only ever be one tiny step from the abyss. He really believes that. He despises impotence, dependency, and weakness because he has always had to be so strong himself. I guess that's typical for . . . what's the word? Mould breakers. Flemming was both father and brother

169

to him, and without Flemming, he's vulnerable and exposed. He'll do anything to safeguard himself and Sonartek."

"Anything?"

She looked at him. Apparently unaware, she pulled up her leg again and Michael could see her beautiful, well-trimmed sex. He averted his eyes. Monika Schmidt frowned at him, then the penny dropped and she wrapped the bedspread around her legs.

"Right! Now we can talk without you getting distracted. And without me getting distracted. My apologies, Michael."

"You said that Victor would do anything?" he prompted her.

"He really would."

"If Victor's a mould breaker, surely he can identify with Jakob?"

She pulled a face.

"Victor doesn't get why Jakob won't come and work for Sonartek. He feels that Jakob has rejected him as a father and mentor, and he doesn't understand why his son won't do his duty, seeing that he has given him everything. That is to say, everything *he* didn't have. Material things, ultimately unimportant things, but like I said, he doesn't get it."

"And he's jealous of Jakob?"

"I think so. He envies Jakob his freedom, but doesn't realize that he can never know what that feels like because he doesn't feel secure within himself. Jakob feels secure. Victor has to learn to see himself in both his sons rather than regard them as strangers. Do you like my boys?"

"Yes. Very different and very alike, I think. But is that all there is to it?"

"All what?"

"The tension between Victor and Jakob. They don't resemble each other physically. I would have thought it went deeper. That it's about more than just the choice between a comfortable life and one that isn't. Or doing your duty."

The bedside lamp drew golden squares on her brown irises.

"Oh, Michael . . ."

"What?"

She poured more whisky into her glass and ran a weary hand across her face.

"Michael, I think you're a dangerous man."

She spoke his name in Swedish where the *ch* became a short *k*, and she stressed the second syllable. It sounded really rather charming.

She yawned and stretched out. Her negligee gaped, and a hard, dark brown nipple peeped out. No matter which direction Michael looked, his gaze still landed on something. It was very distracting.

"I don't think so," he mumbled.

"But you *are*. You *see* things. I understand why Elizabeth hired you."

She looked into space.

"Something is wrong, Michael. Something terrible is about to happen. I know it."

Slowly, she wiped away the tears from her cheek with the back of her hand and looked at her moist hand in wonder.

"Tell me what you think is wrong," he said softly.

"I don't know. Everything. The hunters at Pederslund."

"The hunters?"

"There used to be so many. Now they hardly ever come. They were soldiers—Jakob's and Henrik's friends. Later, it was mostly Henrik's, even though he was never in the army. The boys loved hunting. They started some kind of boys-only club. Women were banned from their lunches and parties. Only high-class hookers and strippers were allowed. Men need space. A woman needs to respect that, or a man feels suffocated and trapped. Most young women today don't understand. They castrate their men by making them feel guilty. Don't you agree, Michael?"

"Absolutely," he nodded. "But Jakob, where does he go when he can't find a disaster zone to work in?"

She sighed.

"Jakob is Jakob. I don't think he has ever needed anyone. He never cried when he was little. He preferred to play alone, and yet he was the most popular boy at school because he never made any effort. Is there anything more attractive to the rest of us than someone who is self-sufficient and is at peace with themselves? We think they have a secret that they could share with us. We're attracted to them because we hope some of it will rub off. He reminds me of Flemming. And of you."

"How do you mean?"

She didn't reply.

He repeated the question and was rewarded with a low snore. Monika Schmidt was asleep.

Fuck . . .

Fuck, fuck, fuck!

He got up and bent over her. Watched her peaceful, quiet face. The years faded away: Monika Schmidt looked like a sleeping child. The irises twitched under the thin eyelids, the mouth was relaxed and the lips blood red. She smelled of woman and expensive perfume.

Shit!

Was he supposed to carry her back to the marital bed to her drunken, unconscious husband? Wherever he was. Or prop her up against the door, knock on it, and then do a runner? Or should he just put her on the sofa in the drawing room downstairs?

He left her where she was.

Michael took a small digital camera, a leather case, and a thin Maglite flashlight from the inside pocket of his jacket, opened the door, and glanced at Monika Schmidt once more. He decided that she was fast asleep. He tiptoed down the corridor, opened the door to the main staircase and continued across the landing to the opposite corridor. The house was completely silent.

Outside Jakob Schmidt's room he stopped and examined the door frame for hairs or folded pieces of paper that would fall to the floor when the door was opened. He couldn't see any tell-tales so he pressed down the handle. The door was locked; Michael squatted down on his haunches, put the leather case on the carpet, and opened it to reveal the slim, steel instruments it contained. It was an old lock and it took him less than a minute to pick it.

Though he was sure that Jakob had left Pederslund, he held his breath when he opened the door and slipped into the quiet room. He leaned against the door and got his bearings in the almost total darkness. Then he switched on his flashlight and looked around a young man's room where time had stood still for many years. There was a narrow, old-fashioned iron bedstead covered with a patchwork quilt, a bookcase with such classics as *Moby Dick*, *Kim*, *Treasure Island* and *Lord Jim*, and various military educational books that he recognized from his own bookcase. A bamboo fishing rod was mounted on the wall above the headboard and below the rod, he saw the photo of the

Swedish summer afternoon with Henrik and Jakob Schmidt that Flemming Caspersen had had hanging in his library. Even the frame was the same.

There was a desk marked with years of knife carvings, burns from forbidden cigarettes, and rings from forbidden beer bottles. A laptop sat on the desk. Michael opened the lid and was asked to type in a password. He closed the lid again, and instead, opened a wardrobe filled with outdoor equipment: climbing ropes, a harness, karabiners and hiking boots, waders, sailing jackets and old uniform items, camouflage jackets and camouflage trousers, but not the military kind. There wasn't, for instance, anything he recognized from Elizabeth Caspersen's DVD. A sabre and a modern bayonet in its sheath hung on the inside of the wardrobe door. He found the Royal Life Guards' full dress uniform in a plastic bag, and on top of the wardrobe a tall, fabric-covered box, which probably contained Jakob Schmidt's bearskin headgear.

If the man with the dark, animal eyes were to find him in here now, he would be lucky to get away with a visit to Casualty, he thought. He was more likely to end up in intensive care with feeding instructions on a Post-it note slapped on his forehead.

Gripping the flashlight between his teeth, he lit up the photographs on the wall and took out his camera. The curtains were closed, but even so the camera flashlight would be visible from the outside. Never mind, it couldn't be helped. He photographed each picture several times and checked the resolution on the camera's LED screen before he moved on.

Officer School, Class of 2001: Jakob Schmidt stood in the middle of the back row, wearing the uniform of a first lieutenant. His expression was neutral. Michael took a small step to the side and looked at a photograph of five half-naked warriors with long hair and beards standing in the desert. Their faces were partly shaded under their hats and the men's eyes were hidden behind sunglasses. He concentrated on the man standing by himself on the far left. Tattooed, a lazy half-smile, muscular, broad shoulders, and long legs. He was almost certain that it was Jakob Schmidt. Michael recognized the type: not a team player, but a useful loner. The scorpion raised its sting along the man's neck.

Then he studied various hunting pictures from the estate. To his surprise, he recognized Henrik in several of them. Sonartek's sales director hadn't struck him as the outdoor type, but he seemed perfectly at home among the others at the display of the day's bag. One of the boys. Jakob didn't feature, and Michael wondered whether he had taken most of the pictures.

Michael frowned and went back to the picture from the unnamed desert. He compared it to one of the hunting pictures taken in front of Pederslund. There was something ceremonious about it. The gun dogs were lined up at the foot of the steps, and Mrs. Nielsen was holding a silver tray with shot glasses with morning bitters before the hunt. Victor and Henrik Schmidt were standing at the top of the steps and eight younger men were posed in two rows; one standing, the other kneeling.

Kim Andersen. The dead Royal Life Guard who committed suicide. He appeared in both the hunting and the desert photograph. There was no doubt. He was dressed for hunting—oilskin jacket, hunting trousers, and boots; he had a rifle over his shoulder and was smiling at the photographer without a care in the world, exactly like the other men on the steps of Pederslund—and he was standing in the middle of the row of sunburned combat soldiers in the desert; probably somewhere in Afghanistan or Iraq. Michael recognized the tattoos from the newspapers; especially from today's photograph of him on the bonnet of an armoured personnel carrier outside Baghdad, with a small Danish flag fluttering from the aerial.

He straightened up. He tried to remember the newspapers' verdict. Suicide or crime victim? The Rigspolitiet's Homicide Division was involved.

Michael listened to the sleeping house and opened the door to Jakob's bathroom, which was basic compared to the luxurious bathroom further down the corridor. A white medicine cupboard over the sink contained some paracetamol, a deodorant, and an unopened tube of toothpaste. Michael ran a finger across the toothbrush. It was dry as a bone and there was a thin layer of dust at the bottom of the bathtub, so it probably hadn't been used for months.

He took one last look at the photographs in the light beam. A boys-only club, Monika Schmidt had called it. But that wasn't what Michael saw in the photographs; he saw a ruthless longing for Arcadia with its own laws, a golden age that had never been. Dreamers, warriors, and killers.

CHAPTER 25

Monika Schmidt had turned onto her side, but she was still asleep. Michael tiptoed inside, returned the camera, flashlight, and pick-locks to his jacket pockets and covered her with the bedspread. He smoked a cigarette by the window, had a mouthful of Talisker and wondered who had sent her.

Somebody, someone not very far away, might have worked out that Michael wasn't there to assist in a paternity case. It was certainly one possible explanation.

He felt someone was looking at him and turned around. Monika Schmidt was lying with her hands folded under her cheek, watching him. She didn't move a muscle.

"It's all right, go back to sleep," he said.

Her gaze swept across his naked torso.

"You look like someone who has been through the wringer, Michael. Where did all those scars and that Homer Simpson tattoo come from?"

"I'm clumsy. And I got drunk."

She smiled. "Why did you move to England?"

"A girl."

"Why did you come back to Denmark?"

"Another girl."

She closed her eyes, rolled onto her back, yawned, and stretched out.

"I probably shouldn't stay here, Michael, even though it's a lovely, lovely bed."

"I guess not," he said.

She moved her arms up and down like a child making snow angels and stared up at the ceiling.

"Monika?"

"Yes?"

"Who is Jakob's father?"

Her arms were still bent at the elbow and her small hands lay near her dark, smooth hair. Her eyes kept watching the ceiling while her pupils expanded until the black had almost banished the brown. She rose onto her elbows, got down from the bed and gathered the negligee around her, all in one smooth movement. She didn't look at him.

"A man, Michael. A real man. Not a two-faced snooper like you."

Monika Schmidt crossed the floor, steady like a sleepwalker, and left.

Michael looked at the closed door. He sighed, hauled one of the chairs in front of it, and wedged its back under the handle. If anyone, anyone at all, tried to enter his room tonight, he would wring their necks.

He lay down on top of the bedspread with his hands folded behind his neck. Then he reached over and switched off the bedside lamp. He could feel the heat from her body and he could smell her. He thought about the redheaded superintendent who was investigating Kim Andersen's suicide ... Lene ... what? Jensen. He wondered if he should contact her. And say what? That the ex-Royal Life Guard hadn't hurt his leg during an innocent hunting trip to Sweden in the spring of 2011, but was injured when he took part in a depraved manhunt in the north of Norway? Did he have any evidence? Not really. It was more of a hunch.

Would she understand? Michael visualized the superintendent's hard green eyes. Imagined her lips forming the words: "Piss off ... Next!"

Then he thought about Jakob Schmidt. The imperturbable brown eyes. The intelligence.

And finally, he thought of Sara and their children, smiled in the darkness, and fell asleep.

CHAPTER 26

He watched her go through the border between light and shade and stop on the pavement. She glanced around and he let her wait. Her hand tucked some stray hairs behind one ear. She looked up and down Allégade, and directly at him on the other side of the street, but failed to spot him in the shadows. He whistled and she looked up. He waved her over and she ran across the road. Confidently.

Close up, her scent was cool and fresh, and he saw that nothing in her make-up or outfit had been left to chance. The same went for his own appearance, and he was aware he was making quite an impression: the rough motorbiking nomad had been replaced with a smooth stockbroker: silk tie in a tight Windsor knot, single-breasted dark suit, shiny black shoes, a crisp white shirt, and a dark blue cashmere coat. He was freshly shaven, his hair cut was smart, and he smelt discreetly of L'Homme.

"What happened to the biker boy?" she asked.

"It's his night off."

She frowned. "What a pity. I rather liked him."

"Did you?"

"Yes."

"He can come back, if you like," he said.

She just folded her arms and nodded.

"Are you cold?" he asked.

"A little."

He pointed to the long, dark BMW parked a few metres away.

"It has heated seats," he said.

She looked at the car, but didn't stir.

"Nice," she said.

He smiled. "I'm glad you came. My name is Adam."

"Josefine."

He fished out a packet of cigarettes from his coat pocket and offered it to her. She took one and he lit both their cigarettes. He coughed and blinked tears away from his eyes.

"I'm new to this," he said.

"I don't believe that."

She looked away and chewed a nail.

"It's true. I've been travelling for so long that I've forgotten what you're meant to do."

He flashed her a disarming smile.

"Where have you been?" she asked.

"Everywhere. Nepal, New Zealand, North Africa . . . South America . . ."

Josefine's face lit up.

"You've been to South America?"

He grinned and launched into rapid Spanish.

"What?" She narrowed her eyes. "What did you say? What?!"

"That I'm freezing my balls off out here and just what do I have to do to make the beautiful lady get into my car so we can drive somewhere nice and warm and have a drink?"

"Tell me something about South America and you're on. I'm going there in a few months."

"Of course. Whatever you want to know."

He opened the door to her, she got in, leaned back in the passenger seat, and ran her fingertips across the leather while he stayed outside and took a look around. There was no one nearby. He had stolen a set of number plates in a multi-story parking lot at the airport, taking care to stay in the CCTV blind spots. He squashed the cigarette under his shoe, got in, smiled at her, and left his door ajar so that he could see her in the light inside the car. One hand rested casually in her lap, while the other tucked the rebellious lock of hair back behind her ear again. Her nose was straight, her profile young and clean, her upper lip slightly fuller than her lower lip, and her mouth looked permanently on the verge of a smile. Her skin was perfect, practically without pores, and her forehead high and well-shaped. She smelled of girl, perfume, and suede jacket.

"Where did you go?" she asked.

"Costa Rica, Honduras, San Salvador, Argentina," he muttered, and clenched his right hand inside the leather glove.

"Did you dance the tango in Buenos Aires?" she asked.

"I don't dance."

"An old Chilean man who lives here in Frederiksberg is teaching me Spanish," she said. "He's a poet and at least 120 years old. He knew Pablo Neruda."

"Impressive," he said.

He closed the door and looked past her out of the side window. There was no one in the parking lot. Then he punched her as hard as he could, close to her left ear. Her lower jaw snapped under his knuckles, her head collided with the side window and her eyes widened before they clouded over and closed. Her mouth was half open. Then she opened her eyes again and looked straight ahead.

"But . . ." she said, and he hit her again.

She grew limp, slid down the seat, and her face lolled towards him. He pulled her upright and reclined the seat so that she was half sitting, half lying down.

He removed her scarf and jacket. She was smaller than he had expected, and she struggled to breathe through her broken jaw. He put her jacket on the back seat, rolled up her nearest shirtsleeve above the elbow, and opened the glove compartment. The rubber tube was ready and waiting, and he tied it around her upper arm. Then he took a syringe from his inside pocket, removed the plastic cap with his teeth and injected five millilitres of Ketalar into her bloodstream.

The girl would be unconscious for at least half an hour, and should it become necessary, he could top up the injection.

He signalled, left the parking lot, and drove east down Allégade. To the casual observer, he would simply be a well-dressed, young man in an expensive car with a sleeping girl in the seat next to him.

His mobile rang and he glanced at the display with dismay. Allan Lundkvist.

The beekeeper was hysterical. "What are you going to do about it?" he demanded to know. "Just what the hell are you going to do? That superintendent has just rung me again. She has called me ten times today, at least. And yesterday. She's not going to go away and she's never off duty. What the fuck do I tell her? And what are you doing about it?"

"Have you talked to her?" he asked.

"Of course I haven't! We agreed that I wouldn't. But if I don't call her back soon, she's bound to turn up."

He looked down the girl's long thighs in the tight jeans and at the point where they met. He started humming a tune. A song by Bruce. The Boss himself. "Call her and say that you'll meet her tomorrow morning, nine o'clock, okay?" he said.

"Nine o'clock! Tell me, do you have a paper round?"

"No. Or nine thirty. What time do you get up?"

"Seven o'clock."

"Are you alone?" he asked.

"Yes! What do I tell her? What does she want?"

He beat out the rhythm on the steering wheel and tried to remember the lyrics. He wished the other man would shut up for a moment.

"She wants to talk to you about Kim, obviously," he said. "She wants to find out how well you knew him and learn something about the rest of us."

"Then that's what I'm going to tell her. Thanks a lot. We're gonna have a great time."

"It's no harder than some of the other stuff we've done, Allan. It's nothing. This is the Kim you knew: he helped you with odd jobs on the farm and you gave him some honey from your busy little bees. You served together at Camp Viking, but not in the same unit. And he didn't invite you to his wedding."

"But I'm in the pictures. In the videos. From Qala. We all are."

"That could be anyone. We all looked the same back then."

"And everyone is dead."

He laughed to calm him down. "You're not dead, Allan, and neither am I. Nor is the photographer."

"So what really happened?" the beekeeper asked.

"When?"

"To Kim, damn you."

"He hanged himself."

"And what am I supposed to do? Stick my head in a gas oven?"

"Of course not. Why would you want to do that, Allan? And do you even have a gas oven?"

180

The other voice sounded more distant—reassured, but still distant, as if he were walking away from the telephone and had no intention of coming back.

"Nine o'clock, did you say?"

"For example," he said.

"And where will you be?"

"Nearby, I expect."

"You're not thinking of . . . of taking her, hurting her while she's at my place, are you? You're not going to do that, eh? You don't work for those crazy companies any more, remember that."

He took another look at the unconscious girl. "Of course I won't. We're in Denmark now."

"Just remember that. Sometimes I have my doubts."

The other man grunted. He sounded far from convinced.

"I know where I am, Allan," he said, and tightened his grip on the steering wheel.

"I bloody well hope so. Are you going to talk to her yourself?"

"I was planning to. At some point."

"So, nine or nine thirty tomorrow morning." Allan Lundkvist sounded more remote than ever.

"Call her now and set up a meeting," he said, and hung up.

He pulled the glove off his right hand with his teeth and let the back of his fingers glide across her face. The flesh had started to swell around her jaw and her left eye. In a few minutes her eye would close up. The skin above the eye and the fractured lower jaw was warm, but cooler where her face was still intact. His fingertips brushed her breast. Young. Fine. Such a shame.

He lifted his hand, drummed his fingers on the steering wheel, smiled to himself in the rear-view mirror, and suddenly remembered the song as if it had never left his mind. He sang Bruce Springsteen's "I'm on Fire" at the top of his voice and beat his palms steadily against the steering wheel. He reached out and turned her head forwards, so her eyes were no longer staring at him. Her head rolled back. He tried a second time with the same result. It was as if there were no bones in her neck.

"Bitch," he muttered, and gave up.

Great song. Boring girl.

181

CHAPTER 27

He parked in front of a low, grey concrete building in Sydhavnen, not far from the sea and the mighty, humming H.C. Ørstedsværk power station. Black bin liners had been nailed across the windows of the warehouse so it was completely blacked out. He crossed the forecourt, locked the barred gates with a chain and padlock, stood for a moment between the overflowing rubbish containers and stacks of damaged Euro-pallets, and looked about him.

The nearest residential properties were a long way away and the only people who ever came here were graffiti artists and vagrants. He opened the car door and pulled out the girl, threw her over his shoulder in a fireman's lift, kicked the car door shut, and carried her up the loading ramp. He knocked three times on a metal door while he glanced around once more.

The door was rolled up. The man inside looked at the girl over his shoulder and smiled. Then he gestured him inside the harshly lit hall behind him.

"Problems?"

"No."

"Ski masks," his boss said.

"She's unconscious."

"Don't care."

He put the girl down on a battered sofa they had found behind a container. Josefine Jensen's head lolled to one side and her hand hit the floor. His boss had rigged up photographic lamps around the sofa and under one of the loading beams. An old, but still working winch, with a chain that reached the floor, was hanging from the beam.

"How much did you give her?"

"Five millilitres. She'll wake up soon."

He turned his coat inside out, folded it and placed it on the floor. His boss handed him a ski mask and he adjusted the holes over his eyes and mouth.

The man looked at him.

"And Allan?"

"I've spoken to him. He'll call the superintendent and arrange a meeting tomorrow morning."

"Good. We don't need any more people developing a guilty conscience or getting depressed, starting to spend money or making phone calls. Like Kim."

They helped each other undress the girl. Her slim limbs were floppy. They looked at her naked body on the sofa, but said nothing. His boss grabbed her under her arms and pulled her further up on the sofa. The uninjured eyelid twitched and she started muttering incoherently. Her lower jaw was askew and her left eye black and closed.

The man straightened up.

"She's waking up," he said, and crossed the floor to adjust the floodlights. "Good-looking girl."

"Yes."

"I mean, she's *too* good-looking. Hit her."

He didn't move and the other man watched him. His eyes were clear and blue.

"You want to make an impression, don't you? Isn't that why we're here?"

"Yes."

"Then hit her."

He went over to the sofa, put the leather glove on his right hand again and punched the girl in the middle of her face. Her nose broke to the right and blood poured from her nostrils.

He rubbed his knuckles. It was no longer so easy.

"Again," the other said.

"That's enough."

"Then I'll do it."

His boss found a short iron bar on the floor and bent over the girl.

He turned away, but heard the blow land with a moist smack, and something give.

The man pointed to the chain hanging from the loading beam and passed him the handcuffs.

"Hoist her up so she doesn't choke."

The girl's slender chest pumped oxygen to her lungs and her body glistened with sweat. The blood from her nose and mouth flowed between her breasts and gathered in her belly-button, along with her broken teeth. He slipped the handcuffs around her wrists, attached the hook at the end of the chain between them and raised her up slightly. Her arms grew unnaturally long, before her long, slim body started rising from the sofa. Her head slumped forwards between her shoulders and down on her heaving chest, her ponytail loosened and her hair swung forwards and covered her face. He tied the chain around a concrete pillar to secure it.

His boss lifted up a heavy, professional video camera on a tripod, slotted it in place, looked in the viewfinder and nodded. Then he kneeled down in front of a laptop on the floor and clicked until the picture from the camera appeared on the screen.

"I have an idea for the soundtrack," he said, and told his boss about the song.

The other nodded happily. "We'll take it from YouTube. It'll be brilliant. Irresistible, I think we could say."

He found the girl's mobile in her jacket, opened the *sent* box and read the last dozen messages to get an idea of her texting style. He smiled when he read the message that described him—favourably and with a hint of irony—to someone called Laura. Then he sent a text to her mother, dropped the mobile on the concrete floor, and crushed it under his heel.

"There's coffee in the pot," he said, pointing to a makeshift office behind a partition wall.

He looked at the girl who was half lying, half hanging, over the filthy, green sofa.

"She's shivering," he said.

"I have some blankets somewhere."

They wrapped her in grey, stiff blankets.

He inserted a cannula into the girl's wrist, rigged up a saline drip, and pushed a small dose of diazepam through the tube. The liquid turned milky and then clear and the girl's whimpering stopped.

His boss held up his hand.

"Easy now. We want her to feel something, don't we?"

"Of course."

Lene tried concentrating on her book, but discovered she had read the same page at least three times without the words making it past her eyes.

The telephone rang.

"Lene."

"Allan Lundkvist. You've called. And called."

The man's voice sounded faint and distant, as if he were on another continent.

"Allan? Thank you. Sorry . . . are you here? In Denmark, I mean?"

She put her book aside and sat up in bed. Her ankle was itchy so she stuck her leg out from under the duvet and scratched it.

Nervously.

"Is it too late? Did I wake you? I've just come back from Jylland," he said. "I thought I had better ring straight away."

"It's not too late. I'm glad you called. Very much so. I'm sorry if I've been a pest."

He didn't say anything.

"It's about Kim Andersen," she said.

"Kim Andersen?"

"Private. The Royal Life Guards. Holbæk. Camp Viking. Helmand."

"Kim, yes, I just needed . . . Yeah, sure . . . What about him?"

"He hanged himself the day after his wedding."

"Hanged himself?" A long, airy pause followed. "Louise. He married Louise, didn't he?"

"That's correct. It sounds as if you didn't go to the wedding?"

"No, Jesus Christ . . . The day after, you say? That makes no sense."

"No."

Allan Lundkvist sounded genuinely shocked, baffled, and a little tired. He searched for the words in just the right fumbling manner.

"Why the hell would he do that?" he then said. "He was crazy about her. And the kids. He was always talking about those kids."

"I don't know. But I'm in possession of a photograph from Afghanistan,

185

Allan. There are five men in the picture. Robert Olsen is dead, Kenneth Enderlein is dead, Kim Andersen also, as I've just explained, and then there's you and a fifth man, whose name is . . . what, exactly? It would seem to be very bad for your health to belong to that group, Allan."

His breathing sounded steady, but shallow. She was scared that he might hang up.

"Musa Qala," he then said. "The picture is taken outside Musa Qala."

"Which is?"

"A kind of town. More dead inhabitants than live ones. The only reason anyone still lives there is because the Taliban have moved back in. We've taken it from them five times, but every time they come back. They killed Amir, the district governor, and Abdul Quddus, the district chief, in March 2006. Then the Brits moved in and threw out the Taliban, then the guys from Bornholm—we call them the Boy Scouts—arrived to bail out the Brits and so it went on. The Americans droned Mullah Gafoor just outside the town recently. It just drags on."

"Is that right?"

"It's been like that since Alexander the Great. Afghanistan isn't a country; it's a piece of fossilized, medieval shit."

"So why go there?"

"Because it's fun!" He laughed. "I'm going back again for six months come January, and I can't wait."

"Who is the fifth man, Allan, the one with the scorpion on his neck?"

"Oh, I don't know. Loads of people came and went. I guess he was just someone who was there that day. I can't remember. Can we meet tomorrow? I'm knackered."

Lene looked out of her dark living-room window and thought about Josefine.

"Yes, of course, but all five of you have long hair and beards. It looks as if you've been in the same place for a while with no access to a razor."

"Yeah . . . I guess you're right. Sure. We probably visited bazaars or attended tribal meetings. And they told us a lot of crap. They don't have clocks out there, Lene. They rely on their memory. And they've got a bloody long memory, let me tell you. They talk about things that happened two thousand years ago as if it was yesterday. They have all the time in the world. They still talk about Sikander and Macedonia and Alexander's horse, Bucephalus, as if Alexander himself might come riding over the mountains with his elephants any minute now."

"The picture was taken in the summer of 2006," she interjected quickly, before the private lost himself in his musing about the passing of the centuries and the futility of it all.

Lene heard a faint rasping of a hand across stubble and the clattering sound of a bottle, hitting a rubbish bin. Or missing it.

And surely it was Hannibal who used elephants to cross the Alps, she thought. Small, hairy ones. Her mother would have known.

"Right . . . yeah," Allan Lundkvist mumbled. "We were probably gone for a few months. I don't remember. Why don't you come over tomorrow, Lene? I'll check my diary. I try to write something every day, even when I'm out in some crappy desert."

"Okay," she sighed. "When?"

"Nine or nine thirty," he said. "I need to be somewhere by half-eleven."

He gave her his address.

"How is the honey business?" she asked.

"The honey business is great, Lene, just great. So I'll see you tomorrow, okay?"

She looked at her watch.

It was midnight. Josefine had left work two hours ago and Lene had heard nothing from her.

"Good night," she said.

"Pleasant dreams," he said.

"Allan . . . ?"

"What?"

"Who took the picture?"

"No one. Self-timer."

Lene leaned back against the headboard and switched off the lamp on her bedside table. She was busy staring up at the ceiling when her mobile buzzed with a text message.

Hey, Mutti. Got lucky!
Staying over. Having a lovely, lovely time.

Sleep tight and don't let the bed bugs bite.
Jose

It was followed by the usual two smileys.

Lene put down the mobile and drank a mouthful of water from the glass on her bedside table. She fluffed up her pillows, lay down, and pulled her duvet up to her chin.

"Got lucky?!"

Would she sleep tight? She highly doubted it. In her mind, she went over the conversation with Allan Lundkvist. He had sounded tired but otherwise normal, so why was every alarm bell going off at the back of her head? She should have insisted on the name of the fifth man, but she had been scared of alienating him.

She tried finding some nice, peaceful places for her thoughts to go to, but the usual safe havens fled in every direction whenever she came near them. For the umpteenth time she thought about Kim Andersen's little cottage in the forest and suddenly she knew what was wrong. At last she had nailed the discrepancy she had been struggling with in the last few days.

The chimney. The log pile. The neat and tidy log pile under the lean-to. But no fireplace.

She smiled into the darkness.

She still had it.

CHAPTER 28

The farm looked like thousands of other traditional Danish farms, with four wings round a yard. It had a sagging thatched roof and crumbling white walls in between the black-painted timbers. Lene had passed a smart new sign advertising organic honey when she turned off the main road.

She wondered how bees could tell the difference between flowers that had been sprayed with pesticides and those that hadn't. And could they be trained to only gather nectar from "clean" flowers?

The lane leading to the farm hadn't been tarmacked. It was little more than a cart track between the fields, and the grass brushed the underside of the car. She slowed down when she spotted a white figure walking between dozens of small, white beehives on a meadow behind the farmhouse. The figure was wearing a loose-fitting canvas suit and wore a broad-brimmed hat with a protective veil on his head. She sounded the horn and he looked up, waved, and disappeared behind the house. Allan Lundkvist was taller than he had appeared on the desert photograph.

Lene parked outside the arched gateway in one of the wings, got out, and took in her surroundings. One man's hopeless fight against decay, she concluded. No wonder he had sounded resigned and beaten. There were half-finished repairs to the brickwork and the wooden fence, small heaps of building materials everywhere, covered by tarpaulin, battered by the winter storms, and an old blue tractor with no wheels, still attached to a rusting harrow. The sky was clear and blue, and swallows swooped out of the air and sliced sharply over the roofs and trees. The only evidence of strict order and regular maintenance was the ruler-straight rows of beehives.

She walked through the gateway and into the cobbled farmyard. She had expected the beekeeper to meet her, but there was no sign of anyone in the uneven farmyard or in the shadowy rooms behind the barn doors. She crossed the farmyard and tried the front door to the main building. It didn't budge.

Lene wondered if she should ring Allan Lundkvist—but for crying out loud, she had only seen him a moment ago. She stepped onto a raised manhole cover below a window, reached up on her toes, cupped her hands around her eyes, and tried to peer inside, but the casement windows were dark and strangely lacking in transparency, and she couldn't see anything. She walked along the house and continued through an opening between the main building and one of the barns. There should have been a door in the gap, but it was leaning up against a shed without its hinges. There were posts for a washing line, but no line, a lawn invaded by weeds, and some old, spreading fruit trees that should have been pruned long ago. She dragged a plastic garden chair up to the house, climbed it, and tried looking inside again.

Yellow curtains with brown edges covered the window. Lene frowned when she heard a dull, low-frequency hum behind the glass. Then the glass moved and she could suddenly make out individual insects in the living mass right in front of her face. She pulled back her head and nearly fell off the chair. Yellow and black, crawling and fighting individuals: tens of thousands of bees were teeming and scrambling all over each other's bodies in a thick carpet.

She hauled the chair to the next window and saw another quivering, undulating mass covering the glass. She tapped the pane gently, the bees retreated and she caught a glimpse of the white figure with the beekeeper hat, sitting on a chair in the middle of the room. She couldn't see the face behind the veil. The bees covered up the hole again so she knocked on the glass a second time. Harder. The swarm pulled away. The man didn't move.

Lene ran around the house, stopped outside the front door, took a deep breath, and kicked the wood below the lock as hard as she could. The wood splintered and the door opened until it was halted by a security chain. She kicked it again, and the chain was torn off the door frame along with its fittings.

"Allan? Allan?!"

The intense hum from thousands of buzzing insects filled her ears. The sound was like water being forced through a concrete pipe.

In the hall she saw a rug, and a row of pegs holding an oilskin jacket and empty dog collars. Lene took out her pistol, went through the loading procedure, released the safety catch, but kept her index finger away from the trigger and along the barrel, and raised the weapon in the prescribed two-hand hold with the muzzle pointing to the ceiling. The noise rose and fell. She decided to take a step back rather than run straight into . . . what?

"Allan, for God's sake! It's me, Lene!"

A staircase led to the first floor and there was an oppressive and muggy smell. There was a white door to the left. She pressed her ear to it and the infernal humming rose. She looked at the door handle, carefully put her hand on it, and hesitated again. Did bees attack? What an absurd idea. Surely only if provoked? Busy little workers, that they were. Slowly, she opened the door to the living room fully; all the insects froze for a moment and watched her as one.

Then the room became alive once more. The bees covered the window-panes and the curtains like a carpet, and formed thick, moving cakes in every corner. The angry buzzing was deafening and the brown-and-yellow swarm had swaddled the man's legs and lower body like cloth. The floor, however, was clear, and Lene approached the figure from behind in a large arc. She was terrified that the insects might view her as a threat, come at her and crawl into her ears, nose, and mouth. Smother her.

The man was sitting on an ordinary, high-backed dining chair, and Lene could now see the strips of silver gaffer tape keeping him tied to it. His head slumped down onto his chest, with a deep, dead sigh when she put a hand on his shoulder, his hat cocked over one ear. The hands on his lap were covered with bees and in between his hands she could make out the obscenely bloated, white, egg-laying rear bodies of the queens, surrounded by hordes of serving drones and workers.

This was why the bees had clustered together: to defend their queens, which someone had removed from the beehives and put in the man's lap.

She stopped on the bare wooden floor and looked at the man's profile behind the veil. The face was reflective and solemn. Dried blood had trickled from a small, ridiculously small, circular hole between his eyebrows. His eyes were half open and seemed to study his hands and the living, squirming queens they were cradling. The blood had stained the suit all the way to his lap.

Lene was about to touch the body again when the realization hit her: the man in the chair had been dead a long time. And she had seen a figure dressed in white walk up and down between the beehives only minutes ago.

She never heard a noise, and the moment between insight and darkness lasted only a fraction of a second.

CHAPTER 29

Opening her eyes intensified the pain at the back of her head to an unbearable level, but she had to keep them open. She would never do anything more important than this in her entire life. She owed it to herself, to everyone, to the whole world, to keep those eyes open. It felt as if someone had rammed an iron bar through her head and down her spine. She had bitten her tongue and the blood tasted warm and salty. It was completely dark outside her field of vision and nothing would have been easier, nothing would have made more sense, than to embrace the darkness and let it carry her away. Her stomach heaved and bitter gall trickled from the corners of her mouth and her nostrils. Lene spat it out and breathed in spasms.

She was sitting on a hard chair. She was completely naked and she saw in disbelief the strips of silver tape keeping her legs together and tied to the chair, exactly like the dead man in the living room. She couldn't move her head and, for a moment, she believed that she was permanently injured, that her neck was broken and that she would never walk again.

She closed her eyes and thought furiously. Reconstructed the events, forcing herself to feel everything. A hard edge chafed her chin and she realized that her unseen attacker had fitted her with the kind of neck collar paramedics used to stabilize the vertebrae of people injured in car crashes. She could move her feet, she could press her lower legs against the unforgiving tape and she could feel the rough floorboards under the soles of her feet. She wasn't paralysed. Her neck wasn't broken.

She sensed the stranger behind her, even though he had no sound or smell. A floorboard moved under the chair and she tried to turn her head until the sharp, white pain shot up her neck and out through the back of her head again. She groaned softly in time with her laboured breathing. She couldn't help it. The pain demanded an outlet.

"Can you see, Lene?"

She opened her eyes and spotted a computer on a chest of drawers right in front of her. Something white and red was moving across the screen, and a voice was coming from the laptop: metallic, flat and not of this world. She stared at the screen and identified a raw, concrete wall, with a high ceiling and deep shadows, which the floodlights carved out of the darkness.

The camera settled on a pair of suspended, bloody feet tied to a broom handle, which kept them apart. The feet were swaying lightly and there was the faint squeaking of a chain. The camera zoomed in on a slim, right foot. Neatly applied, coral nail polish. Nice, even toes.

Her tears blurred her view of the computer, and the lightly swaying feet on the screen, and she blinked hard.

The voice spoke. "Can you see?"

Lene blinked harder and stared.

The white toes were pulled into view. The nail polish. She refused to recognize the colour. She refused to recognize a foot that looked so much like her own.

"Can you?"

Her muscles tensed against the unforgiving tape, and the chair rocked. She tried to get away from the picture, though she knew that it was forbidden, and heard movement through the air right before her attacker's clenched fist hit her ear. The chair jerked sideways and she heard her own scream.

"Do you see, Lene?"

"YES! . . . yes . . ."

A warm trickle of blood ran from her ear and down her neck. A shrill howling came through the perforated eardrum and she could hear the vibration and friction of every air molecule.

Or so it felt.

"YES!!"

The camera zoomed out. The body appeared on the screen, one centimetre at a time, a hanging, bound, graceful, and slim body, white and brown where the blood had dried in a pattern that looked like the veins on a leaf. The camera lingered on a narrow strip of blonde hair over her groin. Her stomach raised and fell slightly with the body's shallow breathing. The legs were spread wide apart by the stick.

A black, gloved hand at the end of a dark sleeve appeared in the picture. The fingers spread across the girl's abdomen and pushed it. The body moved back, the hand disappeared from the picture and the body swung forwards.

Lene cried out again and heard movement behind her despite her screams. She expected another blow, but it didn't come.

They let her scream.

The body on the screen swung back and forth: a strange fruit hanging from a branch, drooping in the wind. The camera slowly moved upwards. Lene closed her eyes and the camera stopped.

"Lene," the voice said. "I can see you, you know. There's a camera in the laptop in front of you and I want you to open your fucking eyes right now."

She shook her head vehemently.

"No? Oh well, we'll do it as a radio play," the voice said. "You keep your eyes closed and I'll try and get you to open them. It's a good game. I know you can't see it, but I'm showing you a piece of freshly cut bamboo. It's old school, but still the best."

Lene heard the bamboo swish through the air.

The voice sounded flatter, more dispassionate.

"Let's try it out on her. See what she's made of, eh, Lene?"

Lene flung herself against the back of the chair when the cane struck the girl's flesh with a wet smack which went right into Lene's brain and soul. The deepest, the very deepest of places.

And she heard the raw cry from a young woman who was beyond all consciousness and whose body could react only to even stronger pain.

Lene opened her eyes. A fresh, red welt had been drawn across the body and groin of the suspended girl. The cane had cut through the thin skin and blood was pouring from the edges.

"Can you see it? Lene?"

"Yes . . . oh, YES!" she sobbed. "Stop!"

"Do you want to see the rest?"

"Yes. Oh, God . . . yes."

She heard a click from the loudspeakers. Music? Lene was convinced her mind must be playing tricks on her, that something inside her had broken, but the music continued and grew louder and louder. It bounced off the walls in the hall and gathered around the young, suspended body.

She had danced to this song with Niels. At one of the first parties where he had noticed her and she had noticed him. They had smiled to each other across a table covered with glasses and bottles—and he had nodded his head in the direction of the small dance area in the living room of a mutual friend, and she had got up. The camera zoomed in on the body, picking out and highlighting details: a pink nipple, a shaved armpit, an upper arm whose muscles twitched and pulsed under the skin. Long trails of blood down her arm, a wrist with a piece of surgical tape and a cannula, white hands, broken and blue below the shiny handcuffs, a rusty chain that continued upwards into the darkness. The camera rested on the hands and paused before finding blonde, bloody and matted hair and an earring with a pearl and a small dolphin.

The camera zoomed out; she couldn't see the face behind the hair. The chin had fallen down on the chest. The gloved hand gathered up a handful of blonde hair.

"Can you see it, Lene?"

"Yes."

"Those are your earrings, aren't they?"

She whispered something.

"I can't hear you. This is very, very important for you. And . . . for her."

"YES . . . They're my earrings."

The head was yanked up and the hair fell away from the girl's face. Lene moaned.

"Jose . . . oh, God, Jose . . ."

It was no longer a face; it was no longer her daughter's face, but a swollen, discoloured, grotesque, and disfigured lump. A broken mask. The intact eyelid twitched, the eye opened, and the green iris was aimed at the camera and at her. There were haemorrhages in the white membrane of the eye and it was stripped of expression. The crooked, swollen mouth opened to reveal a black hole where her teeth used to be.

The hands let go of the head and, without support, it flopped back onto the chest. The song continued, but the camera had shifted from the hanging figure to the floor where blood and urine had gathered in a puddle.

"Lene?"

She shook her head.

196

"You can stop this now," the voice said calmly.

"There will be others," she said.

"*You* can stop it now, Lene, close the case. I'm talking about *you*. No one else. If anyone takes over, we'll communicate with them. Do you understand? Do you want it to stop, Lene?"

The cane swooped through the air before making contact.

"YES!"

"Thank you. Thank you for that."

A man appeared on screen, but all Lene could see was a black boiler suit, black gloves, a shapeless outline, and a strange, tight-fitting black leather mask of the kind bondage aficionados and fetishists would wear, with a zip in front of the eyes and mouth. He lifted her daughter's head by her hair again, pressed a gag, in the form of an obscene, red rubber ball, into her bleeding, distorted mouth, and tightened it behind her neck with a leather cord.

"She's a lovely girl, Lene. Aren't you lovely, Josefine?"

"DON'T TOUCH HER!" Lene screamed, but the man ignored her. She saw his gloved hand glide up her daughter's thigh and two fingers being pressed hard up and inside.

A low, mournful sound erupted from her daughter.

The man walked up close to the camera. The leather mask filled the screen. She looked at his smiling, blue eyes behind the slits. He showed her a narrow, double-edged knife, went back, and placed the tip of the knife under Josefine's breastbone. The tip made a depression in the elastic skin.

"The strange thing, Lene, is that they always . . . always hope. They keep hoping that it isn't going to happen, even when it does and the knife goes in. They're so surprised, so incredibly confused and disappointed when their life ends, and it was all for nothing."

The screen went blank.

CHAPTER 30

The superintendent didn't notice him, even though he stood only one metre away from her. Her eyes were fixed at the black, shiny computer screen.

He saw only defeat and shock in her face, and he left the bedroom. He walked round to the back of the farmhouse and called his boss.

"It's done," he said.

"Sure?"

"Totally. She's finished."

"Right, then I'll get out of here," the other one said. "You should probably do the same."

"Do what?"

"Make yourself scarce. I'll contact you if I need you. I probably will."

"Are you sure?"

"Quite sure. Goodbye."

"What about the other one?" he asked.

"Michael Sander?"

"Yes."

"I'll deal with him. At least he's interesting. Safe trip."

"Thank you. But why does he show up now?"

"I've no idea. Really I don't. I found his homepage with a specialized search engine. He's a professional and we shouldn't underestimate him. But we could let him lead us to Kim's stuff."

"The movies?"

"Kim was the only one who knew where those sodding films and pictures are," the other one said.

"Let's hope so."

"Perhaps I should have a word with Kim's widow," his boss wondered out loud.

When he returned to the bedroom, he put a blackout fabric hood over the superintendent's unmoving head and tightened the cord a little. Then he packed his things into a suitcase, put the suitcase by the door and looked around. The angry bees were still buzzing around the living room.

He put a handwritten piece of cardboard on the floor next to her chair with the address of the abandoned warehouse in Sydhavnen, cut the cable-ties around her wrists and put the craft knife next to the chair. He turned her chair so that she would see the knife, and removed the hood from her head.

Then he picked up the suitcase and left the farmhouse.

CHAPTER 31

"Good sleep?"

"Not really," Michael replied.

He sat down opposite Elizabeth Caspersen at the kitchen table. The indefatigable Mrs. Nielsen was busy at the Aga, and there was a lovely smell of scrambled eggs in the kitchen.

Elizabeth Caspersen spread a thin layer of butter on a piece of toast very methodically and gestured towards a jar of marmalade near Michael's hand. He passed it to her as the housekeeper came over to the table.

"Scrambled eggs?" she asked him politely.

"I won't, thanks. Just some black coffee, please."

She poured him a cup and left the kitchen. They heard her clatter about in the utility room.

"Did anyone disturb you last night, Michael?"

Elizabeth Caspersen's suggestive eyebrow technique was unsurpassable.

He added milk and looked around.

"Where are they all?"

"Victor always leaves early to avoid the traffic, the boys didn't come back, and Monika . . . either she's still asleep or she's out with the horses. What did you think of the family?"

"If they were a place, they would be the Balkans," he mumbled, and sipped his hot coffee.

She laughed and said something, but he wasn't listening. He felt restless. Again, he thought about the redheaded superintendent, Lene Jensen. She was important.

"Pardon?" he said.

"I was just asking when you want to leave."

She took a bite of her toast and wiped a crumb off her upper lip with the napkin. She looked as unflappable, efficient, and impeccable as always. Perhaps because she was going straight to the office. Elizabeth Caspersen had applied elegant make-up; her lips were painted a shade of dark red that complemented her finely arched eyebrows and her grey eyes. She wore her pearls today, a grey silk blouse, and a jacket and skirt that fitted her long figure like a glove.

"As soon as possible," he said.

She nodded, emptied her coffee cup, and got up. They both knew that they couldn't discuss anything sensitive while they were still at the estate.

They walked out into the hall together, and Michael looked at the antlers on the wall.

"The gamekeeper, Thomas. Do you know him?" he asked.

She nodded. "I've seen him a couple of times. Big man. Handsome. Dark . . . He's moody and likes to keep to himself. Hard to get to know, I think. Something of a hermit."

"But a friend of Jakob's?"

"Yes, one of the blood brothers. They're a secret society."

"Forged by fire and blood?"

She looked at him.

"Yes, you could say that. Wasn't it like that for you?"

He smiled.

"I was more of a desk soldier, Elizabeth. I arrested drunken soldiers and banged them up. That kind of thing. It was peacetime back then, if I can put it like that. It's different for them—Jakob Schmidt and his friends. What about Peter, the temp?"

Elizabeth Caspersen bent down and picked up her overnight bag.

He noticed that today's nylon stockings had a fine, black seam at the back. He opened the door to her.

"More forthcoming," she said. "Light-hearted and quite cheerful, as far as I remember. I don't hunt, Michael."

"But your father must have known them quite well," he insisted. "He spent a lot of time here, didn't he?"

"Indeed he did. But I very rarely spoke to him. Like I said."

She pointed. "There's Monika."

Michael paused on the steps and held up a hand to shield his eyes. The blue spring sky looked freshly washed and the sunbeams fell diagonally through the tall branches of the oak trees and across fresh, green pastures.

Perhaps it was a cliché, but horse and rider appeared to be one, and Monika Schmidt looked as if she had been born in the saddle. Her face was serene and an invisible plumb-line began with her head, went straight through her neck and body, and continued into the horse's chest. The long-limbed, dark brown animal trotted forwards and sideways in some kind of well-schooled gait, and the rider was in motion just as much as the horse was. The sun bounced off the mother-of-pearl hairclip at the back her neck when the horse pirouetted and trotted back.

"She's good, isn't she?"

"Yes."

"And tragic," Elizabeth Caspersen said.

"Undoubtedly," he said. "But are we referring to the same thing?"

"No, Michael. Yes, or . . . No, the tragedy is that she didn't know she could ride until she was in her early forties. She had never been on a horse until then. If she had started like all other girls when she was ten years old, she could have . . ."

"Broken her neck and been in a wheelchair she could only move by blowing into a tube," he said. "I don't like horses. Do they even have a brain?"

"Ask Monika," she said.

Horse and rider came back towards them and Elizabeth Caspersen waved. There was no reaction on Monika Schmidt's face. She was totally focused on what she was doing.

He looked past the enclosure, past Monika Schmidt and Cavalier of Pederslund, if that was who it was, past the stable buildings and towards a distant figure standing very still on the edge of the forest. Flat cap, boots, tweed jacket, and a spotted hunting dog at his feet.

And a pair of binoculars in front of his eyes.

"That's Peter," Elizabeth Caspersen said.

She waved, and the man lowered his binoculars and disappeared into the forest.

"Not very welcoming," Michael said.

A line appeared in her brow.

"Oh. How strange. He's usually . . . different."

"Time to go?"

They walked down the steps. Elizabeth Caspersen headed for the enclosure; Michael followed with some reluctance. The horse reared in front of them. It came down on its front legs, tossed its head, and trotted towards the fence posts, where Monika Schmidt swung her leg over the horse's croup and let herself glide to the ground. She landed, perfectly balanced, and pulled the horse along. Without the horse and her high heels, she looked tiny. He had expected a look of mild contempt, or at least reserve, but the Swedish woman's features were still characterized by that strange wistfulness he had seen the night before.

Elizabeth Caspersen bent down for a quick embrace, after which Monika Schmidt offered him a gloved hand.

"It was nice to meet you, Michael."

"Thank you, likewise. And thank you for a great meal last night. I hope that everything works out."

"With Charles Simpson?"

Her face had a natural redness after the ride, and he could detect signs of her age around her mouth and eyes in the daylight. But he thought she would always be beautiful.

"With Simpson Junior and everything else," he said politely.

"Are you leaving now?" she asked.

"We're sending Michael to New York," Elizabeth Caspersen said.

Monika Schmidt smiled and looked down.

"You're always welcome here, Michael." She laughed, sounding a little husky. "As are you, *snälla* Elizabeth, obviously."

"Thank you," he said.

She pulled the horse's head over her shoulder and stroked its muzzle. Its eyes were the size of apples.

"Cavalier?" he asked, and she laughed out loud and shook her head so vehemently that her hair barrette fell to the ground.

He picked it up and handed it to her.

"Oh, Michael. Even you can't be that innocent! This is Zarina, Cavalier's little friend from Germany."

He softened his knees slightly and peered between the horse's hind legs.

"Of course."

"You'd be able to tell the difference," she said.

"I'm sure I would."

He turned in the Opel's passenger seat and looked back as they drove through the park. Monika Schmidt was back on the horse and the gamekeeper had appeared out of nowhere. The dog sniffed around and relieved itself against the post while the two people were deep in conversation. Monika Schmidt sat straight in the saddle and stared right ahead while the man gestured with his hands.

Michael's mobile pinged to tell him that a fresh e-mail had landed in his inbox.

The message was from Dr. Henkel, the forensic examiner in Berne. Michael clicked on the attachment to open it, read the eminent professor's conclusions, leaned back and rubbed his eyelids with his fingertips.

"What is it, Michael?"

"The lab in Berne," he said.

"Are they done?"

"Yes."

He looked across the fields of Jungshoved and the blue, glittering water of Bøgestrømmen.

"Your father's fingerprints were on the cartridge shell from the Mauser. They match the prints from the whisky glass."

"And the jewellery box?"

"Only your prints, Elizabeth."

"No hair or skin cells?"

"No."

"And you can't send him the DVD?" she said.

"The only prints on it were yours," he said. "I checked it myself with a bit of evaporated iodine powder and some tape."

"I'm an idiot, Michael. When I found it in the safe, I didn't think anything of it."

"Of course you didn't. You couldn't know what it was. It could have been anything."

"So my father went to Sweden in Sonartek's jet in March, and you've found his fingerprints on a cartridge from the rifle which you think was used for hunting and killing up there. But you're saying it sounds too good to be true. You're not happy, Michael? Have I got that right?"

"How did he get from Stockholm to Norway and Finnmark?" he wondered out loud, then shifted in his seat.

"I don't know. Maybe he just got in a car and drove there with the rest of them. It's not the best-guarded border in the world. It's not North Korea."

"But who were the others?" he said. "That's the question."

"Will you find out?"

"Of course. Have you heard from your father's accountant?"

"About any bizarre transactions with the Cayman Islands, Cyprus or Liechtenstein?"

"Yes."

She glanced at her watch.

"He said he was going to ring this afternoon. He has been going through my father's bank statements and credit cards with a fine-tooth comb since our first meeting."

"Great."

Nothing else was said until they reached the outskirts of Copenhagen.

"Now what?" she wanted to know.

"There are a couple of other things I want to look into," he said vaguely.

"What about Norway?"

"I'll go up there as soon as I can."

"It's been two years, Michael. What on earth could possibly be left in those godforsaken mountains?"

"Nothing, but if I don't go up there, I'll always be wondering, what if there were some sort of evidence? Or remains that the families could bury? I have to go."

"Of course," she said, sounding tired. "I'll drop you at your hotel."

When he had got out, he leaned inside the car and smiled.

"Speak to you later," he said.

She looked at him. Her eyes were slightly narrowed, and she didn't smile.

"It *was* him, Michael. It's what he became. It's what they become."

"You're probably right," he said.

He waved after the car as it pulled out from the curb and she looked at him in the rear-view mirror and held up a gloved hand. Then Michael turned around. He was no longer smiling.

Who the hell wipes their fingerprints off their own DVD before returning it to their own, private, high security safe?

CHAPTER 32

He had laid down on his bed, a brief nap that turned into three hours of dreamless sleep. Michael rose stiffly, stumbled into the bathroom, and didn't wake up properly until he mistook the hot tap for the cold in the shower.

He dried himself meditatively in front of the mirror and wondered whether to shave, but couldn't be bothered.

Superintendent Lene Jensen. The little voice that kept telling him to contact her had grown stronger, though every unwritten rule in his profession warned him not to involve outsiders. But he had to place Kim Andersen and his suicide somewhere in the picture. And soon.

The superintendent wasn't in her office . . . And no, the Rigspolitiet did not give out the private numbers of its staff. And, yes, that included former staff members. If he would like to leave a message, the superintendent would ring him as soon as she could.

Michael declined, thanked the secretary, and hung up.

He thought he had been able to detect a slight, dry tension in the secretary's voice. She had asked him twice to state his name, and he had heard the keyboard clatter when she entered his name and telephone number. He fiddled with the mobile in his jacket pocket while he tried to remember his old colleagues from the Hvidovre Police. He had worked there for three years as a very green police sergeant. Who had shown the least initiative? Who might still be hanging around?

They had been a bunch of young sergeants—still wet behind the ears, but ambitious—and he couldn't imagine that any of them would still be working in the same police district, but there had been a couple of older police sergeants who had seemed happy to stay put. They lived nearby and their wives worked at Hvidovre Hospital. Nurses and cops had always made a natural and stable combination.

He was in luck. Daniel Tarnovski was still there; he was in his office and he remembered him well. This came as a surprise to Michael, who regarded himself as totally forgettable. After various questions as to how life had treated him, to which he gave non-committal answers, Tarnovski proclaimed Lene Jensen to be one tough cookie. Very energetic. Which was Daniel Tarnovski-speak for a fanatical overachiever. She worked for a posh chief superintendent with a law degree in the Rigspolitiet by the name of Charlotte Falster, whom Daniel Tarnovski was also happy to hold forth about. Why did Michael want to know?

Michael closed his eyes and tried hard to come up with a good story.

He had met the superintendent at a party and had fallen in love?

Unlikely.

He had a hunch that her current investigation into the suicide of an ex-soldier in Holbæk actually ran parallel to his own investigation into a group of psychopathic veterans who were organizing industrial-scale man-hunts in the globe's most inaccessible corners?

That would raise an eyebrow or two out in Hvidovre.

Michael flipped the situation one hundred and eighty degrees and said that the superintendent had contacted him the day before to find out if—in his capacity as a former military police captain with the Horse Guards—he knew of a group of privates who had been involved in the black-market sale of medicines and military supplies in Sarajevo. Kim Andersen, the man who had killed himself in Holbæk, was one of those whose name had cropped up. The Public Prosecutor had handed Lene Jensen the file and Michael had been listed as the original case officer.

Michael laughed sheepishly.

"I was all over the place when she rang, Daniel. The kids were bawling their eyes out, the washing machine was flooding the utility room, and the dog was having eight puppies, so I'm afraid I told her to get lost, which was unfair, really, when she was just trying to do her job. I can remember her name, but not her number. And I do know one or two things about the case which might be important. You know how it is . . ."

"No, I don't," Daniel Tarnovski said. "Yelling at her when she's just doing her job is out of order. I mean it, Michael."

"And that's why I'm calling. Sorry," he mumbled remorsefully.

"Don't apologize to me. Apologize to her."

"Yes, and I've tried calling her. But Lene Jensen? There are millions with that name."

"Send flowers," the other suggested.

"Where to?"

"Just a moment."

Tarnovski gave him an address in Frederiksberg and a private mobile number.

"And I expect you to call her right now," he said.

The digital age had made life easier for investigators like Michael. Today anyone with Internet access and around 150 kroner could buy an effective and reliable GPS transmitter that could be attached to the underside of a car with Velcro or slipped into the bottom of a bag. You could then follow anyone's movements from the comfort of your own home on Google Maps. It had become so much easier to find people—or for them to find you, which was the flipside, and one of the reasons he replaced his mobile daily and always used unlisted numbers.

Michael opened up www.mgoogle.com/latitude/ on the mobile's web browser, entered Lene Jensen's mobile number, and two seconds later knew that the mobile, and therefore presumably its owner, were currently at the Rigshospitalet, 9 Blegdamsvej, Østerbro, somewhere in Stairwell 2 of the hospital's main building.

He studied the location with a frown before he ran down to the hotel reception and asked them to get him a cab.

Thirty minutes later, Michael leaned his head back and looked up at the ugly grey façade of the Seventies hospital. Lene Jensen's mobile hadn't moved. He continued through the revolving door and entered a lift along with silent patients, staff in white uniforms and glum-looking relatives.

He was the only one to exit the densely packed lift on the seventh floor and he looked about him. There were several options. He opened a glass door and was enveloped in the familiar hospital smell; he walked through a waiting area at a leisurely pace while he looked out for a certain shade of chestnut-red hair. He continued down a corridor until the next landing with lifts and tried a parallel corridor: the Ear, Nose and Throat surgical unit. A nurse behind a glass window looked up at him. A couple of mummified patients at a nearby table were eating slowly and in total silence, as if the wrong chewing motion or a rash word could make the brackets, screws, elastics and carefully restored skull bones fall apart, but even they stared at him, and Michael felt conspicuous. When his mobile rang, the nurse shot him an angry look, raised a finger to her lips and pointed to a sign on the wall banning mobiles in the ward. They apparently interfered with respirators or other vital equipment.

Michael half ran down the corridor and out of the ward. He found an empty common room with a magnificent view across Fælledparken and the towers, spires and roofs of Copenhagen. A pigeon on the railing outside the windows watched him with blinking, red eyes. One of the bird's claws was deformed by a large tumour and he wondered how it managed to balance on the railing, let alone how on earth it was still alive.

"Michael," said a voice.

"Keith. How are you?"

"Great."

"Are you sure?"

"Of course," he said.

The invalid bird took off and a couple of feathers fluttered into the gap between the wall and the railing. They twirled around themselves before settling between cigarette butts and empty juice cartons.

"Running Man Casino," the Englishman said. "The West Indies. Antigua and Barbuda. North of Venezuela and west of Puerto Rico. Pirate country. A micro state. That's who is financing your man hunters."

"A casino?"

"It's a poker website. They've become a West Indian speciality. And it's a great idea, if you ask me," his old mentor said. "A really great idea. Strange that no one has thought of it before."

"Perhaps they have."

Michael thought about the crescent of Caribbean islands, former Spanish and British colonies that stretched from Florida in the north to Venezuela in the south like a scimitar. The area was politically, geologically, and meteorologically an unstable nightmare: sugar plantations, slaves, rum, dictators, tropical hurricanes, earthquakes, cocaine, wonderful beaches, and Armani-dressed pirates of the modern type with dreadlocks, gold chains, Bentleys, and machine guns.

"It's an independent state," Keith Mallory said. "Commonwealth, beaches, reggae, steel bands, drinks with little parasols, Rastafarians and—"

"Small banks and poker websites," Michael said.

"Small banks with very big private accounts that make their living by never, ever providing information about their clients to anyone." The Englishman completed his sentence. "The Colombian and Mexican drug cartels have to invest their coke dollars somewhere and online casinos are a great way to launder money. All you need is a bamboo hut on the beach with one heck of an Internet connection, a couple of high-spec, water-cooled servers, a small, friendly bank, and you're in business."

Michael nodded to himself.

It *was* a good idea. The question was now, whose was it? Flemming Caspersen's? He was probably pally with the richest and most influential people on the planet: top lobbyists in Washington, Mumbai billionaires, Russian oligarchs, the CEOs of oil companies. They all depended on Sonartek's products and every one of them would surely like nothing better than to do Flemming Caspersen a favour . . . such as helping him set up an online casino in the West Indies. The next question was if he was its only client, or if it had become a supplier of exclusive leisure activities for old and weary but mighty men seeking increasingly bigger thrills.

"Christ, Keith. I . . ."

"What?"

The encrypted telephone the Englishman was using crackled and howled.

"Who is your source? Is it reliable?"

"Who is? You and I are. I trust no one else, Mike. But as a source, it's good enough. My source was contacted by some guys from Running Man who asked him if he fancied being a tour guide for some very special hunting trips for super-rich clients; he declined. Later, he got curious and discovered that their website offers a special bonus for regular high-rolling players on games where there's no limit. They also advertise unique experiences on scrolling advertisements that don't appear to relate to the casino itself, but which I haven't been able to find on any other website, either. The ads offer safaris for the discerning customer."

"And you pay for them by losing a hell of a lot of money playing poker?"

"I would think so."

"And if you win?"

"You don't win, Mike. The whole thing is as fake as Cher's tits. It's just a scheme to enable the select few to meet up, arrange, and pay for events. Everything is encrypted, and then double encrypted. Unbreakable algorithms."

"Running Man Casino?"

"Great name, isn't it?"

Michael thought about Elizabeth Caspersen's DVD, Kasper Hansen's face, and the empty cliff edge.

"How apt," he said. "Thank you, Keith."

"Don't mention it."

There was another small pause.

"I wasn't going to tell you," the Englishman then said. "But I think this is very different from your usual work, Mike. What I'm saying is, this is . . . big. Do you understand? Very big indeed."

Michael nodded. The pigeon had returned and was sitting a few metres away on the railing. It watched him as if he were a large burger bun for which it had unrealistic plans.

"Yes, but I think it comes with this particular job."

"Are you sure? There's a job with S&W right now if you want it."

"Uzbekistan?"

"Worse. Nigeria."

"I thought they were in the middle of a civil war there? The locals are setting fire to oil barrels?"

"It's our bread-and-butter, Mike. We guard the oil so your kids won't be cold in winter. Have you forgotten that?"

Michael had a flashback to the bitter, choking smell of burning crude oil. As if a furious mother Earth were spewing flames to swallow up greedy humans drilling holes several kilometres into her abdomen.

"Thanks, but no thanks, Keith. I like Denmark in springtime. Besides . . ."

"Wife and kids," the Englishman said. "I understand. Bye, Mike, and send the money straight away."

CHAPTER 33

Michael stood for a moment with the mobile in his hand, staring blankly into space. Nigeria? The Dark Continent. The name suited the place all too well. He had been there many times.

Then he wondered what it was that had struck a chord in his subconscious as he had raced down the corridor to get outside with his offending mobile. He looked at the door to the ward again. A colour. He had caught a glimpse of chestnut red when he passed the door to one of the side wards. The right shade. He switched his mobile to silent and opened the door to the ward of the country's finest Ear, Nose, and Throat surgeon.

He headed down the corridor and found the door, which was still ajar. The colour matched. He could see some hair, part of a low armchair, a small section of a deathly pale face and a dark blue hoodie. He knocked carefully on the door and watched the figure inside. It didn't move. He knocked harder and looked around. The mummies at the dining table had noticed him again. One had inserted a drinking straw in the middle of a metal construction and he thought he could see a woman's eyes behind the bandages.

He pushed open the door and found himself in a passage outside a small bathroom lined with linoleum.

"Excuse me?"

He cleared his throat. The figure in the armchair by the window didn't stir. The hair was still beautiful, red and vibrant, but the face was empty and turned to the floor. It was a single-occupancy room, but there was no bed. There was only the woman in the chair; Michael squatted down in front of her.

Very carefully, he placed a hand on the jeans-clad knee, but withdrew it immediately.

"Lene?"

The superintendent's left ear was covered with a compress and there was dried blood on her neck below it. Her head lifted slightly from her clenched fists on which it had been resting and her green, dry eyes were aimed at him, but didn't seem to register him as relevant. There was nothing in her eyes.

"Lene? My name is Michael Sander. I'm . . ."

What could he say?

He got up. The superintendent didn't move and her eyes returned to the floor. From his wallet, Michael took one of his rarely used business cards, which stated only his name and nothing else. He wrote today's mobile number on the card and put it on the armrest.

"Call me. It's about Kim Andersen. I think we can help each other."

He shrugged helplessly, stuck his hands in his pockets and made to leave.

Then he changed his mind and turned to her again.

"Erm . . . I don't think we have an awful lot of time, so please call me when . . . well, when you're feeling better."

He had put his hand on the door handle when she whispered something. He took a step back and looked at her.

"What did you say?"

"I can't talk to anyone," she said, slowly shaking her head. "I can't talk to anyone."

"Why not?"

Lene Jensen's green eyes filled with tears and she wiped them away mechanically with the back of her hand. Her hands were filthy and several of her nails were broken.

"I can't," she said.

She took the business card from the armrest and looked at it.

"Who are you?"

He moved closer and balanced between necessary closeness and a safe distance. Lene Jensen looked like a hunted animal.

He hesitated before taking a deep breath.

"I'll try to do the talking for both of us, Lene. You can interrupt me if you like, and you can nod if you think what I say makes sense, or shake your head if you think it doesn't, okay? Kim Andersen was a Royal Life Guards veteran. He was deployed in Afghanistan, Iraq, and Bosnia. He was also a member of a group of ex-soldiers who arranged a safari—hunting a couple

214

of human beings in northern Norway. I'm talking about a young engineer, Kasper Hansen, and his Norwegian wife, Ingrid Sundsbö, aged thirty-one and twenty-nine years old. The hunt took place on March 24, 2011. I don't know when exactly Ingrid Sundsbö was killed, but Kasper Hansen was shot at six thirty in the evening. They left behind two-year-old twins."

Michael paused and looked at the superintendent. Had she taken anything in at all? There was no expression on her face, but was it possible that there was a tiny flicker deep in her green eyes?

"I believe that Kim Andersen injured his leg during the hunt. There is a . . . a recording of the end of the hunt. It's a trophy of some kind for the client. I don't know if the two murders were a one-off or if the killers have organized human safaris before, but they seemed experienced. I work as a private investigator for a client who has come into possession of the film and wants to find the hunters. I believe that the gang operates from a country house on south Sjælland. I think they're Danish army veterans and that they were recruited from the estate's shooting syndicates. I've learned that their fees were paid out as gambling prizes from an online casino in the West Indies, Running Man Casino. What I don't have is evidence and more information, especially about Kim Andersen. Did he hang himself or did someone lend him a hand? It would be good if we could join forces . . . a huge help, to be honest."

"Are you one of them?" she asked the floor.

"One of whom?"

"Is this a test? I won't say anything. I've told you already. I promised you . . . Please don't hurt her."

Fresh tears ran down her face.

Michael wondered what in God's name they had done to her. He remembered the photographs of the superintendent from the newspapers and Daniel Tarnovski's opinion of her as a woman who was hard as nails. And famous for it.

He squatted down in front of her again and tried to catch her eye under the red hair, but it was impossible. She refused to look at him.

"No, I'm not one of them, Lene," he said in his kindest voice. "I work alone. I don't know what has happened to you or why there's no bed in this ward, but like I said, I believe we can help each other. Please call me when you've had a chance to think." He smiled to her. "I'll answer your call, day or night, and I really want to talk to you."

Michael got up, looked down at her and was about to add something when there was a knock on the door. Whoever knocked didn't wait for a reply, but walked straight in. The slim, grey-haired woman in the dark suit stopped when she saw him. Her bob haircut was perfect and her eyes were clear and critical behind her glasses. Michael smiled to the new arrival, but his smile wasn't reciprocated.

He held out his hand. "Michael Sander."

"Charlotte Falster. I'm sorry, I thought . . . So you're not Josefine's father?"

He hadn't heard the superintendent get up and was taken aback by the strength in the hand which she placed on his upper arm. He was pushed to one side by Lene Jensen, who still didn't look at him, but only at the woman with the grey hair.

"He's leaving," she said.

A couple of embarrassing seconds passed before Charlotte Falster was the first to pull herself together.

"I'm happy to wait outside, Lene, until you . . ."

The superintendent looked past Michael and nodded towards the door.

"You can stay, Charlotte," she said. "Goodbye, and thank you for coming, Michael."

He looked at her.

"You're welcome."

Michael smiled briefly to the grey-haired woman as he slipped past her. He shut the door behind him and heard Charlotte Falster start to ask questions in a loud and clear voice. And he heard the police superintendent burst into tears.

He smiled to himself. Not that there was anything to smile about, but he had noticed Lene Jensen's stealthy movement when she slipped his business card into the pocket of her hoodie.

CHAPTER 34

The glass doors of the imposing office block in Bredgade opened automatically. Michael walked past showcases with exquisite ceramics and hand-woven rugs and onwards through a covered atrium at the heart of the building. He smiled at a young woman stepping out of a cylindrical glass lift at the far end, entered and pressed the button for the third floor: *Holm, Joensen, & Partners. Attorneys at Law*. He exited the lift, entered a tasteful reception area, and addressed the young woman behind the counter.

"Michael Sander to see Elizabeth Caspersen."

"Sander?"

Michael nodded, and the receptionist gestured towards an armchair in black leather and chrome.

"Five minutes," she said. "Help yourself to coffee or water."

"Thank you."

He sat down and glanced at the usual architecture magazines spread out in an inviting fan on a low glass coffee table between the armchairs. The air was dry, the temperature pleasant, and there was a faint hum of air conditioning.

Michael rubbed his unshaven chin and thought glumly about the traumatized, broken superintendent at the Rigshospitalet. Despair had covered her like a heavy cloak: she had reached some sort of limit, and there was nothing on the other side.

He heard hard heels on the polished granite floor tiles and got up.

"Elizabeth . . ."

"Michael."

She was serious and focused while she led him through the glass doors and down a long corridor. She opened the last door and held it open for him.

There were bookcases full from floor to ceiling with law collections and bound legal journals, a worn Persian rug on the floor, and basic office furniture: Elizabeth Caspersen clearly didn't feel the need to impress anyone. She sat down on a low sofa and offered him a seat at the other end.

She found it hard to sit still.

"I have news, Michael," she said eagerly. "I really do, some good and some more problematic. Thanks for coming over straight away."

"Not at all," he said, trying to mobilize an enthusiastic smile.

"I've spoken to my father's chief accountant in Denmark, or rather . . . It's an international firm, but he heads the Danish division."

"I understand," Michael said.

"Good. I had to give him various passwords, otherwise he couldn't . . ." She blushed even more deeply as if confessing to sniffing lighter gas when she was fifteen.

Michael wished she would get to the point.

"He has discovered a way of transferring money to the men who . . ."

"Killed Kasper Hansen and Ingrid Sundsbö," he said.

"Quite. The accountant found a channel, a private route through which very large sums could be transferred. You probably won't believe it, but—"

"Running Man Casino, Antigua and Barbuda?" he suggested.

Her eyes widened and she shut her mouth with a smack.

"How the hell did you know that? How could you possibly . . ."

He shrugged his shoulders, and she exploded.

"For fuck's sake why didn't you tell me, Michael?"

Her knuckles were white and she shifted in her seat as if she were about to hit him. She was tall, slim, probably very fit, and had large hands. He had no doubt that Elizabeth Caspersen would be capable of hurting him if she lost her temper. And could he permit himself to strike a client who had hit him first? Probably not.

He held up his hands in a gesture of surrender.

"Because I only found out a few hours ago. Promise. I spoke to an old colleague, and I'm sure that he only knew for a couple of minutes before he called me."

She looked at him. Her already narrow lips were pressed together in a line and the fists in her lap were still clenched.

He flashed her a conciliatory smile. "But it's good to have it confirmed from other sources. It really is."

She closed her eyes and took a deep breath.

"Good? Right, it's bloody brilliant."

Michael laughed and scratched the back of his head.

"What are you laughing at?" she asked suspiciously.

"You, sorry. Given that you're a lawyer and a barrister who appears in the Supreme Court, and that you grew up on Richelieus Allé, I wonder why you swear like a trucker."

She blushed and looked down at herself. Then she smiled shyly.

"Is this how you talk in court?" he asked. "I can just imagine it. God help anyone who gets on the wrong side of you."

"These days I rarely go near a courtroom. I'm a corporate lawyer. All I do is find legal loopholes for rich people."

"What did the accountant say about the casino? Does he know who owns it?"

"Transparency isn't really a feature of the West Indian banking sector. Practically anything goes out there. I think the accountant used a hacker."

"Excellent," Michael said.

"Not one of those pizza-eating, Coca-Cola-guzzling ones with a snazzy nickname, but someone from an IT security company. Someone very good."

"Go on."

"Running Man Casino was started five years ago in Antigua," she said. "It offers online poker, blackjack, roulette, slot machines, and so on. It's part of a group of international gaming sites. They open and close, appear under new names and with fresh contact details. Like porn sites, the accountant, said."

"Porn sites?"

"Don't say you haven't come across porn sites."

"I've heard of them," Michael said.

"The casino is owned by a company in Panama City—Pan Pacific Equity. That means a secretary in an office with a computer and an answering machine."

"A shell company."

"That's a common structure." She nodded. "But now I've found the answer to something that has always puzzled me . . ."

"What's that?"

"How Sonartek pays bribes. It's obvious now. And rather neat when you think about it."

Michael nodded. Of course. Although Sonartek enjoyed a virtual monopoly in its niche, it didn't trade solely with states that complied with every international convention. It counted both democracies and dictatorships among its customers. The arms industry wasn't for the faint-hearted. If you wanted the order, you had to play the game.

"How much are we talking about, Elizabeth?"

"Around thirty million dollars every year in the last five years."

Michael whistled. It was more than enough to make all the tough guys in the world do what you wanted and grease the palms of high-ranking civil servants in any defense department.

"Is there a Danish side to this?"

She didn't reply, but got up and went over to a filing cabinet in the corner of her office. She placed a Copenhagen tabloid in front of him. A newspaper Michael knew very well.

"Kim Andersen," she said. "I knew him from Pederslund, but he hadn't crossed my mind until I saw this. Nor would I have paid much attention until I spoke to the accountant. Do you know the case?"

"I do, as a matter of fact. A Royal Life Guard. Veteran. Suicide."

"He died a relatively wealthy man," Elizabeth Caspersen said drily.

Michael looked up from the newspaper's front page. Lene Jensen was caught in midstride in the parking lot outside Holbæk Police Station. She looked at the photographer without smiling, wearing the same hoodie she had huddled inside at the hospital ward.

"Did he now," he said.

"He was paid 200,000 Swiss francs just over a month ago by Credit Suisse in Zurich."

"From Running Man Casino?"

"Exactly. And the payment was authorized by Victor Schmidt in July 2011."

Michael dropped the newspaper and he leaned back in the uncomfortable sofa. "Victor?"

"His very own internal, digital signature. It can't be faked."

"That's interesting," Michael said. "That's very, very interesting indeed. Proof, in fact."

"Yes, I know," she said. "Coffee? I'm afraid I haven't got anything stronger, though Christ knows I could do with a drink right now."

"Yes, please," he said absent-mindedly.

"Milk?"

"Please."

Elizabeth Caspersen got busy with the Thermos flask, two cups, and a sugar bowl. She poured his coffee, sat down again, and crossed her legs.

"Why a month ago?" he asked.

She put down her cup.

"He was married the day before he hanged himself," she said. "Weddings have become showpieces these days, where people compete to outdo each other and prove all sorts of things. It costs a bomb."

"Of course."

Twelve people had attended his and Sara's wedding in a country church in Devon. Afterwards they had all gone to the pub—and later he was carried to his bed by the host and Keith Mallory, while Sara danced the night away downstairs. He smiled at the memory. The whole thing had been unforgettable and cost them a few thousand pounds, including bed and breakfast.

Michael pointed to a small photograph of Lene Jensen on the front page.

"This woman is a superintendent with the Rigspolitiet and is said to be strong, determined, and good at her job. I met her earlier today at the Rigshospitalet. She's broken. Something or someone has broken her."

"We can't go on like this," Elizabeth Caspersen said quietly. "You don't seem to trust me even though I hired you and face terrible consequences if that film comes out."

"Of course I trust you, but I'm also a professional and I see no reason to risk you making a slip of the tongue or for one of our conversations be to accidentally overheard by someone. It could be catastrophic."

Elizabeth Caspersen pointed a well-manicured fingertip at her chest: "Why would I tell anyone that my father was a murderous psychopath?"

He calmly returned her furious stare.

"Not deliberately, of course. And I might be the one who screws up. I'm not superhuman, far from it. But the fewer people who know what we're doing, the better our chances. It's a fine line, of course, because someone clearly has to know what's going on."

"Communication, Michael. That's what I was brought up with, just as you were brought up to keep your mouth shut. We're on a bit of a collision course here."

He smiled.

"In my opinion communication is overrated," he said. "Excessive communication is the scourge of civilization. Meetings for the sake of it. Information without knowledge . . ."

Elizabeth Caspersen provided further evidence of her superior eyebrow technique.

"You may be right." She picked up the newspaper and studied the front page. "Lene Jensen? Why are the police even investigating a suicide?"

"I don't know, but last night I found several photographs of Kim Andersen in Jakob's room," he said. "Photographs from Iraq, Afghanistan, and in front of Pederslund. Happy faces. Mrs. Nielsen with a silver tray. Bugles and morning parade."

"You went to Jakob's room? If he had found you, you would be dead. He's the most private person I've ever met. He loathes people. In general, I mean."

"Of course I went to his room. Why do you think I wanted to visit Pederslund?"

She stared at him.

"How the hell would I know?! You told me you wanted to meet the people who were close to my father. You told me so yourself, God damn you."

"Did I? Anyway, I was there for several reasons."

"So it would appear. You said she was broken? By what? An accident? What's going on, and why do you want to talk to her?"

She put down the newspaper and stared at him in alarm. "You're not going to tell her anything about the hunt, are you? About the film? You can't do that, Michael. You just can't!"

"The thought hadn't even crossed my mind.' He stirred his coffee. "Of course not. But Kim Andersen is dead, so I can't talk to him and I have to find out where he fits into the picture, the big picture, with the casino in the West Indies and the 200,000 Swiss francs from Credit Suisse. You must admit that it's getting a bit complicated."

"Or perhaps it's very simple, Michael. A big game hunting club. A club for men bored with conventional hunting. Who wanted to try something new and found a way of doing it."

He looked grimly at her and drank his coffee.

"Maybe. In any case, I was too late. She's the most traumatized person I've ever met."

"So what do we do now?" she asked.

"Jakob Schmidt . . ."

"What about him?"

"Does he have any tattoos?"

She thought about it.

"I think so. Most people do these days, don't they? Why?"

Michael pointed to his own neck. "A scorpion, for example? Here, below his ear. I couldn't find him in any of the photographs in his room. He really is a ghost as his father said."

Elizabeth Caspersen nodded. "That's how he wants it. A scorpion? No, I don't think so, but I've hardly seen him in the last few years, so he could have got one. Do you want me to ask him?"

"God, no. Forget it."

Michael looked out of the window. The light in the covered atrium had been switched on. Darkness was falling, and he was exhausted.

"You asked me just now what we're going to do. I think the time has come for us to take the lead, Elizabeth."

"How?"

"You said you were willing to spend everything you own, didn't you?"

"And I meant it, Michael," she said firmly. "I know I complained when you wanted to charter helicopters, but it's fine. Fire away."

"Excellent. Because I'm very good at spending other people's money. I have an idea. An expensive idea. A very, very expensive idea."

"What do you have in mind?"

He leaned back and looked absent-mindedly at the Persian rug.

"I want to smuggle someone into the Running Man Casino," he said. "A Trojan horse."

She nodded.

"Do you have someone in mind, Michael?"

"I know a really good guy."

CHAPTER 35

They spoke for several more minutes, after which Michael made a long call with Elizabeth Caspersen on speakerphone.

In the end, it was her persuasive skills that proved to be the decisive factor. That and the money, of course.

Michael then drank more coffee while Elizabeth Caspersen got to work on her computer. A few minutes later, she looked up, pinned her gaze on him, hit *enter*, leaned back and exhaled.

She rubbed her upper arms nervously.

"So this is how it feels to sell 50,000 Sonartek shares. My father would kill me if he knew."

Michael smiled to encourage her. "I hope you think it's worth it, Elizabeth. Will Victor know?"

"I do think it's worth it, Michael. And no, he won't. I'll split the portfolio into smaller transactions through different stockbrokers in the next few days. Sonartek shares are traded thousands of times every day across the globe."

"I guess they are," said Michael, who still had his doubts. It was Elizabeth herself who had told him never to underestimate Victor Schmidt.

For a moment both were lost in their own private thoughts.

"So what was the problematic news, Elizabeth?" he then said.

"I'm sorry?"

"You said you had good news and some that was more problematic."

She sighed and flattened the thick white envelope on the blotting pad with the palms of her hands.

"This. Today, the Probate Office appointed me to be my mother's legal guardian and executor. The probate panel and the judge agreed unanimously. Here is a statement from a clinical psychologist and a medical expert's report from a professor of neurology."

"Should I congratulate you?"

"I really don't know."

"I imagine you'll have considerable influence over Sonartek now."

She nodded.

"Judging by Victor and Henrik's reaction, I do." Her face was stripped of enthusiasm, let alone triumph. "They cornered me in the underground parking lot this afternoon and invited me for a drink. Practically forced me. Victor already knew about the probate decision. I've no idea how he could have."

"What did he want?"

She offered him a pale smile.

"He wanted my assurance that I would vote for him as the new chairman at Sonartek's extraordinary board meeting."

"And what did you say?"

"What could I say? They seemed desperate. Oh God, Michael, I don't want to join my own company. I just want to live my own life. Don't you see?"

Michael nodded, but was really thinking: How hard can it be to have half of sixty-five billion in your hand?

"So what did you say?" he asked.

"That of course I would vote for him. That continuity was important for Sonartek, company culture . . . whatever crap he wanted to hear. I think I'm scared of him, Michael. Both of them."

The confident-businesswoman side of the barrister had evaporated. The light from the desk lamp reflected in a thin layer of perspiration on her forehead.

"Including Henrik?"

"Pardon?"

"Henrik. Are you scared of him too?"

She shrugged her shoulders: "No . . . Yes! I don't know. He has changed. Become obsessive and jumpy. They both have. Victor has never liked me and my mother all that much. I think he was jealous of us. So was Henrik. He worshipped my father."

"Jealous?"

"Is that so hard to understand? My father and Victor had a very deep, but also complicated friendship. I don't think Victor has any other friends. He trusts no one. Probably not even his own children, and certainly not Monika.

He hated having to share my father with anyone. Now Victor is no longer young and Sonartek is his life's work. It must continue, and it must continue in Denmark. He suffered when they outsourced production, even though he could see it was the right thing to do, financially speaking. But he's a patriot and he was absurdly proud when Jakob became an officer, and absurdly disappointed when he left the army and started clearing mines and doing logistics for aid organizations."

"And Henrik?"

"Teflon. His father's spitting image and his right hand, loyal till the end. He's a people-pleaser, and terrified of losing his parents' love if he were to do anything to upset them. Such as having a mind of his own."

Michael got up.

"I understand," he said.

She looked up at him. She tried to smile.

"What do I do?" she asked.

"Keep playing the game, Elizabeth. Just for a little longer. Don't challenge them. For your own sake," he said gravely. "And watch your back."

She nodded, took a deep breath, and found a small envelope in her handbag. She blushed as she passed it to him.

"And then there was this small matter, Michael, I'm sorry. I really am. I'm so sorry. Victor gave it to me. He was terribly pleased with himself and I had no idea what to say."

Michael opened the envelope and took out the document with a sense of foreboding. He read the few lines on the single piece of paper and sat down again.

It was a photocopy of surgical notes from Næstved Central Hospital dated May 3, 1997. The day a surgeon had performed a vasectomy on Flemming Caspersen.

"Great," he mumbled.

"I didn't know. I swear," she said miserably.

"How the hell could you not know, you moron?" Michael erupted in anger before he remembered that she was his only client and source of income for the time being. "I'm sorry, Elizabeth, but really."

"That's all right. He never mentioned it to me and I've never heard my mother say anything about it."

"But why . . . ?"

"Why did he want a vasectomy? No idea."

He got up again and looked at her. "One last thing."

"Yes, Michael?" she said, sounding exhausted.

"Who is Jakob Schmidt's father?"

"What?"

He watched her carefully.

"He's not the spitting image of Victor, unlike his brother, Henrik," he said. "All you have to do is look at the portrait over the mantelpiece at Pederslund and compare it with the picture of your father in Hellerup."

Elizabeth Caspersen stared down at her shoes.

"I'm paying you to find the men in the film, Michael," she said calmly. "Not for anything else. Is that clear? It's not important."

"As crystal, Elizabeth."

"Let me show you out," she said.

Young workaholics buzzed around the law offices.

"By the way, she wasn't alone," Michael said on impulse.

"Who?"

"The superintendent. Lene Jensen. A woman arrived just as I was about to leave. She's a chief superintendent and a lawyer. I googled her. I know there are a lot of you lawyers about, but she's Lene Jensen's immediate superior in the Rigspolitiet and I wondered if you know her."

"What's her name?"

"Falster. Charlotte Falster."

Elizabeth Caspersen stopped in her tracks and looked at him.

"Falster?"

"Do you know her?"

"I know her husband: Joakim. He's a permanent secretary. We were at university together. I was at their wedding."

Michael nodded. He had no doubt it had been a very grand affair.

"Do you want me to have a word with her?" she asked.

"Yes, but how will you explain your sudden interest in one of her employees?"

"I'll think of something. You've taught me more than smoking, Michael.

Such as telling a good lie. Just because it didn't stand up to scrutiny doesn't mean it wasn't good."

"Oh, good. You're a quick learner. You'll go to hell."

"And meet up with my father? That would be wonderful."

Michael smiled wryly.

CHAPTER 36

Michael had been sucked into a McDonald's by a sudden, urgent need for salt, empty calories, fat, and Coca-Cola. He had wolfed down his food and felt bloated but still strangely hungry when he crossed Kongens Nytorv, walked down Nyhavn and through the revolving door to the Admiral Hotel. He waited impatiently while an older American couple got answers to a billion anxious questions before asking the receptionist if there were any messages for him. There weren't, and Michael continued to the lift. His stomach churned as it struggled to digest the burger meal.

When he entered the room, he ran his hand across the light switch to the left. Everything was as it should be, except that someone had removed the cover so that his fingers brushed the live wire. They trailed a long, blue spark from the switch and a shocked Michael snatched back his numbed hand and swore.

While he was shaking his hand in the unlit hallway, his attacker came flying out of the dark, crashing his shoulder into Michael's abdomen. Michael collapsed with a taste of catastrophe in his mouth and was helped along by a kick to the left side of his head. He saw a black, shiny, and pointy man's shoe, along with strange patterns behind his eyelids. There wasn't one cubic millimetre of air left in his lungs. He instinctively raised his arms to protect his face and consequently never saw the second kick to his testicles. He buckled without making a sound because he had no air left to scream and his attacker flung open the heavy door—into his head. Everything went black. He didn't know how much time had passed when he woke up with the smell of vomit in his nostrils. He tried to get away from it by lifting his head. That proved to be a mistake. A white, searing pain shot through his brain and he fell back into the bottomless darkness once more.

He was obviously a quick learner, because when he regained consciousness for the second time, he stayed very still and breathed through his mouth while ignoring the stench of vomit. His whole body hurt and he decided to examine it systematically. He could move his feet and his legs without triggering insane pain, and he could raise his strangely twitching left hand up to somewhere near his head. His hand buried itself in the carpet pile and a wet mass, which he eventually identified as the undigested remains of fries, burgers, and something else. His fingers sought out the places where he was glued to the floor and realized that it was congealed blood from the deep cut to his temple. It had bonded strongly with the carpet and he freed his hair with great care. Then he slowly pulled himself up on his hands and, after a few minutes, to a sitting position. The movement caused nausea to rise up through his throat, but he steeled himself, rested the back of his head against the wall, and stayed put for several, long minutes.

The door to the hotel corridor had been left ajar. He could hear a couple of happy tourists chatting away outside, the sound of suitcases on wheels and his own, soft groaning.

He struggled to his feet and started looking for the light switch on the wall before he remembered that was a very bad idea indeed. So he located the light switch in the bathroom instead and closed his eyes. Even so, the light cut through his eyelids in every colour of the rainbow and triggered new kinds of pain inside his head.

He eased open his eyelids and saw blood everywhere—in the pale grey carpet next to the pool of vomit, and continuing in several directions on the bathroom tiles. He left moist, red handprints as he fought his way to the sink, turned on the cold tap and grabbed one of the hotel's elegant towels.

Still dazed, he watched the blood trail down the sides of the white china sink. Then he raised his eyes to the mirror and discovered Jakob Schmidt standing right behind him, framed by the doorway.

Michael couldn't remember ever feeling so defenseless.

The ex-officer was wearing the same black roll-neck sweater as the previous evening, a knee-length black leather jacket, jeans and—Michael checked—a pair of battered hiking boots. No sign of shiny black shoes.

Most of the blood seemed to stem from a nasty cut above his left temple.

He pressed a towel against the cut and stared darkly at his unexpected guest.

"What do you want?" he asked. "And didn't anyone ever teach you to knock?"

Jakob Schmidt offered him a minimalist smile. "Didn't your mother ever tell you it's rude to pick locks and search someone's room? Especially when you're their guest?"

Michael made no reply, but held a corner of the towel under the cold tap before pressing it against the cut to his scalp. He pulled a face.

"You can't possibly know if I went to your room," he mumbled. "I'm far too clever."

"I'm sure people call you a lot of things, Michael, but clever isn't one that springs to mind. Two layers of tinfoil with talcum powder under the rug inside my door. There were footprints on them when I came back. Your size, I believe."

Michael looked at the other in the mirror.

"You live and learn," he said.

"Yes . . . so long as you do live."

Jakob Schmidt folded his arms across his chest and watched him dispassionately.

"Do you have a Band-Aid?" he asked.

Michael nodded.

"My travel bag. Left side pocket . . . if it's still there."

He pulled off his shirt, and Jakob Schmidt took a step back. This was a common reaction the first time people saw his naked body. Michael's torso was a topographical map of scar tissue on his back, sides, and chest, and some would be able to recognize bullet entry wounds above his right hip and the slightly larger splodges on his back, where the bullets had exited. Or at least Jakob Schmidt would be able to. There was a fresh blue-and-red bruise across his abdomen.

"You can practically see the shoe size," Michael said. "It's smaller than yours."

"It wasn't me. You look like a train crash."

"I'm clumsy. Band-Aid?"

"Coming up."

Twenty minutes later, he was sitting on his bed with a very small miniature bottle of vodka from the minibar in his hand, wearing a clean, pale blue shirt and with the cut to his scalp deftly closed with Band-Aids by Jakob Schmidt. He had swallowed a handful of paracetamol and ibuprofen and had felt worse. But he had also felt better.

Jakob Schmidt sat in the armchair with a Coca-Cola in his hand. The shadows seemed drawn to him. He was as still as a rock and Michael surmised that he was probably a first-class hunter. Patience personified.

"What do you want?" Michael asked.

The other said nothing.

Michael sighed and emptied the vodka bottle, opened the door to the minibar without leaving his slightly swaying bed and found a miniature bottle of gin. He unscrewed the cap and looked at the empty desk. His laptop was gone. The envelope with the constellations from Finnmark and the location of the crime scene which he had placed under the rug by the door to the corridor was gone. He hadn't checked the beam above his head yet, but he knew that Elizabeth Caspersen's DVD was gone, too.

"I think the right question is: What do *you* want, Michael? If that's even your real name," Jakob Schmidt said softly.

"Me? I don't want anything at all," Michael said. "I'm just the hired help."

"Hired to do what?"

"To uncover the facts in a paternity suit."

Jakob Schmidt drank his Coke.

"Number one, Flemming had a vasectomy fifteen years ago; number two, the letter from Miss Simpson wasn't written by an American, but by an Englishman, or someone well-educated with a good command of English," he said steadily. "An American would never spell 'summarize' with an *s*, but with a *z*, nor would an American ever say 'a drop in the ocean,' but 'a drop in the bucket.' And especially not if this person was an editor and a seventh-generation New Yorker, as you claim. So my question is still: What do you want?"

Michael looked at him.

"Have you talked to Elizabeth about this?" he asked.

"Not yet."

"Is it common knowledge that Flemming Caspersen had had a vasectomy, and why did he?"

"My mother thought it would be a good idea. And no, no one else knows. I think. But it's probably not hard to find out."

Michael wondered if the man was bluffing.

"Your mother?" he asked.

The figure moved slightly in the shadows. The Coke bottle was put down on the windowsill.

"Yes."

"Because they were in a relationship?"

"Why did you go to my room?"

"I got lost," Michael said.

"Through a locked door?"

"I walk in my sleep. I don't always know what I do. I wake up in the weirdest places."

The other man got up.

"I recommend tying your foot to the bed the next time you're sleeping in a strange place," he said.

Michael smiled, even though it hurt.

"I need to be able to move. Besides, it's hard to defend yourself if you're tied down."

"You don't appear to be very good at it, even when you're not."

Fair point, Michael thought.

Then Jakob's brown eyes disappeared in laughter lines, something that transformed him.

"It's all about picking the winning horse, isn't it?" he said.

"If time is on your side, then it's a really good idea," Michael said gravely.

The other man nodded. Then he walked across the floor, carefully avoiding the blood and vomit in the passage. He turned around in the doorway to the hotel corridor.

"You don't have very many friends, do you?"

"No, do you?"

"I don't know any more," he said, and closed the door behind him.

Michael hobbled to the door to make sure that it was locked. Then he pulled the desk into the middle of the floor, put the chair on top of it and climbed up with considerable effort. He sweated nervously as his fingers scuttled like frightened spiders across the beams. Nothing. The envelope with the DVD was gone. How the hell had they found it? Black defeat and blistering self-reproach washed over him. Along with the fear that Keith had been right: that he and his opponents were in different leagues. That he was now playing in a division where he was out of his depth.

Even though it was almost impossible, he pulled himself up on the beam and studied its dusty surface, inspecting the empty crack.

His attacker had to be the most pedantic and methodical person on the planet.

He lowered himself with shaking arms, nearly lost his balance, and wobbled for a few seconds on the smooth seat of the chair and the edge of fresh disasters before finally regaining his balance.

When he had returned the furniture to its original position, he undressed and headed for the shower cubicle. He turned on the cold tap, shielded the cut to his temple with one of the hotel's ridiculous shower caps, and watched the water swirl between his feet, clear at first, then rust-coloured before it turned clear again.

Afterwards, he dried himself with the speed of a Parkinson's patient, and every movement hurt. His testicles were twice their normal size and turning blue. Blue testicles? Great. He opened his mouth, studied a cut to the inside of his cheek with some dismay, and wobbled a loose molar. He couldn't pull it out or turn it, and hoped that it would grow back by itself.

Then he gave in to a sudden impulse, draped a towel around his shoulders and located the trimmer in his wash bag. His longish, almost black hair landed on the tiles in front of his feet. He winced whenever the machine came near the cut to his temple and let only millimetre-long stubble remain on his head. He put on the ugly glasses with the plain lenses that he had worn for his visit to the Niels Bohr Institute and studied the result in the mirror. He looked like a lifer from Siberia. The guy none of the other prisoners liked.

The porter eyed him anxiously.

"Have you hurt yourself, Mr. Sander?"

Michael smiled stiffly and spread his legs to ease the pressure on his genitals.

"A brief encounter with a bike messenger," he said. "Please, would you prepare my bill? I'm afraid I have to check out sooner than expected. Family illness."

The woman nodded.

"These things come in threes," she said, and started typing on the keyboard. "Minibar? . . . Movies?"

"One vodka, one gin, two Cokes, one tin of peanuts," Michael forced a smile. "No naturist films."

He paid with his MasterCard and put a banknote on the counter. The woman smiled and the note disappeared.

"You're always welcome back, Mr. Sander."

"Thank you."

He returned to the stairs, thinking that she would probably regret her last remark when she found out about of the state of his room.

On the first floor, he picked up his travel bag and his shoulder bag from where he had left them in a linen cupboard. Then he glanced at the map of fire escape routes and chose the back stairs, which he knew would lead him through the kitchen and out to the back of the hotel. Once outside, he pulled up the collar of his coat and walked briskly towards Sankt Annæ Plads. He kept listening out for measured footsteps behind him and he glanced over his shoulder a couple of times before he disappeared through the glass doors into the new Danish National Theatre.

Tonight's performance was about to begin and he mingled with the excited theatregoers who filled the foyer. He left the theatre through a side exit, a few metres from a cab rank.

The cabbie folded his newspaper and watched him in the rear-view mirror.

"Where to?"

"Good question," Michael said.

The man smiled.

"And what's the answer?"

Was Elizabeth Caspersen still at her office? And if not, then where did she live?

He gave the driver her office address in Bredgade.

The driver didn't move.

"You can walk it in three minutes, mate," he said.

Michael found his wallet and passed a folded 500-kroner note over cabbie's headrest.

"Just drive, will you," he said, "and keep the meter running when we get there."

CHAPTER 37

Michael's eyes were on Elizabeth Caspersen as she walked down the ramp to the underground parking lot, greeted the attendant in the glass cubicle by the barriers and headed towards her Opel. When she got in, she leaned back in her seat, lit a cigarette, and inserted a CD of a piano concerto into the car stereo. She was driving towards the ramp when she spotted him in the back; she screamed out loud and dropped her cigarette.

"Only me," he said. "I was attacked in my room and hoped you'd still be here."

She scrambled around her feet and pedals for the glowing cigarette; found it, burned her fingers, and straightened up with a jerk only a second away from crashing into a concrete pillar.

"Christ Almighty, Michael. What the hell . . . I mean, what are you doing here?!"

He looked miserably at the back of her head and ran his palm across his stubbly scalp.

"Trouble, I'm afraid. They're on to me."

She turned around.

"Then get down and shut up," she ordered him.

He curled into a fetal position obediently and pulled a blanket over his head.

"What happened? . . . Michael?"

"I was careless," he said. "Someone was waiting for me. Someone who decided to use my head as a football. He knew what he was doing."

"But surely you had expected some kind of reaction?"

"Yes, only not so soon. Which reminds me . . . Did you get hold of Charlotte Falster?"

"I've spoken to her. She's going to talk to Lene Jensen and try to persuade her into some kind of partnership. It didn't sound as if it was going to be easy."

"He took everything, Elizabeth," he said.

She turned off at Frederiksborggade and drove along the lakes.

"All of it? What do you mean? Sit up!"

"The location in Finnmark . . . the DVD . . ."

He could see her jaw muscles quiver and her mouth was a tight, red line, but she didn't utter a single word.

"I wish you'd say something," he said.

"I don't know what to say."

"Where are we going?" she asked him after a pause.

"I need a place to think," he said.

"Shit, Michael! Shit, shit, shit."

She banged her hands on the steering wheel.

"I couldn't have put it better myself," he mumbled.

"This was exactly what couldn't happen! This very thing," she yelled.

"I'm sorry. I really am."

"Who attacked you?" she asked.

"I never saw his face, but he wore pointy, black shoes. I have an imprint of them on my abdomen and on the side of my head. The strange thing is that Jakob Schmidt turned up afterwards. He had found out that I had been to his room at Pederslund."

"I thought you were supposed to be clever, God dammit! I pay you 20,000 kroner a day to be clever!"

"Am I fired?"

"Perhaps you should consider getting a real job, in a care home, for instance. Or as a gravedigger. Somewhere you're not constantly outwitted."

"So I *am* fired?"

She shot him a withering look in the rear-view mirror, tossed the cigarette out of the window, and lit a fresh one.

"You're fired when I tell you you're fired. What did Jakob want?"

"I think he had come to beat me up himself. He seemed disappointed that someone got there first."

"I know exactly how he feels," she grunted.

"Incidentally, he told me about your father's vasectomy. Everyone, except you, appears to have known about it. Jakob said his mother had suggested it. He had also noticed a couple of linguistic errors in our letter."

237

"So we can conclude that neither of us is especially clever," she said, taking a deep drag on her cigarette.

"So it would appear."

"What did he really want, Michael?"

"To find out who's going to win. You know him better than I do. He actually looked like someone who wanted to do the right thing."

"I can't see him as a cold-blooded killer, Michael. I just can't. Not Jakob."

"Countless relatives, friends, and acquaintances of cold-blooded killers have said that time and again," he said. "How well do we really know other people?"

She indicated right and pulled up at the curb of a quiet, residential road in Frederiksberg, turned off the ignition, and switched off the headlights.

"Can you spare a cigarette?" he asked, patting his pockets.

She turned around, gave him one, and lit it for him.

"Get in the front," she said. "I'll get a crick in my neck."

He got out and looked up and down the road before he got in beside her and rolled down the window. They smoked in silence.

"So what do we do now?" she asked some minutes later. "And, yes, I'm officially giving you a second chance to prove yourself."

"Thank you. Let's start by looking at the plus points," he said.

"Well, that shouldn't take long," she said after a good look at his battered face.

"What does Victor want?" he asked.

"That's easy," she replied. "He wants to preserve and expand his life's work. Same as my father. Victor is a determined and very vain man. If I play along and back him as the new chairman of the board, I'll be fine . . . if I don't, he'll destroy me."

"And what do *you* want, Elizabeth? I mean as things stand right now?"

She furrowed her brow and looked at him.

"I want the hunters found, Michael. I don't see that your news has changed anything. If what we're both thinking, but not saying, is correct, then Victor knows no more than he already did. There has to be something else from that manhunt. More evidence. I don't know who attacked you, but I presume it was one of the hunters from the film. So the question is, how far will you go, Michael? I know that you have a wife and children, but there is still a job for you, if you want it. And I'm not talking about a trial, but justice. For Kasper Hansen, Ingrid Sundsbö, and their children, and possibly others whom we don't know yet . . . I've begun to appreciate you," she continued. "You've actually exceeded my expectations. If anything were to happen to you, I'll do whatever I can to ensure that your family never wants for anything . . . financially speaking, of course. You can have that in writing, right now, if that helps."

She handed him an envelope with the logo of her legal firm containing an official document signed by her, two of the firm's senior partners and a public notary. The document laid out the terms and conditions for a one-off payment followed by regular payments of a lifelong pension to . . . Michael could insert the names of the beneficiaries himself. There were spaces for three names and civil registration numbers, and he did a double take when he saw the amounts.

"I could do everyone a favour by jumping off Rundetårn," he muttered.

"Oh, I think they would prefer to keep their husband and father."

"I sincerely hope so."

He stuck the envelope into his inside pocket and patted it.

"Lene Jensen is one of their victims," he said. "Or someone who is close to her. My guess is they blackmailed her into stopping her investigation into Kim Andersen's suicide. I don't know if she's married or has children, but this is how they work: they go for your family."

"According to Charlotte Falster, she has a twenty-one-year-old daughter, Josefine," she said. "Do you really think they would threaten a superintendent?"

"They're not ordinary criminals," he said. "They think they're above the law. I have to talk to her."

He rubbed his face and winced when he got close to the cut to his temple.

"I can't think. I need some sleep, Elizabeth. Smoke cigarettes. Drink coffee."

She started the car.

"Were you ever a boy scout?" she asked.

He lowered his hands and looked at her: "A boy scout? Of course I was a boy scout! I'm the last real boy scout there is."

She rummaged around her handbag, found a key, and gave it to him. A lily, the symbol of the Danish Girl Scout Corps, was burned into a small leather tag.

"Both of my girls are scouts so I know a place you can go, and I guarantee that you'll feel right at home."

"A scout hut? I was hoping for an executive flat . . ." he began.

"Man up."

CHAPTER 38

Was it possible to die from grief and guilt? To be eaten up by shame, for it to hollow you out until the shell collapsed, until you turned into something no one wanted to bury or sing hymns for? Lene had prayed. She had said the Lord's Prayer dozens of times while she listened to Josefine's breathing, and the regular beeping of the heart monitor, until the morphine had been washed out of her daughter's body, the pain returned, her heartbeat accelerated and Lene pulled the bell cord.

She had listened to the nurses' and doctors' cautious knocking on the door, their footsteps across the linoleum, and their attention to her daughter, who was sleeping in the hospital bed next to a guest bed for Lene that had been rolled into the ward along with her daughter's. She had turned her face to the wall when they came in because everything was her fault. Her eyes were dry, and chaotic thoughts and images tumbled over each other. They had asked if she wanted something to help her sleep, but she didn't think she deserved rest and oblivion.

She had barely uttered one word all day, but she had heard every word that had come out of Charlotte Falster's mouth. And she was ashamed. She was ashamed that she had made fun of her boss, at her own lack of trust, her inferiority complex, her arrogant attitude towards a bureaucrat who had never had to find dead children.

She was ashamed because Charlotte Falster had been compassionate and patient. She had stood by the window and waited for hours until Josefine came out of surgery. She had spoken to the doctors and translated their information into snippets that Lene could take in. She had brushed over difficulties and complications and focused on the positive: the MRI scan had shown no signs of brain damage. Josefine would be able to see and hear, taste and speak normally again. In time. They had put small titanium braces on her facial bones, so that everything was neatly in place again. In a couple of days the maxillofacial surgeon would measure her for implants to replace the teeth that had been left behind in the warehouse in Sydhavnen. Cosmetically, she would be fine. No one would be able to tell that they were not her own. The Ear, Nose, and Throat specialists would fix her broken nose, and hand surgeons had said that Josefine had suffered pressure lesions to her hands as one would expect, but that all muscle and nerve tissue would return to normal and the bones would heal by themselves.

Charlotte Falster had kneeled down by her chair. One of the doctors happened to touch Lene's shoulder and from then on everyone knew not to get within arm's length of the redheaded superintendent in Side Ward 12. It was said that the superintendent was armed, and moreover there were now two vigilant, short-haired, and very fit young men from the armed response unit sitting outside the ward with machine guns on their laps. Charlotte Falster had seen to that.

Niels had been there and spoken to the superintendent. And cried and cried. Lene had peered furtively at her ex-husband and caught a glimpse of pure, unadulterated hatred even though he was usually the mildest and gentlest of men. He had sat by Josefine's bed for an hour before a nurse had said Josefine needed rest, and had asked both Charlotte Falster and Niels to leave. He had bent over Lene on his way out, and had started to say something in a low, hoarse voice, when the chief superintendent dragged him out of the ward.

Lene swung her feet down onto the floor and went out into the small bathroom. She avoided looking at herself in the mirror, but relieved herself and washed her hands. She drank a mouthful of water from the tap, went back to the window and looked out at the city. The sky was orange and violet; she heard a helicopter preparing to land on one of the other buildings. The navigation lights glowed red, green, and flashing white.

She pulled a chair up to the bed and carefully caressed one of Josefine's bandaged hands. Her daughter's face was discoloured from blood effusions and yellow iodine, and waxy where it was still intact. Lene held her daughter's hand and continued to look at her. She must have dozed off, but woke up when she felt a presence. The bedside lamp was aimed at the floor. Its light was dim and yellow. Lene looked at Josefine's healthy, open eye and watched the pupil expand and seek something in the air. She leaned closer to her.

Her daughter's grotesquely swollen lips moved painstakingly.

"You don't have to say anything, darling," Lene whispered.

Josefine nodded slowly and stubbornly. "Stupid," she mumbled indistinctly.

Her breath smelled of blood.

"I know, darling. I'm sorry."

The head moved from side to side.

"Me . . . Stupid . . ."

Lene had thought she had no more tears left, but she was wrong. They dripped down on her daughter. Josefine's hand moved, tried to free itself and Lene let it go. Very, very slowly it rose up into the air and came to rest softly on her cheek, and something inside Lene broke. She started sobbing.

Her daughter let her hand fall down on the duvet and Lene looked at the broken face. It was calm and the eye was starting to close again. Then it opened and the corner curled very slightly upwards as it always did whenever Josefine smiled. It wasn't much, but it was enough. She knew it would be okay. Josefine was still in there.

Her daughter fell asleep again and Lene got up, folded her arms, and rested her forehead against the cold windowpane. A pigeon with a deformed claw was sitting on the railing outside the window. It tucked its head inside its feathers, cooed softly and closed its eyes.

"Coffee?"

The voice sounded right behind her and a moment ago Lene would have jumped out of the window or shot the silent intruder. But something had changed.

"Yes, please," she said, without turning.

Charlotte Falster was back.

A brown paper cup came past her and was put down on the windowsill. The door to the corridor was ajar and Lene nodded at the other woman in the dark window. One of the bodyguards outside the side ward shifted in her chair. Two women had replaced the men; Lene could see her pistol holster and the elbow of one of them.

"Has she woken up yet?" the chief superintendent asked.

"Yes."

"Did she say anything?"

"'Stupid.'"

Lene eased the lid off the cup and took a sip.

"What time is it?" she asked.

"Ten thirty. Why did they do it, Lene?"

She opened her mouth, but no sound came out. She couldn't speak. She cleared her throat, drank some coffee, and tried again with the same result. The chief superintendent watched her agonized face.

"Can't you write it down?" she asked impatiently.

Lene smiled angrily.

"I can't," she murmured.

The chief superintendent sighed.

"Okay. Then I'll try to reconstruct it for you. Allan Lundkvist was killed by a .22-calibre bullet to his brain. He had been dead for about an hour when you turned up. We almost failed to get him out of the living room. The bees kept attacking the CSOs until one of them had the bright idea of chucking the queens into a corner, so they could get access to the body. There was no sign of a struggle; there were no other injuries and nothing under his nails. We presume that Allan Lundkvist knew his killer."

Lene started to cry again.

The chief superintendent fell silent.

"I'm sorry, Lene. And it's not the real reason I'm here. I'm here because I've had a call from one of my husband's old university friends, someone I haven't seen for years. Her name is Elizabeth Caspersen. It was a very surprising conversation and it was mainly about the man who was here today. Michael Sander. Are you listening? Black hair. Blue eyes?"

Lene nodded.

"It was also a rather frustrating conversation. She was very secretive and I'm not sure that she was being entirely honest. I've checked out Michael Vedby Sander. He was a military police captain in the Horse Guards, and later a promising police sergeant in Hvidovre, before he fell in love with a British girl and moved to London. He was called something else, then. For almost eleven years he worked as a security consultant for one of the big, international security companies over there, Shepherd & Wilkins. They don't hire fools, Lene. They really don't. He now works for Elizabeth Caspersen on some kind of investigation where Kim Andersen's name has cropped up. It turns out that Kim Andersen was a member of a group of veterans from the Royal Life Guards, who went hunting on an estate belonging to her late father's business partner. It would appear some of the group's activities were not entirely ... sound. That was the word she used. And there's another thing. My husband has made some enquiries in the banking world, don't ask me how, but the two hundred thousand Swiss francs that appeared in Kim Andersen's account can be traced back to the West Indies. Kim won it in an online casino called Running Man Casino. It's registered in Antigua and Barbuda and would appear to be legal and above board. The money was paid out via a British bookmaker, so European sales tax has been paid. Like I said, it's legal, but it stinks."

Charlotte Falster paused and sought out Lene's eyes in the window.

"What did Sander say to you, Lene?"

"I wasn't listening."

Charlotte Falster heaved a sigh.

"You'll never learn to trust others, will you?"

"Probably not. Thanks for everything you've done, Charlotte. And I'm sorry I've been such a bitch to you. You didn't deserve that."

The chief superintendent shrugged it off. "I don't think you've been that bad. I've never found it to be much of a problem. You're good, Lene. I wish I had more people like you. Articulate officers who didn't always play the Lone Wolf. The time for that has passed on this occasion."

Lene laughed bitterly.

"True, and now when I really want to tell you something, I can't."

"Let's start over some other time," Charlotte Falster said. "Like I said, I know Elizabeth Caspersen and she knows quality when she sees it, she's generous and she's stinking rich. I'm certain that she picks only the best—including when it comes to private investigators. I'm aware that we don't usually work with amateurs, though in this instance Sander would probably regard *us* as the amateurs."

She put a note on the windowsill next to the coffee cup and hid a deep yawn behind her hand.

"If you think there is any way you can continue with this case, perhaps you should speak to Michael Sander. I don't think it can do any harm and it's okay as far as I'm concerned. His number is on that piece of paper. One of his numbers. Elizabeth Caspersen's private mobile number is there as well. She knows where he is."

"But if I talk to him, they'll find out, Charlotte." Lene gestured towards the figure in the bed. "They'll hurt my daughter again. Not now, perhaps. But some day. One day she won't come home because I wouldn't back down. That was the deal."

The chief superintendent nodded. "I have children of my own, Lene. I'll understand if you don't want to go on. Of course I will, and of course it's all right with me. However, that doesn't really make it all right. I've spoken to my superior and he has promised me full cover from the armed response unit as long as we deem it necessary. That means that they'll watch you and your daughter, 24/7, anywhere."

"Thank you."

"Sleep tight, Lene."

"Thank you."

"I'll just leave the note there, okay?"

"Thank you."

"Well, good night, then."

"Good night."

Finally she left and Lene crawled back into her bed, pulled the duvet up to her chin and stared at the ceiling.

And she looked deeply into herself. She thought about Kim Andersen. About the shiny 9-mm cartridges on his children's pillows. About the choice he made. An old rock song on a CD. His tattoos. *Dominus Providebit*: "The Lord will provide." That was the test she was facing. If she passed it, Josefine would be safe. If she failed it, everything Lene believed in would come crashing down, and Josefine would still be a victim because there would be nothing to stop them carrying out their threats in the future. And she thought about the serious man with the black hair, Michael Sander. And about the Running Man Casino in the West Indies.

And though it was hard, she banished Josefine, Michael Sander, and Charlotte Falster from her mind. Instead, she looked for a flicker of anger in the midst of all her guilt and fears for her daughter, and when she finally found it, she blew on it, carefully, very carefully until it started to glow and turn into a small flame, which she nurtured and fed with thoughts about what she was going to do to the man with the smiling blue eyes behind the leather mask and to the man who had waved her inside Allan Lundkvist's house.

She sat on the edge of the bed for a long time with her face cradled in her hands.

Josefine mumbled something in her sleep and Lene's sweat ran cold in the darkness at the thought of the terrors her daughter's subconscious was fighting. The door to the ward opened and one of the bodyguards slipped inside with her machine pistol raised. Lene looked at her.

"What?"

"You were shouting," the young woman said, and lowered her weapon. She was dark-skinned and had short hair. Indian or Pakistani. Nimble.

"Did I? I'm sorry. I didn't realize."

The teeth in the girl's dark face were very white.

"Is everything okay? I mean . . ."

Lene nodded.

"Everything is okay. What's your name?"

"Aisha."

"I would like to speak to a doctor, Aisha. One who can make things happen. And I'd like to borrow your mobile."

The young woman took a mobile from the thigh pocket of her combat trousers and handed it to her.

"The code is 1882 and I'll get you a doctor. One who can make things happen."

She disappeared.

Charlotte Falster sounded wide awake, even though it was now one-thirty in the morning.

"It's me," Lene said.

"How are you?"

"I'm going to need some guarantees," she said.

"Start talking."

They spoke for a long time. On certain points the chief superintendent was very accommodating; on others she bridled—mainly because there were no precedents for Lene's requests. And they were all expensive and required substantial manpower. But Lene didn't care. It was all or nothing.

Finally, Charlotte Falster promised that she would try.

"By the way, I'm going to need clothes," Lene said, "and some things from my flat. The neighbour has a key."

"I'll go there myself."

"Thank you. And you'll talk to that Caspersen woman?" Lene asked.

"Of course."

Afterwards, she sat down on the chair by the head of her daughter's bed. The sky was getting light, but for some strange reason she didn't feel tired. Adrenaline was a wonderful invention, she thought, but she knew she would pay the price eventually: when the stress hormone ran out, she would collapse like a rag doll. She caressed Josefine's cheek and the healthy eye opened, focused, and recognized her. Again, there was this hint of a smile at the corner of her eye, and Lene breathed deeply and managed with considerable effort not to cry.

There was a knock on the door, and Aisha ushered in a middle-aged man in a hospital coat. His hair stuck out on all sides and the eyes behind his spectacles were dull and red-rimmed.

"I found you a consultant, Lene."

The consultant held out his hand and introduced himself.

"You know her story?" Lene asked.

He nodded. "Of course. I was one of the surgeons who operated on her. She'll be fine. Eventually."

"Can she be moved?"

"Where to?"

"Another hospital."

"Which one?"

She told him, and he left the side ward and returned with Josefine's notes and a nurse. He sat down on the chair by the headboard and read her notes from beginning to end. Then he said, "One moment," and took the nurse outside where they held a whispered conference before he came back.

"We'll send an anaesthetic nurse with her, just be sure, and she'll need blood thinners to prevent embolisms. Excellent place you suggested. I've been there myself. Their people are very good."

"And her nose and teeth?"

"They can wait. In fact it's better to wait until the swellings have gone down. But not so long that the nose grows back crooked, of course. That would be unfortunate. No more than a fortnight, in my opinion. Do you want to go ahead?"

Lene nodded. She wanted to hug him, but felt it was probably not a good idea.

When they were alone once more, she started stroking Josefine's cheek and hair again until her eye opened.

"Thirsty," her daughter murmured, and Lene held up a cup with a spout so that she could drink.

"Thank you."

"Can you hear me, Jose?"

Her daughter nodded.

Lene moved her face very close to her.

"You've always wanted to visit Greenland, haven't you?"

"No."

"Come on, Jose. Of course you have. Who doesn't want to go to Greenland?"

"Not me. Cold."

"Not where you're going, darling."

"Mum?"

"Yes."

The eye closed. Her daughter grunted something without opening it again. "The man. That night at the café. He was waiting for me. And he had been there before."

Lene's eyes were stinging and she gently placed her finger on Josefine's lips. "We'll do it later, darling. You don't have to . . ."

"Yes! The drinks menu. He had oil in his fingers. Ask them if they still have that menu."

"I will, sweetheart. And now I want you to shut up!"

There was a hint of a smile at the corner of her daughter's mouth, but she did as she was told.

CHAPTER 39

At 8:10 the next morning paramedics rolled a bed into a Copenhagen Fire Service ambulance, which stood waiting in the courtyard outside the Rigshospitalet's trauma centre. A nurse in an orange parka, pushing a trolley stacked with monitors, medication, and personal belongings, accompanied the bed. The ambulance proceeded to drive to Copenhagen Airport. It went through a guarded entrance in the steel mesh fence surrounding the runways and continued until it reached one of the Danish Air Force's Challenger 604 aircrafts, fuelled and ready for take-off, on runway 22L. The patient was moved to a transport stretcher and lifted up into the aircraft.

Twenty minutes later, the aircraft was given permission to begin its four thousand-kilometre journey to the Thule Airbase at the far north of Greenland; a base that counted a well-equipped hospital among its facilities. The only people on board were the nurse, the patient, and the two pilots. No flight plan was ever filed.

A hand on her shoulder woke Lene up. She had fallen into a deep, exhausted sleep a few minutes after Josefine had been collected. The knowledge that her daughter was safe and out of harm's way had been like a switch being flicked off.

She lashed out after the hand without opening her eyes, but it returned like an irritating fly. She got the feeling that it had been there for some time. As had the voice.

"Lene!"

"What!"

"Open your eyes."

"Why?"

She opened her leaden eyelids and looked without enthusiasm at Charlotte Falster's face. The chief superintendent looked just as exhausted and her hair was messy.

"I packed your clothes," she said.

Lene sat up and hid a yawn behind her hand.

"Thank you."

"Someone had been to your flat and left the door open so I didn't need to disturb your neighbour after all."

Lene was instantly wide awake.

"I've been burgled?"

The chief superintendent nodded. She positioned herself by the window and folded her arms folded across her chest. She yawned as well.

"Christ, I'm glad I have a desk job," she said emphatically, and Lene couldn't help smiling.

"Well, it's important to know your limitations," she declared.

"But you shouldn't be bound by them," Charlotte Falster said. "And that's what I'm trying to do. Move out of my comfort zone."

"And you have done," Lene said. "I'm deeply grateful for everything you've done for Josefine. I won't ever forget it, Charlotte. Never."

The chief superintendent blushed.

"They didn't damage anything, Lene, but the whole place had been searched." Charlotte Falster hesitated. "There were hidden wireless cameras everywhere."

"So you were filmed?"

"Yes."

Lene shrugged and got up from the bed. "Not that it makes much difference, in my opinion."

"I agree," Charlotte Falster said. "Shall we?"

Lene nodded. "Five minutes."

She took a very hot shower and quickly towel-dried her hair. She stuffed a fresh ball of cotton wool into the ear with the burst eardrum. It no longer hurt and the doctor had said that it would heal of its own accord in a week. If only the blasted howling would go away.

Charlotte Falster had brought her clean underwear, and Lene put it on and brushed her teeth. No make-up. Members of the armed response unit never wore make-up. She stared straight ahead and nodded to the chief superintendent, who dragged the chair into the bathroom. Charlotte Falster wiped the mirror with a hand towel and draped it over Lene's shoulders.

"Are you ready?"

Lene made herself comfortable, looked into the mirror, and nodded grimly.

Charlotte Falster combed Lene's long, damp hair and assessed it critically. Then she grabbed a sizeable handful, held up a pair of scissors and looked at Lene in the mirror.

"Are you quite, quite sure? Some people would give a kidney for a mane like this."

"Do it."

Ten minutes later Lene had a practical, but not terribly well-executed short haircut. She bent her head over the sink while her boss rubbed in the dark hair dye with steady, unhurried movements. There was an intimacy, a warm companionship between them, which was completely surreal given their usual antagonism and reserve, Lene thought. It would end when it became necessary to restore distance and lines of authority between them, but right now they were just two women helping each other in a bathroom.

Once the colour had taken, Charlotte Falster supported Lene's head while she rinsed out the surplus dye with the shower head. Then she took a step back while Lene dried her hair, combed it behind her ears, and looked blankly into the mirror.

"Christ on a bike," she said.

Charlotte Falster leaned her head to one side.

"I think the colour suits you," she said.

They looked at each other.

"When is she coming?" Lene asked, and at that moment someone knocked on the door.

"Now, it would appear."

The chief superintendent opened the door to a woman dressed in the black uniform of the armed response unit. She had short, dark hair roughly the same shade as Lene's, green eyes and regular features; she was 1.75 metres tall and weighed 65 kilos—and her real job was as a senior civil servant in the Rigspolitiet. The woman put a black sports bag, a machine pistol, and a belt with a pistol holster on the floor and quickly took off her uniform.

Lene found a long-haired chestnut wig at the top of the sports bag and handed it and a pair of sunglasses to the now undressed civil servant. None of the three women spoke while Lene put on the black uniform, clicked the belt in place and pulled the strap of the machine pistol across her shoulder. She picked up the sports bag and looked at Charlotte Falster, who handed her a set of car keys.

"White Passat, registration BK 46 801 at Stairwell 3. Look after it. It's my own car."

"I will. Do you have the address?" Lene asked.

Falster gave it to her.

"What's that?"

"A scout hut in Herfølge. He doesn't have a mobile at the moment."

"A scout hut?"

"I suppose that's appropriate. He's a boy scout. Or so he says. The last real boy scout. Good luck."

They looked at each other and there was a suggestion of movement by both of them, an awkward hug, perhaps, but it stayed at the thought.

"He always works alone," Charlotte Falster said with a tiny smile. "And you hate confiding in anyone. You'll make a great team."

Lene smiled back at her, put on the sunglasses, and left the side ward.

She took the lift to the hospital basement, found the right door and opened it with the key card that Charlotte Falster had obtained for her. She carefully closed the steel door behind her and walked quickly through the several hundred metres of the tunnel that connected the hospital with the Faculty of Medicine on the other side of Tagensvej. A tunnel normally used only by porters taking dead bodies to the Institute of Anatomy. At the end she took a sharp left, opened another steel door to an underground parking lot, and found the chief superintendent's shiny, white VW Passat parked close by.

CHAPTER 40

He had spent the night on a rickety sleeping loft in the unheated and gloomy scout hut in a sleeping bag, which would have suited him perfectly if he had been a seven-year-old dwarf, and on a camper mat as thin as paper. Even though he had gone to bed fully clothed, the cold had woken him up several times.

Before he had settled down for the night, he had found a headlamp in a cupboard and searched the hut for something to eat. The result had been depressing. Michael had ended up heating a tin of tomatoes over a Trangia burner, adding noodles and macaroni he had found rolling around in the bottom of a drawer.

It was the dawn chorus in the nearby forest and the sunbeams creeping in between the roofing panels that had woken him up the last time. He had tossed and turned before he gave up trying to fall asleep again, then climbed down the hen-coop ladder on stiff legs to the icy rooms below. He looked around with dismay at the troop's limp flags, a couple of clumsily stretched-out animal hides in frames, and discarded papier-mâché figures, before removing the boxer shorts from his head and the woolly socks from his hands. He rinsed out the tomato tin because he couldn't find any mugs, and lit the Trangia burner. He poured water into a small kettle, put it on the burner and searched for the lemon tea bag he knew was there somewhere. He had hidden it last night so as not to give in to the temptation to drink it there and then.

He saw her come through the trees along the narrow path that led through the forest to the nearby main road with scattered houses and farms. She moved with relative ease, even though the path was deep and slippery, and the black sports bag seemed to be heavy, since her left shoulder hung much lower than her right. She had a carrier bag from a petrol station in one hand

and her face was serious and introverted. The woman was wearing a dark green hoodie, a black anorak, jeans, and sneakers, and Michael had never seen her before. The water boiled and he poured it distractedly into the tin, adding the tea bag to the reddish liquid. The woman pushed the sunglasses up into her short, dark hair and looked straight at him through the filthy kitchen window.

Michael frowned. Then he burned himself on the kettle and suddenly recognized the woman outside. He swore and opened the door to her. The mid-morning sun fell across her head and shoulders and made her seem smaller and thinner.

She stopped on the doorstep and looked at him.

"May I come in?"

"Of course."

She glanced around and measured him from head to foot.

"You look different," she said, without returning his gaze.

"Shall I take your bag?" he asked.

"No, thanks."

"You look a bit different yourself," he said lightly, then went back to the kitchen table. "Tea? Red tea? Tomato-lemon flavour?"

She put the carrier bag on the kitchen table and Michael sniffed the air.

"I heard that you were spending the night in a scout hut," she said. "So I brought coffee and fresh bread. And some cigarettes. My boss says you smoke."

"God bless you," Michael said warmly.

He found the paper cups of coffee and eased off the lids. The aroma was heavenly. The superintendent opened the bags of bread and butter and cut the rolls with a rusty scout sheath knife. Her movements were unhurried and assured and she looked at her hands rather than at him.

Michael buttered half a bread roll, put two slices of cheese on top, swallowed the food, and sipped the still very hot coffee. He closed his eyes.

"Ah, that tastes good," he said.

She retreated to a corner with her coffee, blew on it, folded her arms, and almost looked him in the eye. Michael threw a glance at the black sports bag.

"I had to talk to you," he said. "I'm sorry for bursting into your room at the hospital."

"How did you know I was there? My mobile?"

He nodded, tore the cellophane off the cigarette packet with his teeth, picked out a cigarette with his lips, and looked around for the kitchen matches. He lit a cigarette, inhaled deeply, and peered at her.

"They took my daughter and tortured her," she said. "They made me watch on a computer. I was somewhere else. That's how they work. They push your buttons. My love for my daughter."

Michael nodded.

"I know. Why don't we go outside? I think it's actually warmer."

Outside the hut, directly in the sun, there was a bench made from branches tied together with rope. Someone had truly earned their proficiency badge, Michael thought. He leaned his head against the wooden wall, which was warming up and smelled of tar. Lene Jensen sat down and put on her sunglasses.

They sat in silence for a while before she asked, "Who are you?"

"I'm a security consultant. A one-man band. With one client."

"Elizabeth Caspersen?"

"Yes."

"Why does she need you?"

He looked at her.

"It's difficult to . . ."

"It's all bloody difficult, Michael," she said. "And it's just as hard for me. They told me you work alone, and so do I. It drives my boss up the wall, but as long as I get results, she's prepared to put up with it. At least up till now. It's no longer trendy, apparently."

Michael watched her. She had crossed her arms and her legs and was crouching like a pregnant woman. Perhaps that was how she felt. They really had got to her.

"So what's it about?" she asked.

"A secret," he muttered.

"Everyone has secrets."

His laughter was mirthless. "There are secrets, and then there are big secrets. Trust me."

She sighed. "So it's a big secret. Great. What kind?"

He smiled. "One man's big secret. A family's secret. Or . . . that's what I thought, to begin with. It turns out it's a part of something much bigger. He's dead now, by the way."

"So you've found something out?"

"Yes. Do you know Elizabeth Caspersen?" he asked.

"No, but she appears to know my boss."

"She's a corporate lawyer and Flemming Caspersen's daughter. You must have heard of him. A billionaire. He started a company that produces rangefinders, lasers, and sonars for arms manufacturers all over the world. It's a huge, widely diversified business and they make equipment for fighter jets, drones, satellites, and nuclear submarines. Almost everyone depends on their technology. But he was also a big game hunter. His house is full of skulls, horns, and antlers from dead animals. He's the Pol Pot of the deer family."

"I think I've heard of him. But you say he's dead now?"

Michael nodded.

"He left behind a DVD that his daughter happened to find when she was clearing out his safe. A DVD showing the final minutes of a hunting trip in north Norway. It would appear that Flemming Caspersen had become . . . degenerate. He had lost interest in shooting dumb animals and preferred more challenging prey, i.e. young, fit people who could run far and fast, and were used to the terrain."

"Degenerate?"

"Insane."

"Kasper Hansen and Ingrid Sundsbö?"

"Yes."

Michael was impressed. She had actually listened to him while she sat in that side ward.

"I think I remember their names," the superintendent said. "Wasn't that a couple of years ago?"

"March 2011 in Finnmark. North of the Arctic Circle. They were never found."

Michael closed his eyes. Being warmed up by the sun was wonderful. He could happily have sat here for the rest of his life. His headache was also starting to clear.

"Everything fits," he said. "It's almost too good to be true."

"When something sounds too good to be true, it's because it is," she said.

Michael looked at her with gratitude. "Thank you. Did Kim Andersen really kill himself?"

"Yes."

"You're sure?"

"I'm sure, but then again, he didn't have a choice. Someone had left a couple of live cartridges on his children's pillows and played a CD with an old rock song . . . a song he and his mates sang when they went to war. The message was loud and clear. His trained reflexes kicked in."

"'We Will Rock You?' Queen?"

"Yes. How did you know?"

"It's their song. But why now?"

Lene leaned back as well, and raised her face to the sun.

"He needed money for his wedding. And for presents. It had to be a big do, he had pulled out all the stops. He was terrified of losing his wife. Or he just couldn't wait. He was paid the krone equivalent of 200,000 Swiss francs from Running Man Casino one month before his wedding. He bought his wife a car, a Rolex, and a diamond ring. I think he transferred the money without asking for permission first and they found out."

Michael lit another cigarette and she looked at him.

"This is a trade. You understand that, don't you, Michael? I know that you'll insist on client confidentiality and all that, but we're both here because we're in seriously deep shit. And because it has become personal. They took my daughter. That's unacceptable. I wish I could forget all about it and find a way to move on, but I know that I can't, no matter how much time I give myself. I'll always fear that they might take her again."

"I would feel the same way," he said. "And I'll answer all your questions. Kim Andersen was a Royal Life Guards veteran who belonged to a group of ex-soldiers who took part in a manhunt in north Norway up by Porsanger Fjord. Kasper Hansen was chased over a cliff edge and his wife disappeared. Kim Andersen injured his leg during the hunt. You can see a bandage on the DVD and I'm absolutely sure that he was there."

"The forensic examiners said that he had a gunshot wound to his leg." She nodded. "It was never treated by a doctor. They're certain. He told his wife that he hurt himself falling over a tree while hunting in Sweden. In March

2011. He came back from Afghanistan in 2008, but wasn't treated for depression until June 2011. His wife told me he changed after that hunting trip."

"That would imply the hunters armed Kasper Hansen," Michael said, after mulling it over.

"How very sporting of them," she remarked.

"Yes."

"But why?"

Michael got up and started pacing up and down. "Because they could? Because they were bored? Because they were psychos? Or adrenaline junkies?"

A suggestion of a smile appeared at the corner of the superintendent's mouth.

"Probably all of the above," she said. "Plus, Flemming Caspersen was paying them shedloads of money."

"That's the conclusion I'm coming to. But why did he do it?"

Lene sat for a while before speaking.

"I've learned that men can be extremely vain. They all run marathons these days, don't they?"

"Yes."

"They think they can outrun death."

"Flemming Caspersen did actually run a marathon a few days before he died," Michael remarked.

Lene nodded. "Perhaps killing others reduces your own fear of death? Or maybe there is no explanation, even though we think there has to be one. Perhaps we'll never know."

"What do you mean?"

"First comes motive, then planning and committing a crime. That's what we're used to dealing with, but it's too simplistic in this case. I don't think you or I will ever be able to understand people like them. I spoke to a psychologist at the Institute for Military Psychology the other day. She seemed very insightful. According to her, Kim Andersen and Allan Lundkvist were quite normal, psychologically speaking, even though they had lived under extraordinary conditions and could do extraordinary things."

"Normal?"

"Normal, yes. When measured with the tools available to psychologists, tools devised by normal people. They weren't obsessive or hallucinating, they weren't paranoid or babbling about conspiracy theories, nor were they driven by an urge to isolate themselves—even though Kim Andersen came close. They weren't clinically insane, but even so a normal—or relatively normal—person would find them impossible to understand."

She got up.

"Wait here," she said.

"I'm not going anywhere," Michael said.

A moment later Lene returned with a photograph in her hand. He took it from her and studied it. The left third had been folded back.

"I've seen this picture before," he said. "The other night at Pederslund, a hunting lodge owned by Flemming Caspersen's business partner, Victor Schmidt. Kim Andersen also appeared in some of the hunting photographs there. Royal Life Guards veterans work on the estate as gamekeepers or belong to one of the shooting syndicates. One of Victor Schmidt's sons was an officer in the Royal Life Guards."

"Which one?"

"Jakob Schmidt."

"Is he in the photograph?"

"Perhaps. I'm not sure. They're hard to identity. Who are the others?"

Lene pointed. "Kim Andersen. Suicide. Left of him is Robert Olsen, the guy with the red beard, and next to him Kenneth Enderlein, with the dragon tattoo on his chest. They were both killed in May 2011 by a roadside bomb in Afghanistan. The man to the right of Kim Andersen is—or was—Allan Lundkvist," she went on, "a thirty-five-year-old beekeeper and private first class in the Royal Life Guards. He lived near the RLG Barracks in Høvelte. He was shot through the head with a .22-calibre bullet yesterday. I found him. I was meant to find him. The whole thing was a set-up."

"So that was where you . . . ?"

"Saw my daughter being tortured, yes."

"How many were they?" he asked.

"Two. One killed Allan Lundkvist and beat me up; the other assaulted my daughter in an abandoned warehouse in Sydhavnen. There could have been more of them, of course, I don't know."

"You watched it via an online link?"

"Yes."

Michael nodded. "Right, let's try to do the maths here. Allan Lundkvist is dead, as are Kim Andersen, Kenneth Enderlein, and Robert Olsen. So who is left?"

The superintendent's fingertip hovered over the last man in the photograph. The survivor.

"He would appear to be the only one still alive," she said. "He has a tattoo on his neck. A scorpion. Kim Andersen's wife thought his name might be Tom, but she wasn't sure. Nor did she know if he was even Danish. The photo was taken outside an Afghan town called Musa Qala. Could that be Victor Schmidt's son?"

"Jakob?"

"Yes."

Michael scrutinized the photograph.

"He's standing apart from the others," he said. "Something Jakob Schmidt would undoubtedly do. I've met him. He's a very cold young man. And intelligent. It could be him. It's the right hair colour. And build. He's the right height."

"But you're not sure?"

Michael lowered his gaze.

"No. The gamekeeper at Pederslund is called Thomas. I haven't met him. He runs a safari business. Thomas Berg."

"How many people were on the film?" she asked.

"Seven, including the client."

She nodded and counted on her fingers: "Kim Andersen, Robert Olsen, Kenneth Enderlein, Allan Lundkvist, the man with the scorpion tattoo, and Flemming Caspersen. Who's the seventh man?"

He looked at her and shrugged. "I guess it could be Jakob Schmidt."

"Was he the one who attacked you?"

Michael touched his head and carefully pressed the cut with his fingertips.

"No. But I think he wished he had. He had found out that I had searched his room. The person who attacked me took my computer and the DVD . . . and slammed a door into my head before he left."

"You kept the DVD in your room?" she said in disbelief.

"I was working on it. I had to have it nearby, didn't I? I had hidden it."

"Hidden it?"

"Yes, of course I bloody had."

Michael was aware that he was reddening. He wasn't used to this. Previously, he had always been able to charm people, but Lene was immune. Not one aspect of her was susceptible to that charm, and Michael's vanity was suffering, even though he realized why she was so intent behind her grief. He was beginning to see why you should never come between a female bear and her cubs. It was a bloody dangerous place to be. The hunters had made an incredibly bad mistake by taking her daughter, he realized. They had messed with the controls in nature's engine room. And they hadn't understood how fatal that could be because they were men.

"So we carry on?" he asked.

"What with? You already know who they are."

Michael thought it was obvious: some hunters, some army veterans, and a bloodthirsty, deranged billionaire. A fertile environment for the realization of sick fantasies at an enchanted, isolated castle. A discreet payment route in the West Indies. He could visualize it: the euphoria after that day's shoot and the triumphant display of the bag, the thrill of increasingly frowned-upon masculinity, the lunches, the bragging, the fascination with weapons, and their finely honed skills. Feelings of superiority had flourished under far less favourable conditions.

"I think I do. But there must have been someone higher up who organized it. Have you ever met the man with the scorpion tattoo?"

"I saw him in a car parked outside a hotel in Holbæk where I spent the night after Kim Andersen's suicide. I saw him from the back."

"Were you meant to see him?"

"I don't think so. I went for a walk after dinner. It was a spur-of-the-moment thing."

"Why were you even there, when it was a suicide?"

She looked annoyed. "The wife handcuffed him."

"What?!"

She sighed and yanked a short, dark brown lock of hair in anger. "To attract our interest, I presume."

"In what?"

She looked at him. "In the money, Michael. The change in his personality. The car and the diamonds. She knew something was terribly wrong with

Kim. The injury to his leg. His depression. Part of me totally gets where she's coming from. She, too, was trying to protect her children."

"Have you seen the guy with the scorpion since?"

She hesitated.

"I don't think so. My daughter met a man at the café where she works. She thought . . . well, she believed she was going on a date with him. People in the café must have seen him, but I haven't spoken to any witnesses yet."

"Was he at Allan Lundkvist's place?"

"He might have been. I never saw him. I waltzed straight in and found Allan dead in the living room. Covered by a hell of a lot of bees. I was an idiot."

She described the attack, being naked, the collar around her neck, how it had taken her a long time to knock over the chair, get hold of the craft knife, and free herself. She had called Charlotte Falster, who had found Josefine for her.

"Did you see his hands?" he asked.

"Gloves."

"How about his wrists?"

"I don't think so. Why?"

Michael remembered Jakob Schmidt's distinctive twist of the hand when he pulled back his sleeve to check his watch, and the white mark under the strap on his tanned skin.

"Jakob Schmidt wears a stainless steel Rolex on his left wrist," he said. "He's tanned, but the skin under his watch is white."

He saw her trawl though her memories. Then she shook her head: "No wrists. I'm sure. I'm usually good at noticing things . . . or at least recalling them later . . . when it's too late. Gloves, ski masks. The man who tortured my daughter wore a black fetish leather mask, one of those with a lot of zips. He had very clear blue eyes. Smiling, blue eyes, in fact."

Lene fell silent and Michael watched her closely. The tears crept out behind the sunglasses and trickled down her cheeks.

"You're crying," he said.

"Am I?"

She dried her tears with her sleeves.

"They had added a soundtrack. A song. 'I'm on Fire.'"

"Springsteen?"

"He caned my daughter to the beat of the song."

Michael said nothing.

"I'm truly terrified of them," she said, looking down at her lap. "I am. Their methods really work."

"I'm scared of them too," he said. "And we have every reason to be. But someone has to stop them. If they think they're smarter and cleverer than anyone else, their actions will only get worse. It's inevitable."

She took a deep breath and looked at him with eyes that glowed green like water.

"So you know who they are, you know what they do and have done, you know how they transfer the money, and you almost know who is behind the organization. All you're missing is . . ."

"Evidence," he said. "Though I'm starting not to care very much about the law."

She smiled. "Me neither. But I don't suppose we can just find them and shoot them."

"No," he conceded. "Even though it's tempting."

"I think there might be some evidence in Kim Andersen's cottage," she said. "We missed something when we were there, the CSOs and me."

"What?"

"Their laptop was gone. It would be good to find it. And they have a chimney and a fine lean-to with a perfect log pile—but no fireplace. Only an oil tank. What if Kim Andersen built a place . . ."

"He was a carpenter, wasn't he?"

"Yes."

Michael got up.

"It's worth looking into," he said.

"I agree," she said.

"I presume you didn't walk here," he said.

"I borrowed my boss's car."

"I need to buy some supplies," Michael said. "Including a sleeping bag that fits me."

She put the car keys in his hand. "White Passat, a few hundred metres down the road. Please, would you buy two sleeping bags while you're at it, and do you need any money?"

Michael patted his pocket.

"For once, that's the only thing I have plenty of," he said.

"Shout out when you come back," she said. "Or you risk a bullet to the head. I mean it. And if you see a flashlight, buy it."

CHAPTER 41

When Michael returned to the scout hut a few hours later, laden down with sports bags, carrier bags, and with a rucksack on his back, the bench outside was empty. Nor was Lene inside. He sat down and put his bags on the floor while needle-sharp claws played the xylophone up and down his spine.

He went out into the sunshine and looked around the clearing.

Nothing.

She had told him to call out when he came back if he didn't want to get shot, so he had shouted out his name a couple of times, stood very still and listened to the birds and the distant hum of transmission cables. He walked into the wood and a few minutes later, he found Lene at the foot of a tree in a sunlit clearing—fast asleep.

Michael breathed a sigh of relief and tried to hide his annoyance as he walked up to her. Lene was sitting in between the roots of the tree with her knees pulled up to her chest and a black Heckler & Koch MP5 machine pistol on her lap; the favoured close-combat weapon for all soldiers and police officers. A twig snapped under his foot and the sound was followed by the click of the machine pistol's safety catch being removed—a sound with which Michael was extremely familiar. He now looked straight down the barrel of the gun, which was aimed at a point between his eyes. Over the fore sight the superintendent's eyes were narrowed, but strangely cloudy as though she weren't fully conscious. A finger curled around the trigger and Michael closed his eyes.

"It's me," he said wearily, and held up his hands in front of his face, as if they could stop a bullet. He pressed his eyes shut, turned his face away and waited . . .

The shot never came and he opened one eye very slightly. Lene had got up and was looking at him without expression.

"You should have shouted," she said.

"I did," he snapped.

"Sorry."

His knees were shaking.

She secured the weapon and walked past him with strangely wooden movements.

"I bought sleeping bags," he said angrily to her back. "And a flashlight and a new laptop . . . and a bottle of wine."

"Wine?"

"Châteauneuf-du-Pape."

"And a corkscrew?"

"There's just no pleasing you, is there?"

She didn't reply and carried on walking.

Michael took out his new mobile and looked at the display. The first thing he had done was send a text message to Keith Mallory in London, and the Englishman's one-word reply was: *Contact*. Michael smiled and nearly tripped over a tree root. He tried Sara's mobile and was in luck.

"Hi, darling, it's me."

"I've been calling and calling, Michael. Has something happened to you?"

Her voice was trembling, and Michael knew that she was close to tears and fighting it as hard as she could. Sometimes she succeeded, other times not.

"I'm fine, darling. Really I am. I'm all right."

Lene was swallowed up by the scout hut.

"Are you sure? What happened?"

Michael ran his hand over the stubble at the back of his head and considered various responses.

"I was attacked and someone took my laptop and some other important stuff," he said.

"Attacked? Who by, when, where . . . ? Are you hurt?"

"I don't know who it was, Sara, but it happened last night at my hotel room. The only thing to suffer permanent damage is my pride."

There was a long pause. He could hear only her breathing.

"Michael . . ."

He looked up at the bare treetops. Sara and he had been here before and he didn't want to go there again. Not right now. He didn't have the energy. And he didn't have the time.

"I'm trying, I really am," she said.

"I know you are. You're doing really well, Sara."

"When will you be done?" she asked.

"It'll be some time. Your brother's holiday cottage . . . Could you go there with the kids?"

"Now?"

"I think it might be a good idea."

It wouldn't be the first time he had asked her to leave the house when he thought someone was getting too close. It helped him to know that they were out of harm's way.

"For how long?"

"A week, I think."

"I'm so tired of this, Michael. Really. I'd love to be upbeat, ironic and brave and all that, but quite frankly I'm starting to—"

"Not now, Sara."

"Are you alone?" she asked.

"No, for once I'm not. There's a police officer here. She's trying . . . We're trying to help each other."

"Great," she said in a flat voice, and Michael sighed.

"Cute?" she wanted to know.

"Super-cute. Stop it, Sara."

She sniffed, and Michael looked down towards the hut. Smoke was rising from the chimney. The superintendent had found something with which she could start a fire. Why hadn't he thought of that last night?

"I'll ask him. About the cottage," she mumbled.

"Thank you. That would be good, Sara."

"Take care," she said.

"I love you," he said.

"Bye. . . ."

Michael looked at the phone and stuck it in his pocket. He walked down the path and into the hut. Lene had hammered the cork down the neck of the bottle and was pouring wine into paper cups while holding the cork back with a pen. The wine sloshed into the cup and ran down her hand. She finished pouring and washed her hands in the sink.

"It should be scientifically impossible," she muttered.

"What?"

"For liquid to run upwards."

She handed him a cup and raised her own. "Cheers. Was that your wife?"

"Correct."

She smiled faintly. "I bet you're not easy to be married to. Given your line of work, I mean."

"Probably not. I don't suppose you are, either."

"We're divorced. Do you have any children?"

"Eighteen months, and four years."

Michael took the cup and wandered over to an old oil barrel that acted as a stove in the common room and whose bottom had started to glow red. He positioned himself with his back to it, closed his eyes, and savoured the heat. He was still chilled to the bone, but knew it wasn't purely because of his night in the sleeping loft and the gaps between the roof panels.

Lene sat down on a bench by the wall and ran a fingertip along one of the inscriptions which generations of scouts had carved into the table top. She drank wine and her finger found another inscription.

"Was there any firewood?" he asked.

She shook her head.

"I used some of their banners and animal hides and a chair that was starting to fall apart. It was for the scrap heap."

Michael looked at the empty walls.

"I bet the scouts will be thrilled," he said. "Your daughter . . . Josefine. What's going to happen to her? Will she recover?"

An ominous look flared up in her eyes and she eyeballed him as if he were a cardboard cut-out criminal on a shooting range.

"She'll recover, they say. As far as her soul, mind, psyche, whatever . . . because that's what you're really asking, isn't it?"

"Not just hers."

"No. I know. Thank you. What's done is done, isn't it. You can't turn back time. I don't think either of us can pretend that it didn't happen. Ever. We're not like that."

She rose quickly, walked out into the kitchen, and returned with the wine bottle. She waved it. And he held out his cup.

"Thank you. Is she strong? Mentally?"

"I think so. But her confidence . . . whether she'll ever trust a man again, that's another matter."

She wiped a tear brusquely from her cheek with the back of her hand.

"Of course," he said.

"Let's not talk about it," she said. "I'm shattered."

Michael nodded, and pressed his tongue against the loose molar. He started unpacking the bags on the table while she watched him. He handed her one of the sleeping bags. She opened the packaging, got up, and shook it out. She held it up to her nose.

"It smells good," she said.

"Goose down. The best that money can buy. I bought inflatable camper mats too," Michael said, draping his own sleeping bag over a chair near the stove. "Food. A flashlight. I also bought a couple of T-shirts, which I think we'll both fit. Underwear. . . ."

"For me?"

He held up a pair of white men's underpants. "Large."

"You're saying I have a big arse?"

He looked at her and put the underpants back in the bag. Women. They get everything out of proportion.

Later, she yawned and stretched out while he sat on the chair next to the oil barrel, wrapped in his sleeping bag. They had emptied the wine bottle without him really knowing how that had happened.

"What if you're wrong and there's nothing in Kim's house?" he mumbled with closed eyes.

"I'm not wrong," she said. "What about the man with the scorpion tattoo? Do you think we'll bump into him?"

"I hope not. At least, not yet. He's dangerous. They all are."

"We're armed to the teeth," she said.

"Are we?"

She unzipped the black sports bag and rummaged around for a moment before pulling out the pistol holster and putting it on the table. Michael looked at the weapon.

"For me?" he asked.

"If you like. It's a service pistol with eighteen shots. It's fine, I'll take responsibility."

Michael got up and took the pistol out of the holster, clicked the magazine out into his hand, went through the unloading drill, and looked through the barrel. Heckler & Koch. Same make as the machine pistol. Good, heavy, and ugly. He replaced the clip, stuck the pistol in the holster on the table and looked at it.

"I don't know," he said. "I don't like guns."

She returned the pistol to the black sports bag.

"It's there if you change your mind. How about a siesta? I'm bushed."

"Will you be able to sleep?" he asked.

"Probably not. But I'm willing to give it a try."

He took her sleeping bag and hurled it up onto the sleeping loft.

"How about you?" she asked.

"I'll stay down here and keep watch."

She nodded and disappeared.

Michael stretched out on the bench, still wrapped in the sleeping bag. He knew he wouldn't be able to sleep. He turned on his side and watched the red glow behind the stove's damper. He heard the planks squeak under Lene's feet, a sigh—and then he fell asleep, like a trapdoor shutting.

CHAPTER 42

She had driven for a long time in silence. Michael knew that the superintendent was still angry with him.

"You fell asleep," she reproached him when she woke him up later that afternoon. "You promised you'd keep a lookout."

He had mumbled an apology, but she was frosty and monosyllabic as she boiled water for their Nescafé, and Michael carried their equipment out to the car. They had drunk the coffee in silence and she walked in front of him down the path and drove off before he had time to shut the door.

On one occasion Michael had tried to strike up a conversation, but he hadn't been very successful. While they drove west through the afternoon rush-hour traffic, he had made a half-turn in the seat and sent her stony profile his most infallible wry smile.

"What do you do when you want to go to sleep?" he had asked.

"What are you talking about?"

"When you want to go to sleep. I think of images, scenes from my childhood. An attic filled with old junk, my grandmother's sitting room. She had a grandfather clock that always ticked even though time stood still in her house and I never saw anyone wind it up. What do you do?"

She glanced at him sideways while she made sure to concentrate on her driving.

"I imagine I'm lying on my back on a guillotine looking up at the blade. It falls . . . and just when it hits me, I fall asleep."

"Okay . . . That's . . . very interesting, Lene."

"I'm taking the piss, Michael. It's none of your business what I think about when I go to sleep. I've enough strangers in my head right now. Got it?"

"Of course."

"Good."

One hour later, she stopped in a lay-by with a view of Holbæk Fjord. She turned off the ignition and put her hands on the steering wheel. The lay-by was a few hundred metres from the dead-end road that led to Kim and Louise Andersen's small cottage.

"Do we walk the rest of the way?" Michael asked.

"Yes."

Michael looked at her.

"I could go there first to see if it's safe," he said.

She shook her head.

"It's okay. I just need a . . ."

A drop of sweat trickled from her hairline and down her temple.

They put their bags in the back. Michael took the flashlight and slammed the trunk shut.

"There's a police car outside," he said as they came nearer to the cottage.

"I asked them to keep an eye on it."

She pressed down the front door handle and frowned.

"They must be in the garden," he said.

They walked in the direction of the voices. The young, bearded officer who had first drawn Lene's attention to the missing jib sheet on the dinghy was sitting at a garden table. The dog handler she had met in the kitchen of Holbæk Police Station sat opposite him. The Alsatian was standing in the middle of the lawn, watching them with pricked ears. A yellow tennis ball was lying on the grass in front of the dog. The two police officers looked up, but failed to recognize her.

"It's me," she said, showing them her warrant card.

The bearded officer smiled cautiously. "I see that. Now."

Michael cleared his throat impatiently.

"Has anything happened?" she asked, ignoring him.

"Nothing," the officer said. "Louise Andersen dropped by a couple of times to pick up some stuff. Clothes for the children, that kind of thing."

"How did she look?"

"Sad."

"You can go now. We'll guard the house. In fact, there's no need for you to return. Please, would you tell them back at the station?"

"Of course. But are you sure?"

"Absolutely," she said.

The policeman nodded, and collected the Thermos flask and the coffee cups from the garden table; the dog handler picked up the puppy's water and food bowls from the grass. It had pricked up its ears again and turned its attention to the forest that started behind the meadow. The dog handler watched it. The dog took a couple of paces forwards and emitted a low growl.

"What is it, Tommy?"

Michael looked in the same direction and spotted a roebuck slowly and cautiously making its way to the meadow. Its ears were turned backwards towards the forest.

"I know that roebuck," Lene said.

"You do?"

"It so tame you can touch it. I almost shot it the other night. It was standing right behind me, sniffing me. Nearly gave me a heart attack."

They waited until they heard the patrol car reverse out of the driveway. The branches of the trees were darkening against the deep blue evening sky and the sun hung low. It was a lovely scene, Michael thought. Peaceful. It reminded him very much of his own home. Further down the meadow, the roebuck was foraging.

"Nice place," he said, while Lene shivered in the cold. "But perhaps you're more of a city girl?"

"You could say that," she said, and walked up to the cottage.

They stopped in front of the impeccable log pile,which reached right up to the roof of a well-constructed lean-to, covered with roofing felt, at the back of the cottage.

Michael opened a shed next to the lean-to and saw a couple of large yellow gas canisters. One of them supplied the cottage through a rubber tube connected to a safety valve, while the other was still sealed. He looked through the window to the small, but neat kitchen: gas cooker, round table, two chairs, and two Tripp Trapp children's chairs. Everything ready for the family.

Lene tugged at a beam and ran her fingers along the inside of the lean-to. The sun was sinking fast, and Michael lit the flashlight and inspected the underside of the roof. As far as he could see, there was nothing wrong with it.

"Try removing the log pile," he suggested.

"All of it? There are several cubic metres. There has to be an easier way."

"I don't think so."

Perhaps it really was just a log pile, he thought, and tapped his foot on the concrete floor in front of the lean-to. It made a hollow noise. He went into the garage, edged his way past the dinghy, and found a rusty iron bar lying next to a jack. Michael weighed the bar in his hand. It should be strong enough. He went back to Lene, who was pulling logs off the pile, tossing them over her shoulder.

He bashed the end of the iron bar against the concrete floor, which stretched a couple of metres out into the lawn, and was rewarded with a thudding echo. Lene stopped and looked at him.

"It sounds like a well," she said.

"Perhaps he's hiding a whole family down there," Michael said.

He ran his fingers along where the lean-to met the half-timbered cottage. There was a gap one finger wide between the roofing felt and the wall; odd, really, because rain and other forms of precipitation would seep down behind the log pile and make it rot. He stuck the iron bar in between a beam in the wall and the roof of the lean-to, placed his foot against the wall, and pulled until his head started spinning and he could feel the cut to his temple opening up. The construction moved a little, but something near the ground was blocking it. He wiped the sweat off his brow and looked at the roof of the lean-to.

"I think our approach is wrong," he said. "We don't need to move the log pile; we need to shift the whole damned lean-to. There's some kind of locking mechanism at the bottom. All we have to do is find it."

He kneeled down on the grass and started scraping away the soil where the lawn met the concrete. Lene squatted down next to him to help. She smelled faintly of shampoo and something more bitter. Hair dye, possibly. Michael used the end of the iron bar to dig, and, after a couple of minutes, hit something metallic. He put down the bar and uncovered a black steel ring in the soil under the turf with his fingertips. A flat piece of iron had been welded to the ring and it disappeared into a crack in the concrete.

Michael leaned back on his heels and studied the device.

Lene looked at him.

"What are you waiting for? Pull it, for God's sake! It's got to be some kind of lock."

He nodded and pulled. The ring, and the well-oiled steel mechanism beneath, slipped a smooth twenty centimetres out from the foundation, and she nodded to encourage him.

"What are you waiting for?"

"Do you want to have a go?"

He got up and held out the iron bar to her, but she shook her head.

"Just get on with it."

Michael wedged the bar behind an upright post and employed all his strength.

The entire lean-to swung across the concrete with surprising ease and speed, and he fell backwards and banged his head against the concrete edge.

Lene turned away while Chinese fireworks exploded behind his eyelids. He had bitten his own tongue and felt the taste of blood in his mouth.

Michael rose up on his elbow and rubbed the back of his head with his other hand, looked at his palm, and groaned. If he carried on like this, he would end up in a home for people with brain injuries. Perhaps that wouldn't be so bad after all: peace and quiet, regular meals, and stimulating conversation.

He realized that she was bent double, crying with laughter, and he sat up, rested his forehead on his arms, and looked down between his feet.

Lene eventually regained some measure of self-control, straightened up and turned to him.

"I'm sorry, Michael. You just looked so . . . so incredibly surprised."

She dried the tears from the corners of her eyes.

"That's all right," he said darkly. "It's natural to become hysterical and mean when you've been through what you've been through. I'm really glad you found it funny. That you take pleasure from my pain. Really I am."

She stuck out her hand to help him back on his feet, but he shook his head.

"No, thanks, I'll manage . . . go away. . . ."

"Michael . . . I'm sorry. . . ."

He ended up accepting her hand, and was pulled to his feet. He nearly blacked out and had to rest his hands on his knees while she pushed the construction the last stretch across the concrete.

The lean-to proved to be hinged on one side and fitted with wheels or casters under the bottom planks. A galvanized steel sheet appeared where the lean-to had been. The sheet was hinged on its longer side, which faced the cottage, and a heavy padlock was attached to the side that faced the garden. A channel had been moulded along the sheet to divert rainwater away from the cavity underneath it.

Lene looked at him. Her face had regained its colour and her eyes sparkled in triumph.

"Yes, you told me so," Michael muttered to beat her to it.

"Yes, I told you so," she said contentedly.

He stuck his faithful iron bar through the loop of the padlock and wrenched it open with a bang. Lene bent down, slipped her fingertips under the sheet and tried to pull it upright.

"It weighs a bloody ton," she said.

"Just get on with it."

She glowered at him and lifted with all her might. The sheet crashed against the cottage wall, and they stepped closer and stared into the hole.

Kim Andersen didn't have a family living down there. At most, a couple of woodlice that curled up when the flashlight hit them. The concrete-lined cavity was roughly a metre and a half deep, well-drained, and some kind of metal grille had been cemented into the house wall, which presumably led to a crawlspace or cellar under the kitchen.

Lene held her flashlight while Michael jumped down and lifted out a rucksack made from dark green camouflage fabric.

"Is there anything else?" she asked.

"This."

A small, green money box wrapped in strong, clear plastic. She took it from him and tucked it under her arm. Apart from that, the cavity was empty. He bent down and shone his flashlight through the grille, but couldn't see anything other than a darkness that seemed to continue under the house.

"It's a basement of some sort," he said. "Did you know that it was here?"

"There's a trapdoor in the kitchen floor and a ladder down to a crawl-space," she said. "We didn't find anything down there. Just a few bits of junk, that's all. Water pipes."

"But you didn't notice the grille," he said. "Why don't we carry this stuff inside the cottage and take a look at it?"

CHAPTER 43

Michael discovered a heavy-duty jacket with an arctic-grey, white-and-black camouflage pattern at the top of the rucksack. He spread it out on the kitchen floor and searched its many pockets without finding anything.

Meanwhile, Lene had unwrapped the small, green money box and was going through the kitchen drawers, looking for a suitable tool to pick the lock.

He looked inside the rucksack and pulled out a pair of hunting trousers that matched the jacket, and held them up to the light. Michael was able to push a finger through a jagged hole halfway down the thigh. The fabric around the hole was stiff and dark brown.

"Talking about evidence, this should help," he said.

Lene looked at the trousers, his finger and the two holes in the fabric.

"What else is there?"

"A cap, gloves, ski mask, a headlamp, water bottle. In fact, everything your well-equipped human hunter would need in the Arctic."

He opened a zip at the top of the rucksack and found three folded, plastic-laminated maps in the scale 1:50,000: *Statens Kartverk series M711: Porsanger Fjord, Alta Fjord*. He pinched them between two nails and put them on the PVC cloth on the kitchen table.

"Finnmark," he said tellingly.

"But you already knew that. Anything else?" she asked impatiently.

He glowered at her.

"I'm starting to understand why you work alone," he said.

"Likewise. Anything else?" she repeated.

Michael aimed the flashlight beam inside the rucksack and looked in all the pockets he could find.

"Nothing, I think. Hold on . . . There's another pocket."

He had felt a small zip under his fingertips in the rucksack's waterproof cover piece. He unzipped it and found a single A4 sheet.

Lene tried to force the lid of the money box with a kitchen knife. It slipped and she cut her finger.

"What is it?" she asked, and stuck her finger in her mouth.

"The floor plans of Flemming Caspersen's mansion. There was a break-in a couple of months ago. Someone sawed off the horns of a rhinoceros and ran off with them. They came from the sea at two o'clock at night in a rubber dinghy, cooled the alarm system with liquid nitrogen, and nothing else was taken. The house was empty."

"Horns?"

She furrowed her brow.

"Rhino horns with a combined weight of eight kilos. They sell on the black market for around $50,000 per kilo. If you know the right people," he said.

"Do you think Kim did it?"

"Well, he's got a map of the house showing the alarm system and the location of movement sensors and surveillance cameras."

She wrapped a tea towel around her finger and glared with hatred at the unbreakable green money box.

"Just to steal a couple of horns?"

Michael shrugged. "It's not a bad hourly rate, in my opinion. I wouldn't mind doing it myself, if I knew where to sell them."

"You're no thief," she said earnestly.

"No, I'm not," he said. "How are you getting on with that box?"

"Not very well. I need a skeleton key or something. A crowbar or a screw-driver."

"Do you mind if I have a go?"

"Be my guest."

She pushed the box across the table; Michael got up and hurled it against the floor. The lid sprang up and its contents spilled out.

Lene didn't even flinch.

"Neat," she said. "I could have done that."

"Just taking a short cut," he said and squatted down on his haunches.

The loot was disappointing: a CD in a plastic cover and two colour photographs. Michael placed the items on the table and pointed at the first picture.

"That's Pederslund in the background. And there we have Kim Andersen with a hunting dog and . . . is that him?"

Lene had jumped at the sight of the other man in the photograph: tall, dark-blond hair, broad shoulders, white teeth, dark, possibly brown eyes, open-necked, checkered shirt, oilskin jacket, corduroy trousers and hunting boots. And the end of a tattoo that reached up under one ear: the articulated tail of a scorpion. Michael had never seen him before.

She nodded and gulped.

Michael turned over the photograph: *Pederslund 2008. Max and T.*

"I guess Max is the dog," he said.

"And the 'T' stands for Thomas."

"Yes. When you know it, you can see that he's the man at the far edge of the picture from Afghanistan," he said. "Withdrawn, isn't he? Thomas Berg, I mean."

"Exactly."

"And it's not Jakob Schmidt," Michael said.

The other photograph was blurred and taken from an angle. Part of a hand covered the lens. There was a black, slanted bar on one side of the photograph that must have been the column of a car roof. The picture had been taken late at night. There was a deserted, grey and rain-sodden parking lot in the foreground, and the camera focused on a woman in a red parka, who had just turned into the doorway to a yellow wooden building. She held a rucksack in one hand while holding open the door with the other. Her mouth was halfway through a smile and a word to a lean, dark-haired man behind her. She had smooth, black hair and regular features. Her expression was simultaneously loving and impatient. Her companion was wearing a black parka, had a rucksack on his back and was leaning a pair of cross-country skis against the wall next to the entrance.

Porsanger Vertshus, it said in the red neon writing mirrored in the wet tarmac.

He leaned back.

"Is that them?" she asked.

"Kasper Hansen and Ingrid Sundsbö." He nodded. Everything fell into place at this moment, he thought with a strange melancholy.

He stuck the photographs in his inside pocket and took the CD out of the plastic pocket.

"Shouldn't you have checked for fingerprints before you did that?" she asked.

Michael held the plastic disc at eye level and studied the surface in the light from the lamp above the kitchen table.

"There won't be any, and does it matter now?"

He pushed back the chair and looked at her. Into her green eyes that didn't blink.

"Does it really matter now, Lene?" he asked her again with emphasis. "More evidence, I mean? They did it. The question is what are you going to do about it? Do you want to see them in court?"

"I don't know yet," she mumbled.

She pushed her chair back as well and stared at the floor.

"It's hard," she then said. "Have you ever seen anyone get killed when you could have prevented it?"

Michael felt his face get hot. He thought about the two kidnappers in the Netherlands, and the abandoned farm outside Nijmegen; and about Pieter Henryk's usually kind and youthful face, which had been haggard and grey when Michael, after the rescue operation, had met him on the steps outside the Slotervaartziekenhuis in Amsterdam where his daughter was being treated. The Dutchman's shirt was one size too big and the navy blue coat hung loosely from his shoulders. Henryk had handed Michael an envelope with his fee. He had turned into an old man in a matter of only a few weeks. His eyes were dull, he moved slowly and unsteadily, and his voice was reduced to a crisp whisper.

"Thank you, *mijnheer*. Thank you. Also from Julia, my daughter. Thank you."

"You're welcome." Michael had looked up at the concrete front of the hospital. "How is she?"

The Dutchman dried his eyes with a handkerchief and looked down at the paving stones.

"She was always delicate," he said. "Very shy. A dreamer . . . difficult and artistic. She was a flautist with the Koncertgebouw, Michael. She was a virgin, even though she is nineteen."

"But much loved," Michael said, hoping.

The billionaire inflated his lean cheeks. "Absolutely! When we had time, and it wasn't too difficult to love her."

"Perhaps she'll get over it," Michael said.

"Yes, perhaps."

The father didn't look as if he believed it.

"But I think she'll go insane," Pieter Henryk said.

Michael grimaced.

"What is it?" Lene asked.

"Nothing."

"And what I just asked you?"

"I've done it. I have killed people. And I never regretted it," he said.

"Never?"

"They deserved it. They had lost all humanity. Beyond redemption."

He brought his newly acquired laptop into the living room and inserted the CD.

The disc held numerous files in various formats. Michael clicked on a random file—"Sagarmatha 2006-23-10"—and leaned forwards.

CHAPTER 44

They watched the ninety-second movie and fell silent.

"Johanne Reimers," Lene said at last. "The woman who flew with black kites in the Himalayas."

The young Dane had won the World Paragliding Championship before she started flying with the famous black kites in Sagarmatha, a national park in northern Nepal, not far from Mount Everest. However, in October 2006, she had vanished without a trace along with Ted Schneider, an American photographer from *National Geographic*. Several search and rescue teams had looked for them in vain.

"No one ever found out what happened to them, did they?" she asked.

"Now we know why," Michael said.

Lene looked up Johanne Reimers on Wikipedia and also found half a dozen good photographs of her on Google. Johanne Reimers was smiling in all of them, but was always deep in concentration. She was not only of this world, but also of others. She must have been absolutely fearless, Lene thought, or rather too wise to be fearless. She had had the mental strength to cut through the fear that anyone suspended some kilometres up in the air underneath a thin nylon parachute must inevitably feel, or perhaps the thrill of flying with the kite's perspective, agility, and company was simply too magical to give up.

And it wasn't a freak storm, a miscalculation, a technical malfunction, a gust of wind, or an unexpected hole in the thermal systems that had killed the twenty-seven-year-old woman. It had happened one day in October 2006, on a narrow path carved into the raw granite of the rock face, high above a valley where a silver stream wound its way through the mountain ranges until, a thousand kilometres to the south, it merged with one of India's mighty, holy rivers.

It had rained that afternoon, the rocks were glistening with moisture, the air was dense and grey with humidity, and a stream trickled down the middle of the path. They could hear quick, rasping breathing and see two dark figures stumbling along. Upwards, all the time upwards, following the sharp bends of the path. The man, who had to be the American photographer, called out to the woman in English. Johanne Reimers slipped and fell on her hands and knees; he stopped as well and rested his hands on his side. His face was pale and he was wheezing.

The person holding the camera also stopped. The picture heaved and sank with his laboured breathing.

The American watched the woman a few metres behind him who was trying to get up. Then he looked back at his pursuers on the path and undoubtedly calculated his chances of getting away—with or without her. He staggered back, put his arm around her and dragged her with him with superhuman effort. He continued to stagger upwards, but stopped halfway through his third step when a bullet tore through his chest. His anorak billowed slightly on impact, but his body didn't move.

Johanne Reimers fell to the ground, raised herself up on her hands, and looked at the American. He was rigid and stared straight ahead with puzzled eyes as if he had forgotten something or wanted to tell her something important. She got up on her knees and reached out her hands to him as he slowly fell through the air, across the path and tumbled down towards the river far, far below them.

Johanne Reimers stood up and faced her pursuers. Her arms fell down her sides. Her face was a pale oval and her hair hung in dark, wet strands.

The others copied her and became just as inert and still. Like an audience watching a chamber play. The cameraman didn't move and the camera was steady.

Johanne Reimers furrowed her brow and her gaze became alert; she opened her mouth as if she wanted to ask a question, but then she closed it again. She shook her head while someone loaded a rifle. She walked over to the cliff edge and stared into the abyss.

"I can't," she called out very clearly to them.

In Danish.

The camera zoomed in until her mouth filled the picture.

"I can't," she called out again.

The picture zoomed away from her face with dizzying speed, a shot was fired and Johanne Reimers fell to the ground and stopped moving.

Lene buried her face in her hands. She had recognized the woman's expression from Josefine's one open eye on the computer screen. The emptiness, the lack of understanding. Her own daughter's face slipped effortlessly in place under the hood of Johanne Reimers's anorak when Lene closed her eyes.

"Bastards," she muttered, and stared at Michael's battered, but composed face. Somehow it was reassuring, almost comforting to look at him. He was close and he was real.

He stretched his hand across the table and grabbed hers for a moment.

"What did her last words mean?" Lene asked.

"I think they gave her the choice between jumping into the void . . . or getting shot. But someone like her would never kill herself."

"And they knew it," she said.

"Of course."

"They're insane. Totally insane and sadistic."

"Not according to the psychologists," Michael said.

"I doubt the psychologists have seen this movie," she said.

Michael nodded. She noticed that a nerve was throbbing below one eye. The skin around his eyes was dark and sunken, and he looked just as exhausted as she felt.

"They certainly have an unusual urge to document their cruelty," he mumbled.

"Is it that unusual? It reminds me of those pictures and films from ghettos and mass graves which the Nazis took. Perhaps they met up to view the recordings."

"The Nazis?"

"The hunters, Michael."

"And Kim filmed the killings?"

"What if he wasn't supposed to keep or copy the recordings? What if he only did it as an insurance policy? So that he could expose the others if they threatened him. Perhaps the plan was for the client to have the recording and for the original to be destroyed."

"You're right," he said. "The client's trophy was the recording. That was what they paid for. To own something no one else had."

Michael pulled the laptop across the table and his index finger hovered over the files.

"Another one?" he asked.

Oh, God, no, she thought desperately, but knew very well that she had to. That it was her agonizing duty.

Lene got up and looked over his shoulder at the screen.

"Musa Qala," she said, and pointed to a file. "Allan Lundkvist talked about that place. I believe it's some kind of regional capital in Afghanistan. The Taliban and the Allies take it in turns to gain control of it."

"The picture of the five men was taken outside Musa Qala," he said.

After the dark, wet afternoon in the Himalayas, the desert was very bright. Two of the four soldiers were bare-chested despite the fierce sun, the third was wearing a khaki T-shirt and shorts, and the fourth had a loose uniform shirt hanging outside his baggy camouflage trousers. All of them had chequered, black or red partisan scarves—keffiyehs—tied around their necks or faces because the desert wind whipped up sand and dust from the empty, white road and the bleak, scorched fields.

Lene recognized all four of them: Robert Olsen, Kenneth Enderlein, Allan Lundkvist, and Thomas Berg.

The camera moved in a restricted arc and the recording was speckled with green reflections.

Michael pointed to the shadow on the road in the foreground.

"A Humvee," he said. "A light armoured vehicle with a heavy machine gun on its roof. The cameraman is filming from inside the vehicle. The reflections are from the bullet-proof windows."

The four men were armed with automatic carbines, which they never put down. Two were deep in conversation in the foreground while the others squatted patiently in the shadow of the Humvee without talking.

In the distance, blue wood smoke hung over a cluster of low, clay houses with flat roofs, which were the beginning or maybe the end of the town called Musa Qala. A narrow, green ribbon crept past the buildings and lost itself in the horizon. They could make out some scrawny scrub and bushes growing along the river.

"What on earth do people live on in a place like that?" Lene wondered.

The soil looked as if it couldn't support thistles.

"Opium and goats," Michael said.

Lene pointed to one of the two standing men.

"Thomas Berg," she said.

"Talking to Allan," he nodded.

"They're waiting for someone," Lene said.

The two men stopped talking and turned towards the desert. The other two got up and dusted themselves down. One of them tossed a pair of binoculars, which Allan Lundkvist caught in mid-air and held up to his eyes. The camera zoomed in on the tall, swaying column of dust balancing on the heat haze in the distance. At the bottom of the column something white was moving swiftly. The men got ready.

They loaded the carbines and one of them—whom Lene recognized as Kenneth Enderlein—went back to the Humvee. He opened the door and flashed a broad, white grin at the camera before pushing his way past the cameraman. You could see his legs and boots. A bolt was pulled back and released with a bang.

"He's standing in the gun turret," Michael informed her. "And he has just loaded his machine gun."

The white dot grew larger and turned into a Toyota pick-up that seemed to sail across the road in the shimmering, metallic heat.

None of the soldiers spoke to each other. Everything seemed practised, unhurried, and routine. The man with the scorpion on his neck raised his hand and waved to the pick-up, which was approaching at high speed. His muscles rippled under the tattoo when he called out something incomprehensible by way of greeting. An arm came out of the Toyota's side window and waved back. The arm stayed outside and a brown hand tapped the warm, white car door in time to the music from the car radio. The car skidded to a halt on squealing, worn tires. The white column of dust travelled on, overtook the car, and dispersed.

"They're nervous, but don't want to show it," Michael said, pointing to the two people in the pick-up.

"They have my sympathy," Lene said in a hollow voice. There was something ominous and inevitable about the soldier's movements. They were natural born killers, she thought, and no longer of this world.

Allan Lundkvist also greeted the new arrivals and in the same movement pulled his red chequered scarf over his mouth and nose and tightened it. His sunglasses were silver and reflected the surroundings. He looked at his partner for a moment and then he nodded.

They walked up to the pick-up, which had no registration plates or other identifying features. The two middle-aged men in the Toyota were dressed in traditional, loose-fitting, and baggy Afghan clothes. They got out with the engine running and the atonal music continued to blare out from inside the car. White turbans, black waistcoats, Kalashnikovs strapped across their shoulders, broad smiles. The smaller but sturdier of them wore black sunglasses. The men embraced each other. The four of them appeared to communicate without difficulty in a mixture of English, Farsi, and gestures. The taller of the two Afghans had a short, black beard, a sharp, birdlike face, and narrow, dark eyes. He looked at the Humvee, spotted the camera and the man holding it inside the vehicle and started gesticulating while a stream of angry words poured from his mouth, which had only three teeth. He covered the lower half of his face with one end of his turban. Allan Lundkvist placated him with smiles and gestures. The smaller of the two Afghans didn't seem to mind being filmed. He waved to the camera and took out his own mobile to photograph the Humvee. The two Danish private first class soldiers watched him. Their smiles had frozen.

"He shouldn't have done that," Michael said.

"Taken the picture?"

"He's mad. What an amateur."

"What are they doing?" Lene whispered, and wondered why she was whispering, but somehow it seemed appropriate.

"Raw opium. Afghanistan is the world's biggest exporter. How do you think it gets out of the country? They fly it out with damaged equipment, with the wounded, or in sealed coffins with dead soldiers."

Michael was whispering as well.

"Are those goats at the back of the truck?" she asked.

They could hear a faint, tremulous braying from the densely packed, long-haired animals behind the barred sides of the pick-up.

"Camouflage."

The Afghan with the bird-of-prey face pointed to the back of the pick-up and his stocky companion leaped with remarkable agility over the side, forced his way through the noisy, skinny, and filthy goats and started passing down small brown bags. Allan Lundkvist and the man they knew as Thomas Berg took the hessian sacks and stacked them in a pyramid on the ground. The man on the pick-up lifted up an animal by its horns and threw it to the back to make room.

"Poor creature," Lene muttered.

"Twenty-four sacks," Michael said.

The short, stocky Afghan jumped down from the pick-up, and his Kalashnikov swung round in its shoulder strap and hit him in the face. For the first time his companion let his guard down. He threw back his head, laughed out loud, and slapped his thighs.

The two Danes didn't move a muscle.

Lene held her breath. She expected that blood would be spilled at any moment, but the clumsy opium smuggler merely rubbed his bearded cheek and joined in the laughter. She remembered reading that the ordinary Afghan was the most hospitable, humorous, and lovable person you could hope to meet. Hospitality was a sacred duty and whoever showed a stranger the door or turned his back on him was the lowest creature on Earth.

Michael put his hand on her forearm.

"Something is wrong," he muttered. "Who the hell is that?"

A fifth soldier had appeared on the scene. He was carrying two aluminium boxes that looked heavy. He put down the boxes in front of the group and greeted the smugglers, who appeared to know him since a round of fresh handshakes and brief embraces followed, and they showed no surprise at seeing him. The new arrival positioned himself next to Allan Lundkvist while Thomas Berg, as usual, stood slightly apart from the others.

The man turned around. Long hair, desert hat, long beard, the usual sunglasses, but his naked upper body was covered with easily recognizable tattoos. The camera swept across the tableau and zoomed in on the opium sacks.

"Kim Andersen," Lene said.

"Yes. So who the hell is inside the Humvee operating the camera?"

"No idea. The fifth man, it would seem," she said.

"The sixth."

"Yes. Thomas Berg, Kenneth Enderlein, Kim Andersen, Allan Lundkvist, Robert Olsen and . . . ? How many were there in Norway?"

"Seven, including the client. If we presume that Flemming Caspersen was the client at Porsanger Fjord, I'm missing a sixth man. We're one short."

"Jakob Schmidt?"

"Good question," Michael said, and pointed at the screen. "By the way, I think they're nearly done, poor fools."

Kim Andersen unlocked the boxes and flipped open the lids. The two Afghans looked inside and grinned to each other. Again they shook hands with the private first class, who closed the lids and helped them carry the boxes to the pick-up. He passed them up to the stocky smuggler who had jumped up on the back of the pick-up again.

"What's in the boxes?" Lene wanted to know.

"Some kind of military hardware. Plastic explosives, hand grenades, rocket equipment, night vision goggles . . . stuff like that. Stingers."

"And it'll end up with the Taliban?"

"I can't think of any other buyers, can you?"

She looked Michael in disbelief.

"So they sell weapons and get paid in opium? Weapons that will end up being used against themselves or other Danes? Or their allies?"

He let out a weary sigh.

"I don't think they're going to get that far, Lene. Either they'll get mowed down in ten seconds, or the Danes have agreed with the CIA or MI6 to hide an electronic tracker in the boxes which can lead Special Forces up through the food chain. Or they'll detonate the explosives in the boxes remotely when they have got away. My money is on the latter."

"My money's on the first," Lene said, looking at the screen. "Look at Thomas. And how the hell do you know that?"

"Military Police. I was a captain. I'm not a complete amateur, Lene."

The tall, sturdy soldier scanned the sky through his binoculars as the white pick-up started driving back to the road. Once again, the passenger's brown hand beat the side of the car rhythmically and the music from the car radio mingled with the braying of the goats. Thomas Berg turned to the armoured vehicle and ran the edge of his hand across his throat.

Michael gulped.

Twenty metres. Thirty. Dust started rising from the wheels of the Toyota, the hand in the white sleeve waved goodbye and they could hear an electric hum close to the camera's microphone.

"The machine gun," Michael said, and Lene jumped when the salvo exploded from the laptop's speakers. They saw the individual bullets hit the white road. They caught up with the back of the pick-up, went through the animals and reached the driver's cabin. The shells ate the car. The frame wobbled and shook in time to the long machine-gun salvo. The Toyota keeled over; for a moment its rear end seemed to hover above the road, before the car skidded diagonally down the high verge and slowly, tragically slowly, turned onto its side.

"Jesus," Michael said while Lene instinctively covered her ears with her hands. Her bad ear was ringing. The film was shocking, but she couldn't take her eyes off the screen.

The man with the scorpion tattoo walked through the dust cloud, jumped across the ditch, and approached the upturned car. A couple of metres behind him, Kim Andersen appeared with his service gun at the ready. They instinctively avoided each other's firing lines.

By some miracle, the car radio was still working somewhere inside the wreckage. A few fortunate goats scarpered noisily across the bare fields; others lay still next to the Toyota or had been crushed under it. One animal with a broken front leg hobbled towards the soldiers. Small flames from the engine started to lick the car. Kim Andersen aimed his gun and shot the goat through its head. He said something to his colleague, who laughed.

There was movement on the driver's side of the car and the lean opium smuggler elbowed his way up through the side window with considerable effort. He cut his hands on the window frame and they started bleeding. His turban was gone and his long, blood-stained hair had come loose and was falling across his face. He said nothing, but fought gravity with silent, grim determination. He had managed to free his upper body and twist, so that he could pull himself out by holding on to the undercarriage, when Thomas Berg reached him. The Afghan turned his face towards the Dane and hung without moving, half in and half out of the car. No expression.

Thomas Berg stopped a few paces from the smuggler, took out his pistol from his hip holster, flicked aside the safety catch and assumed the classic shooting position with legs astride and his arm fully outstretched. He sent a bullet through the smuggler's head at close range. The man's head was flung backwards; his body straightened out like a rubber band before flopping down, while the glass in the window frame held it in place. The Dane looked inside the car and fired two shots in quick succession—probably at the trapped passenger, the fat, cheerful one.

Kim Andersen recovered the two aluminium boxes some distance from the crashed Toyota, tucked one under each arm, and walked back to the Humvee and the camera.

"You were right," Michael said.

Lene shook her head: "I don't understand how that can happen. That they're prepared to run the risk. I thought the sky was packed with drones, planes, and satellites scanning every corner?"

"It's a bloody big country," Michael said slowly. "Firstly, the soldiers probably know the flight plan and positions of the drones and the satellites, secondly . . . well, secondly, it's a bloody big country. If it really was possible to watch every inch of it from the sky, the Taliban wouldn't be able to plant a single roadside bomb."

"What's he doing now?" she asked.

"Covering his tracks. With a shock grenade."

Thomas Berg had unscrewed the cap on the Toyota's listing petrol tank, which was gulping its contents down on the ground. He walked away from the wreckage and tossed something that looked like a white beer can in a lazy arc towards the trunk of the car. Then he covered his ears and closed his eyes.

They heard a sharp bang followed by a blinding white light and the Toyota was engulfed in flames.

The film ended and Lene wanted to throw up.

"He's unbelievably inhuman and callous," she mumbled. "I thought I'd met my fair share of psychos, but that one . . . Thomas."

"He's bordering on unique," Michael conceded.

"Have you ever met anyone like him?" she asked.

"Yes."

"What did you do to them?"

He shrugged his shoulders. "Either I worked for them or I fought them. One or the other."

"I feel sick," she said.

"Would you like a glass of water?" he asked.

"Yes, please."

He went over to the kitchen sink and opened a couple of wall cupboards before he found a water glass. Lost in thought, he held his finger under the tap, waiting for it to get very cold. Lene studied his profile. He was gazing out of the window when he suddenly straightened up. His eyes narrowed and he leaned forwards. Something luminous and white like a shooting star flew past the window and crashed into the outside wall.

Michael spun around and opened his mouth, but Lene never heard his warning. He placed a hand on the kitchen table and scaled its entire width. Lene had never seen anyone move so quickly and with such coordination. He hit her mid-chest as she was about to get up, and they fell to the floor, tangled up in each other. Michael's face was a few centimetres from hers. He looked down at her, opened his mouth and shouted something about the gas canisters outside, a fraction of a second before everything exploded, the kitchen became a bell jar of fire, and a big, hot hand flung them against the wall.

They flew through the room, along with the furniture, and she couldn't breathe, didn't know which way was up or down, if she was dead or alive. She must be dead, she thought and was grateful because everything had turned bright and warm and then all of a sudden it grew black, everything hurt, and the air she inhaled into her lungs was scorching—so blistering that she must still be alive, but even so she longed for the beautiful light.

CHAPTER 45

Michael was blinded and it terrified him. He dug his fingers into his eye sockets and sobbed with relief when he was able to scrape away a sticky mess and see again. He looked at his hands, but couldn't work out what had covered his eyes. Dust, mortar, or blood? Or perhaps a mixture of all three. Lene was soft, hard and warm underneath him.

He got up on his hands and turned his face in the direction of the garden. The wall was gone. The trees outside were lit up by the flames that were consuming the cottage and he could see stars above the trees. Determined armed figures walked slowly across the lawn, blurred shadows at first, until they turned into two men wearing sophisticated camouflage clothing and ski masks. They carried military carbines in their hands.

He heard a dry crack from the beams as they gave way above him, and the sky, the trees and the killers were erased by a cloud of embers when the lean-to collapsed in front of the wall that had been blown away. The heat was indescribable and he could feel his eyebrows and eyelashes burning. Lene looked at him with wide-open eyes. Her mouth was also open and he realized that she was talking to him, but he couldn't make out the words. He got up on his knees and then onto his feet, pulled her upright, put his arm around her, and spotted the doorway to the living room in front of them.

"Out!" he shouted.

She lashed out at him and he nearly punched her until he realized that she was trying to extinguish the embers on his shoulders and his head. They stumbled through the doorway into the cooler living room, where Lene bent double and coughed and spluttered while Michael got the first mouthful of air into his lungs after what felt like forever. He looked back over his shoulder. The kitchen was an inferno. The glowing mass that was the thatched roof had cascaded into the gap left by the missing wall and was obscuring his view of the killers.

He grabbed hold of her hand and they staggered through the living room towards the sanctuary of the porch, where the windows overlooking the garden had been blown in. With a strange sense of detachment Michael noted a perforated stripe being drawn across the white wall. Fountains of plaster and brickwork erupted at waist level and came towards them at speed. Glittering shards of glass flew through the room.

"Get down!" he shouted, and kicked her feet away from under her.

With deep sighs the bullets passed right above their heads. He covered her with his body and pressed her face against the floor. They were trapped between the fire and the killers' automatic weapons. Every thought of escaping through the hallway, the children's bedroom or the bathroom was dead in the water. Lene turned over underneath him. Her face was powdered with tiny glass fragments which he carefully brushed them away from around her eyes with his fingertips. She opened her eyes and looked up at him. The flames changed her irises from green to twinkling gold.

"What do we do?" she asked. "What happened?"

"They threw a stun grenade or a hand grenade at the gas canisters," he said. "Now they're waiting for us outside."

"So what do we do?" she asked calmly. She tried to get up, but he kept her pinned to the floor.

Michael ducked as a new salvo was fired from the meadow to the right of the house. The old half-timbered cottage and the wall offered little resistance against the bullets, which tore another dotted line across the living-room wall.

"Back to the kitchen," he said and started moving backwards and away from her on his stomach.

"What?! Are you out of your mind!?"

He crawled back to her and put his mouth right up to her ear.

"If we stay here, we'll die! The basement. Now!"

He grabbed her by her jacket collar and dragged her along. The kitchen was a wall of fire and sparks flying in the draught created by the hole in the wall and the broken windows in the living room. The smoke was a thick carpet above their heads and sent tears streaming down their faces. Michael coughed in spasms and couldn't stop, and yet he continued to make his way to the doorway. Finally, his obstinate companion started working with him rather than against him. He got up on his hands and knees and pulled her level with him.

"Grab hold of my foot! Take a deep breath, close your eyes and follow me, Lene, now, it's our only chance! Understand?"

He blinked away his tears and could see that she nodded with her eyes closed. She breathed in.

The heat was dense and textured like a wall. Michael pushed aside tables and chairs and burned his palms; his eyeballs dried out and shrank in the fierce heat and he struggled to see. It was Lene who located the iron ring that was sunk into the floorboards and who managed to raise the heavy trapdoor to the crawlspace under the kitchen. She must be incredibly strong, he thought. She slid down the short ladder on her stomach and Michael followed right behind her.

There was air down there and they curled up, coughing, pumping oxygen to their lungs while the tears flowed. He was able to see again and gazed at the white trails that the tears drew down her sooty face. Her hair was still filled with glass fragments. The floor groaned and warped above them when more of the roof fell into the kitchen and a cloud of sparks landed on Michael's back. He instinctively rolled onto the concrete and threw his shoulders against the floor to extinguish the embers. Lene pulled him towards the wall and away from the trapdoor.

He hawked, spat soot out of his mouth, and got up on his hands and knees.

"I've got to get back up there," he grunted.

"What?! What did you just say?"

"Got to go back up. The CD."

"*No!*"

He pulled off his anorak and wrapped it around his head. She tried to restrain him, but he pushed aside her hands and began climbing the ladder. The top steps were on fire.

Michael raised his head up above the floor and felt like a clay figure in a kiln. He watched the hairs on his hands curl up and fall off. The once white kitchen walls were blackened, golden and ablaze. He hadn't known that stone and mortar could burn like that. He stuck his head back down in the basement, swallowed a mouthful of air and went back up straight away because he knew he would never be able to do it if he allowed himself time to think. He crawled across the black, smouldering floorboards and spotted the computer under one of the Tripp Trapp highchairs. Without thinking he reached for it and howled in agony when melting plastic stuck to his fingers and palms. He grabbed a tea towel, wrapped it around the laptop and dragged it back to the trapdoor. Michael had almost reached the ladder when something heavy and burning crashed down from the roof and landed diagonally across his shoulders. He couldn't move and knew that the clothes on his back were on fire. He pushed the laptop towards the opening and spotted Lene's face in the gap.

Michael stared at her, and signalled that he very much wanted her to take the damned laptop, disappear with it, and leave him to his fate.

Small, blue flames started frizzing her hair, but she reached her arms across the floor, got a hold of his shoulders and the anorak around his head, and dragged him across the floorboards and down through the hole. The trapdoor slammed shut behind them.

He hit the concrete floor in the basement headfirst and was granted a few seconds of merciful darkness. He desperately wanted a break, some peace and quiet, but it was not to be. She was just as brutal as he knew she would be. She kept hitting him on the back with the palms of her hands; she pulled the anorak off his head and continued putting out the flames in his shirt and hair.

"Leave me alone," he mumbled.

She wouldn't appear to have heard him because he was dragged further into the darkness and laid down along an end wall where there was still a small amount of oxygen. Then the indefatigable superintendent started bashing the water pipes under the ceiling with a hammer she must have found down there.

A dazed Michael watched her efforts uncomprehendingly until she suddenly cried out in triumph. Something metallic gave way with a welcome bang and cold, wonderfully cold, water splashed down in a wide, hard stream from the broken water pipe. He elbowed closer, stuck his face under the water and let it wash over his back.

He had never been this close to paradise before and knew that he never would be again.

Lene sat with her back to the wall. She had pulled her knees up to her chest and poked her head straight into the jet. She smiled. Michael smiled too. The water rose and it was black and filled with golden reflections from the fire raging above them because strips of light fell through the floor planks. It was the most beautiful sight he had ever seen.

Then he rolled onto his back and sat up.

The laptop.

He looked around frantically and spotted it on an old crate. He put it on his lap, out of the water's reach, opened the lid, and saw with almost religious awe the little lamps and buttons glow white and blue under the keyboard.

He clicked the CD out of the drive and looked around for something that could protect it from the fire and water. He emptied a plastic bag of old toys, carefully wrapped the bag around the disc and his wallet, and stuck it into what was left of his anorak. The water now reached to his knees and poured foaming white from the broken pipe with remarkable force. He drank a little from his cupped hands and looked at Lene who was still sitting up against the wall, now resting her chin on her chest and with her eyes closed.

"Thank you," he said.

She raised her head and looked at him. Her face was ghostly white and occasionally golden when the reflected flames danced across it.

"You're welcome," she mumbled. "How did they know we were here?"

Michael flinched instinctively every time something heavy hit the floor above him. He reached out his hand and touched the rough floorboards with his fingertips. They were warm, and the ladder below the trapdoor was steaming, hissing and contracting.

"Your boss's car," he said. "I was an idiot; I should have checked it for GPS transmitters."

"So they could have attacked us in the scout hut while we were asleep. While *you* were asleep!"

He shook his head. "They had no reason to harm us until we found Kim Andersen's hiding place. In their own insane way they're rational, so they must have been disappointed that they failed to scare you off."

The water now reached up to his armpits. He let his hands glide through

298

it and clenched and unclenched his fists. Right now they didn't hurt, but he knew that the pain would return later when they dried.

"I'm thinking of something," he said a little later. "Or rather . . . two things, Lene."

She smiled. She actually had a lovely smile, he thought.

"Two things? Well done, Michael."

His hands were like two white fish in the black water.

"Yes. One, we're going to drown shortly, which is ridiculous, and also really rather embarrassing. Drowning in a burning house—I mean, who does that. Wouldn't you agree?"

Lene considered it before she nodded. The water now reached up to her chin.

"It *is* a bit ridiculous, Michael. What was the second thing?"

"I don't understand why we can still breathe. It shouldn't be possible because the fire should already have consumed all the oxygen down here. Technically, we should have died a few minutes ago. At least."

He pulled one hand out of the water and looked at it. It dried faster on one side than the other. Down here in their sanctuary there was a draught. Above them the fire sucked up all the oxygen there was, but it also drew fresh air through the crawlspace from another source.

"Perhaps we should turn off the water," she suggested.

"Yes, if you would be so kind." He nodded amicably and lifted up his chin. He was floating now and his forehead bumped against the warm floor planks above him.

Armed with her hammer Lene made her way through the water. She located the broken pipe and covered the hole with her hands. The water flowed with undiminished force past her palms. She tried pressing the handle of the hammer into the pipe, but the pipe simply broke off near the wall. The pipe would appear to have been badly corroded.

"It's not going very well," she said.

"If you try to locate the grille," Michael said, "I'll try to stop the water."

She nodded and moved slowly through the black and orange water with her nose above the surface. There were only ten centimetres between the water and the burning kitchen floor.

Michael covered the pipe stump with his hands and managed to stop the flow, but water continued to seep in from the crumbling wall in several places. He fumbled for anything he could find in the water and got hold of some wet newspaper which he squashed into a ball and pressed against the hole where the pipe used to be. He couldn't turn around, but he could hear Lene gurgle as she bashed away at the wall at the end of the crawlspace.

"I think you need to hurry up," he called out in desperation.

She made no reply, but started hacking at something that resisted. Michael stretched out in the water, succeeded in pressing the soles of his feet against the opposing wall and forced the ball of newspaper into the open pipe until his arms quivered.

"Now!" she shouted.

He closed his eyes, gritted his teeth and kept pushing. There was no more clear space in the basement, they were both underwater and the only air he had left was in his lungs. He could feel air bubbles seep from his nose and disappear past his eyes and forehead. His badly scorched lungs stung, and strange visions started playing at the back of his eyelids. His arms let go, he flapped impotently through the water, but he had neither the energy nor the willpower to find the pipe again. His oxygen-starved brain was shutting down in preparation for unconsciousness and the great darkness. He thought about Sara, their children running across the lawn in front of their house, and he smiled to them from the garden gate, the warm sunshine, he would just wave to them and then be on his way . . .

Michael gulped helplessly and could do nothing but take the last, big, final breath which would fill his lungs with water.

But it wasn't cold water that flowed into his empty lungs; it was air—lovely, lovely, sooty, warm, and filthy air, that couldn't have tasted any better if he had been in the Alps. He tried breathing again and more of it came. Lots.

He opened his eyes, kicked off with his legs, and drifted down to Lene's head.

Michael embraced her wet figure and, little by little, his embrace was reciprocated. Just.

Her eyes glittered yellow and green, but her face was waxy, and her teeth chattered from the cold.

She took his hand and guided it to an opening in the wall. Somehow, she had managed to tear out the grille between the crawlspace and Kim Andersen's hideout, and smash through part of the breezeblock wall, so the water could drain out of the basement.

"The water is no longer rising," she called out.

"Can we get through there?" he asked.

She pressed the hammer against his chest under the water.

"Your turn," she said.

The remains of the roof collapsed with a boom that could be felt through the soles of their feet. Sparks whirled up against the dark sky and were snapped up by the light breeze. The sky was orange and deep blue. The two men in the forest heard the sirens in the distance and saw the first orange and blue flashing lights through the trees.

"They're finished," the taller of them said.

"About bloody time," the other said. "Let's get out of here."

He pulled a mobile out of his pocket and looked at the screen.

"It's a client," he said. "An Englishman. Norwegian ancestry. Magnusson. An oil man from Aberdeen. Big shot. Filthy rich."

"Has he been checked out?"

"Of course."

They started walking. They still carried their automatic carbines ready and loaded. The barrels were smoking hot.

"What does he want?" the smaller of the two men asked.

"One, preferably two."

"Where?"

"He likes Norway and Finland. Alaska, possibly."

"Let's find him a treat," the other said. "Fancy a trip to Norway?"

CHAPTER 46

"Is that her? Kim's wife?" Michael asked, and hugged himself tightly. The shivers came and went. Right now they were very violent and he could barely talk.

"That's Louise Andersen. Kim's widow. And her children."

Lene was also shivering like a wet dog.

The cottage was still burning under the long cascading jets of water from the fire hoses. Wherever the water landed, sparks flew and white steam rose towards the sky, which was cloudless and clear.

He leaned against the nearest tree and watched a young, slim woman, with two small children pressed against her legs. The younger, a girl, had wrapped her arms around her mother's legs and refused to look, while the boy stared numbly at the fire with a thumb in his mouth. The woman just stood there, her face impossible to interpret in the flickering light.

The ambulance had left and the bearded police officer and the dog handler stood with their hands in their pockets, saying nothing—silent, black silhouettes against the flashing blue light from the patrol car.

Finally, the last big flames began to die down. Clouds of sparks settled on the ground, and the firemen reduced the pressure of the jets.

"Let's go," Lene said. "I'm freezing cold."

"Yes."

They walked in among the trees and in a wide curve behind the meadow. They stooped as they walked, lost in their own private world. Michael kept checking if the CD was still in his inside pocket, one of the few parts of his anorak still intact.

They had had a brief, heated exchange, teeth chattering, about whether they should make themselves known to the firemen and the officers from Holbæk Police or simply disappear. Michael preferred the latter. Being dead gave you a certain amount of leeway, he argued; room for manoeuvre that he regarded as essential right now. Lene had given in eventually, but whether it was because of his powers of persuasion, or because she was too exhausted to carry on arguing with him, was hard to say.

They left the forest a few hundred metres from the lay-by and ran the last stretch. Lene's numb fingers dropped the car keys and Michael picked them up and managed on his third attempt to unlock the car. He sat down behind the steering wheel while she curled up on the passenger seat next to him. He started the car, turned the heating to maximum and held his hands above the warm air vents. Flat white blisters had started forming on his fingers and palms, but they didn't hurt very much.

"The seat heating! Hurry up," she urged him.

"Hang on . . ."

Michael turned off the engine when he saw the fire engines and the patrol car in the rear-view mirror pull out onto the main road with their flashing lights switched off. Shortly afterwards, a white Alfa Romeo appeared, indicating right before disappearing behind a hill.

"The wedding present?" he asked.

"Was it a white Alfa?"

"Yes."

"She paid a high price for that," she said. "Let's drive. It'll help us warm up."

"Lene . . ."

"Sorry. The GPS transmitter. I had forgotten all about it."

"Unless we have a serious death wish, we have to leave here on foot. I don't know about you, but I was actually hoping to live a little longer."

"So what do we do?" she asked. "We can arrest Thomas Berg. We have the film . . ."

"And the others? He can't be the only one left," Michael said.

"I expect he'll confess."

"I wouldn't bet on it. They have their crazy warrior code. I want to get everyone who belongs to that insane organization. Dead or alive. Thomas Berg clearly isn't the only one. There were at least two of them at the cottage."

"Dead or alive?" she asked.

"Exactly. Preferably the latter. But the former will do."

She was silent for a long time. Perhaps she was thinking about her daughter. Then she took a deep breath. "Okay."

"Okay?"

"Yes, Michael. Okay. So what do we do now?"

"We walk."

"Where?"

"To the scout hut," he said.

"But they know about the hut!"

"They think we're dead. So why would they watch it?"

"You hope."

"I hope," he admitted.

"How about a hotel?" she pleaded. "A lovely, warm hotel with real beds and duvets and . . . room service . . . and . . ."

"We're dead, Lene. Dead people don't book hotel rooms."

She gave him a hateful stare.

"If you have a better idea, then by all means let me hear it," he said.

"I can't think. I'm cold. I'm hungry. I miss my daughter."

"She's fine, Lene," Michael said. "Flying her to Greenland was a good idea. It really was."

"Do you think so?"

"I'm absolutely sure."

She pulled her wet jacket around her more tightly.

"Five more minutes?" she asked.

"Of course," he said. "Five more minutes won't make any difference."

They changed into dry clothes from the supplies Michael had bought earlier that morning. Lene went behind some trees to change and Michael shook his head at her modesty, which he regarded as rather misplaced. They had almost burned up and drowned together. How much closer could two people get? Then he searched their bags, weapons and wet clothes for electronic tell-tales without finding anything; afterwards he examined Charlotte Falster's Passat and found the first bug a few minutes later: a small, black Garmin GTU-10 the size of a packet of cigarettes attached with Velcro to a dark, inaccessible corner of the spare tire compartment. A small LED light bulb flashed green and happy at the back of the sender. The gadget was ideal to monitor teenage daughters claiming to be staying the night at a girl-friend's—or stubborn superintendents and interfering security consultants.

He put it back where he had found it. The whole exercise was pointless. Even if he found one, there could be many more. There were literally hundreds of hiding places in an ordinary sedan car.

Afterwards, they walked the four or five kilometres into Holbæk and found a taxi outside the railway station.

Michael called Elizabeth Caspersen from a payphone, giving her a status report and a description of the contents of the CD. He didn't give her the chance to ask questions, offer suggestions or raise objections before he hung up. He was going to leave the CD for her in the scout hut, he said, and described the location of the hiding place he had in mind.

The taxi dropped them half a kilometre from their destination. They walked quietly and avoided the path between the trees. Lene had the machine gun loaded and ready in her hands, while Michael carried her service pistol, also loaded and ready. The scout hut lay dark and deserted in the moonlight. He touched her shoulder and signalled that she should head to the right while he walked in a wide curve around the hut to the left. They met in the deep shadows at the campfire area behind the hut without having seen or heard any other living creatures.

Michael kneeled down outside the front door and opened it with one finger while Lene pressed herself against the wall with the machine pistol at shoulder height. There was no welcoming committee.

She turned on her flashlight, put down the bag, and checked the sleeping loft, the kitchen, and the lavatory.

"It's not much, but it's home," she said.

Michael broke up the bench and tore down the last banners in order to sacrifice them to the stove. He feared there would be tearful faces all around at the next scout meeting.

He got the fire going and stood for a moment with his back to the open grate and inspected his hands with his flashlight. The blisters were proud and waxy. A couple of them had burst and plasma seeped down his fingers.

Michael heaved a sigh and went out into the kitchen.

Lene had put a camping lantern on the table and was heating a tin of minestrone on the Trangia, stirring the contents without expression. Her hair was considerably shorter after the fire and the ends were black, crispy and singed. Michael sat down at the kitchen table, instinctively ran a hand over his scalp and winced. He was bald, and skinless patches stretched from the neck and over his ears. He wondered if hair would ever grow back from those charred stubble fields.

Lene looked at him while he fished his most recent mobile out of his trouser pocket. He removed the back cover and tipped the water out on the table. Then he stared forlornly at it and put it to one side.

"Do you have any electronic equipment in working order?" he asked.

"I wouldn't have thought so. Are you tired?"

"You're asking if I'm tired?"

She smiled and served up some minestrone.

"Yes."

"I'm quite tired," he admitted.

"Me too," she said.

"Wait a moment," he said.

"I'm not going anywhere," she said.

He squatted down next to the bag and found Elizabeth Caspersen's document, which left a fortune to Sara and the children if he got himself killed.

Michael unfolded it on the kitchen table, took a pen, which was attached to the wall by a piece of string, and looked at Lene.

"What's your daughter's full name and civil registration number?"

"Why? What's that?"

"Something I should have done sooner," he said. "This is a document drawn up by my client. It has been witnessed by her partners and registered with the public notary. If . . . well, if anything should happen to me . . . if I die, in other words, your daughter will get a lifetime pension from Elizabeth Caspersen or her estate. I can add her as a beneficiary."

"Are you serious? Can I see it?"

He pushed the paper across the table and she read it carefully.

"Josefine Ida Thea Jensen," she then said.

She gave him her daughter's civil registration number, reached her hand across the table and put it on his forearm. It was the first time she had touched him—except for putting out the flames when he was on fire.

"Thank you, Michael."

"She can afford it; really, she can, in fact . . ."

He fell silent when the realization hit him like a punch to the stomach.

"In fact what?"

"Nothing."

He tried smiling, but knew he hadn't succeeded. Michael shook his head, despairing at himself. He was tired, exhausted . . . borderline insane, possibly. And no wonder, given what they had been through. But the nagging thought refused to go away. Was he being used? Was he simply the means to clear away the opposition in Sonartek so Elizabeth Caspersen could take charge with her own and her mother's majority share? Was that her real goal, rather than expose a gang of psychopathic man hunters? And had she known all the time who was behind the murder of Kasper Hansen? No one would have been in a better position to plant that DVD. She knew the code to the safe. She could have put the Mauser in Flemming Caspersen's weapon room, couldn't she? It was as easy as 1-2-3.

Nonsense. He was paranoid and seeing conspiracies everywhere.

"What's wrong, Michael?"

"What do you mean?"

"You look as if you've seen a ghost. What's happened? I mean, apart from lots of men trying to kill you?"

He pulled himself together and returned her smile.

"Nothing . . . nothing at all. I'm fine. Great. Absolutely. Super."

She threw him a worried look.

She hadn't said "kill us." He hoped that one day he would be just as unselfish.

"You're right," she said later.

"About what?"

"Thomas Berg and the others. It's not enough. Arresting them is not enough."

"Are you sure?"

"Yes, I agree with you. You're a very bad influence on me, Michael."

"So everyone says."

They ate their soup in silence because there was nothing else to be said. Michael hid the CD under a loose floorboard, as agreed with Elizabeth Caspersen, while Lene washed up. They carried their sleeping bags upstairs, unrolled them, and switched off their flashlights.

They lay next to each other and were warm inside their sleeping bags. Michael had to lie on his stomach to protect the burns on his back. He rested his forehead on his forearms and listened to Lene's breathing getting slower and slower.

Then he heard her murmuring and it took a while before he realized she was saying the Lord's Prayer. She finished the prayer by holding up her folded hands in the darkness before she placed her arms along her sides.

"You pray?" he asked.

She said nothing.

"My father was a vicar," he mumbled.

"I'm a believer," she said. "You think about the grandfather clock in your grandmother's sitting room, and I pray. It doesn't make me less able, Michael."

"Of course not," he said. "Good night."

"Good night."

She jerked violently a couple of times and the whole sleeping loft shuddered while she balanced on the edge between sleeping and awakening. Michael imagined that her subconscious was desperately working overtime.

She twitched again in her sleeping bag and muttered something pitiful and incomprehensible; Michael sighed. It was like trying to sleep next to an anxious dog reliving that day's hunts. He stared down between the planks. The faint glow from the stove spread across the floor and he was reminded of the flickering, restless surface of the water in the crawlspace in the forest while the cottage burned above them.

CHAPTER 47

Michael sat up, but she wasn't there. He stared at her empty, flaccid sleeping bag, looked at his watch and groaned. It was ten thirty in the morning and the night and the early morning had been an endless series of shifting, awkward sleeping positions.

"Lene?"

He swung his legs over the sleeping loft and looked down between his feet, but could sense that the hut was empty. The sun was out, and he touched one of the warm roofing panels with his fingertips. Today was Friday. He had been away from home for seven days, and it was two years and one month since Kasper Hansen and Ingrid Sundsbö were killed up in Finnmark.

Michael gingerly climbed down the ladder and straightened his back with a series of small cracks. He looked out of the kitchen window and spotted Lene walking up and down a small mound with some trees. She was talking on a new mobile, gesturing with her free hand, and would sometimes pause and look up at the blue sky as if imploring it for help. Once she stamped her foot in anger.

As if they had telepathic contact, she suddenly stopped, turned her head and stared at him. Her facial expression didn't change, but she greeted him with a "Hang on a minute" hand signal and carried on walking. He held up the aluminium kettle, pointed to it, and she nodded and almost granted him a smile.

Michael thought that Lene was the most direct and uncompromising person he had ever met. He could see why she was good at her job and had reached the rank of superintendent while still in her early forties . . . but a little bit of . . . a little bit of warmth and human kindness wouldn't go amiss.

Michael poured water into the kettle. Then he remembered Josefine and felt ashamed. It was a miracle that Lene could even put one foot in front of the other.

He carried the mugs filled with Nescafé outside and put them on the bench. There were already a couple of carrier bags there and a brand-new rucksack. She had been busy. A nice blue ladies' bicycle was leaning up against a tree down by the path.

She ended the call, shook herself as if she were wet, and marched towards him.

"Your boss?" he asked.

"My ex," she mumbled, and took the mug.

"He wasn't too happy, I presume?"

"I don't want to talk about it," she said. "Show me your hands."

Michael held them out obediently and she delved into the plastic bags.

"I went to the pharmacist while you were sleeping," she said. "Burn ointment, bandages, Band-Aids, anaesthetic cream. You really ought to wear plastic bags on your hands for a week. I think you have third degree burns on the back of them."

"Plastic bags on my hands will only get in the way," he said. "But is there enough anaesthetic cream for me to swim in it?"

"No, but I can always cover your head and mouth with bandages," she said, and tore off strips with her teeth. She got to work on his hands, applying ointment to the raw, weeping blisters and covering them with cold compresses. Michael watched her with gratitude. She knew what she was doing.

"How did you reach civilization?" he asked, and she blushed.

"I nicked a bicycle."

"Good move," he said. "What else did you get?"

She handed him a box.

"A new mobile with a prepaid SIM card and a small laptop. I don't think I make as much money as you do, so I've kept the receipts."

"Of course. Thank you."

He turned over the box with the mobile in his hands. He was actually able to bend and stretch his fingers now.

"They're great," he said. "My hands."

She warmed her hands on her coffee mug and stared into space.

"Did you get some sleep?" he asked.

"A bit. And you?"

"A little, I think."

"What do we do now, Michael?" she asked; she sounded calm.

He leaned back and looked up at the sky. The weather was excellent. He wondered what it was like in northern Norway. Cold, probably. Snow. Ice on the lakes. Cold, basically.

"I'll take it from here," he said, then drained the mug and carefully avoided looking at her.

"No way," she protested.

Michael smiled sternly and something burst on his cheek. He raised his fingers to his face and felt a scab and fresh plasma seep out.

"Lene, this isn't a democratic forum. I'll take it from here. And that's how it's going to be," he said.

"I can arrest you," she said.

"What for?"

"Vagrancy."

Michael stood up and looked gravely at her.

"Lene, you'd be walking straight into a kill zone. An arena. You've seen what they're capable of. And they have plenty of practice. They won't care that you're a police officer, trust me. They'll do whatever it takes to eliminate you. You've seen for yourself how good they are. Besides, you wouldn't be much help. You don't have the right training or the experience to take them on."

He regretted his next words even before he had uttered them.

"And think about your daughter, Josefi—"

When he regained consciousness a few seconds later, he was lying on the threshold without knowing how he had covered the distance. It didn't hurt very much and by now he was so bruised, battered, and burned that he couldn't tell new injuries from old ones. His central nervous system was overloaded and sparked impotently like a short-circuited transistor. He looked up at Lene, who was standing by the bench with her arms by her sides and her fists still clenched.

Michael rocked his lower jaw from side to side. He was able to close his teeth together and open his mouth. Almost normal functioning.

"But I'm open to suggestions," he mumbled.

Her shoulders heaved and sank, and the flames in her green eyes slowly died away.

"Then I suggest that you bring me along, and I'm asking you again: what do we do? And why did we have that cryptic conversation about Thomas Berg if you weren't going to take me? And I actually do think about my daughter, Michael. In fact, that's all I do."

Michael got to his feet and tried focusing on the bicycle. Something fixed and real.

"Why don't we sit down?" he asked. "Again?"

"It has to stop, do you hear me? It has to stop. Now!"

He nodded.

"All right then! I think it's time to flip the game, Lene. And as regards the hunters, dead or alive, I don't expect you to do anything incompatible with your role as a Danish police officer."

"Excellent," she said. "Great . . . How do we flip the game? And forget about my job. Maybe I just quit."

"Bait," he said. "Irresistible bait."

"What do you have in mind?"

"Us, who else? Besides, we don't have a choice. We need to lure them out in open terrain where we can see them. It's our only chance."

"What terrain? Where?"

He told her and she didn't interrupt him. When he had finished, she looked at the ground, massaged her forehead with her fingertips, and nodded. Her face gave nothing away; neither doubt nor enthusiasm.

"That's what I want to do," he said. "That's where I want them."

"If that's where they want to go," she said tentatively. "If all your one million and one assumptions are right and all your predictions come true."

"I don't see that they have a choice, either. The difficulty lies in preventing them from sabotaging our game plan before we get there."

"Do you think there's anything up there?" she asked.

"I'm not sure if that matters," Michael replied. "As long as no one can be sure that there *isn't*, we all have to play the game to the end. Those are the rules. Unless the hunters discover a sudden urge to emigrate. We can't prevent that, of course."

"To Antigua and Barbuda?" she suggested. "That's what I would do. They have plenty of money in the banks out there and they probably can't be extradited unless they do something really bad, like cut off someone's dreadlocks or burn portraits of Haile Selassie."

"Never underestimate male vanity," he said. "It's a strong driving force. For better or for worse. They'll be there."

"Remember Berlusconi."

"Remember Napoleon," Michael said. "Do you still want to come? You'll be risking your life. You have a secure job. You have a future and a career, whereas I'm being paid extremely well to do this."

"I want to come. I *have* to come," she said emphatically. "And how did you get to decide the rules?"

"That's just how it has turned out. Or, at least, I hope so."

"There's a word for unfounded omnipotence, you know."

"Megalomania?"

"I was going to say insanity."

Thirty minutes later, Michael left the forest track and joined the main road on the bicycle. It was half an hour's ride from the scout hut to the nearest railway station. He hoped that he wasn't arrested before he got there because he looked exactly what he was: an escaped, desperate burns victim with bandaged hands and balding, black patches where his hair used to be. And he was riding a stolen blue ladies' bicycle.

He had been lying when he told Lene they were not in a hurry. The truth was that they had very little time if they wanted to keep the initiative—too many things of vital importance had already been left to other people.

CHAPTER 48

He managed not to get arrested before he reached the station, but his fellow passengers eyed him suspiciously and stayed well clear of his seat, even though the train was packed. He didn't blame them. He thought it likely that small plumes of smoke were still rising from his head.

Michael got off the train at Nørreport Station and walked down Nørre Voldgade to a menswear shop on Jarmers Plads. The shop assistants must have been exquisitely polite, well-trained, or just strangely lacking in curiosity, as they made no reference to his appearance whatsoever. His various credit cards, however, were scrutinized, a control call was made to his bank, and they asked politely to see his passport—something that hardly ever happened. The edges of Michael's wallet were singed, but its contents had survived the fire and the flood. Half an hour later, he left the shop dressed entirely in new clothes and carrying several shopping bags.

From Nørrevold, he took a taxi to a specialist shop on Østerbro. The shop was run as a kind of wholesale business by two seasoned mountaineers, and Michael moved slowly through the basement, followed by one of the owners who pulled down goods from the shelves: two coils of eleven-millimetre climbing rope, sixty metres long, tubular tapes, climbing harnesses, belaying ropes, nuts, bolt anchors, a hammer, Jumar grips—useful for ascending ropes—a two-person tent, a couple of rucksacks, an iridium satellite telephone, hiking boots, and more.

The bearded owner hummed happily to himself when Michael swiped his red-hot MasterCard through the terminal, and helped him carry everything up the basement steps to the pavement. Michael called a cab and smoked a cigarette while he waited. He thought about the superintendent and wondered where she had learned to fight so well. And about her other skills. She wasn't the kind of woman you bumped into every day and that was probably just as well: too many bruises.

The awkward pantomime at the menswear shop repeated itself at the Hertz counter at Copenhagen Airport. Even though Michael was now well-dressed, the sight of his face, hands, and scalp was enough for the young woman to call over her supervisor, who scrutinized Michael's documents, passport, and credit cards.

"What did you have in mind?" the supervisor asked him nervously. "We have a special deal on a fine Ford Focus."

Michael acknowledged the offer without interest and looked at a laminated list of car models.

"I was thinking of something a little faster," he said. "How about that one?"

His bandaged finger landed on the last car on the list. The supervisor took a sharp intake of breath, and the junior didn't move at all.

"The Audi A6, V8-engine, 400 hp? Nought to 100 in 4.6 seconds?" The supervisor gulped.

Michael looked at him.

"That sounds nice. Is it available?"

"Yes, but . . ."

The other man must have seen something implacable in Michael's eyes because he began to nod.

"Nothing. It's available, absolutely. For how long will you be needing it?"

"A week, I would think."

The man smiled and produced the keys.

"Take good care of it," he said, tight-lipped. "There aren't many of them around . . ."

He looked at Michael's equipment on the luggage trolley and pulled another anxious face.

"Mountaineering?"

"That's what I had in mind."

"Take good care of it," he said again, and asked the young woman to photocopy Michael's passport one more time.

*

They put the last of the bags into the trunk of the Audi, and Michael made sure that the safety catch on the superintendent's service pistol was on before he put it in the pocket in the car door—close to hand. Lene got in on the passenger side and placed the machine gun between her feet. She ran her fingertips across the seat's exclusive golden leather.

"Why don't I get to drive?" she asked.

Michael pressed the red start button, and the engine's eight turbo charged cylinders awoke with a tiger roar.

"We've been through this, Lene. Besides, it's my name on the rental documents. It's an insurance thing."

She muttered a protest, but he revved the engine and drowned out her words.

A few minutes later, they joined the Holbæk motorway. It was growing dark and the traffic had eased off. The road conditions were ideal and Michael put the Audi through its paces. He enjoyed driving, being in total control of a little speck of reality.

Lene leaned back. She seemed to have come to terms with her passive role.

"I've spoken to my daughter," she said.

Michael stole a glance at her.

"Will she be okay?"

Lene smiled and the rays of the setting sun deepened the sparkle in her green eyes. She shook her head in amazement. "She's young. She'll recover. I just know she will. Remarkable, really. She was upset, but at the same time, she was fine. She'll be all right."

Michael smiled too.

"Of course she will," he said

He thought about Pieter Henryk's daughter. She had ended up in a secure, private facility in Switzerland, she had stopped playing the flute, and was kept in almost a waking coma to prevent her from harming herself: a kind of pharmacological lobotomy. She had smeared herself with her own faeces to keep everyone—especially male carers—at bay.

He shook off his dark thoughts.

"Have you spoken to your wife?" she asked.

"Not yet."

He pulled out behind a convoy of trucks and pressed the accelerator right down. The car leaped forwards with an offended howl and the motorway narrowed, becoming almost tunnel-shaped. He couldn't handle the guilt, he felt exhausted at the mere thought of his wife's silence or carefully worded reproaches, and he also knew that it was the thin end of the wedge. Didn't a break-up always start with not wanting to call? He knew exactly what Sara would say and how he would respond, and he wondered when it had begun: this tiresome dance that neither of them wanted, but which neither of them had the energy to end.

"Call her, Michael," Lene said as if she had read his mind. "She must be beside herself with worry. The fire is all over the Internet and on TV. You did tell her about me, didn't you?"

"I didn't tell her your name," he said.

"Surely she can put two and two together."

Charlotte Falster had announced that Police Superintendent Lene Jensen had been killed in a gas explosion in a house near Holbæk Fjord. It had been on the news. Falster had prepared a short press release and Lene had smiled when she heard herself described as an inspired and dedicated investigator. Police were treating her death as an accident, but were still carrying out technical examinations at the scene.

"You're right," he said. "Okay. Please, would you check what the weather is like up there?"

"Of course."

She got busy with the laptop and the wireless Internet modem and started looking for a suitable meteorological website, while Michael pulled over to call home.

Afterwards, he put the mobile back in the inside pocket of his jacket.

"Thank you," he said.

"*De nada*. Was it all right?"

"Yes," he said. "It's fine, really."

And it had been. Sara had cried, but not railed against things that couldn't be changed. The children were great. They loved being at her brother's cottage. There was a farm nearby they could visit whenever they wanted. There were kittens and puppies which the toddler could put on her lap like dolls and play house with, and there were pigs and sheep for the four-year-old to chase after, and a sea which Sara could gaze across. She said she knew that he would be back. She was sure of it.

He loved her and knew that he would never be able to get enough of her.

He glanced at the computer screen on Lene's lap.

"So what does it look like?"

"Everything is fine right up to the border between Sweden and Norway," she said. "But after Kiruna everything turns white and it's minus six degrees. In the daytime. Spring appears to be very late this year."

"But the E10 is passable?" he asked.

"Yes."

Kiruna. Would they even make it that far? It seemed an incredibly long way away: 1,500 kilometres. At least. And from then, several hundred more kilometres across the mountains before they reached their destination. Anything could happen. The opposition had the advantage and all they could do was drive—and improvise.

Again, Michael checked the inbox of his mobile for messages: the last one had arrived two hours earlier and its brevity had been just as nerve-racking and frustrating as the previous ones: *Stand by.*

He knew it was how these things were done, but even so he was seething with impatience and every imaginable worry.

"There it is," she said, forty-five minutes later.

Michael drove the Audi up a small, dark hill and stopped a hundred metres from Charlotte Falster's white Passat, which was still parked in the lay-by near some tables and benches.

There were no other cars around. The area was deserted. No dog walkers, joggers, or mountain bikers.

He turned off the engine and they sat quietly, watching their surroundings.

Michael got out, leaned against the warm bonnet, and lit a cigarette. The sun had gone down behind Tuse Næs; the smell from the burned-down cottage still lingered in the air, but the birds were singing, unperturbed by it all, and the world seemed at peace. Holbæk Fjord extended its glittering surface beneath the dark blue sky and he watched a small, white ferry sail towards a distant, dark shape dotted with light from the islanders' houses.

The first stars had come out. He flicked aside the glowing cigarette butt and walked across to the Passat. He tried with every fibre of his body to detect whether he was being watched, but could sense no alien presence.

Charlotte Falster's car was covered with dew. It was cold and wouldn't appear to have moved one millimetre since they abandoned it last night.

Again, his gaze scanned the tables and benches, and the trees near the lay-by. Nothing. He lay down on his stomach, switched on a small flashlight and carefully inspected the undercarriage, the silencer, the exhaust pipe, the suspension, and the wheel bays. Everything looked perfectly normal. There were no blocks of plastic explosive, or a digital timer counting down to a deadly explosion if anyone tried to start the car.

Michael got back on his feet and looked at the motionless figure in the Audi. He waved to her, but she didn't react. He opened the trunk of the Passat and found the small Garmin GPS transmitter exactly when he had left it last night. It was still flashing its green, cheerful light.

Inside the car, he checked under the seats and under the dashboard, and examined all stitching and welded seams before he was satisfied. Then he went back to the Audi and Lene got out and started dividing up their equipment.

She covered her mouth with her hand, yawned, and arched her back. She looked up at the stars and the white band of moonlight across the fjord and shivered.

"Sixteen hundred kilometres?" she asked, even though she knew the answer. "And we can't stop to sleep at any point?"

"I don't think it would be wise," he said, and swung a rucksack up on his shoulders. He swore when the strap pressed against the burns on his back. "We've been through this countless times, Lene."

She stared at the ground and her shoulders slumped.

"I know, but . . ."

"But what?" he asked.

"Nothing. The GPS?"

"Ours or theirs?"

"Both."

"Theirs is still in place," he said. "And this one is for you."

He handed her an ordinary sat nav.

"It covers all of Western Europe. All you have to do is type in 'Kiruna,'" he said.

"I know that."

She picked up a rucksack, slung the strap of the machine pistol over her shoulder, and they started walking towards the Passat.

"There were no bombs under the car?" she asked.

"None that I could see," he said.

"What does that mean?"

"That I couldn't see any."

They put her kit in the trunk of the Passat; she wedged the machine pistol in between the front seats, got in the driver's seat and looked up at him. He handed her the key and she immediately stuck it in the ignition, and turned it while she pressed her eyes shut. The engine started humming. That was all it did.

Michael stared at her.

"Couldn't you have waited until I was gone?" he asked.

"You said there were no explosives."

"I said that I couldn't see any."

"Same thing, surely."

"I don't think so," he said.

"Do you want to swap?" she asked. "And I'll drive your fancy car."

"No, thanks."

"Are you sure that they're still checking for a signal? I mean, they think we're dead," she said sceptically.

"I don't think they monitor the bugs 24/7, but I'm sure that alarms will go off on various computers, smartphones, and tablets the second that Passat is on the move."

"But if you're—" she began.

"Drive safely," he said, and slammed the door shut. She shouted something from inside, but he just cupped his hand behind his ear, shook his head, and turned on his heel.

CHAPTER 49

Sweden was endless. And boring beyond belief. Lene drove the white Passat a few hundred metres in front of Michael. For hours they had followed the ruler-straight E45 through snow-powdered pine forests. The sun had shone through the right side window, but was now at her back. Michael's only distraction had been the changing regional accents on the radio up through various Swedish counties.

They had stopped at the same petrol station, had drunk the same weak, Swedish coffee, and eaten the same bland sandwiches, but had ignored each other's presence. Michael had waited until she had filled up the car, been to the lavatory, and bought supplies. He had stayed close, but in the background, with a loaded pistol tucked into his belt behind his back, ready to blast anyone who approached her to the ends of the earth. He had monitored traffic patterns, memorized registration numbers, car models, and was convinced they had not been followed at any point.

South of a godforsaken place called Porjus, his mobile vibrated against his thigh.

"Michael? I need to sleep. I mean it," she said.

"Now? I don't think that's a very good idea, Lene. I really don't."

"I'm pulling over at the next lay-by, Michael. I'm shattered. I need a break. This is going to kill me otherwise."

"All right then," he grunted.

The lay-by had a view of a small, dreary town by a dried out riverbed. Michael parked fifty metres from the Passat. Two sturdy truck drivers in green body warmers and clogs were chatting next to a couple of incredibly long trailer trucks loaded with pine trunks. The men held tall, steaming Thermos mugs in their hands and looked like they were enjoying themselves. Michael's mouth watered at the sight. He hadn't had a decent cup of coffee since the scout hut.

The Passat had stopped under the snow-covered branches that reached across the lay-by. White smoke was pouring from the exhaust, but he couldn't see Lene inside. He tightened his parka around his neck, plodded across the tarmac and cupped his hands against the side window of the Passat.

She lay curled up in a foetal position on the back seat with her hands between her knees and her eyes closed. Michael could hear faint harmonica music from the car radio. He rapped his knuckles on the window, but she didn't move. Then he opened the door and turned off the engine.

"Lene?"

"Go away."

"You'll freeze to death," he said.

"Turn on the engine," she mumbled without opening her eyes.

He straightened up and looked at the unbroken cloud cover. The truck drivers were watching him. Not much happened around here.

"This is . . . not okay," he said.

"What?"

"Just lying there with the engine running."

One angry, green eye opened a fraction.

"Are you worried about global warming? Tell me you're joking, Michael. Please."

He opened the trunk and found a sleeping bag.

"I'm going to stand here until you climb inside it," he said.

"Die," she said.

He waited.

"I'm still here, Lene. The door is open and the engine is turned off."

He closed and locked the door when she had obeyed orders, and walked back to the Audi. The truck drivers left the lay-by with hissing air brakes and swaying cabins. He got into his own car, drummed his fingers indecisively on the steering wheel, yawned, and realized how exhausted he was. Thirty minutes? What could go wrong in thirty minutes?

Everything.

He thought about the indefatigable GPS transmitter in Chief Superintendent Charlotte Falster's white Passat fifty metres away, and muttered curses under his breath. One of them had to stay awake. He swore again and pulled his collar up around his ears. He opened the side window so the cold would keep him awake and turned on the laptop.

He would allow her a few hours' sleep while he kept watch and felt very Christian, almost altruistic. They wouldn't reach Lakselv until late evening anyway, and whether it was this side of midnight or the other really didn't matter. All they had left to do was drive through the small Norwegian town at the bottom of Porsanger Fjord and onwards up Route 98 to Børselva. From then on, it was roughly forty kilometres north-north-west to their destination. On foot.

He had studied every available map and satellite photo in detail, and the landscape looked terrifying: deep ravines with meltwater rapids, glaciers—and glacier crevasses—ridges . . . wild, scattered, impassable moraine ground, with thousands of rocks the size of anything from a car to a tower block. And only a few mapped paths.

Right now, hiking across Finnmark seemed utterly impossible to him, even if he had been well rested or relatively unhurt. But he was neither. They had everything they needed in terms of supplies: good boots, warm, waterproof clothing, a small Trangia, a tent, freeze-dried food, energy drinks, sleeping bags and more—but it wasn't about having the right gear. There was also the human factor. Especially his. Lene had the strongest possible motive for being here and to go on long after her body had hit a wall: she wanted to avenge her daughter but, more importantly, she wanted to stop the men from hurting anyone else ever again. His own motives were rather more prosaic, almost tawdry by comparison.

He closed Google Earth with the depressing satellite photos of the frightening landscape up north and looked instead at the sunny beach in the Seychelles he had chosen as the background screen on the computer. You could almost warm your hands on that picture, he thought. Then he sensed movement through the windscreen and saw Lene walk along the lay-by with her hands tucked under her armpits, and the short, stiff gait of someone who feels the cold and has just woken up.

Without a word she got in next to him and stared straight ahead.

"Ready?" he asked.

She shuddered and hugged herself.

"Turn on the heating," she said.

Michael complied and switched on the engine. He handed her a Snickers bar, she tore off the wrapping, and devoured it ravenously.

"How far is it from here?" she asked, and folded the chocolate wrapper neatly before putting it in her pocket.

"Around four hundred kilometres," he said. "As the crow flies."

"Christ. I had no idea Sweden was so . . . vast."

"It's a huge country," he agreed. "Haven't you been up here before?"

"Me? Why on earth would I want to do that?"

He shrugged his shoulders.

"It's beautiful and clean and . . . practically deserted," he said. "You can go hiking, skiing. Fishing. People actually live here, Lene."

"What do they live on? And how do you know?"

"Judging by the trucks, I'd say they make their living from forestry. Once we pass Lakselv, it's only forty kilometres. On foot," he added with a hint of sadism.

"Jesus Christ . . ."

". . . and the Holy Ghost. There are no roads where we're going."

"And then what happens?" she croaked.

Michael leaned back and folded his hands in his lap.

"Interestingly, the best and the worst outcomes are one and the same," he said. "It's unique. A classic dilemma. I've given this a great deal of thought. The exact circumstances can play out in a number of ways, depending on the opposition."

"The opposition? Is that how you refer to a bunch of psychos? I'm sorry, but that all sounds terribly academic, Michael. Hasn't it crossed your mind that they might just have hired a guy to lie in wait and shoot us without bothering with questions?"

"Of course. But I'm betting that they can't resist the temptation to gloat, boast of their cleverness to us—and besides, they'll want to watch. Like you say, they're psychos."

"If they're there."

Michael nodded.

"True."

He thought about the small group of Serbian mercenaries whom Pieter

Henryk had hired to free his kidnapped daughter. Europe had been flooded with operatives from the Balkan wars; from every corner of the kaleidoscopic conflict in the nineties. They spoke the same language, they were cheap, worked hard, and got on with each other, though they might have been on opposite sides in Bosnia-Herzegovina or Kosovo, and they got the job done without drawing unnecessary attention to themselves.

But it wouldn't be the hunters' style to hire someone to do the killing for them, he thought.

"It's an assumption," he said. "A hypothesis. You can see that, can't you?"

"A hypothesis?"

Michael flared up.

"I'm not clairvoyant. I can't read their minds, Lene! I'm doing my best here with whatever facts I happen to have available. It's called improvising. And I'm sorry if I'm so bloody academic."

"No, I'm sorry." She put her hand on his forearm. One of her rare physical gestures. "Are you scared?"

He turned in his seat and stared at her in disbelief.

"Of course I'm scared, woman! If I wasn't, I'd either have had a lobotomy or swallowed a handful of Valium."

"I didn't mean it like that. I'm sorry."

She looked down.

"It's just that I still don't understand why you do this. Why do you?"

"It's one way to make a living," he grunted. "Might not be a very good one, but that's how it turned out. It's the one thing I'm fairly good at."

She let out a hollow laugh, and her breath came out in small clouds.

"I refuse to believe that's true, Michael. You're resourceful. Surely you could do anything you wanted."

"I'm almost forty-four years old, Lene. I did try to get other jobs at one point, but it didn't work out. I've finally learned to accept that this is what I was meant to do. It's important to believe that. If you don't, you won't last very long in this business."

She smiled.

"How are your hands? Do you want me to change the bandages?"

Michael spread out and bent his fingers on his lap. The bandages were filthy and damp, but he wasn't in much pain.

"Later, perhaps," he said.

She opened the door and put a foot on the tarmac.

"You just let me know."

She looked up at the low sky, which had turned cloudy.

"Four hundred kilometres, you said?"

"Give or take," he replied. "Let's stop and get a decent meal soon. According to the sat nav, there's a town with a restaurant in seventy kilometres."

"Our last supper?" she asked.

"I hope not," he said.

CHAPTER 50

Could sounds be trapped in a landscape? And could they one day be set free? Lene wondered. Because whenever the path steered away from the thundering river that flowed to her right, their footsteps echoed between the walls of the ravine, making it sound as if they were being followed. Then the path returned to the foaming river and the boiling, frothing water would wipe out all other sounds.

The river crashed through a narrow ravine between steep rock faces. The path mostly ran parallel to, or over, the fast stream, and had been eroded by spring meltwater in several places. In other parts, it veered away from the water and was hidden behind the tall, wet rocks that were scattered chaotically between the rock walls.

The path lay in constant shade, so it was cold down here, but at least they were sheltered from the strong north-easterly wind that tore through the cloud cover above their heads.

She looked at her watch. It was almost eleven o'clock, and they had been hiking for four hours since leaving the parking lot in Børselva. There they had spent the last few hours of the night in separate cars, until Michael had stuck his hand inside the Passat and sounded the horn. She had jerked upright and banged her head against something hard.

The ground began to crumble under her feet and she clung to the rock face. Gravel, soil and pebbles slowly broke off and tumbled into the river, before being carried away by the current with incredible speed. A tree trunk crashed into the bank just below her and knocked off her last bit of footing. Lene leaped forwards and managed to reach firm ground as the path behind her collapsed. The tree trunk rotated on its long axis, collided with the opposite bank, tore itself loose, and smashed with a splintering crack through the next waterfall. Her pulse was pounding in her ears, but some distance in front of her Michael turned around and beckoned her on impatiently before marching ahead. Lene felt like screaming at him that she had almost just died, but gritted her teeth and walked on. All talking, all sudden and uncontrolled noises were strictly banned by Michael.

They were also forbidden from approaching each other. Michael kept far ahead, usually out of sight, and Lene felt exposed and alone whenever she couldn't see his dense, dark figure. He was armed with the machine pistol, which he carried on the shoulder strap, loaded and ready, while she had the pistol in her hip holster. For someone who had stated on more than one occasion that he didn't like firearms, he was handling the machine pistol with ease and routine expertise. Lene and the police's firearms instructor both regarded her as an excellent shot, but she had an inkling that they were both complete novices compared to Michael Sander.

She speeded up until she spotted him again behind the next bend. The gorge widened and became more even, the distance between the big rocks on the bottom grew greater, the river itself broadened and the current slowed down. She could see more of the sky. Then she suddenly lost sight of him and felt her panic soar up her chest and tighten her throat.

She started jogging. There was vegetation now, low willow thicket and pine scrub in small clusters in between the moraine blocks. She considered calling out to him, but knew that he would be furious. She passed a rock the size of a family house and let out a startled cry when someone put a hand on her shoulder and she was pulled behind the rock.

"Jesus Christ, Michael!"

"Easy now . . . and keep your voice down."

There was shelter from the wind behind the rock and a small area the size of a table-tennis table with dry gravel where they could sit without being watched by . . . the opposition.

Lene leaned her back against the dry rock. The granite was reddish, raw, and young, and it would be fiery red and orange when the rays of the evening sun hit it. Michael was surveying the terrain in front of them through a pair of small but powerful binoculars.

"Where are we?" she asked.

She was sitting on a rolled-up camper mat and could feel her thigh muscles twitching. If she made it back alive, she had sworn to herself that she would start running again, perhaps go hiking. The landscape sapped all the strength from her legs and made her blood scream out for nourishment. She felt nauseous due to low blood sugar, and bowed her head between her knees.

"What's the matter?" he asked.

"Low blood sugar."

Michael rummaged around the rucksack and handed her a couple of energy bars and a Snickers. He took the kettle from their Trangia kitchen and squatted down by a babbling brook and filled it. Then he lit the Trangia, put the kettle on top of it and placed tea bags in their plastic mugs. He found a bottle of acacia honey and Lene stared at the golden stream being squirted into the mugs as she munched.

"Thank you," she said.

"You're welcome."

"It comes on suddenly," she explained. "My blood sugar plummets and it feels as if my skeleton is being pulled out through my feet."

"I know what you mean," he said. "I'm the same."

"And what do you do?"

"Keel over." He grinned.

He handed her the mug and blew on his own.

Lene looked down her red parka and then at his light grey one, which blended into the landscape much better. She felt as conspicuous as a monk setting fire to himself at a summit meeting.

"Why am I wearing the red coat, Michael?" she asked. "Even a blind man could see me from fifty kilometres away."

He looked at her parka without expression and sipped his tea.

"I think you look nice," he said.

"But red."

"Mmm, quite red."

"In fact, there's nothing bright red up here except my coat," she said, and took in the horizon with a sweeping gesture.

Every trace of merriment or sympathy vanished from his face, which became tight and sombre once more.

"The best and the worst, Lene," he said harshly. "Two sides of the same coin. We want to be found. In fact, it's up to us to make sure that we are. I had hoped that you understood that. So, what do you want?"

She looked down, gathered up a handful of gravel, and let it trickle through her fingers.

"I want to be found," she mumbled. "And stop being so bloody patronizing. Where are we?"

Michael unfurled the map and consulted a hand-held GPS. He pointed to a long, narrow stretch of water.

"We're roughly six kilometres south of a lake called Kjæsvatnet. That's where the two disappeared. The Norwegian police or army found a creel up there with Kasper Hansen's initials."

"And after that?"

"Eighteen kilometres, give or take. We've done very well, all things considered."

Lene swallowed the last of the chocolate bar, scrunched up the paper into a ball and was about to wedge it into a crack in the rock when she felt a look of disapproval. She sighed, stuck the wrapper in her pocket, and got up.

"It's uphill from here," he informed her. "This is where the plateau begins."

"Uphill? That's just what I need right now, Michael."

CHAPTER 51

Lake Kjæsvatnet appeared to be alive. The north-easterly wind pushed the water onwards in small, white horses, and the wind cut through their clothing whenever they weren't sheltered by stretches of valley and rocks, or when they plodded through small willow thickets in heavy melting slush. The ice constantly cracked underneath their boots. Lene took care to tread in Michael's footsteps, one hundred metres behind him, visible for miles around in her red parka. The sun was still high in the sky; it was a beautiful, yet utterly bleak and strangely oppressive landscape.

Even though it was heavy going, they had made surprisingly good progress, he realized after a fresh look at the map. He raised the binoculars to his eyes and studied the shores of the lake. Nothing. Not so much as a migrating bird on the restless, black water, and nothing moved between the frozen rushes or in the small birch thickets along the shore.

This is where they spent their last night, he thought. Kasper and Ingrid. By a campfire, he remembered. The weather had been fine and the night sky endless and starry.

He heard Lene's boots in the soft snow behind him.

"Are we going down to the lake?" she asked.

Michael looked at his watch.

"Why not? We have almost four more hours of daylight left."

"Is anyone here?"

"Not a living soul."

They walked through the birch trees and down to the stony shore where the ice had started to melt between the tussocks. There were only a few crisp and perforated ice floes left along the shore.

Again, they stood beside each other and looked across the narrow stretch of water that disappeared towards the north-east.

Lene shuddered.

"You could lose a whole army up here," she said. "There is . . . nothing here."

"There are the Sami and their reindeer," Michael said.

She stretched up on tiptoes and looked around.

"Where?"

"In theory," he said.

"But the two of them were here?"

He nodded. The article in *Verdens Gang* had only stated that the search-and-rescue team had found an empty creel and the remains of a campfire that Kasper Hansen and Ingrid Sundsbö had left behind, but hadn't specified where around Kjæsvatnet the findings were made.

"They were abducted somewhere near the lake," he said.

"I can see how that would be possible," she said. "Anything could happen up here."

"Just like in the Himalayas," he said.

"And in Afghanistan. Nobody ever sees what they do."

Michael looked at her.

"Exactly. No one ever sees it. That's how they get away with it. Let's walk on."

"Is this it?" she asked. "Is this the place from the DVD?"

Michael ran his hand down a boulder scoured by a glacier. Where the boulder faced Porsanger Fjord, the ice and the wind had polished it to a deep curve. At its foot lay scree broken off by the frost, pebbles, and gravel. And that was it. An anti-climax, just like he knew it would be.

"This is it. He was standing right here when they found him."

Michael pointed.

"And he ran over the cliff there."

He walked right up to the edge, and the wind that blew up the side of the hundred-metre-high rock face filled his trousers and jacket until the seams strained. The north-easterly wind, which had pushed the waves along the surface of Kjæsvatnet, whipped up tall waves in the fjord that marched steadily south-west in long, white bearded rows. Huge mountains rose on the other side of the fjord, many of them still snow-covered. Peak after distant peak. There was snow in the saddles between the mountain tops as well. An endless wasteland. He leaned into the wind and looked down at the shore below. The meltwater brook had left white stalagmites up against the cliff face in many melting layers and while he looked, a chunk of ice the size of a car broke off the wall and crashed into the black fjord below. It disappeared under the surface and reappeared further out, shaking off cascades of saltwater. It bobbed up and down, looking for a new equilibrium in the water as it drifted out to sea.

A couple of curious terns dived down to inspect the new attraction, but quickly lost interest and flew away.

He heard her call out and turned around.

"Get back here, Michael!"

He looked down between his boots and realized he was standing on the edge of the crumbling, eroding cliff.

He walked over to Lene, who was cowering behind the boulder.

"I'm sorry," he said.

Her lips trembled.

"I thought you were going to fall! . . . What were you thinking, man? What use would you be to anyone if you fell?"

"None whatsoever. Sorry. And yes, this is where it happened."

Lene was still fuming. And she was frightened.

"How can you be so sure?"

Michael looked at the sun on the other side of the fjord. It drew long, blue shadows across the distant valleys and left the peaks glowing.

"You'll be able to see it in a couple of hours," he explained. "When the stars come out. You can see them in the last frame on the DVD. I got an astronomer to calculate the position based on the altitude of the stars and their individual position. It's very accurate indeed. In fact, it was the easiest task of them all."

Lene wiggled out of the rucksack strap, laid it on the scree and sat down.

"Clever thinking," she said.

"Thank you."

She patted the ground beside her.

"Sit down. It'll be dark soon. And then you can tell me all about it."

"All about what?"

She smiled to him.

"Your surprise, Michael."

He raised a singed eyebrow.

"You think I have a surprise for you?"

"I know you better now. Or at least I think I do . . ." She nodded to herself. "A bit better, I mean. And I know that you wouldn't just wander up here, enter this arena without an exit strategy, make yourself a target, without having something up your sleeve. Please tell me you have something, Michael!"

He gestured towards the empty horizon. The wind tugged at his sleeve.

"Like what? A buried tank? An F-16 fighter squadron? The Frogmen Corps?"

"Yes!"

Michael shook his head.

"I'm afraid not, Lene. It's just us."

She looked at him for a long time. Her green eyes widened slowly and her hands flopped between her knees.

"Just us? Are you serious?"

"Yes."

"Then God help us," she muttered.

He nodded. "I certainly hope he's manning the switchboard."

She gestured towards the cliff edge.

"I don't suppose we dragged all that rope up here unless you were thinking of using it?"

"I am, as it happens. I have to get down to the shore."

"Did you see something? Right now when you nearly succumbed to your death wish?"

He hesitated. He couldn't explain it. It was a hunch. She would think he was out of his mind.

"There's a frozen waterfall below the edge created by that brook over there," he said. "You should take a look at it. It's magnificent."

"No, thanks."

She pressed herself closer to the boulder.

He nodded and looked across the fjord. The superintendent suffered from vertigo.

"There's nothing down there," he said. "Rocks, water, ice . . . nothing."

She got up, and he looked at her rucksack and then at her face.

"Let's get out of here," he said. "We'll find somewhere to pitch the tent and cook some food. This is a bad place."

"Especially if you're prone to sleepwalking," she said.

"Quite."

He stepped out into the howling wind and gazed at the distant slopes of the basement rocks from where a glacier must once have transported the giant boulder which was now standing like a lonely, forgotten sentry at the edge of the world. He surveyed the upland. Moss-covered ridges, some willow thickets, and bare, stony plains with snow in the hollows as far as the eye could see. But Michael sensed something further inland even though nothing moved; there were no noises or reflections, only this faint humming, watching presence.

Then his concentration gave way to a semi-conscious flashback. He had caught a glimpse of cobalt blue; a colour that had no business being here.

Lene was standing with her thumbs tucked inside the straps of her rucksack, ready to go.

"What is it, Michael?"

"Blue," he muttered.

"Blue?"

He snapped his fingers impatiently.

"Cobalt blue. Like they use in ceramics. The colour everyone wore in the Eighties."

"Where?"

He pointed to the boulder.

"Over there."

Michael walked around the monolith and pulled off his rucksack. He kneeled down and narrowed his eyes against the sun's reflection in the glittering silicon specks in the granite.

"Michael?"

Carefully he brushed pebbles and gravel aside at the base of the boulder and felt something soft under his fingers. A shoelace or a piece of string. He pulled it out into the light. The cobalt-blue shoelace was trapped under a stone, which he brusquely pushed aside. He yanked the shoelace and lifted out a sturdy grey-leather and Gore-Tex hiking boot from the hollow. He looked inside it.

"Scarpa, size ten," he said. "Right foot. It's a fine boot. And new. Look at the sole."

"It's damaged," she said.

The small metal eyes that kept the bootlace in place had been blown clean off the leather.

"A bullet would have left a mark like that," he said. "It's dark brown inside. It's full of dried blood."

They looked at it in silence. Her shoulder touched his and he could smell her. She smelled of wind and sunshine and sweat. It was a nice smell.

He cleared his throat.

"Do you think it was his?" she asked.

"I'm absolutely sure of it. He must have buried it before they found him."

"And hoped," she said.

Michael nodded.

"He hoped that one day someone would find it."

"It's evidence," she said. "We can get DNA confirmation from the blood."

"We can prove that Kasper Hansen was here, but we can't prove who killed him," he pointed out.

"But now you won't have to scale down that wall, Michael!"

"We'll discuss it tomorrow," he said. "Come on."

They pitched their tent on a fairly level piece of ground among willow thickets half a kilometre from the cliff edge and the lonely boulder. Michael cleared away the scree and erected the tent, which involved nothing more than feeding two flexible aluminium rods through channels in the canvas and laying out the groundsheet and their sleeping bags inside it.

They had heated up some food and eaten it, though neither of them was particularly hungry, and they had boiled water for tea, to which Michael added brandy from his hip-flask.

Keith Mallory had given it to him for his thirty-fifth birthday. It was silver, flat, and concave, with a fine, aged leather cover, and embossed with a warm inscription over the winged dagger from the Englishman's old regiment—the 22nd SAS—and their motto: *Who Dares Wins*. He unscrewed the cap again and waved the hip-flask.

"More?"

Lene was now a dark shape that blocked out the first stars on the northern sky. She stuck out her cup.

"Yes, please. What a fine hip-flask."

He held it up and looked at it. He could feel the inscription under his fingertips.

"A present from a friend," he said.

"A friend?"

"I have friends."

"Of course you do," she said in a neutral voice. "I suggest we take turns to keep a lookout?"

"I'll take the first four hours," he volunteered.

"What's your friend's name, Michael?"

"Keith Mallory."

She looked at him, and on a sudden impulse asked, "Is he in the same line of work as you?"

"He is, as it happens. Only he's better at it."

She drained her cup.

"We're not alone," she said quietly, and Michael watched her calm, clear profile against the still bright evening sky. There was no anxiety in her voice. At most, it was stating a fact.

"We're not?"

"No."

Michael pulled his knees up to his chest, reached inside the dome tent for a sleeping bag, and wrapped it around himself.

"Have you seen . . . or heard anything?" he asked.

"Nothing. I just know it. Someone is up here."

"I've never believed in a sixth or seventh sense," he said.

"Perhaps now is a good time to start," she said. "I'm fairly certain. Good night."

"Sleep tight."

She slipped through the tent opening, zipping the flaps down behind her, and he heard her rustling around inside. There was something comforting and normal about the sounds she made.

Michael picked up the machine pistol, checked that it was loaded, and flicked aside the safety catch. He unzipped his sleeping bag, pulled it up around his legs and lower body, zipped it up again and tried to find a comfortable position against a wide willow trunk. He placed the machine pistol across his lap. It was heavy and felt very real. He could just about see his own cloudy breath and he pondered what she had said.

There was nothing out there. Even the car headlights across the fjord had disappeared. The boulder down by the cliff edge stood out sharply against the dark grey waters of the fjord. Taut, upright, and black, like a Chinese character.

Perhaps he had nodded off for a moment. Or maybe he had got out of the habit of keeping watch. The last time had been with Keith Mallory in that sodding church loft in Grozny.

Half asleep, he watched a star on the western sky. It appeared brighter than the others. Or maybe it was a planet? One of the gas giants?

The star moved. Quickly.

He opened his eyes wide and observed the phenomenon. It moved with unnatural speed, it turned green, and began flashing and then he heard the rotor sound . . . faintly, like a trapped insect.

Michael straightened up, now completely awake.

The helicopter's navigation lights reflected spookily in the fjord. At times the engine sound disappeared, but it always came back. There was no hesitation or indecision about the flight. The helicopter vanished behind the nearest mountains towards north-east and the noise grew more distant before it faded away altogether.

He jumped when he sensed her right behind him. He hadn't heard her leave the tent and was impressed by quite how still and silent she could be, while at the same time she had scared him half to death.

"Would it kill you to cough or make a noise before you sneak up on me like a sodding ninja?!"

Even Michael could hear the crisp crack of fear in his voice.

"Sorry," she grunted, and put her hand on his burned shoulder. "Was that them? The helicopter. Are they here?"

"Yes. Please, would you move your hand?"

"Sorry. Are you happy now?" she asked.

"No."

CHAPTER 52

Lene had a walkie-talkie in her pocket and an earpiece in her left ear. And empty, useless hands.

Michael hadn't uttered one word for the last ten minutes. She could hear his rasping breathing as he abseiled down the frozen waterfall on the cliff wall. The thin red-and-blue climbing rope quivered like a bowstring on top of the camper mat Michael had placed between the rope and the cliff edge. At times it would move slightly to one side or the other, as if he were swinging in large arcs across the wall. He had seemed calm but distant as he hammered in pitons and anchor bolts to the mountain to attach the rope. Then he had flung the coil into the abyss, strapped on the climbing harness, and disappeared over the edge after one last, expressionless gaze at Lene, who was sitting behind the boulder. No power on Earth could make her walk up to that edge, whereas Michael looked as if he had lowered himself down vertical cliff faces his whole life.

He had left the machine gun with her.

How long did it take to abseil a hundred metres? One minute? Twelve minutes had passed. She took the walkie-talkie out of her pocket and pressed the *send* button hard.

"Michael?"

The rope gave the most violent jerk she had yet seen. The chafing of the rope was starting to wear through the camper mat. If the rope came into direct contact with the cliff it would probably fray and then snap.

"... Yes ... ?"

"What are you doing? Are you there yet?"

She heard a cross between a grunt and a sigh.

"Most of the time ... I just hang here. The end of this sodding rope has looped itself around some of the icicles and got wedged under a protrusion ... I can't get the bloody ..."

Lene heard the sharp sound of an ice axe in action and closed her eyes.

"Can't you just jump the last stretch?"

"Thirty metres? I don't think so. I'll call, or whatever it is you do, when I've landed, okay?"

"Okay . . ."

She sat down behind the boulder and delved into her pocket for the last Snickers. She had to do something.

Michael dangled his arms along his sides. They ached with lactic acid, and he was forced to take a break from hacking away with the ice axe. Overall, he was comfortably suspended and nicely balanced with the iron spikes from his climbing boots against the ice wall, but an offshoot from the meltwater stream sent a constant spray of icy droplets over his helmet, head and shoulders. The water found its way under his collar and down the warm skin on his back, past the rubber cuffs on his sleeves and down his chest. He raised his face up into the spray, blinked hard, and stared imploringly at the rope which was trapped somewhere above him.

He looked down between his boots at the narrow shore below him. Rocks. Ice. A sliver of snow on the north face of the cliffs. Nothing. He bent his legs, pushed his climbing spikes against the ice and slowly and diagonally kicked off the wall. When he hit the wall again, he grabbed the rope above his head and started running across the wall, hanging horizontally with one hand on the rope and the other wielding the ice axe. He reached the limit of his swing, set off again with all his strength and whacked the ice axe into the far end of the curve.

He started climbing upwards to offset the terrible pull of the rope. The ice axe bit deeply into the porous ice. The rope slackened and he could breathe more freely. He could see every detail of the rock behind the thin shell of clear ice. Michael climbed past the looped rope, leaned forwards, yanked it free, and was finally able to lower himself down.

He stood on the shore for a long time, with his hands on his knees, breathing in quick, hard gasps until he could speak normally again.

"I'm down," he said into the walkie-talkie.

". . . Down . . . ?" he heard.

"Yes, down!"

". . . Good . . . fine . . ."

He silenced the radio.

"Right, bloody brilliant," he muttered, and looked about him.

The ice lay like duvets on the shore and in between the rocks in the shallow water. The beach was six metres at its widest. Michael skirted around the frozen waterfall. This, he thought, must have been the very spot where Kasper Hansen hit the ground.

There wasn't so much as a seabird landing or the sound of a distant boat engine. The fjord was deserted as far as the eye could see. He waded out into the water to the top of his boots and studied the seabed. The water was greenish, but blue and shimmering further out where the sun hit the surface. He walked back past the frozen waterfall in a northern direction and stopped and stared up at the wall twenty metres on. A narrow, straight ravine stretched from the shore all the way up to the plateau. It was just as inviting as a staircase, and a geriatric with a Zimmer frame could easily scale it.

Something round and white at the foot of the cliff caught his attention. The shore was covered with surprisingly uniform, dark grey stones the size of potatoes and polished by the water, and the spring snow was grey and grubby, but in the shade something bright white glowed. He bent over the object and frowned. It was shiny, and domed, and stuck out of the surrounding gravel. It gave a crisp, hollow sound when he tapped it with the ice axe. Carefully he started removing pebbles and sand and discovered that the bony dome was really the tip of a large, irregular block of ice, which was almost buried in a hollow: in eternal shadow, and isolated by the gravel and the sand. The ice was greenish and long, and black veins ran through it. Michael surmised that the block could have lain there for years. He began digging it out with the broad blade of his axe, easing the handle under the lump, lifting it up from its nest, and then fell backwards onto the ice. Shocked, he raised his hands to his face and closed his eyes while his heart pounded dry and hard in his chest. He gulped several times before he was able to open his eyes again.

Inside the block was the perfectly preserved head of a woman: regular features, and smooth, black hair that floated eternally inside the green ice. The head was balanced on a short neck that had been severed cleanly, right below the throat, with near-surgical precision. The woman's eyes were half closed, with a meditative, almost dreamy expression. There was a hint of a sleepy smile around her bloodless lips. A young, black-haired woman. Ingrid Sundsbö.

Michael's fingers shook, and he felt hot tears stream down his cheeks. Her scalp had been exposed to the elements; wind, ice and water had scoured away the crown of her hair and the skin, so only the white scalp, as smooth as porcelain, was left. The rest of her head was intact.

Piano wire, he thought automatically. The hunters had garrotted her with a thin wire, probably while pressing a knee into the back of her neck. Suddenly, he knew which one of them had done it. Afterwards, they had put her head in a sack and tossed it to her husband, a few seconds after the time when he had cried out in triumph—in the belief that she had escaped. When he had seen the contents of the sack, his soul had been snuffed out like a candle. Kasper Hansen had jumped: Michael knew that now. He had done what Johanne Reimers couldn't do. He had never been hit by a rifle bullet.

Michael sat for a long time with his back against the red granite, staring at the ice block by his side. Then he stuck his hand in his pocket and found and drained the hip-flask.

He covered the ice block with grey, round stones, gravel and sand before he left the shore. She should stay here, he had decided. As close to her husband's body and spirit as possible.

He had climbed almost seventy metres up through the narrow ravine, and it was just as easy as it had looked down from the shore. His walkie-talkie crackled; perhaps it had done so for a while without him being aware of it.

"Yes?"

Michael held the walkie-talkie to his ear and thought how absurd it was to make radio contact when all she had to do was walk up to the edge and call out to him in a normal voice.

"Someone is coming, Michael, where are you?!"

"Who?"

"Get up here . . . now!"

He began to hurry. There was plenty to hold on to, so it would take at most twenty seconds before he could push his way through the turf a few metres from Lene, who was shifting from foot to foot by the rope with her back to him.

He put his hand on her shoulder.

She spun around with her pistol half out of the holster. Her eyes were blurred and intensely focused at the same time, and her face was deadpan.

"Easy now. It's me!"

Her eyes lit up and she stamped the stony ground.

"Jesus Christ, Michael! How the hell did you get back up here?"

He made a half-turn and pointed.

"From over there. Nature's up-escalator."

"How . . . ? Never mind. Someone's coming."

She dragged him behind the boulder and handed him the binoculars.

"Where?"

"There." She pointed north-east, and he stepped out into the sun with the binoculars to his eyes.

There was nothing stealthy about the man's approach. He walked briskly and in a straight line across the stony plateau, as if taking a stroll in his lunch break, and he was approximately three hundred metres from their position. He was alone, and Michael recognized him instantly.

Lene watched Michael and suffered with him. His face had gone pale and drawn, and his hands, still holding the binoculars, were shaking. He had stopped breathing.

"Who is it, Michael? Don't forget to breathe."

"Be quiet."

The straight-backed man stopped fifteen metres from them. His grey eyes watched them with interest, but his mouth was a straight, anxious line under his moustache. His face was narrow and gaunt. He shifted his gaze from her to Michael, and the lines of his mouth and face softened. He folded his hands behind his back and nodded briefly, army-style.

"Tell me how you do it, Mike?" he asked very clearly in English.

Michael smiled faintly, but he didn't move.

Lene took a step forwards, and the stranger immediately took one step back. Michael yanked her arm hard. The two men looked at each other, and not at her.

"Do what, Keith?" he asked.

"We're close to the North Pole in this godforsaken wasteland, and yet here you are in the company of a beautiful woman."

"I guess I'm just lucky. Lene is a police superintendent. What went wrong, Keith, and can they hear me?"

Keith? Keith Mallory, Lene thought. Michael Sander's friend. The trump card. She had known all the time he must have something up his sleeve; he was far too wise and experienced to walk into an ambush without having a backup plan.

"They can't hear us, Mike."

He held up his left hand. The last joint of his ring finger was missing.

"Everything was fine until I bumped into them at Gardermoen Airport in Oslo. Old pictures from a forgotten past. My cover was blown immediately. They had really done their homework. All the arseholes I served with have written books about the regiment's heroic deeds—including quite a few who were never even there. Pardon my French, miss, but they really were arseholes."

"That's okay," she mumbled.

"They recognized me from a picture in a bloody book, Mike. That sodding finger I left behind in Iraq. So . . . Well, goodbye Magnusson, Norwegian-Scottish oil billionaire. An otherwise nice guy. S&W has done a fair amount of work for him over the years, so he was happy to have a doppelgänger for a couple of days. I'm the spitting image of him. Great idea of yours, Mike. And like you said, the money is good. But . . ."

"Nobody's perfect, Keith."

"Speak for yourself." Keith Mallory laughed a mirthless laugh. "Do something to them, Mike. Especially the young one. He's pure evil. A sick fucker."

"I'll try," Michael said.

Michael Sander raised his head and looked over the Englishman's shoulder to the higher ground, with moraine debris and willow thickets further up.

"How many, Keith?"

"Three."

"Where?"

The Englishman smiled, but he didn't move.

"Somewhere right behind me. I'm sorry, Mike."

"So am I, Keith."

Mallory started to turn, to indicate a spot behind him, when the shot was fired. The bullet arrived at the same time as its echo. It hit the small man between his shoulder blades, then passed through his chest, and Lene heard and felt a spray of blood hit her face and clothing. The Englishman's knees buckled and he stumbled forwards without trying to cushion his fall. His legs lay tangled under his body, and his arms parallel to his sides, as if he had fallen while kneeling in prayer.

She started screaming, and looked down to her blood-splattered hands. She was about to run to the dead man when Michael grabbed hold of her. He was phenomenally strong and she couldn't move.

"Stand still, for Christ's sake, woman!" he hissed. "Look! Look, God dammit."

"What?!"

Michael held his hand in front of her chest and caught a quivering red and a green dot in his palm.

"Laser sights. Two of them. Right above your heart. Now do you understand?"

She nodded and her legs nearly gave way under her.

The red and green dots wandered up to the machine pistol she carried over her shoulder. Very carefully Michael removed it, emptied out the ammunition with exaggerated, slow movements and tossed it aside. The busy little dots dived down to the pistol in her hip holster and he repeated the procedure. The pistol pinged when it hit a stone some metres away.

Then he meshed his fingers behind his neck and nodded to her.

She copied him.

"Michael, can't we . . . ?" she began.

"No."

"He was your friend," she said, looking at the crumpled, immobile body.

"Yes."

"So what does it mean, Michael?"

"Nothing. It means nothing at all. We're finished. They won."

Two figures began to emerge from the rocks and the crippled willow bushes half a kilometre away. They strolled along at a leisurely pace. They had all the time in the world.

CHAPTER 53

Victor Schmidt walked at the front with long strides and he carried a hunting rifle in the crook of his elbow. He was wearing the same camouflage clothes that Michael had seen on Elizabeth Caspersen's DVD and had found in Kim Andersen's rucksack: jagged lines and patterns in white, grey and black, well-suited to northern Norway. He had put up the hood of the jacket and a pair of sunglasses hung from a string around his neck. Henrik Schmidt, wearing an identical outfit, followed behind him. He didn't wear sunglasses and his blue eyes sparkled.

Lene jumped when she recognized those eyes, and Michael prayed that she wouldn't lunge at him. Henrik Schmidt carried a loaded army carbine in his hands. The barrel was pointing right at her stomach and the young man's finger was on the trigger.

Father and son stopped three metres away. Henrik Schmidt smirked and Victor Schmidt pushed down his hood. They spent a moment looking at the dead man.

"I hope your daughter is better, Lene," Henrik Schmidt said. "You should have listened to us. I'll find her again. I promise you. What's left of her."

He grinned at the superintendent.

Michael glanced at Lene out of the corner of his eye. Her body was rigid, her face deathly pale, and her green eyes flat and icy.

Victor Schmidt swung the rifle over his shoulder.

"I'm sorry about the girl," he said in a low voice. "It was unnecessary."

He shot his grinning son a disapproving look.

"Henrik . . ."

"Why don't you introduce us to your friend?" Michael interrupted him and nodded to the landscape behind them. "Thomas Berg."

Victor Schmidt peered at him and checked his wristwatch. Then he shrugged and murmured a few words into a VHF radio.

"Yes, why don't I? In fact, he ought to be here, we all should. I like neat endings, even though explanations are really for children." He smiled to Michael. "I have to hand it to you, Michael, you did a great job. In some respects. I can see why Elizabeth hired you. She's a great judge of character."

"She didn't know her father very well," Michael said casually.

"Flemming?"

Victor Schmidt stuck the radio into his jacket pocket and kept his hands there while a tall, powerful figure emerged from the willows five hundred metres away.

"I knew Flemming," Victor Schmidt responded. "He would have liked you, Michael. He judged a man by his skills."

"My skills don't appear to be worth much," Michael said, and his knees felt like rubber. "If they were, I'd be on a beach in the Seychelles rather than here."

He couldn't help looking at Keith behind the two men's legs; boundless grief and guilt threatened to overcome him. He thought like crazy about Sara and his children. It was like staring into a black wall.

"Being outnumbered isn't the same as incompetence," Victor Schmidt said kindly. "Any organization will usually beat an individual, Michael. Ultimately, it's a simple question of resources. Flemming . . . he was a remarkable man. I don't think I ever found out what drove him . . . and kept driving him . . . He never stopped until he had got what he thought he wanted, and he was fantastic at overcoming setbacks."

"And he enjoyed killing people," Michael added, and managed with a huge effort to keep his voice under control. "Right here, in fact. You all did. Caspersen, Allan Lundkvist, Robert Olsen, Kenneth Enderlein, Kim Andersen, Thomas Berg and . . . your son, Henrik, I presume?"

Victor Schmidt nodded, and smiled faintly. His glass eye was aimed at the ground, while his working eye sized Michael up. There was something regretful in his manner. He wasn't crazy like his son, Michael thought.

"When you're rich . . . when you've tried most things . . . I think you need to have experienced it to understand. Personally, I never got it. That urge. I have to admit that. I didn't join in, as you know. Never."

He gestured towards his son.

"Henrik was different. He and Flemming were as thick as thieves. Always. Flemming took care of him while I looked after the business. I made Sonartek what it is today. Anyone can get a good idea, Michael. That's the easy part. Bringing it to fruition takes talent, luck, and hard work."

He fell silent and stared into space.

"Flemming also took care of Jakob?" Michael asked.

A cloud passed over Henrik Schmidt's sky-blue eyes. The barrel of the carbine swung around and pointed at Michael's groin.

"Easy, Henrik," his father said, but he sounded distracted. "Sander is just trying to provoke you. Don't allow yourself to be provoked, Henrik. It's childish."

Michael stole a glance at the machine gun on the ground before his gaze returned to Henrik's face. It was out of the question. Henrik Schmidt never took his eyes off him. He might well be stark staring mad, but there was nothing wrong with his reflexes or marksmanship, and the machine pistol was at least four metres away.

Victor Schmidt smiled to Michael. "Yes, Flemming took care of Jakob as well, that's right. We all did, though it turned out that he would rather we didn't. As you've already worked out, Jakob was the son Flemming so desperately wanted. We shared most things, Flemming and I, though I didn't always realize what that actually implied."

"Did Jakob know?" Michael asked.

"Of course he did. He never liked me."

"Personally, I'm beginning to warm to him," Michael said.

Victor Schmidt turned around at the sound of boots on rock.

"Thomas. Let me introduce you to Michael Sander," he said, "and you already know Lene . . ."

The new arrival stopped next to Victor Schmidt and his son. He had a straight back with a muscular neck and broad shoulders. He looked very much like Jakob Schmidt, Michael thought. His camouflage jacket was open and his shirt buttoned up to his neck. The scorpion tail curled up under his right ear.

"It was you," Lene whispered, and her mouth contorted.

"Don't . . ." Michael began, but Victor Schmidt held up his hand.

"It's all right, Michael. Let the superintendent speak. I think she has earned the right."

"It was you," she repeated, and stared furiously at the gamekeeper. "You took her. You took my daughter, you fucking arsehole!"

"I hope she'll be all right," Thomas Berg said with a pleasant, deep voice. "She's a fine girl."

"Lene," Michael warned her again. "Stop it."

Victor Schmidt watched the exchange with interest. Then he smiled at Lene.

"Perhaps you really should stop it now," he suggested. He pulled his other hand out of his pocket and looked at his wristwatch again. "The CD, Michael, where is it? Kim's CD. I presume you escaped through the crawlspace. In the nick of time—to judge from your lack of eyebrows and hair."

Michael stared at him.

"It was lost in the fire," he said.

The financier nodded pensively and sent the gamekeeper a sideways glance. A black automatic pistol appeared in Thomas Berg's hand as if by magic. The muzzle pointed right between Lene and Michael.

"The CD, Michael?" Victor Schmidt asked him again, but more harshly this time. "Now!"

"So Flemming Caspersen really was the client?" Michael asked.

Victor Schmidt seemed genuinely surprised.

"Of course he was. But he got the trip for free. It was a good hunt. Everyone was very excited about Kasper Hansen. He made a fine trophy. And his wife was almost better. Henrik found her."

"And cut off her head?"

The financier made an almost conciliatory gesture.

"Is there any need for these details, Michael?"

"And Caspersen died peacefully in his sleep?"

Schmidt pursed his lips and looked at him closely.

"He did. His time had come and I don't suppose the devil was prepared to wait any longer. We didn't help him on his way, if that's what you're implying."

"And you intended to use the DVD to blackmail Elizabeth Caspersen once she had been appointed her mother's legal guardian," Michael said. "You planted the DVD in her father's safe during the horn theft? Isn't that right?"

He looked from one to the other, but no one said anything.

"Answer me, please."

Victor Schmidt seemed genuinely puzzled. Thomas Berg looked across the fjord and didn't appear to be listening. Even the fanatical Henrik Schmidt looked mystified.

"Isn't that right?" Michael asked again, and even he could hear how shrill his voice had become.

"Horn theft?" Victor Schmidt asked. "Is that what that bloody woman told you? Flemming had that damned DVD all along, but even in my wildest dreams I didn't believe that he would ever put it in his own safe."

Michael felt as if he had been hit in the solar plexus with a battering ram. All his instincts screamed that Schmidt was telling the truth. His hands started to release their grip at the back of his neck, but some friendly encouragement from Thomas's automatic pistol made him interlace his fingers again.

And yet he repeated stubbornly, "Did Kim Andersen break into Flemming Caspersen's house and steal a pair of rhino horns? I mean, they're worth $50,000 per kilo?"

Victor Schmidt looked blankly at him. Then he turned his gaze, reluctantly, towards his son and the gamekeeper.

"Henrik? Thomas? Rhino horns? Any ideas?"

"Absolutely not," Henrik Schmidt said. "If he had, he wouldn't have needed to clear out his account with the casino to pay for his wedding. And, anyway, he wouldn't have known how to go about it. Flemming always had the latest in security systems."

"I agree," Thomas Berg said. "If he had sold ten kilos of rhino horn on the black market, he wouldn't have needed his Running Man money. He knew that we weren't to touch that money for the next five years. At least. He knew what would happen if he did it and was found out. But why does that matter now?"

Victor Schmidt turned his attention back to Michael.

"The CD? I'm not going to ask you again."

Michael's mouth was as dry as sand. So this was the end.

"One more thing . . ." he said.

"Dad . . ." Henrik Schmidt whined. He sounded like a child who had been refused his Christmas presents.

"Hang on," Victor Schmidt said and ran his palms over his stubble. "What?"

Michael looked at his dead friend behind the trio. His eyelids stung, but he would rather die than show them his grief. No regrets, nothing. Suddenly that became terribly, terribly important.

Victor Schmidt followed his gaze.

"One of your former colleagues from Shepherd & Wilkins, I presume? Elizabeth must have written one hell of a cheque to get him up here. Senior consultant, I believe? Christ, I can't even begin to imagine his hourly rate. Because I don't suppose he joined Running Man as this Magnusson from Aberdeen for sentimental reasons?"

He stared hard at Michael.

The man was a pedant, Michael thought. An anal, vengeful, and rejected little man. He could see why his wife had ended up the way she had and why Jakob despised him.

"Not exclusively," he said.

Which was true. Keith Mallory had been his friend, but the Englishman was also a professional, and he never mixed business with pleasure.

Victor Schmidt finally looked at his son with a hint of approval in his working eye. Henrik Schmidt blushed faintly.

Michael shuddered at the sight.

"It was Henrik," the financier smiled. "He claimed to know everything about this Magnusson and I challenged him. I said that you can never know everything about someone. Fortunately, Henrik rose to the challenge and decided to investigate Running Man's latest client."

He smiled to Michael.

"It was a good ploy. It really was. The timing might have been a little too convenient for it to be entirely convincing, but it could have worked out. For you."

He turned and looked at the dead Englishman.

"And then it would have been us lying dead over there. Henrik, Thomas, and me, wouldn't it?"

"That was the plan," Michael nodded.

He could feel Lene's eyes on him, but he didn't look at her.

"But Dad," Henrik implored him again, and Victor Schmidt nodded.

"Where is the CD?"

"I . . ." Michael began, but was interrupted by a shot from Thomas's pistol which sounded as if it was fired inside his own head.

Lene screamed and Michael watched her collapse. His hands reached out for her, but Thomas took a step forwards and kicked his feet away from under him. He hit the rocky ground with his shoulders and back first and the air was knocked out of his lungs. He ignored it and looked around for Lene. He scrambled around on his stomach while his chest pumped in vain to get air into his lungs.

Her ashen face was turned towards him and her eyes sought out his.

Michael gasped like a new-born baby and finally managed to open his throat.

"Lene . . . Lene, Jesus Christ," he whispered. "Lene . . ."

She was lying on her back and looked at him with eyes wide with shock. She sent him an embarrassed smile.

"I'm sorry, Michael . . . I'm sorry."

Her hands were clutching her right thigh, just above the knee. Michael pushed himself up on his burned hands and saw the blood pour out between her fingers. Somewhere above him, he heard Victor Schmidt speak and he rolled over.

"That was the knee, Michael. Next shot will be to her cunt or her head. You've seen her cunt, Thomas. It's a nice cunt, isn't it?"

The gamekeeper nodded.

"Yes," he said evenly. "I suppose so."

Victor Schmidt's breathing was strained now.

"Now do you understand, Michael? What's it going to be?"

Michael nodded. His head was heavy as mortal sin, but he managed to raise it up and turn his face towards the older man.

"A scout cabin," he said. "There's a scout cabin in a forest . . ."

Henrik Schmidt bent over Lene. His expression was closed and intent, and he was no longer smiling. At long last.

Michael reeled off addresses and information about the sleeping loft and the crack to buy time and neutralize the insane son. Henrik Schmidt moved closer, raised his carbine and pressed the muzzle against Lene's hands on the wound. He forced her fingers aside with the barrel and grinned at her while he rested his weight on the carbine. She tried to push it away, but screamed again.

And again, when the next shot was fired.

Michael blinked and looked at Lene's hands. They were still there, but the barrel was gone.

"Henrik . . . ?" Victor Schmidt said into the air above Michael's head. "Henrik . . . ?"

Michael realized that the shot had come from afar. Everyone looked at Henrik Schmidt's right hand. His thumb and index finger were missing and small arteries sprayed fine, red arcs into the air.

"Dad . . ."

The carbine had landed a few metres away.

Then everyone turned their gaze inland, to the low ridges, the moraine blocks, and the willow thicket. A flash lasting only a second appeared from that direction. Like the sun bouncing off the telescopic sight of a rifle, Michael thought.

Thomas Berg was in the process of turning around when his head was yanked backwards by an invisible hand. It swelled and burst like an overripe fruit. He fell forwards and the dust rose. The back of his head was a wet crater.

The crack of the invisible sniper's rifle echoed across the terrain and Michael and Lene stared at each other.

Victor Schmidt had got his own rifle down from his shoulder and was oblivious to the two of them. He aimed it at the moraine and the rocks, but there was no movement there, nothing to shoot at.

"Who are you?" he screamed. "Who are you?!"

There was no reply and he spun around and raised the rifle.

"You . . . ! You bastard!" he screamed at Michael. "All the time, it's you . . . You bastard . . ."

A second later Victor Schmidt lay across Thomas; the two men formed a cross on the white snow.

Michael got up and hobbled past Henrik Schmidt who was bent double with his damaged hand pressed against his stomach. The young man didn't see him. His blue eyes kept staring at the two bodies on the ground.

Michael picked up Lene's service pistol, walked behind Henrik and kicked him at the back of his legs so he fell to his knees. Then he pulled a bootlace out of one of Victor Schmidt's boots and tied the son's hands behind his back. The blood was warm and sticky under his fingers. He took the other bootlace from the financier's boots and ran over to Lene, who had got to a sitting position. He stuck his finger into the holes in her trousers and ripped open the fabric. She bit her lower lip and looked at his hands, but didn't make a sound. The bullet had gone through her quads, but the wounds were no longer bleeding very much. The bullet hadn't hit the thighbone or any of the major arteries, he concluded. He tore the bottom off her trouser leg, folded it into a compress and tied it tightly over her injuries with the bootlace.

"It's going to hurt like hell, but it isn't fatal," he said.

She had gone white and she nodded, but she was looking over his shoulder at Henrik Schmidt.

"Are you able to stand?"

He helped her to her feet, and her face contorted violently when she put her weight on her right foot in a hesitant step. She turned her face towards him and he slowly let go of her, ready to catch her again.

"It's okay," she said in a low voice.

"Are you sure?" he asked.

"Yes."

"Totally?" he asked, and looked her right in the eye.

She nodded and touched his arm.

Michael turned away and looked across the plateau behind them.

"You were right."

"About what?"

"We weren't alone," he said.

Michael pointed to a figure far away. Impossibly far away. The man had got up between some rocks and was strapping a rucksack to his shoulders. Unhurried and methodical. He straightened up and Michael knew that the sniper was watching them. Michael slowly raised his hand; a couple of seconds later the stranger returned his greeting. Then he disappeared between the rocks.

"Do you know him?" Lene asked.

"I don't think so," Michael said.

There was a faint smile around Lene's lips, but it disappeared when her eyes fell on Henrik Schmidt.

"Are you absolutely sure you want to do this?" Michael asked her again, very gravely. "You'll have to live with it for the rest of your life, Lene."

"I know. And I'm absolutely sure," she said.

He handed her the pistol.

"I'll wait here. I won't leave unless . . ."

"I'd like you to stay," she said.

Henrik Schmidt lifted his head and looked from one to the other. When she limped closer, he started to cry.

Lene stopped a few metres in front of him and raised her pistol.

Henrik Schmidt stared up at her, but found nothing in her face he could use, so instead he looked at Michael.

"You have to do something," he said, still smiling. "She's going to kill me."

"What can I do, Henrik?" Michael asked. "You're incurable."

He paused for a long time and looked at Lene who was struggling to stay upright.

"You cut off her head, didn't you, Henrik?"

The young man didn't reply, but looked into Michael's dark blue eyes.

"Who?"

"The woman, Henrik. Ingrid Sundsbö."

The boy smiled at the memory. He nodded eagerly: "Flemming always said, "Destroy what they love and you castrate them. They won't be back." It was good advice, don't you think?"

He looked up again with his smiling, pale blue eyes.

"We found her quite quickly and Flemming gave me permission to kill her. He said it was my right."

"Goodbye, Henrik."

Henrik Schmidt's jaw muscles quivered. He tried to swallow, but failed. Again, he glanced briefly at the superintendent's face before staring down at the ground. He closed his blue eyes, Michael closed his, and the shot cracked.

Michael had counted to three when the fatal second shot echoed across the rocks and the fjord and reverberated between the hollows. A few seagulls on the black water took off, only to settle a little further out.

CHAPTER 54

As Michael collapsed from exhaustion outside their tent, drank some water or ate one of the optimistically named energy bars, which tasted like crunchy loft insulation, Lene was morose and silent. She either sat on a stone some distance from the tent with her face turned away or laid curled up inside it, staring at the canvas. It was understandable and Michael had no great urge to talk either. Chewing alone hurt enough.

He lay on his back on one of the camper mats which they had rolled out in the sun and stared at the blue sky while his pulse and blood pressure returned to almost normal levels and the sweat dried on his body. Before his muscles seized up completely, he got up with a groan and walked back to the cliff edge to fetch another body, which he threw over his shoulder in a fireman's lift and carried up to a hiding place he had found behind the big moraine blocks.

Victor and Henrik Schmidt were heavy but manageable, while Thomas Berg nearly killed him. The man was a giant, heavy and long, and one of his feet scraped along the ground behind Michael's boots.

He put Berg's body down at the foot of the moraine blocks and paused to get his breath back. He was smeared with the dead men's blood, urine, and faeces which made it almost impossible for him to manoeuvre them. He grunted, grabbed hold of the gamekeeper's jacket and started dragging the body by its shoulders up through a small ravine. Sweat was dripping from his face and he sobbed from fatigue before he was finally able to roll the body of Thomas Berg down into a shaded, damp chamber under a low rock face where he sincerely hoped all three of them would remain undisturbed until Judgement Day, together with their rucksacks and the rest of the weapons he had found in the willow thicket. He had smashed their mobiles and satellite telephones and searched their clothing and rucksacks without finding anything of interest—with the exception of Elizabeth Caspersen's

DVD, which was in a pocket in Henrik Schmidt's rucksack, or at least one with his name on it.

Michael got up, stretched his aching back, and started throwing small rocks and stones down the slope. It took him an hour to cover the bodies and seal the chamber.

Then he staggered back across the plateau. The last body was Keith Mallory's, and Michael had found a special place for his old friend, far, far away from his executioners.

When he got there, he dried the blood from his face and picked up Mallory in his arms as if lifting a sleeping child. The Englishman was light, much lighter than the others, and his face was strangely serene, strangely disciplined, even in death. Keith had mastered every situation, he had never had doubts or been at a loss or behaved inelegantly. His eyes and mouth were closed and he smelled only of his aftershave; the most expensive, obviously, that money could buy.

Michael had no qualms about burying him up here. The Englishman had been married once, but hadn't seen his ex-wife for thirty years. He had no children. Many people would undoubtedly miss him, but no family members.

An hour later, Michael placed his hip-flask on Mallory's small chest, arranged his open hands across it and stroked his old friend's cheek with his fingertips one last time. Then he said a short prayer and covered the body with earth, rocks and, finally, turf. It was a good, high location; a small mound with grass and heather in between the rocks and with a view of the fjord. It was the best he could find.

"Lene?"

"What?"

"Please, would you toss me my rucksack?"

His rucksack was passed through the tent opening and Michael tore it open. He was naked and had washed himself, screaming, in the meltwater brook and rubbed himself with handfuls of snow, after which he had sprinted across the plateau to the tent. Right now his skin was red and glowing, but very soon it would turn cold and blue.

He took out some clean thermal underwear, a fleece jumper, some socks, and a pair of jeans. He buttoned them with shaking hands and picked up his relatively intact parka from the ground. He laced his boots, squatted down on his haunches outside the tent and started heating water.

When the water boiled, he poured it into their mugs and chucked in some tea bags.

"Tea?" he called out over his shoulder.

There was movement inside, but no reply.

He was just about to repeat his question when she crawled out of the tent and sat down not far from him. He handed her a mug. She took it from his hand and stared blankly into it.

"How are you?" he asked, and looked across the fjord. It was getting late and he would hate to have to spend the night here.

"I don't know. All right, I suppose. Christ . . . I don't know."

"I would have done the same," he said quietly. "Exactly the same."

"Yes."

She shifted. She didn't move further away, but she didn't move closer, either.

"What do we do now?" she asked.

Michael looked up at the sky.

"I think Elizabeth Caspersen would be prepared to spend a helicopter on us," he said. "We have a satellite telephone."

"I'd prefer to walk back to the cars," she said.

"You've been shot in the leg," Michael reminded her.

"It doesn't hurt very much."

"Tomorrow you'll be begging me for a morphine drip, trust me."

"I still prefer to walk, Michael. Have you buried them?"

"They're gone," he said.

"Completely?"

"They're completely gone."

"And your friend?"

"In another place. Far away. Honey?"

"Yes, please," she said.

Michael squirted a jet of acacia honey into her mug.

"Who was he? The miracle that saved us? I know that you know, but you won't tell me because I'm a cop. Was he Plan B?"

"The sniper? Possibly, but he wasn't *my* Plan B. I didn't get a proper look at him. Hat. Sunglasses. A camouflage net over his hat. I walked over to the place where he must have been hiding."

"Did you find anything?"

He smiled. "Nothing. Not even a flattened blade of grass. Or a cartridge shell or a footprint in the snow further in between the rocks. Nothing. A ghost, Lene."

She shook her head.

"Who the hell can hit anything at that distance? It must be at least six hundred metres from the cliff edge to his location."

"It's 816 metres," Michael said. "Thomas Berg had a rangefinder in his rucksack."

"Eight-hundred . . .?"

Michael nodded and lit a cigarette.

"A very skilled shot."

"Do you think Henrik Schmidt will haunt me?" she asked. "That's what worries me most. That he'll always be there."

"Christ . . . Lene. I don't know. I think hell will keep all three of them under lock and key. You think you did the right thing, and I think you did the right thing. I'd have done exactly the same if they had hurt one of my children like they hurt Josefine. And I'd have been grateful for the chance. If you hadn't, Henrik would simply have been sent to a secure hospital and you would have had to live with the knowledge that he was still out there. This is better."

"What do I tell them at home?"

"Back at the station, you mean?"

"Yes."

"Nothing."

"Don't you think people will notice that the founder of one of Denmark's most successful companies and his son have vanished without a trace?"

He looked across the plateau at the snow-covered, mystical mountains on the other side of the fjord that continued as far as the eye could see.

"You said it yourself, Lene. You could lose a whole army up here. What's a few hikers and hunters?"

They agreed a plan, and Michael entered the lawyer's number on the satellite telephone. The call was answered immediately and the connection was first-class.

359

Elizabeth Caspersen was satisfied. Without saying anything incriminating on the open line, Michael accounted for the situation and she grew happier and more grateful as the conversation progressed. She would be delighted to charter a helicopter to pick them up and it would fly them anywhere they wanted. Michael told her they only wanted to be flown forty kilometres to a parking lot.

She rang back ten minutes later. Her voice was tense, but clear, and she had been just as efficient as she always was. One and a half hours, she promised them.

"Thank you," he said.

"It's wonderful," Michael," she said. "It's all really rather wonderful."

"So have you got what you wanted?" he asked and a small pause followed down the other end.

"I suppose, I guess I have. Did you find anything up there?" she wanted to know.

"Nothing," he said.

"Nothing?"

"No."

"Well . . . All right, then. The helicopter is on its way."

"Thank you."

"I think we should drive home in the same car," said Lene who had half followed the conversation.

"Then we'll take the Audi," Michael said.

"Okay.' She looked at the satellite telephone in his hand. "Do you trust her?"

Michael lit a cigarette, one of the last four of that day's ration, and stretched out on the camper mat with one arm behind his head.

"If that helicopter really does show up, I don't suppose I've anything to complain about," he said.

"But do you trust her?"

He waved the cigarette and yawned.

"Does it really matter? If you're asking me if she'll be discreet, I trust her one hundred percent. If you're asking me if I think she has had her own agenda all along, and used me to get what she wanted without at any point giving me the full picture, then I'm quite sure that she isn't just a penitent daughter trying to atone for her father's sins out of sheer piety."

"But doesn't it piss you off to be used like that?"

Michael looked at her and laughed out loud. She sat with her injured leg stretched out in front of her and the other pulled up to her chest. She rested her chin on her knee and carefully massaged the muscles around the wounds with her hands. He had found an excellent first-aid kit among Victor Schmidt's belongings and cleaned and disinfected the bullet wounds while she bit her lips until they bled. Then he had given her a handful of ibuprofen and paracetamol and some broad-spectrum antibiotics. She was rubbish at swallowing pills.

"What's so funny?" she asked.

"I'm being paid for this, Lene. It's a job. If I only worked for Nobel Peace Prize winners or saints, I'd have a lot of time on my hands."

"That's rubbish, Michael," she said with a small smile. "If that was true and you really were just some hired fixer, you wouldn't have brought me along. You would have tied me up and left me in that scout hut. You wouldn't have cared about my daughter, you wouldn't be calling home all the time, and you'd never have risked your life abseiling down that cliff because it didn't matter whether or not you found anything down there. It made no difference to your assignment. The hunters would have shown up anyway. And you wouldn't be mourning your—"

"That's enough!"

Michael raised the hand with the cigarette to warn her and she fell silent.

"Do you think you could let me have a moment's peace, woman," he said, and closed his eyes. "I'm not always as professional as I would like to be, okay? Not yet."

"And fortunately you never will be," she said.

"Right, but do you think that we could shut up now? Both of us? Please?"

"Yes. Did you find anything down on the shore? You said something about a head earlier?"

Michael sat up and stared wildly at her. Then he got up and started dismantling the tent without saying anything or dignifying her with a glance.

One hour later, they heard the helicopter come in from Porsanger Fjord.

CHAPTER 55

Three days later, Michael was back behind the desk in his usual room at the Admiral Hotel. The hallway carpet had been replaced. There had been no complaints or compensation claims from the hotel management and the porter was just as polite and welcoming as always. She was used to rap and rock stars, she said, and nothing Michael did could ever compare to the total vandalism which the music industry's current wunderkinds subjected hotels to—if only to keep up their image. Even so Michael felt compelled to tip her and the other staff generously at every opportunity.

And he could afford it. Sara had called the same morning and told him in a breathless voice of the astronomical sums pouring into his business account. His accountant had hummed a little tune when he rang her, she said. In addition to his agreed fee and reimbursement of various expenses, Elizabeth Caspersen had decided that he had earned a bonus. Of the seven-figure variety. A seven-figure sweetener to buy his silence, Michael said to his wife, but she wasn't listening.

She couldn't wait to see him.

"I can't wait to see you either," he said.

"And the children?" she asked.

"Sod the children. I can't wait to see *you*," he said.

There was a smile in her voice.

"Thank you. When will you be home?"

"Tomorrow."

"Not today?"

"I've got a couple of things to do here, Sara. Little things. But important."

"I'll see you tomorrow," she said. "How will I recognize you?"

"Look for my ears," he said.

*

He had visited Elizabeth Caspersen the day before at the Caspersen mansion in Hellerup. Her black Opel was parked on the gravel below the main steps, but the garage was empty; the Maserati, the Mercedes, and the Rolls-Royce were gone, and inside the house the wall above the stairs was bare. There was a faded rectangle left by Flemming Caspersen's portrait. The man was systematically being erased, Michael thought.

Klara Caspersen still missed her husband and continued to ask for him in her darkened bedroom where a nurse tried gently to distract her. In the library, the light and the view were still sensational, but the bear had gone along with the photograph from Sweden. The endless summer afternoon in the canoe had been taken down.

"Will you be moving in here?" he asked Elizabeth Caspersen.

"I would rather die," she said and took a seat. "Do sit down."

Michael sat down on the armchair next to the lawyer. She was wearing a well fitting, pinstripe suit and a collarless white silk blouse; her expression was neutral.

"Will it grow back?" she asked.

"What?"

"Your hair."

Michael ran his palm over the short stubble. His hands were freshly bandaged and the plastic surgeon had been hopeful. He didn't think Michael would have much in the way of permanent scarring.

"So they tell me."

"I'm glad to hear it," she said and her fingers found the string of pearls around her throat. "It was nice. Your hair."

"Thank you."

Michael looked out of the windows. Something was missing.

"Where is the dog?" he asked.

"Nigger? I had to have him put down, sadly. The neighbours complained. Michael?"

He looked at her.

"Yes?"

She blushed faintly.

"Did he do it?"

"Yes, he did."

She closed her eyes for a moment and sank back into the armchair. "Why?"

Michael lit a cigarette and offered her one. She hesitated before taking one, then she got up and found an ashtray which she placed on the armrest of her chair.

"I'm trying to quit," she said. "Again."

"So am I," he said. "Henrik Schmidt was the driving force, I think. It might have been your father's idea, but it was Henrik who organized it, set up Running Man Casino for the financial transactions and screened the clients. I guess they thought they might as well make money out of their sport while they were at it. They were business people through and through, your father, Victor, and Henrik Schmidt."

"But why?"

"Henrik was insane. Textbook psycho. And he desperately wanted to be close to your father and his own. He wanted to be important to them and surpass his brother. That was probably his primary motive."

He looked at her.

"By the way, thanks for your help," he said. "We were as good as dead. They had seen through Keith, or Henrik had. They killed him."

"I'm sorry to hear that, Michael."

"How did you convince Jakob to help us?"

She narrowed her eyes and studied him for a while before she replied.

"Deep down Jakob is a survivor. I imagine he could see where it was heading with his brother and his . . . Victor."

"His half-brother, you mean?"

"Yes."

"I don't think that's the whole story, Elizabeth."

She winked, but then she smiled to him. A genuine smile.

"You're sharp, Michael. The girl. Henrik took her from him. He was jealous. He loved Jakob. And hated him because Jakob was the favourite even though Henrik was the one who always did as he was told and what he was expected to do and worked day and night for Victor and my father."

"Johanne Reimers?"

"Yes. Jakob met her in Nepal. He fell in love with her, but he was in the army at that time so he had to go back to Afghanistan."

"And Henrik Schmidt found out about her?"

"They were close back then, so of course Jakob told Henrik about her. Henrik organized the hunting trip with his friends from Pederslund. Perhaps it was the first of many, and I presume it was that trip which prompted Henrik to create the set-up. I picked up the CD in the scout hut where you had hidden it and I called Jakob. I told him about Nepal and he saw the film. You could call it an incentive."

"And you gave him the coordinates for Porsanger Fjord?"

"That was all he asked for. He's very good."

Michael nodded. "He's very, very good indeed. But couldn't you have told me that he was coming?"

"I suppose I could have, but you might not have needed him, it might have been enough for him to observe and then go home. Or perhaps your reactions might not have been so convincing, if you knew that he was there. Perhaps the others wouldn't have felt so confident."

"And perhaps he could have shot Thomas before he executed Keith Mallory," Michael said harshly.

"There are a lot of variables here, Michael. I did the best I could. I can't mastermind everything."

She stared out of the window and he sensed a steely will and hard quality that he should have detected long ago.

"Of course not, Elizabeth. I'm sorry. He saved our lives, there's no doubt about it. Thank you."

"Did you find it?" she asked.

He stuck his hand in his pocket and handed her the DVD.

She held the plastic disc carefully between her fingertips.

"And you haven't made any copies?" she asked with a smile as if the question had been asked in jest.

"No."

She nodded and her knuckles whitened as she snapped the DVD in half. An almost serene expression spread across her face.

"I'm so relieved," she said. "Thank you."

"You're welcome." He smiled faintly. "I presume it's yours?"

"What on earth do you mean?"

"All this time I've been wondering why the only fingerprints on the DVD were yours. Who the hell wipes their own fingerprints off their own DVD? And who would store a film like this in a safe in their own home?"

The lawyer managed a guarded smile, but she had stopped looking at him.

"That's an interesting question, Michael. It really is. One of those that can never be fully answered."

"I guess not. You're right."

She got up and Michael rose to his feet as well.

"I'd like to recommend you to others if I may," she said. "To people with special problems."

"You may. Only they don't have to be quite as complex. The problems, I mean."

"You don't always get to choose," she said.

Michael held out his hand.

"The files?"

Elizabeth Caspersen's eyes narrowed.

"What do you want with them?"

"Satisfy my own curiosity, that's all. Round things off."

"I don't expect to see them on YouTube, Michael."

She placed the small USB stick in his hand.

"Of course not. They'll be deleted as soon as I've finished with them. How do you truly feel about it?"

"Which?"

"That it was your father . . . that he . . ."

"Killed people?"

Her face was in profile against the grey windows. The light was pleasant, subdued, and softened the lines. Her gaze was distant and aimed at something across the sea. Her pulse beat slowly under the delicate skin above the string of pearls.

"Yes, that he killed random people," he said.

"It's no longer important," she said. "Not in that way, and not any more . . ."

"I see. Was it expensive?"

"Was what expensive?"

"Getting someone to break into the house and steal the rhino horns? I presume that was why the dog wasn't here."

There was no reaction in her broad face. She was formidable, he thought.

"It was money well spent. Goodbye, Michael."

"Not *au revoir*?"

"I can't imagine. Unless you do something very foolish, and I know that you won't."

"One last thing," he said.

"Oh, I really hope it is, Michael."

"What about Tove Hansen and the twins?"

Elizabeth Caspersen nodded gravely. "Now that *is* important. They'll want for nothing. Ever. An anonymous benefactor will remember them in his will. A rich man with no children of his own or any other family. He had read about their parents' disappearance and was deeply touched by their story."

"Excellent," Michael said, and left the big, empty house.

Michael inserted Elizabeth Caspersen's small USB stick into his new laptop and clicked on a high resolution picture. A very familiar photograph appeared: Five soldiers in the Afghan desert—Kim Andersen, Kenneth Enderlein, Robert Olsen, Allan Lundkvist, and, standing slightly apart, Thomas Berg. The young warriors. The photo had also been on Kim Andersen's CD.

He had invested in a professional picture editing program and selected and cut a section from the picture: Robert Olsen's reflective Oakley sunglasses. Pasting the segment into a new file, Michael cut and pasted one of the lenses, zoomed in . . . and kept zooming.

His heart started to beat faster. Allan Lundkvist had told Lene that the photograph had been taken with a self-timer, but like everything else in this case, it had been a lie. The photographer was reflected in the Oakley sunglasses, a sixth man with a camera which obscured half, but only half his face. A desert hat lay at his feet along with his carbine, and he was wearing a sand-coloured T-shirt and loose-fitting camouflage trousers.

Jakob Schmidt.

Michael clicked to close the picture and opened the only other file on the USB stick: the recording of the smugglers on the desert road outside Musa Qala. He drummed his fingers until the taller and more watchful of the two opium smugglers aimed an accusing finger at the Humvee and the picture frame wobbled. Then he froze the recording and studied the image. There was a green reflection in the side door's thick, bulletproof glass. Michael cut and enlarged it repeatedly until he was finally able to lean back in his chair and stare at the screen.

Once again, Jakob Schmidt was the man who had filmed the exchange and the killing of the smugglers. He was reflected in the window of the Humvee.

A chameleon. A ghost.

Michael got up, opened the balcony door and lit a cigarette. The sea breeze swept into the room. He furrowed his brow and recalled the evening Henrik Schmidt had attacked him and taken Elizabeth Caspersen's DVD, and Jakob had found him bleeding in his hotel room. Jakob had said something about picking the winning horse. And Elizabeth Caspersen had described him as an opportunistic survivor.

Michael closed the balcony door, went back to the desk and shut the laptop. He hadn't finished with Jakob Schmidt, he thought. He would find him one day.

He watched his own reflection in the balcony door. He was homesick. He really was. But even so, he would miss the case. The excitement. The investigation. The opposition. The chase. Even the introverted and irritatingly headstrong police superintendent whom he had taken to Copenhagen Airport that morning. No power on earth could keep her from her daughter any longer.

They had exchanged a few muffled words and almost hugged in front of the escalator to the departure lounge, but at the top she had turned and waved to him. Stony-faced.

He had grown used to her. Like you learn to get along with a bad-tempered cat.

Michael sighed, turned away from his reflection and started packing.

EPILOGUE

Three weeks later

In the doorway to Elizabeth Caspersen's office, the young woman cleared her throat and the lawyer turned round with a smile.

"Take a seat, Louise."

The woman sat down in one of the visitor's chairs and crossed her legs while the lawyer took a good look at her. Louise had changed in the weeks that had passed since she last saw her. Her skin was clear and glowing, and her dark, curly hair looked fantastic as always, but was now cut in a simple, classic style.

Louise Andersen gestured towards the removal boxes.

"You're packing," she said.

The lawyer nodded, took the last papers from a drawer and put them in a box. She inserted a picture of her husband and daughters carefully into a padded envelope and placed it on top of the papers.

"I've been promoted," she said. "Or rather, I've now got my own business."

Louise Andersen smiled.

"You're the new Chairman of Sonartek, Elizabeth. Is that what you call getting your own business?"

Elizabeth Caspersen returned her smile.

"In a way, yes. You're busy packing, too, I gather?"

"There's not much to pack. Most of it was lost in the fire."

"Of course. When are you leaving?"

"Monday. For a month to start with. I've always wanted to see Switzerland. I think the Alps will be good for my asthma."

The lawyer sat down behind her desk, then she leaned forwards and pushed the box to one side.

"Your bank is Allgemeine Genève, Louise, and your bank manager is Dr. Steinschweiger. Remember to address him as Herr Doktor. The Swiss are very particular when it comes to titles. It's a small, very discreet bank, also used by Sonartek, incidentally. They value us and would do almost anything for us."

"Thank you."

Elizabeth Caspersen smiled again, but shook her head.

"I should be thanking you, Louise. If you hadn't found those films and brought them to me, I definitely wouldn't be sitting here now, and certainly not as Sonartek's new chairman. Perhaps I wouldn't be here at all. I can never repay my debt to you. The DVD and the other films in your husband's hiding place made Lene Jensen and Michael Sander take an interest in the case, and they forced my enemies to make mistakes. Did you know that your husband was going to kill himself?"

The widow looked out of the window. Her face was relatively composed.

"He was a murderer. I don't know how many people he and the others killed, and I don't want to know. But he loved the kids. I knew exactly what he would do when he heard the song and saw the bullets. He used to say that you were the only normal person he had met at Pederslund, and that's why I came to you when I discovered that was where the hunters were recruited."

Elizabeth Caspersen nodded. "And, like I said, for that, I will be forever in your debt. By the way, Sander didn't buy the rhino horn theft. That Kim did it."

Louise Andersen frowned. "But I planted the floor plans in his rucksack, like you told me to. He must have found them."

"Of course, but Victor or the others must have convinced him that Kim wasn't involved."

She dismissed the thought with her large hand.

"Anyway, it doesn't matter now. It was a detail I believed to be important at the time."

"So they won't be coming after me?" the widow asked. "Michael Sander or the police superintendent?"

The lawyer looked at her with surprise: "Why would they? They've no reason to suspect you. You've done nothing wrong, Louise. You put a stop to it. You should be proud of yourself. Besides, Michael Sander does only what he's paid to do, and no one is paying him to bother you."

The other nodded sceptically.

"Of course. Thank you."

The lawyer put her arm around the young woman's shoulder. She could have chosen that perfume herself.

"So what do the children say to Switzerland?"

"Skiing!"

Elizabeth Caspersen laughed.

"Fantastic."

AUTHOR'S NOTE

The author would like to thank the following for their invaluable assistance:

- Vibeke Schmidt, chief psychologist, Militærpsykologisk Institut;
- Consultant Dr. Dorte Sestoft, Justitsministeriets klinik for Retspsykiatri;
- Major Dr. Dan Volder;
and
- Police Sergeant Naja Svarre.

Any factual errors and misunderstandings are solely the responsibility of the author.

S. J.